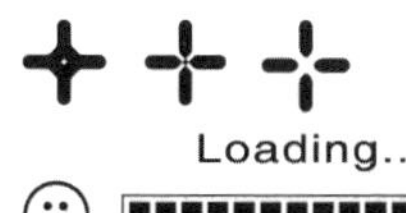

Limerence

▸ Author:Jiang Zi Bei

Via Lactea

Limerence

An imprint of Via Lactea Ltd.

This book is a work of fiction. The characters and events portrayed in this book are fictitious or are used fictitiously. Any similarity to actual persons, living or dead, is purely coincidental and not intended by the author.

Author: Jiang Zi Bei
Translators: Connie; Yolanda
Editor: Michaela M

CONTACT:
Customer Support: info@vialactea.ca
Wholesale & Distribution: market@vialactea.ca
Other Cooperation: https://vialactea.ca/pages/cooperation
Discord Server: https://discord.gg/vialactea

Follow us on Twitter/Instagram/Facebook: @ViaLactea_Ltd
Official Website: www.vialactea.ca

ISBN: 978-1-77408-344-4(pbk)
Printed in Canada

LOCATION:
Shops At Waterloo Town Square
#27, 75 King Street South, Waterloo, ON
Canada
N2J 1P2

Limerence

LIMERENCE
CONTENT

It was during a game of *PlayerUnknown's Battlegrounds* that Pei Ran first realized something was wrong with his boyfriend.

His boyfriend was called Luo Qingshan. They had started dating back in Grade Eleven, nearly three years ago. Later, they had both been admitted to the same university, although in different departments.

It was the weekend, so he was home from campus. After supper, he logged in to start a video chat with Luo Qingshan. However, before they exchanged more than a few words, his boyfriend coaxed him into starting up the game.

The player who joined them was Luo Qingshan's classmate. Pei Ran didn't remember his name. What he did recall was that the boy was not tall, that his skin was white like snow, and that he often went to the library with Luo Qingshan.

Pei Ran was somewhat of a pro at MOBA games, but shooter games were not a strong suit of his. Luo Qingshan used to play PUBG with him quite often, and, to help him out, they usually parachuted into areas with fewer people.

At the start of this round, Player 3 immediately marked out the airport.

"How about parachuting into the airport? I want something exciting." It was the voice of Luo Qingshan's classmate—very soft, a bit nasally, and sounding slightly pitiful.

Luo Qingshan agreed.

Pei Ran stayed silent. They were playing in a squad of four, and he didn't know the fourth teammate. Maybe he was a friend of Luo Qingshan. Like him, that person hadn't spoken a word since the beginning of the round.

It was only after Luo Qingshan and his classmate cleared an entire building that they finally seemed to remember that there were other people in the squad.

"Pei Ran, make sure you've taken cover," said Luo Qingshan.

Pistol in hand, Pei Ran had been hiding in the corner of a room for a while. "Uh-huh."

Luo Qingshan continued, "Su Nian, come here. There's someone in this room."

"Coming, bro."

"I'll run first; you follow me."

"Okay, don't die."

So that person's was called Su Nian.

Listening to the gunfire, Pei Ran suddenly felt a little bored. He shook his mouse. From his angle, he could see the fourth teammate in the opposite building.

His teammate fought alone, swiftly eliminating an entire squad of four until his own health bar went in the red. Then, he calmly walked to the window to bandage himself.

From this angle, Pei Ran had the impression that they were staring at each other.

"All clear," Luo Qingshan said. "You can come out now,

babe."

They never deliberately tried to hide their relationship, and almost everyone around them knew about it. Luo Qingshan had been openly calling him "babe" since senior high school.

Pei Ran collected his wits, left his mic muted, then jumped out of the window holding his pistol.

Su Nian was looting other players' equipment when he arrived. Pei Ran didn't join him. He knew that he wasn't good at the game, so he tended not to compete for gear.

"Bro..." Su Nian asked, "You took the M4?"

Luo Qingshan chuckled, "How did you know?"

"Can you give it to me? I'm not in the zone today. I don't want to use an AK."

"Sure," said Luo Qingshan, "This rifle is yours if you bring me a meal to my dorm later."

"Again..." Su Nian's words sounded reproachful, but his tone was cheery. "Okay, whatever you say."

Pei Ran frowned slightly. He opened the supply crate and saw that they didn't even leave a gun.

He suddenly felt his temper rising, so he turned away to search somewhere else. However, after exploring just two rooms, he was sniped by an enemy from the opposite building. His character abruptly fell to the ground.

The attacker mercilessly shot him two more times, halving his health bar, and Pei Ran hurriedly shuffled into the room's blind spot.

Just then, he heard a scream coming from the voice chat. "Ah—bro! There's someone in this building!"

Immediately after, a message popped up, informing him that Su Nian had been knocked out.

"Ah, that guy sneaked up on me. He's hiding behind a crate

and doesn't have the balls to finish me off. Bro, come quick!" Su Nian's voice grew louder with anger.

Pei Ran was ready to give in. The enemy was too close and would likely lose no time in killing him. What perfect timing, since he wasn't in the mood to play games.

However, at the sound of a gunshot, another message popped up in the upper right corner of his screen:

111GOD knocked out **zhiyefudi** via headshot with a **Kar98K**.

With a single shot from the fourth teammate located inside a tower, the enemy sprinting towards him dropped stone dead.

Pei Ran was stunned for a moment, but then he felt compelled to check the map. Player 4 was far away from Pei Ran; If he could shoot a running enemy in the head from this distance, he was either a cheater or a god.

But it didn't matter if he was scripting or just that good at the game.

Pei Ran looked away, moving his gaze down to Luo Qingshan's icon. Luo Qingshan was in a delicate position—right between him and Su Nian.

Luo Qingshan only hesitated for half a second. "Hold on, babe. I'll find Su Nian first. I'm worried that someone might kill him."

111GOD knocked out **luwenz6** via headshot with a **Kar98K**.

Just as Luo Qingshan finished talking, the person targeting Su Nian was also shot down by Player 4.

Pei Ran glanced at the map again. Luo Qingshan hadn't slowed down, dashing toward Su Nian without even looking back.

Su Nian was merely down; he wasn't out of the game yet. His enemy had been struck down by Player 4 before he could finish off Su Nian for good. When Luo Qingshan helped him, his health bar was still more than half-full.

On the other hand, Pei Ran's health had almost reached rock bottom, just like his mood.

Luo Qingshan helped Su Nian get up and looked at Pei Ran's health bar. "Fuck."

He was running out of time, so he rushed to the car outside the fence. As he started to drive, he couldn't help but swear again.

The car had both tires blown out; it refused to budge.

"Wait for me, babe. I'll be right there." Luo Qingshan left the car, unequipped his rifle, and sprinted to the building where Pei Ran was.

Pei Ran sighed, "Forget it..."

Before he finished his words, he heard the sound of a motorcycle engine approaching.

Pei Ran was dumbfounded. He shifted his gaze and saw Player 4 jumping off the motorcycle before it could come to a halt, and the shock of landing shaved off half his health bar.

Then, he leaped in from the window and immediately squatted down in front of Pei Ran. Right before the last of his health could trickle away, Player 4 managed to stabilize him.

Pei Ran blinked. Maybe it was because he had just narrowly escaped death, but he felt his heart racing for a second or two.

When his character stood up, he was still a little confused. Player 4 dropped something to the floor, then turned around and ran out of the room.

Pei Ran picked up the dropped med kit. "...Thank you."

Player 4 paused, then suddenly walked back.

Pei Ran thought that he'd changed his mind, so he cancelled the command to heal himself. However, he saw instead an M416 suddenly thudding to the floor.

Pei Ran looked at the 98K left on the Player 4's back and hurried to say, "Don't bother, I can't play that well."

But, without a word, Player 4 jumped out of the window.

Pei Ran was a bit weirded out by this teammate of his, but in the end he could only pick up the rifle. "Thank you."

After a few seconds, just as Pei Ran thought that his teammate didn't have a mic at all, a small megaphone began flickering beside Player 4's icon.

"You're welcome."

The words were hurried, and the timbre was deep.

Pei Ran quirked an eyebrow. Somehow, the voice sounded familiar to him.

"Sick job, *xiao*-Zhun!" Luo Qingshan breathed a sigh of relief. "I'll remember this. Next time, my babe and I will treat you to dinner."

Pei Ran finally recalled. Xiao-Zhun, a.k.a. Yan Zhun, was Luo Qingshan's roommate.

Their university was divided into two campuses. Pei Ran stayed in the western campus, while Luo Qingshan lived in the eastern one. Due to the distance, Pei Ran rarely visited Luo Qingshan's dormitory. Strictly speaking, he'd only seen Yan Zhun twice before. One of those times, Yan Zhun had been playing on the computer. Pei Ran only remembered that Yan Zhun's shoulders were broad and that his arm, which had been holding the mouse, seemed muscular.

The other time was on the floor's balcony. Yan Zhun had been leaning against the wall, smoking. When he'd noticed Pei Ran, he'd frozen for a moment, then he'd quickly turned around and put out his cigarette.

Pei Ran's impressions of Yan Zhun were as thus: a bit aloof, not very talkative, and quite handsome.

Of course, apart from the last point, these impressions meant nothing. Take Su Nian as an example. Pei Ran had once believed Su Nian to be a loner and untalkative, but now it seemed that maybe Su Nian just didn't like talking to him.

"Babe, why do you only have one gun?" Luo Qingshan ran toward him and promptly dropped his weapon to the floor. "Here, take my AK."

At the thought of where the rifle came from, Pei Ran said, "No need, I'll use Yan Zhun's M4."

Bang!

Yan Zhun had barely driven his motorcycle for a few dozen meters. In a moment of carelessness, the front of the motorcycle smashed straight into a tree.

"Yan Zhun, how did you just lose half your health?" Luo Qingshan asked, looking at the lower-left corner.

Yan Zhun replied, "I crashed into a tree."

Luo Qingshan laughed. "So it seems that even pros like you crash into trees sometimes... But say, babe, how did you know xiao-Zhun's name?"

Pei Ran loaded the M416. "I once heard you use it for him."

Luo Qingshan opened the inventory screen, saying, "Okay, AK is hard to aim with; you may not be used to it. Here, pick up this stock and attach it."

"No need." Pei Ran repeated Yan Zhun's movements from just earlier, jumping out the window as he exited the house. "The gun Yan Zhun gave me is fully equipped."

Yan Zhun stopped his vehicle under a tree, grabbed a bottle of mineral water from nearby, and took a sip.

The location of the blue zone was not doing them any favors. Luo Qingshan took a look at the map, noticing that they had to cross most of it to reach the safe area.

The worst part was, just like the car he'd tried earlier, all the vehicles on the road had their tires blown out.

"Damn, what asshole blew out all the tires?!" Luo Qingshan cursed as he kept running. "Didn't we kill all the other squads at the airport? Maybe a lone wolf was able to escape?"

"Whenever you run away from the blue zone, you also tend to blow up every tire you see on the road," reminded Su Nian.

Luo Qingshan chuckled and cursed again before noticing that the icon of Player 2 hadn't moved from the airport. "Babe, what are you doing? Why aren't you running to safety?"

After a long moment of silence, Luo Qingshan checked his health bar. "Su Nian, you go on ahead. He might have disconnected. I'll go back and help him. If there is a car on your way, you can come back and pick us up..."

Pei Ran returned to the call and said, "It's fine, I'm back. You go ahead."

Luo Qingshan asked, "Do you have any healing items on you?"

"Yes." Pei Ran quickly used a first aid kit.

Reassured, Luo Qingshan rechecked the map. "Yan Zhun, did you see any four-wheelers on your way?"

"No."

"Then you could've at least taken someone on your backseat. Why were you running away on your own?"

"Coming." Yan Zhun turned his motorcycle around.

The player closest to him was Su Nian. As the motorcycle approached, Su Nian stopped and was about to climb on it. Instead, the motorcycle didn't even slow down and rolled straight past him.

Pei Ran watched the motorcycle leap off a mountain. When

Yan Zhun braked, the tail spun around in perfect oversteer.

"Hop on."

"Thank you." Pei Ran quickly sat in the back.

This was his third time saying "thank you" to Yan Zhun.

Yan Zhun's motorcycle went fast and steady. With nothing better to do, Pei Ran switched his camera to the first-person perspective. It felt rather exciting.

Pei Ran and Yan Zhun reached the safe zone without a scratch, but, before they could find a place to reconvene, Luo Qingshan got caught in a pickle.

He and Su Nian were just about to step into the circle when they got shot down by a squad hidden just inside the border. Pei Ran and Yan Zhun were left as the only surviving members of the squad.

"I knew it..." Luo Qingshan ran an irritated hand through his hair. "If only I'd known earlier, I wouldn't have gone through that spot... You two hide and try to stay alive. I need a smoke."

"Don't," said Su Nian, "the room's gonna smell of cigarettes when I get there."

"The dorm windows are open."

"It's still gonna stink."

"Wow, you're so delicate. What time are you coming? I'm starving to death."

"Half-past eight. Also, check your WeChat. I just sent you a funny video I came across."

Pei Ran had his character crouch down inside a house, then switched windows to turn down the computer's volume.

By the time he switched back, his character had gotten shot in the head and was falling to the ground.

"Wait for me." Yan Zhun turned on his mic.

Luo Qingshan and Su Nian had continued to chat in the call, and Yan Zhun's voice was almost overpowered by theirs, but, oddly enough, Pei Ran still heard him loud and clear.

Pei Ran wasn't a skilled player, but he was no newbie either. Soon enough, he spotted the enemies who shot him. "Don't come here, at least two players are keeping an eye on me."

"Hide in the corner," Yan Zhun instructed, "and wait for me."

Unfortunately, Pei Ran couldn't see properly from his position. Plus, a knocked-down character was agonizingly slow. He tried, but the enemy didn't give him a chance. They promptly fired several more rounds to finish him off.

Pei Ran clicked into Spectator Mode.

Yan Zhun arrived a moment too late and was now standing before the loot box that Pei Ran had dropped.

"You can get hit from this angle," Pei Ran reminded him. "Don't bother with my crate; there's nothing useful inside, not even a healing item."

Yan Zhun responded with a hum of acceptance, but his character avatar still looted the box.

Pei Ran leaned back. He wasn't familiar with the game, so he couldn't tell what kind of equipment Yan Zhun had taken.

"Su Nian, I just transferred you the money for the meal, make sure to accept it..." Luo Qingshan chuckled before he could finish his words. "Hey, Yan Zhun, why did you take my babe's clothes? Did you get tired of wearing expensive skins and want to go back to basics?"

Pei Ran raised his eyebrows and saw that Yan Zhun's clothes had changed into the default white T-shirt.

Yan Zhun shifted his position and replied curtly, "I pressed on the wrong key."

Pei Ran was in a bad mood. He was about to close the game, but as he watched Yan Zhun, he couldn't bring himself to do it. In that case, he might as well continue watching.

He thought Yan Zhun would start running. After all, he was the only one left in the squad. But Yan Zhun didn't do so. Instead, he entered another house and began to snipe at players across the street.

After Yan Zhun shot down his fourth target, the enemies finally decided to make a strategic retreat. However, as soon as they jumped down from the building, they were mowed down by a hail of bullets from Yan Zhun.

As inexperienced as Pei Ran was, he could still tell that Yan Zhun was very good. If he didn't already know that Yan Zhun was Luo Qingshan's roommate, he'd suspect that he was a professional player.

Skillful as he was, his opponents still had the advantage of numbers and could rescue each other from being knocked down. It would be no easy feat to properly eliminate them all.

"Forget it, xiao-Zhun. Get in the safe zone first. Don't waste your time with them; you won't be able to survive the damage from the blue circle," Luo Qingshan advised. "Go inside the circle and find a good spot. There are only ten people left."

Just as Luo Qingshan finished talking, Yan Zhun peeked to the right and fired at the other side.

"No," Yan Zhun insisted, "they must die here."

A few minutes later, three messages flashed in the top right corner that three players eliminated outside the safe zone.

Yan Zhun managed to wear down the opposing team of three completely.

"Sick job!" Su Nian sounded rather excited, "Yan Zhun, heal yourself ASAP. Do you have any meds on you?"

Yan Zhun stood still and didn't reply to him. Ten seconds later, the blue circle caught up to him, and it was game over.

Pei Ran was a bit stunned. He had never watched such fascinating gameplay before. When they returned to the game lobby, Pei Ran's eyes were still glued to Yan Zhun's in-game character.

"Well, I quit. I'm feeling tired." Luo Qingshan stretched. "Babe, let's video chat."

Yan Zhun's character suddenly vanished—he left the team.

No sooner had Pei Ran turned off the game than Luo Qingshan started the video call.

Luo Qingshan was your typical bad boy. He'd been a bad student since high school, both smoking and drinking. He'd even gotten into fights over Pei Ran. In short, he did all the things that a delinquent would do.

After he'd started dating Pei Ran, his temper had softened up. To enter the same university as Pei Ran, he had pushed himself to his limits, studying fervently. Now that the pressure had gone, he was beginning to revert to his old self.

"Babe." Luo Qingshan stood on the balcony. "When are you coming back to campus? I'll pick you up."

"Tomorrow afternoon," said Pei Ran.

"Oh, afternoon?" Luo Qingshan frowned.

"Why, what's wrong?"

"Nothing..." Luo Qingshan hesitated for a long time, "It's just that I'd planned to play basketball with Su Nian then."

Pei Ran's phone was off center. When he heard Luo Qingshan's words, Pei Ran glanced over at the screen.

"You don't need to pick me up. I have no luggage."

"No way. I'll just bail on the game."

"Don't bother," replied Pei Ran. "Go play. I'll arrive tomorrow. See you then."

Pei Ran ended the call, then he stood up and went for a shower. When he came out, he lay down on his bed and browsed his WeChat Moments.

Luo Qingshan:
Poverty in Today's Male University Students **[image]**

The photo showed Luo Qingshan's supper: a box of rice, two cans of meat, and a side of green vegetables.

The status was posted a moment ago. Only one person had commented underneath.

sn:
I see veggies and meat, how's that poverty **[angry emoji]**

sn:
Are you trying to imply that I'm doing charity work? **[laughing-crying emoji]**

Pei Ran had a hunch. He refreshed his newsfeed and, as he'd expected, saw a new post.

sn:
Look at this hypocrite **[custom emote][image]**

It was a photo of Luo Qingshan devouring his meal.

Pei Ran examined the photo coldly for a few seconds. Then, he clicked on the profile of "sn" and formally changed his alias to "Su Nian."

By the time Pei Ran reached campus, it was pitch-dark outside. He stood on the deserted court and called Luo Qingshan, who was panting when he picked up.

"Babe... you're here already?"

Pei Ran hummed in confirmation. "I don't see you."

"Su Nian sprained his ankle during the game, and I had to take him to the infirmary. He's still getting patched up," Luo Qingshan explained. "How about you go to my dorm first and wait for me? My neighbor borrowed my computer, so the door should be open."

When Pei Ran got to the dorm, the door was indeed ajar.

Since Pei Ran had permission from Luo Qingshan, he didn't bother knocking before walking in.

At the same time, someone pushed open the PVC door of the bathroom. Steam immediately emerged from the bathroom, and a person stepped out.

The only thing Yan Zhun had on was a bathrobe, which had been slung loosely around his waist. His form was striking, with fluid lines contouring his abs and droplets of water still dotting his skin. Hearing the noise of the front door, he intuitively turned his head toward it.

They stared at each other for a few seconds.

Pei Ran immediately dropped his gaze. "Sorry... I saw that the door wasn't closed, so I just came in."

Yan Zhun quickly recovered from the shock. He nodded, walking to his bed as naturally as possible. Then he picked up his T-shirt and put it on.

Afterwards, Yan Zhun glanced at him once again. "Why are you standing there? Come on in."

Pei Ran felt a bit warm in the slightly steamy air.

The air was heavy with Yan Zhun's scent—a subtle fragrance of cologne that was typical of masculine shower gels.

For a moment, Pei Ran felt almost as if he hadn't come over for Luo Qingshan, but instead for Yan Zhun.

Luo Qingshan had forgotten to shut down his computer before he left. Pei Ran took a peek as he sat down and noticed that PUBG was still open in the taskbar.

Luo Qingshan had always been quite scatterbrained. When

they'd roomed together in high school, he'd often leave their dorm without turning off the lights. Pei Ran clicked into the game window, wanting to help him shut down the computer.

When the game window maximized, he realized that Luo Qingshan was not the only one on standby in the lobby.

Su Nian used a female avatar for his character. Both her and Luo Qingshan's character were standing in silence, dressed in the newly released clown costume.

"Do you want any water?"

Surprised, Pei Ran inadvertently let go of the mouse. He froze for a half-second, then turned around.

Yan Zhun had his back towards him, about to launch a game booster. "Your lips look dry."

Pei Ran licked his lips. They were dry indeed—he had forgotten to buy water before he set out for campus.

He eyed Luo Qingshan's cup. Although they'd been dating for a couple of years, he was still not used to drinking from other people's cups. "It's fine..."

"I've got paper cups," Yan Zhun said, "the disposable type."

Half a minute later, Pei Ran sat down next to Yan Zhun with a paper cup in hand.

"Sitting alone gets boring. Can I watch you play?"

Yan Zhun replied, "Suit yourself."

Even during matches, Yan Zhun maintained his cold and quiet demeanor. After a few rounds, Pei Ran noticed that Yan Zhun never unmuted while playing, even though his teammates' microphone icons were flashing nonstop.

As he witnessed Yan Zhun gun down players on the ground before he even landed, Pei Ran couldn't help but blurt out, "You're amazing."

Yan Zhun paused and shot him a questioning look. Just

then, an enemy emerged from behind the corner.

Without thinking, Pei Ran grabbed Yan Zhun's shirt to alert him. "On your right!"

By the time Yan Zhun looked back at the screen, his character had already been reduced to a crate.

Pei Ran frowned and loosened his grip. "Am I bothering you?"

"No." Yan Zhun took off his headset and returned to the lobby. "I misheard the steps and misjudged his position."

Yan Zhun swiftly unplugged his headset. Pei Ran could hear the game's background music and sound effects.

Seeing that he joined another match, Pei Ran asked, "Can you hear the footsteps without wearing earphones?"

"Yes, I'm playing against beginners," Yan Zhun said. "I can't hear you with the headset on."

Pei Ran had to pause for a second. "It doesn't matter if you can't hear me."

Yan Zhun paused for two seconds. "What did you say to me just then?"

"Nothing, I said you're amazing," Pei Ran replied, "same as the last time we played together... You could go pro."

Pei Ran meant every word he said. He accompanied Luo Qingshan to two PUBG global championships. He felt that many of the so-called experts didn't play as well as Yan Zhun.

Yan Zhun turned around and glanced at him for barely two seconds, then looked away and smirked.

"No way, not skilled enough." Yan Zhun retorted, half-jokingly. "I can only win against newbies."

Pei Ran nodded. "Like me."

"No, you don't suck." Yan Zhun's tone became serious. "You don't play often, so you aren't familiar with it yet. You're good at *League*, right?"

Pei Ran was somewhat taken aback. "Yeah... How did you know?"

Yan Zhun went silent for a while, then answered, "I saw you play with Luo Qingshan."

In the final stage of clearing Sanhok, a girl in Yan Zhun's team was knocked down. As usual, Yan Zhun quietly eliminated all the enemies in the vicinity, went back to help his teammate, then tossed her a first aid kit and painkillers.

"Thanks, bro," said the girl. "Let's play together again next round. I'll give you three kits back!"

Pei Ran waited for Yan Zhun's response. After a long time, he couldn't help but tug at his sleeve to alert him. "I think your teammate is talking to you."

"I know, but I don't want to join their lobby," Yan Zhun answered.

Nevertheless, his teammates would not yield so quickly. Pei Ran guessed that they were in a group chat of their own. Every time they spoke into their mic, they were always addressing Yan Zhun.

"Come on! Player 4 has been begging for your WeChat number!" One of them said in a joking tone.

Another voice arose immediately. "Shut up! Don't say that out loud..."

Yan Zhun replied, "Change your gender, and I'll reconsider."

The girl didn't understand. "Huh?"

"I'm into men," Yan Zhun said as he reloaded his gun.

Pei Ran was a bit at a loss.

Even when the words "Winner Winner, Chicken Dinner" appeared on the screen, Pei Ran still couldn't quite regain his bearings.

Did Yan Zhun just come out in front of him? Just like that?

The sound of the door opening interrupted Pei Ran's thoughts.

Luo Qingshan pushed through the door, wearing a baseball cap with his eyes partially covered by the brim. He closed the door and turned around. In the instant that their gazes met, Pei Ran saw a flash of shock in his eyes.

However, before Pei Ran could take a closer look, Luo Qingshan's expression had already returned to normal.

"Babe," Luo Qingshan said as he took off his hat, "did I keep you waiting?"

Pei Ran stood up. "No, I'm watching Yan Zhun play games."

Luo Qingshan glanced at his roommate. Yan Zhun had started another round and wasn't paying attention to him.

Luo Qingshan didn't mind, though, since he knew that Yan Zhun was always like this. He grabbed Pei Ran's waist and bent down to kiss him, but Pei Ran blocked his mouth with his palm.

"You're all sweaty." Pei Ran leaned back. "Go take a shower first. Wanna eat out after?"

Luo Qingshan's lips pouted slightly. "Fine, I'll go shower. Wait for me."

While Luo Qingshan was in the bathroom, his charging phone suddenly chimed.

Instinctively, Pei Ran glanced down at it.

You have one new message.

Luo Qingshan had turned off message previews.

Just a few days ago, while Pei Ran was away from school, he'd used Luo Qingshan's phone to play Tetris. He remembered that the setting hadn't been like this back then.

Done with his shower, Luo Qingshan donned his hat again.

"Come on, babe."

Before Pei Ran closed the door, he couldn't help but shoot a glance at the gamer in the room.

Yan Zhun had once again put on his headset.

Pei Ran opened his mouth. As he hesitated for a few brief seconds, Luo Qingshan gently took his wrist in hand.

"What are you staring at? Let's go before they run out of seats."

When the dorm door closed, the in-game character avatar abruptly stopped. Yan Zhun turned his head, gaze turned to the direction in which they had left.

Luo Qingshan didn't come back until very late at night.

Even still, Yan Zhun was playing video games by the time he got in. Surrounding him were the corpses of his enemies, mowed down by a hail of bullets in a brutal rampage.

Luo Qingshan was talking on the phone. "I got back to the dorm... Dinner? The new restaurant next door is not good. The food were bland. I won't be going back... I didn't turn off the game. It must be Pei Ran who saw that my computer was on and switched it off for me."

After hanging up, Luo Qingshan climbed on his bed and pulled the covers over his head, his mind drifting back to what happened in the afternoon.

That afternoon, Su Nian confessed his feelings to him.

Su Nian and Pei Ran were like polar opposites. When Su Nian confessed, his watery eyes had been on the brink of tears. Even his lips had become redder than usual.

"I thought you wouldn't come back tonight."

Luo Qingshan wasn't expecting Yan Zhun to talk to him. He starled for a moment, but then he pulled down his covers.

"No way, we're in the damned suburbs. Pei Ran says the hotels near the campus are too dirty, so he's never agreed to spend a night in any of them."

Yan Zhun walked to the sink on the balcony and didn't speak again.

Unfortunately, Luo Qingshan was looking for a conversation partner who could help him unclutter his thoughts. After Yan Zhun closed the light and went to bed, Luo Qingshan finally turned around to face him.

"Yan Zhun, what did Pei Ran say to you today?"

"Nothing."

"You didn't say anything bad about me, did you?"

"Like what?"

"Well, not washing socks, things like that..." Luo Qingshan put his hands behind his head and continued. "Jeez, I thought all guys had that problem. But the thing is, Pei Ran is a bit of a clean freak."

"Then no, I didn't."

Luo Qingshan proceeded to bombard Yan Zhun with questions, and Yan Zhun answered every single one of them, although all of his replies were very curt.

"And who do you prefer, Pei Ran or Su Nian?"

With that question, the dorm fell silent for a moment.

Luo Qingshan suddenly realized what had slipped out of his mouth. Flustered, he tried to explain himself. "I was just asking..."

"Pei Ran."

"Huh?"

Yan Zhun shut his eyes in the dark and repeated, "Pei Ran."

Annoyance and indescribable feelings of irritation nagged at the back of Luo Qingshan's mind. He had always seen Yan

Zhun as a log of wood—a man of few words who avoided small talk and spurned gossiping.

Hence, his lips were much looser when talking to Yan Zhun.

"I know, right? Pei Ran is the best-looking guy I've seen in my life," Luo Qingshan murmured. "You didn't see him in high school. He looked so good in a white shirt—his face, his hands, even his neck was hot. Have you ever noticed his legs? They're long and straight. He took dance classes when he was a kid, so he's got a great physique."

Yan Zhun hummed.

Lost in a world of his own, Luo Qingshan didn't realize that Yan Zhun's hum had been one of agreement.

"He's also really clean. Pure from head to toe... When I learned that he was into guys, I decided to pursue him without a second thought."

Pei Ran had been especially hard to woo. No amount of coaxing could make him crack a smile. In the end, Luo Qingshan had fought with the boy who'd outed Pei Ran to the whole school. He'd gotten beaten half to death, but at last he'd persuaded Pei Ran to date him.

The shrill ringtone of a cell phone interrupted Luo Qingshan's speech.

Luo Qingshan swiftly returned to his senses and picked up his phone. "Hello, Su Nian?"

His mind was still full of Pei Ran, so his tone when first answering was standoffish. "I was about to fall asleep; let's hang up—What? Your foot is hurting again?"

They chattered for quite a while before Luo Qingshan threw off his blanket and stood up. "I'm coming to your room to check up on you. Open the door for me."

When Luo Qingshan opened the dorm door, he heard a cold voice behind him. "You're leaving to check on a classmate's leg so late at night?"

Luo Qingshan chuckled. "Hey, don't make fun of me. I'll just have a quick look upstairs. Leave the door open."

After Luo Qingshan left, Yan Zhun got up from his bed, grabbed a cigarette and went out on the balcony.

Enveloped by the darkness, Yan Zhun blew a mouthful of smoke. The fumes cloaked the moon in a white veil, making it seem all the more distant and ethereal.

After a very long time, Yan Zhun stubbed out his cigarette.

He lowered his gaze, concealing the feelings of restlessness and unwillingness that clouded his head.

"Fuck..."

When Pei Ran returned to his dorm, the first thing he did was to take a shower.

The dishes in that restaurant had been fairly bland, but they sure smelled. Pei Ran was certain that his hair reeked of vinegar from the potato stir-fry.

After showering, he stood at his bed and dried his hair with one hand. His other hand picked up his phone and tapped on Su Nian's WeChat Moments once again.

He and Su Nian had added each other on WeChat after their initial meeting, but they never chatted afterward.

He skipped the first Moment and scrolled down.

The chili sauce here is absolutely amazing. **[Image]**

Luo Qingshan had mentioned to him today that he'd recently found a restaurant with very spicy dishes. He also said that it was a shame Pei Ran didn't like spicy food. Otherwise, he would've taken him there to try it out.

Today's workout (1 / 1) **[Image]**

The photo showed the school's basketball court. Pei Ran spotted Luo Qingshan's jersey.

One-day trip to the library.

...

Most of Su Nian's posts from the past two months were related to Luo Qingshan.

Pei Ran raised an eyebrow, but he soon relaxed.

He didn't know why he suddenly decided to check Su Nian's posts.

He had seen these pictures before, but he hadn't care back then. In fact, he hadn't even opened on them.

Well, that wasn't entirely true. The fact of the matter was, Pei Ran already knew about these photos.

However, his suspicions were very impolite, maybe even malicious. He shouldn't be speculating based on mere coincidences and a couple of photos.

He studied the photos for a few more seconds, then closed WeChat.

A week later, Pei Ran's Calendar app sent him a reminder that Luo Qingshan's birthday would be tomorrow.

He was shopping for gifts when Luo Qingshan called him.

"Uhm... babe, I have a request for you."

"What is it?"

"I wanna go to a karaoke box for my birthday, is that okay?"

"It's your birthday, you can do whatever you want."

"But the important thing is that you have to come too." Luo Qingshan confessed, "I know you hate that kind of place... Those dumbasses kept urging me to go. They said that they knew the people who worked there, that there'd be a discounted group meal, so it'd be very cheap. But, if you don't want to come, I'll find another place."

"As long as you're happy."

Thus, the location was settled.

The next night, Pei Ran stared at the mask on his desk and began to hesitate.

He genuinely disliked karaoke boxes. They were noisy, messy, dirty places where body odors intermingled to yield a nauseating stench. Worst still was the smell of cigarettes, confined to a shoe-box sized room... Just imagining it made him wrinkle his brows.

Maybe wearing a mask would make everything bearable, even if he wouldn't be able to breathe as easily.

His phone rang—it was a call from Luo Qingshan. Earlier that day, Luo Qingshan had gone back home. Since he would be leaving directly from home to the karaoke box, the two of them hadn't met up during the day.

"I booked a room. Do you know how to get there? Or should I pick you up?"

"No need." Pei Ran grabbed the face mask and stuffed it inside the drawer. People went to karaoke bars to let loose. He didn't want to ruin the mood by covering himself up in a mask. Then he added, "I'll use a GPS."

"What are you doing here?"

Yan Zhun lifted his head. Sitting next to him was Lin Kang, who was in the same major as him at school. They had also shared a homeroom back in high school. They weren't particularly close, but they nevertheless considered each other friends.

Lin Kang took off his light jacket and threw it on the couch. "I can't believe Luo Qingshan managed to invite you of all people."

"I'm free today," Yan Zhun replied.

"What do you mean, Lin Kang? Yan Zhun and I are bros. Why would it be weird that he's come to celebrate my birthday?" Overhearing their conversation, Luo Qingshan chimed in by speaking right into his microphone. "We even play PUBG together in the same four-squad."

"Careful with your wording! What you actually mean is, Yan Zhun carries you in PUBG," Lin Kang immediately retorted.

"Bullshit."

After some back-and-forth, the two started to bicker. Yan Zhun listened in for a bit before turning his attention back to his phone.

Su Nian looked up from the karaoke machine and smiled. "Yeah, the two of us died instantly."

"Speak for yourself. I'm better than that."

"Yeah, right!" Lin Kang ribbed Luo Qingshan, then asked, "You said you play in a four-squad, so who's the fourth?"

Luo Qingshan chuckled. "Who else? My wife, of course!"

"Pei Ran knows how to play PUBG?"

"Not really, he only plays when I do. Ever heard of 'domestic harmony'?"

Yan Zhun's hand wavered, and he tapped on "Do not bid for the landlord," wasting the excellent hand of cards he had in his game of Doudizhu.

He promptly closed the game.

Within half an hour, the large room booked by Luo Qingshan became packed.

Luo Qingshan was rather well-known throughout the school as having come from money. Hence, the table was covered with the finest bottles.

"Luo Qingshan is so generous." Lin Kang sat next to Yan Zhun, took out a pack of cigarettes from his pocket, and offered one to the other boy. "Here you go."

"No, thanks."

Lin Kang was a little surprised. He flicked the cigarette in a spin around his finger, then stuck it in his mouth. "Why? You quit?"

"No," Yan Zhun answered placidly. "I'm not smoking today."

Lin Kang walked to the karaoke machine, with a cigarette in his mouth. He tapped Luo Qingshan on the leg, gesturing him to move aside. "Get out of the way if you're not gonna pick songs. I'm still waiting for my turn! You don't monopolize a karaoke machine just to play hand games with someone else!"

"Be nicer to the birthday boy, can't you?" Luo Qingshan retorted, smiling. "Fine, you can sit here."

Lin Kang sat down. "Where's your wife? Why didn't you pick him up?"

"The man can take care of himself," Su Nian interrupted with a cheery tone. "Pei Ran won't get lost, right?"

"He'll be here any second now." Luo Qingshan took out his phone. "I offered to come to get him, but he refused. Let me send him a text..."

Someone pushed the door open. When Luo Qingshan saw who had just arrived, he quickly threw aside his dice and ran toward him.

Pei Ran's clothes were no different than usual. His dark jeans accentuated his long, slim legs. Luo Qingshan held his waist and pecked him on the corner of his mouth. "What took you so long? I was about to go fetch you."

Luo Qingshan's mouth reeked of cigarettes. Pei Ran wanted to dodge him, but then he remembered that today was his birthday, so he restrained his urge by sheer force of will.

He was not used PDA, so he just pursed his lips and said, "I saw this place was pretty close, so I walked instead of taking a taxi."

"No need to be so thrifty, Pei Ran." Su Nian grinned. "It took you at least ten minutes to walk here! You could've asked Qingshan to cover the taxi fare, y'know."

Su Nian was about to say something else when Pei Ran suddenly glanced over.

Pei Ran had thick eyelashes and almond shaped eyes, which gave him an air of gentleness and softness, but this glance of his was utterly devoid of emotion, so much so that Su Nian felt compelled to shut his mouth.

Only when Pei Ran sat down on the couch did Su Nian regain his composure.

"Happy birthday." Pei Ran stopped paying attention to Su Nian on his right. Instead, he handed his gift to Luo Qingshan. "I saw the screen on your phone was cracked, so I thought you'd want a new one."

Luo Qingshan was stunned for a moment, then he took the present from him and stole another kiss. "How nice of you, babe."

"Shit, you guys are rolling in cash or what?" Lin Kang looked over and wondered. "Why are you all buying phones for each other? Qingshan, if you don't need two phones, your buddy right here is more than willing to disburden you."

Pei Ran gave Luo Qingshan a puzzled look.

"Ah, right, I also bought him a phone." Su Nian smiled as if he couldn't care less. The light in the karaoke box was rather dim. When a ray or two occasionally hit his face, they reflected off his pitch-black irises. "Oh, and the same model, too. Haha, what a coincidence."

Pei Ran gave no reaction, yet Luo Qingshan's expression shifted minutely.

"I'll give yours back later, Su Nian." Luo Qingshan responded. "I'll be using Pei Ran's gift. I can't carry two phones around. It's too heavy, and I haven't the need."

Su Nian took a bottle of alcohol from the table and gulped down its contents, then shrugged. "Whatever you want."

Luo Qingshan lowered his eyes and asked, "Babe, what do you want to sing? I'll get Lin Kang to pick the songs you want."

Pei Ran shook his head. "I'm not singing. You should drink less."

"Don't worry, I don't have the heart to make you carry me back to the dorm."

They exchanged a few more words before being interrupted by the people around them.

"Lin Kang, switch places with me," Su Nian requested. "I want to smoke, but I don't think Pei Ran can stand the smell."

"Wait a sec, I'm picking a song..."

"I'll switch with you."

Su Nian turned toward that voice by instinct. Then, before he realized it, Yan Zhun had approached him and their eyes had met.

Yan Zhun's face could make anyone fall for him. Su Nian's heart skipped a beat, but he quickly recovered.

Unlike Luo Qingshan who'd become bent over a particular

boy, he had never been straight. Having been aware of his sexuality for longer, he also had the experience of years over Luo Qingshan. Included was the skill of reading people. He knew this type of boys—Yan Zhun was someone to be admired from a distance. The likes of Su Nian shouldn't touch him, not that he could, even if he tried.

It was only when Su Nian took Yan Zhun's spot that Pei Ran abruptly remembered: wasn't Yan Zhun also a smoker?

Luo Qingshan liked to move around and could never stay still. He only chatted with Pei Ran for a short while before leaving for the front seat to fiddle with the microphone.

Pei Ran was looking down at his phone. He didn't actually have anything to play—he had already cleared every single-player game he'd previously downloaded. His goal was nothing more than to avoid having to socialize. Although he knew everyone in the room, he had never bonded with any of them, as the only reason he had a chance to talk to them was that Luo Qingshan was around.

After losing all of his in-game currency, Pei Ran slowly raised his head. He was feeling thirsty and searched for a glass of water. However, he realized that there was neither water nor juice on the table, only alcohol.

Pei Ran hesitated for a moment. Just as he reached for a cup filled with alcohol, a hand tugged on his clothing.

Yan Zhun was sitting beside him. He never made a sound, but his presence was impossible to ignore. Pei Ran could smell his scent—a hint of pine fragrance that dispersed some of the stale air around them.

Pei Ran leaned back inadvertently. "What's wrong?"

Yan Zhun reached into the bag beneath his jacket and took out a bottle of mineral water.

Pei Ran didn't know how to respond.

"I bought it on the way, then forgot about it." Yan Zhun explained. "The cap is sealed. Want it?"

Seeing that it was just a bottle of water, Pei Ran skipped the formalities and held out his hand. "Thank you."

Yan Zhun unscrewed the cap before handing it to him.

Pei Ran took a sip of water and felt alive again. He turned to thank Yan Zhun again, only to notice that the other boy was examining him.

To be precise, his eyes fixated somewhere below his nose.

Pei Ran blinked and instinctively wiped the corner of his mouth. "What is it? Is my mouth dirty?"

Yan Zhun didn't answer. He looked away and swiftly joined the hand game beside him.

Pei Ran was a bit disconcerted. Before he could think properly about what had happened, someone put an arm around his neck.

Luo Qingshan was getting tired of singing, so he naturally returned to Pei Ran's side and started a four-person hand game with Lin Kang.

Lin Kang rolled the dice. "Old rules: one cup at a time, no sipping, and no preferential treatment for the birthday boy! Pei Ran, are you joining us?"

"No, he doesn't drink," Luo Qingshan said. All of a sudden, he remembered something and hastily asked the boy next to him, "Babe, are you thirsty? I'll order you some juice, all right?"

"It's fine, I have water." Pei Ran released himself from Luo Qingshan's embrace. He didn't feel comfortable in that position.

As the main character of his party, Luo Qingshan became

targeted in the hand game. No matter what number he called out, others would make him start another round.

"Shit, I only guessed once, and you want me to start again. Lin Kang, are you crazy? Are you trying to bring me down with you?" Luo Qingshan sneered before chugging his shot.

"Remember what you did to me on my own birthday? You're just reaping what you sowed..."

Pei Ran leaned on the couch and watched Luo Qingshan's face become increasingly flushed.

On the other hand, Yan Zhun barely drank anything. His legs were spread out casually, and his elbows were propped against his knees. His fingers, which held the dice shaker, were clean and slender, lending him an air of dignity even though he was merely rolling the dice.

"Maybe you should let Pei Ran take over. With your level of skill, you won't last until midnight," Lin Kang derided.

Luo Qingshan laughed and cussed him out a little. Suddenly, his phone on the table lit up, notifying him that he had just received a new message.

Luo Qingshan picked up his phone and unlocked it. His grin froze as he read the message. Silently, he moved the screen a few inches closer to his face.

A few seconds later, he put down his phone and replied to Kang. "It's nobo—I mean nothing important. Keep playing."

After another round, Luo Qingshan put the dice shaker upside down on the table.

"Wait a minute, I need to go to the bathroom."

But Lin Kang wasn't about to let him off the hook. "Why? You got scared and want an excuse to flee?"

"Bullshit, I'm going for a piss. By the way, ask the server for some juice." He then prodded Lin Kang with his foot. "Move aside so I can get out."

Luo Qingshan left the room in a hurry. Lin Kang snickered again. "Look at him go with such big steps. He's not leaving to pee. He's chickened out!"

As soon as Lin Kang sat back down, someone patted him on the shoulder.

"Please let me out, I have to make a phone call," Pei Ran requested.

In the corridor, Pei Ran walked slowly with his head hung low.

Since the day he scrolled through Su Nian's Moments, Pei Ran had been reflecting on himself.

First, he should not have gotten suspicious of his boyfriend over such minor details. Second, he should not have made ill-disposed speculations about Su Nian just because he got along with his boyfriend.

Having friends of the same gender was perfectly normal. Girls call them besties, and guys call them bros. He couldn't deprive Luo Qingshan of his right to make friends due to the remote chance that he might become attracted to them.

Besides, gay people weren't that common.

But for some reason, after Luo Qingshan dashed out, Pei Ran's first reaction had been to look for Su Nian. Only, without anyone noticing, Su Nian had already left the room.

When Pei Ran snapped out of his thoughts, he found himself a few meters away from the bathroom door.

He rubbed his temples, chuckled at himself, and decided to go back. But the moment he looked up, his smile vanished.

He saw Luo Qingshan not far away.

Luo Qingshan was standing stock still at the edge of the corridor, posture tall and straight, and his hands hanging at his sides.

Su Nian was holding him in his arms.

They were embracing like lovers, with no space between their bodies. Su Nian's head rested on Luo Qingshan's shoulder, as if he were whispering something.

About ten seconds later, Su Nian raised his head and kissed Luo Qingshan's chin.

Pei Ran was riveted to the spot. Before he could figure out how to react, his vision suddenly blacked out.

A large hand covered Pei Ran's eyes as the crisp scent of pine aroused his senses.

"Don't look. You'll dirty your eyes," said Yan Zhun.

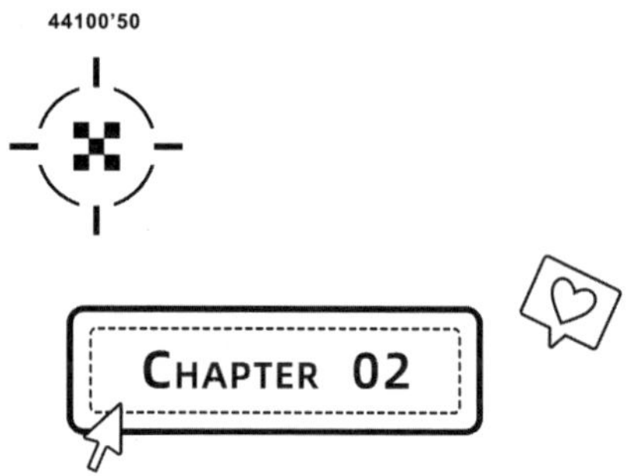

Pei Ran's heart was pounding, but he couldn't tell whether it was because he just witnessed Luo Qingshan and someone else kissing, or because of the lingering warmth on his eyelids.

"What now?" Yan Zhun pulled him around a corner, to where Luo Qingshan and Su Nian wouldn't see them.

Under the dim light, Pei Ran's cheeks became deeply flushed. His porcelain skin reacted strongly to any kind of heat or stress.

"What?" Pei Ran replied mechanically.

"Will you catch them in the act," asked Yan Zhun, "or leave?"

Pei Ran could never have imagined that he would one day catch his boyfriend "in the act."

When he eventually came to himself, he opened his mouth stiffly and, after taking his time, uttered, "Forget it... Let's leave."

It was Luo Qingshan's birthday today. With so many of his friends present, Pei Ran didn't want to make a scene.

“Okay,” Yan Zhun answered.

As they approached the room, Pei Ran was about to enter with his head down when Yan Zhun suddenly turned around. “Wait here; I’ll let Lin Kang know.”

Pei Ran stared blankly at him.

“Aren’t we leaving?” Yan Zhun asked naturally.

And so Pei Ran waited quietly outside. He even pondered what he would say if he were to bump into Luo Qingshan and Su Nian.

Yet by the time Yan Zhun left the room, Luo Qingshan still hadn’t returned.

Yan Zhun came out with Pei Ran’s jacket on his arm. “Let’s go.”

Outside of the karaoke box, as the chilly night air blew on him, Pei Ran finally felt alive again.

He lowered his head and ruffled his hair, then took a deep breath.

Out of the corner of his eyes, Yan Zhun noticed his expression. He pursed his lips several times before asking, “Do you want to cry?”

“No,” replied Pei Ran.

“You look like you do.”

Pei Ran wasn’t on the brink of tears, but he did have a lot on his mind.

“I’m fine,” he assured. “Thank you for accompanying me. I’ll treat you to milk tea.”

There happened to be a bubble tea shop nearby. Pei Ran figured that, after buying their respective drinks, they could go their separate ways. He needed time to digest tonight’s shocking revelation.

Yan Zhun declined: “I don’t drink that stuff. Too sweet.”

Pei Ran nodded. "Then I'll..."

"How about coffee?" Yan Zhun asked. "The café across the street grinds their beans fresh."

Yan Zhun seemed to be friends with the café's owner. They had been chatting at the counter for quite a while.

Pei Ran sat alone, gazing distantly out the window.

The soft clink of cups on the table brought his attention back.

"I asked him not to make it too bitter," said Yan Zhun as he sat down.

"Thank you," Pei Ran answered before realizing that he had been thanking Yan Zhun a lot lately. "Do you know the owner?"

"Yeah, we're friends. He graduated from our school a few years ago," Yan Zhun explained. "I met him through gaming."

Pei Ran wasn't sure if he had been fully attentive, but he still nodded.

He took a sip of coffee. It was bitter, but it had a sweet aftertaste—much better than those sugary milk teas.

After a moment, he put down his cup. "Did you already know about this?"

Yan Zhun stirred his coffee. "No, I'm not close with them."

You're not close, yet you came to his birthday party?

Pei Ran interpreted Yan Zhun's response as him being unwilling to snitch on a friend. His lips twitched and he hummed noncommittally

Pei Ran spotted a napkin near his hand. Yan Zhun had just fetched it and was pushing it towards him alongside the coffee.

Pei Ran felt the need to clarify, "I'm not going to cry."

"Okay," said Yan Zhun. "Is the coffee bitter?"

The subject changed so quickly that Pei Ran had to pause. "A little bit, but it tastes good."

Yan Zhun took out a piece of candy from his pocket and placed it in front of Pei Ran.

It was a piece of White Rabbit—Pei Ran's favorite milk candy. He even kept a few stored beside his computer.

"You can take anything out of your pocket." Pei Ran peeled off the wrapping and put the candy into his mouth without thanking Yan Zhun again. The instant that the milky sweetness of the candy touched his taste buds, his mood lightened considerably.

Unfortunately, he barely had time to relax before his phone started ringing—it was Luo Qingshan.

Pei Ran glanced at his phone for a few seconds, then declined the call. Luo Qingshan didn't give up and called him again, but Pei Ran still didn't pick up. Only after the fifth unanswered call did Luo Qingshan stop at last.

Pei Ran was about to breathe a sigh of relief when his phone lit up again. This time, the call came from Lin Kang.

Pei Ran hesitated for a moment and took it on.

"Pei Ran, where are you?" Judging by the commotion around him, Lin Kang should still be inside the karaoke room. "Hey, turn off the music! I'm on the phone with Pei Ran! "

Pei Ran answered this question with a question of his own, "Is there a problem?"

Lin Kang paused momentarily. "Ah, yes... Luo Qingshan is drunk; he's been asking for you. "

On the other end of the line, Luo Qingshan leaned on the sofa in a drunken stupor. Suddenly, he straightened his back and jumped on Lin Kang. "Pei Ran? Babe? Where's Pei Ran?

Pei Ran... Why don't you answer my calls? "

Lin Kang laughed and let out a curse word. "There, there. Take the phone and explain it yourself."

Before he could prepare himself, Pei Ran was talking to Luo Qingshan.

"Babe? Babe?" Luo Qingshan called out twice, then squinted at the phone to confirm that he was indeed on a call. "Pei Ran, don't ignore me."

Luo Qingshan couldn't hold his liquor very well. Judging by his voice, he seemed a bit wasted.

Drunks were impossible to reason with. Knowing this, Pei Ran sighed softly. "You're drunk."

"I know..." Luo Qingshan slurred. "I know. I'm drunk; you're not happy. I won't drink next time... Babe, come take me home. "

Pei Ran could hear people around Luo Qingshan jeering in the background. Lin Kang yelled that he wanted to record Luo Qingshan in this drunken state.

Pei Ran kept his patience. "I'm not going back. Put Lin Kang on the phone again."

"Why?" Luo Qingshan's drunken babbling continued, "No way! I'll die if you don't come."

The background noise grew louder and louder, to the point of giving Pei Ran a headache.

He didn't want others to make a fool of them both, so he had no choice but to soften his tone. "Will you listen to me or not?"

Leaning against a chair, Yan Zhun stuffed his hands in his pocket and watched him.

Luo Qingshan thought briefly and conceded, "I will."

"Then give the phone to Lin Kang," Pei Ran instructed.

"Good boy."

At last, the phone was in Lin Kang's hand again. Pei Ran told him that he wouldn't be returning for the night and hoped Lin Kang could bring Luo Qingshan back to the dorm.

Until he hung up, he could still overhear Luo Qingshan calling his name.

"Good boy?" Yan Zhun sneered as he curled his lips. "Are you coaxing a child?"

"There's no difference between a drunk person and a child."

"There's a big one," Yan Zhun stated coldly. "A child doesn't cheat on their partner.."

Pei Ran frowned slightly. He had the impression that Yan Zhun's tone changed after that phone call, although he could be mistaken.

Yan Zhun wasn't wrong, but making that observation in this context was like rubbing salt in Pei Ran's wound.

Pei Ran pressed his lips together. "Indeed."

The phone on the table suddenly buzzed—Luo Qingshan sent him a voice message.

Pei Ran clicked on the message. Before he had the time to press the phone against his ear, most of it—illogical, gibberish nonsense—had already played out loud.

Most importantly, he heard Su Nian's voice intermingled with the background noise around Luo Qingshan. The way he called Luo Qingshan "bro" sounded both intimate and lovey-dovey. Pei Ran could hear that these two were close together.

"What is it now?" Yan Zhun scoffed. "The child can't find his toy?"

Many people who were cheated on liked to pour their hearts out to a friend, hoping that said friend would protest their grievances and serve justice on their behalf.

But Pei Ran was not one of those people. He didn't like to expose his vulnerabilities to others; instead, he dealt with them by himself.

Yan Zhun had compared him to a toy. Perhaps he blurted out words he didn't mean. Under normal circumstances, it wouldn't have been a big deal. But in this particular case, Pei Ran felt somewhat offended.

He abruptly remembered that he was not close to Yan Zhun—not even to the point of being ordinary friends.

"Maybe." Pei Ran put away his phone and got up. "It's late, so I'll get going now. We can chat another time. Thank you for helping me tonight."

Pei Ran went to the front desk to pay, stuffing the receipt into his pocket.

He pushed the café's door open and barely took two steps when he once again heard the chiming of the bells that hung on the door. Then, someone grasped his arm.

Yan Zhun's palm was so hot that Pei Ran was startled by his grip.

"I'm sorry." Yan Zhun's expression remained impassive, but he was apologizing. "I misspoke."

Pei Ran blinked, confused by his action. "It's okay; you don't have to apologize..."

Yan Zhun took all the White Rabbit candies from his pocket and put them in Pei Ran's palm.

"These are all yours," he said. "Don't be angry."

Pei Ran returned to his dorm and dumped all the candies in his pocket by his laptop.

When his roommate heard the clatter, he looked behind

and laughed. "Is the White Rabbit Company going bankrupt or something? Are they handing them out on the streets?"

"No, these were gifts."

The roommate let out an "Oh," then continued, "Luo Qingshan only got you a few pieces? What a cheapskate."

Pei Ran was not keen on flaunting his relationship. Whenever his roommate mentioned Luo Qingshan, he would answer with monosyllables to avoid dwelling on the topic.

He walked to the bathroom with his pajamas and explained, "It wasn't him. They're from a friend."

"I see. By the way, I'm going out tonight." The roommate grinned from ear to ear. "It's Luo Qingshan's birthday today, so I thought you wouldn't come back either."

Pei Ran smiled without speaking.

By the time he stepped out of the shower, his roommate had already left. He laid on his bed and checked his phone, only to find his screen bombarded by notifications.

Luo Qingshan had sent him countless voice messages of varying lengths, plus a bunch of stickers.

Most people fall asleep when they become drunk. Luo Qingshan was different—alcohol energized him instead.

Pei Ran carelessly swiped across the screen. He wasn't in the mood to listen to any of them.

He didn't want to hear Luo Qingshan's voice or Su Nian's. He only wished for a good night's sleep.

Pei Ran closed the chat window and was about to close WeChat when he noticed a large "1" next to the Contacts icon.

Approved has sent a friend request.

Approved:
Yan Zhun.

They had plenty of friends in common, so Pei Ran didn't

question who gave his WeChat ID to Yan Zhun. He approved his friend request without a second thought, then swiftly changed his alias.

Yan Zhun:
[voice message]

Illuminated by the light from his phone screen, Pei Ran pursed his lips and pressed on the two-second voice message.

"Sorry; don't be angry. Get some sleep soon."

He heard Yan Zhun's low and deep voice mixed with the sound of water running, as if he was taking a shower.

Pei Ran was suddenly very amused. Luo Qingshan was obviously the one at fault here, so why did Yan Zhun keep apologizing?

Besides... Yan Zhun hadn't done anything wrong.

Pei Ran:
I'm not angry. You should also sleep soon.

On the other end of the line, Yan Zhun stood under the showerhead and read his message over and over.

Luo Qingshan woke up to the first glimmer of dawn.

He narrowed his eyes, stared blankly at the space for a while, then struggled to sit on his bed. He felt as if someone had bludgeoned his head with a wooden staff, and his face became twisted with pain.

Luo Qingshan looked around and realized that he was lying in a hotel room. He was naked above the waist and only wore a pair of underpants. However, his skin didn't feel sticky as he had expected from a hangover—someone must have cleaned him up already.

Something dropped in the bathroom and clattered faintly. Luo Qingshan forced a smile. "Babe, what are you doing? My head is killing me... Damn, that shitty karaoke box must've sold fake fucking wine."

Luo Qingshan scratched his hair and pushed back the covers. Suddenly, he heard footsteps coming from the bathroom.

"Bro, you're awake? Do you feel sick? Need a glass of water?"

Luo Qingshan froze, then turned around in a daze. "Why are you here?"

"Why shouldn't I be here?" replied Su Nian, holding a clean cup in his hand.

"Where's my ba—Pei Ran? "

"He left last night." Su Nian smiled. "I'll pour you some water first. Get up now; we still have class this afternoon."

Luo Qingshan sat up with his legs crossed and repeatedly banged his forehead against his knees. It took him a long time to recall vague memories of last night.

By the time he returned from the bathroom, Pei Ran had already left the room. No matter how he tried to please Pei Ran later, he wouldn't come back.

But the most crucial part was...

Luo Qingshan couldn't resist peeking at the bathroom, then rubbed his face violently.

Shit, he might have made out with Su Nian.

Fake wines ruin lives.

Luo Qingshan saw the incident as nothing more than a mishap, so he soon moved on from his guilty feelings. After charging for an eternity, his phone finally lit up, and he immediately picked it up.

As soon as he opened WeChat, he couldn't stop himself from grinning. Last night, he had sent more than thirty voice messages to Pei Ran. The shorter ones were two or three seconds long, while the longer ones lasted up to forty or fifty seconds.

Pei Ran must've been driven up the wall by him.

Luo Qingshan crossed his legs and started to type.

Luo Qingshan:
Haha babe, did you lose sleep because I kept sending you messages?

Luo Qingshan:
Why didn't you bring me back to the hotel last night? **[crying emoji]**

Luo Qingshan:
You meanie. I kept sending you messages, but you didn't even reply to me once.

Su Nian brought a glass of water, and Luo Qingshan took a sip. "Thanks, how's your leg? Did you hurt yourself carrying me yesterday? "

"Don't worry; it's almost healed." Su Nian smiled, revealing his dimples.

After washing himself, Luo Qingshan checked his phone again. When he saw the complete lack of reply, he couldn't help but frown.

When Luo Qingshan opened the bathroom door, Su Nian was standing beside him, fiddling with his bangs in front of the mirror.

Luo Qingshan asked, "Did you stay here all night? Where did you sleep..."

Then he abruptly fell silent, because Su Nian suddenly approached him and leaned his head close to Luo Qingshan's.

Luo Qingshan jumped back a few steps. "What are you doing?"

Su Nian hesitated a bit. "A good morning kiss?"

Luo Qingshan stared at him, his expression shifting from surprise to astonishment. An eternity passed before he opened his mouth, "Su Nian, are you still drunk?"

The phone rang nonstop for almost 20 minutes before the person wrapped in the bedsheets finally stirred.

Pei Ran opened his eyes and spent a few seconds collecting his thoughts after his dream.

He picked up the phone two seconds before it hung up. He was so sleepy that he could only hum.

"Babe, it's me... Are you still sleeping? Oh, you don't have class today, right?" Luo Qingshan sounded quite energetic. "I only have class this afternoon. What do you want to eat? I'll order it for you."

"No need," Pei Ran answered.

"Yes need. I want to buy you food. So, what would you like?" Luo Qingshan glanced at the food stores around him. "Did you see my messages? Why didn't you text me back? You didn't come back to fetch me either. You're so cold; you don't care about your boyfriend at all..."

"Luo Qingshan." Pei Ran interrupted him.

"Yes?"

Pei Ran paused for two seconds, then replied, "Get me a bowl of wonton, thanks."

"Why are you thanking me?" Luo Qingshan chuckled. "Isn't bringing you meals my privilege—"

Pei Ran hung up the phone.

He rubbed his face as his mind brought him back to last night's dream.

It had been a very absurd dream. In it, he and Luo Qingshan had been climbing a mountain together. They had gotten caught in a landslide, so they'd hidden inside a cave. But then, when he'd turned back, Luo Qingshan had transformed into

Yan Zhun.

In his dream, Yan Zhun had looked as aloof as he did in reality. He had said to Pei Ran, "Don't be afraid," and they had stayed up until dawn.

Maybe Yan Zhun had also said something else, but Pei Ran couldn't remember.

When Pei Ran finished washing his face, someone knocked on the dorm door.

As soon as he opened the door, Luo Qingshan lifted the plastic bag in his hand. "Shrimp wonton with sesame oil and a touch of hot pepper. Is this to your liking?"

Pei Ran stopped wiping his face for a moment, then returned to the washstand. "Come in; I'll join you after I rinse my towel."

After arranging everything, Luo Qingshan pulled the roommate's chair and sat next to Pei Ran. He watched Pei Ran eat with his chin resting on his hand.

Luo Qingshan liked to observe Pei Ran eat. Pei Ran had been brought up very strictly. Even after an exhausting afternoon basketball game, he would still eat in a neat and elegant manner that was pleasing to the eyes.

Therefore, when Pei Ran put down his spoon and asked to break up, Luo Qingshan initially smiled and nodded.

A few seconds later, Luo Qingshan's smile froze on his lips. He asked incredulously, "What?"

"I said," Pei Ran repeated, "let's break up."

"Why?" Now, Luo Qingshan couldn't even force a grin. He gradually straightened his back, visibly panicking. "Babe, are you joking?"

"I wouldn't joke about this," stated Pei Ran.

Luo Qingshan swallowed nervously. He took a long time to

find his voice again. "Why? Did I do something wrong? Did I upset you... because I didn't listen to you last night and drank too much? Or did I annoy you by sending you too many messages..."

Luo Qingshan's gaze then drifted towards the table. "Or is this wonton not tasty enough?"

Pei Ran frowned quizzically. "These trivial things don't upset me."

"I know, I know." Luo Qingshan licked his lower lip. "That's why I have no idea why you're angry..."

"I saw it."

"Huh?"

"I saw it," Pei Ran uttered after a brief silence. "You and Su Nian, in front of the bathroom door."

Luo Qingshan was on the verge of asking what happened in front of the bathroom door when the realization stunned him like a thunderbolt, leaving him incapable of budging an inch.

Pei Ran threw away the wonton container and continued, "We've been together for three years. Throughout this time, you've given me a watch, a few backpacks, and seven pairs of sneakers... I've kept track of everything. When I go home in a few days, I'll do the accounts and transfer you the amount. Oh right—how much did the wonton cost? I'll transfer you immediately."

By the time Pei Ran opened WeChat Pay, Luo Qingshan finally became aware of the seriousness of the situation.

Instinctively, he reached out and seized Pei Ran's wrist.

"No..." Luo Qingshan tried to put his thoughts into words, but he couldn't make any sense. "It's not like what you saw. Listen to me, babe... You meant last night, right? Last night, you were there too... I drank too much; I was dizzy..."

"So you kissed someone else." Pei Ran helped finish his sentence.

"Yes... No, that's not true." Luo Qingshan fumbled. "He kissed me on his own. It had nothing to do with me. I have nothing to do with him..."

"I asked Lin Kang about last night," Pei Ran said. "After you went back to the room, you resumed playing dice with them."

Not expecting that he would be interrupted, Luo Qingshan stared confusedly at Pei Ran.

"Furthermore, you got another person drunk during your game. Only after that did you become plastered and started babbling," Pei Ran calmly said. "Therefore, you couldn't have been completely wasted when Su Nian kissed you. You had enough strength to push him away."

Luo Qingshan was losing his temper. "It was nothing more than an accident! I didn't expect that he'd kiss me. I barely had time to react before it was over!"

Pei Ran pursed his lips. "Su Nian's WeChat Moments are full of your photos."

"He's delusional. I didn't even accept his confession!"

When he heard the word "confession," Pei Ran lowered his gaze.

Su Nian had confessed to Luo Qingshan, and afterwards, not only did Luo Qingshan not distance himself from Su Nian, but he also invited him to his birthday party and chose to spend time alone with him.

Pei Ran felt much more at ease now. Perhaps he had already been thoroughly shocked by what he witnessed last night.

"Luo Qingshan," Pei Ran started, then sighed. "Luo Qingshan, let's break up."

Luo Qingshan's eyes turned red in a split second.

Luo Qingshan gritted his teeth and stayed silent for a long time. At last, he replied, "No, Pei Ran.

"You can't break up with me because of something so small," he muttered. "I became gay because of you. You made me like men. You can't break up with me."

Pei Ran's back stiffened.

"For you, I studied like hell just so that we can go to the same university. Because of you, I refused so many girls. I even broke a finger for your sake."

Pei Ran's face paled as images of Luo Qingshan's hands covered in blood flooded his mind.

Afterward, Pei Ran stopped paying attention to what Luo Qingshan was telling him. He struggled to blot out memories of that grisly scene.

"Pei Ran… I truly love you," Luo Qingshan pleaded. "I know that I made a mistake last night. I was drunk. Don't blame me… I won't do this anymore. I'll block Su Nian when I get back to my dorm. I won't drink again. Forgive me, please?"

Pei Ran eyed him without saying a word.

Just when Luo Qingshan thought he would soften up, Pei Ran quickly looked away and tied up the plastic bag in front of him with a tight knot.

"I'm truly grateful that you helped me get rid of those people back then." Pei Ran chose his words carefully. "I'll repay you five times your medical expenses, all right?

"Or, if you need anything in the future, you can always come to me. I'll do anything within my power to help out. You can also borrow money from me," Pei Ran said softly. "Let's break up, Luo Qingshan."

Luo Qingshan bought a pack of beers and brought them

back to his dorm.

By the time he cracked open the third can, his roommate shot him a look.

Yan Zhun closed PUBG, stood up, and placed a present on Luo Qingshan's desk. He said coolly, "Happy birthday, here's a late gift."

"Thanks." Luo Qingshan mumbled. He glanced at the package—it was the latest model of Apple earphones. Must've cost a small fortune.

He was somewhat taken aback. After all, his relationship with Yan Zhun was far from close. Who knew Yan Zhun would give him such an expensive gift?

Luo Qingshan swallowed another gulp of beer, wiped the corner of his mouth, and suddenly asked, "I heard from Lin Kang that Pei Ran left with you last night. Was he... in a terrible mood? Did he tell you anything?"

Yan Zhun halted. "Why do you ask?"

Luo Qingshan thought he couldn't think straight anymore. He and Yan Zhun were nearly strangers. Judging by Yan Zhun's personality, he couldn't possibly reveal anything to Luo Qingshan.

"Whatever, it's nothing." Luo Qingshan leaned back and let out a heavy sigh.

"What's the matter?" Yan Zhun asked.

Luo Qingshan didn't notice how abnormal it was that his roommate expressed concern for him.

"Pei Ran and I quarreled." Luo Qingshan's face tightened. "Also, he wanted to break up with me... Fuck! It's all Su Nian's fault!"

Yan Zhun subtly raised an eyebrow and waited before answering, "Don't worry, the next one will be better."

"There's no next one," Luo Qingshan fumed. "I'll apologize to him once he cools down."

Yan Zhun said nothing else. He sat down in front of his computer again and clicked on his new WeChat messages.

Not Important:
Boss, you won't play another round? Fine, we'll play together next time. Help me climb up the ranking!

Not Important:
No! Call me next time you're online! I'll be there for sure! Boss!

Approved:
Invite me, I'm still on.

Not Important:
???

Not Important:
Didn't you say that you were done, boss? I'll invite you right away.

Approved:
I'm in a good mood, so I'll carry you for two more rounds.

As the class ended, Pei Ran closed his textbook, took out a face mask from his pocket, and put it on.

"You're leaving early again?" asked his roommate.

Pei Ran nodded.

"You've been leaving early for a few days in a row. If I didn't know better, I'd think you were avoiding someone bullying you after school..."

Pei Ran smiled and didn't say anything. He waited for the moment his teacher turned around to gather his books, then left through the back door.

When Pei Ran was some distance away from the school building, he loosened up at last.

He breathed a sigh of relief and checked his phone. As

expected, he had received several messages—all of them from Luo Qingshan.

Pei Ran quickly scrolled through their chat history over the last few days. Somehow, he had the vague impression of being transported back to high school.

Luo Qingshan:
Pei Ran, wanna have lunch together?

Pei Ran:
No, I ordered take-out.

Luo Qingshan:
OK, which one? I'll order the same.

Luo Qingshan:
[video call request declined]

Luo Qingshan:
Babe, I miss you.

Luo Qingshan:
I couldn't pay attention in class for the whole day.

Luo Qingshan:
I deleted Su Nian already. Feel free to check anytime.

Luo Qingshan:
Wanna eat dinner together? I'll see you in your class.

Back in high school, Luo Qingshan had courted Pei Ran in the same way: he asked the teacher to sit next to Pei Ran; he moved to the bunkbed above Pei Ran's bed; he always ate lunch and supper with Pei Ran. No matter what Pei Ran said, he wouldn't leave him alone.

Pei Ran closed the chat window and unpinned his DMs with Luo Qingshan from the top of his chat list—a feature that that Luo Qingshan had previously set up.

In the evening, when Luo Qingshan pushed open the door of his dorm, Yan Zhun was watching a replay of the PUBG Global Championship.

He only wore one earphone and his legs were spread out

casually, seemingly absent-minded. The creak of the door didn't startle him in the slightest.

With a loud thunk, Luo Qingshan set a pack of beer atop his desk. He asked Yan Zhun, "Want some?"

The cans were covered in condensation, obviously taken out of the fridge only recently. Yan Zhun eyed the drenched tabletop, frowned slightly, then shook his head. "No, thanks."

Thus, Luo Qingshan had no choice but to drink alone.

Halfway through, he reflexively reached toward his phone to call someone who could keep him company. He had just dialed the number when he realized something was off, and he immediately hung up.

At 2 AM, Yan Zhun was woken up by the voice of his roommate.

He slowly opened his eyes, his dark irises filled with drowsiness and irritation.

Luo Qingshan, "Pei Ran, you're so cold-hearted..."

Yan Zhun felt wide awake in an instant.

The lights inside the dorm went out hours ago, so the screen of Yan Zhun's phone became the only source of illumination.

Luo Qingshan's tone sounded very depressed. "Three years... we've been together for three years. You have to forgive me, Pei Ran."

Luo Qingshan mumbled to himself for a few more minutes. Yan Zhun was starting to feel annoyed, so he grabbed his earplugs underneath his pillow. Just as he was about to put them on, he heard a soft rustle.

"Luo Qingshan, it's getting late."

So Luo Qingshan had turned on the speaker mode.

Pei Ran's voice was hoarse and exhausted. "Whatever you

want to say, leave it for tomorrow, OK?"

"You'll ignore me tomorrow," replied Luo Qingshan.

Pei Ran ruffled his hair as he sluggishly recovered his senses.

Luo Qingshan spoke in broken sentences and stuttered quite a bit—clearly, he had been drinking again.

Pei Ran took a sip of water to soothe his sore throat and continued, "Luo Qingshan, that's not the only reason... why I broke up with you."

The other end of the line went quiet—there was no reply.

Pei Ran, "We agreed before, to give it a try."

At that time, Luo Qingshan had been lying on a hospital bed, his hands and arms covered with bandages. The two of them had been about 17 or 18, eyes flickering with agitation.

Luo Qingshan had been grimacing in pain, yet he had still tried to humor Pei Ran, asking if he was moved and if he would promise to marry him.

Pei Ran had stayed silent for a long while. Finally, he had said, "Luo Qingshan, we can try it out."

Afterwards, it had taken Pei Ran three years to understand that love wouldn't necessarily grow stronger over time.

At least, his feelings for Luo Qingshan as they stood were not strong enough to pardon everything he did.

Luo Qingshan still didn't utter a word. Pei Ran lowered his eyes. "I'm sorry..."

"He's asleep." A deep voice came from the other end.

Pei Ran was startled. "Huh?"

Yan Zhun took the empty beer can from the desk and threw it into the garbage bin. "He drank some booze and fell asleep. This is Yan Zhun speaking."

Pei Ran was at a loss for words.

In other words, Yan Zhun had heard each and every word that Luo Qingshan had said to him?

A strange feeling of awkwardness spread upwards from the soles of Pei Ran's feet. He gulped and paused for some time before talking again. "Did we wake you up?"

"No," Yan Zhun replied impassively, "I was staying up late."

Pei Ran let out a soft "Oh."

Silence fell between them, albeit briefly.

"Go to sleep," said Yan Zhun. "Next time, remember to mute your phone before going to bed."

Pei Ran hesitated for a moment, then said, "Alright."

The second before Pei Ran hung up, Yan Zhun dropped a hasty "Good night."

After the WeChat call was over, Yan Zhun looked down and accidentally saw Luo Qingshan's chat list.

The first one was Pei Ran; the second was Su Nian.

Su Nian:
Did you call me? I'll call you back now if that's OK...

He couldn't read any older messages.

Yan Zhun recalled a line from Luo Qingshan's incoherent mumbling, "I already blocked him. What else do you want?"

Suddenly, Luo Qingshan's head—which was facing the desk—turned over, as he blurted out, "Babe..."

Yan Zhun grabbed one of Luo Qingshan's jackets at random and threw it over him. "Don't call him that."

With his eyes still closed, Luo Qingshan muttered under his breath, "Huh?"

"You two already broke up," Yan Zhun had the rare patience to remind him. "He's not your babe anymore."

Pei Ran sat on his bed, staring at the screen of his phone.

Did he hang up too soon? Yan Zhun seemed to have more to say.

After such a squabble, Pei Ran had completely lost the will to sleep. Fortunately, his roommate was out of town for a few days, leaving him alone in his dorm room. Otherwise, he would've had to run to the balcony to answer his phone.

He sat in front of his laptop and looked at the half-done sketch, wondering if he ought to finish it now.

In the end, his laziness got the better of him. Pei Ran snatched his phone and climbed back into his bed.

Pei Ran laid on the side and kept playing on his phone. He casually refreshed his WeChat Moments and noticed a new status published a minute ago.

Yan Zhun:
Gaming companion for hire. Can play any game, available anytime.

Pei Ran clicked on Yan Zhun's Moment, only to realize that post had been swiftly deleted.

Or rather, Yan Zhun had reposted something different...

Yan Zhun:
Gaming companion for hire. Can play any game, available anytime, can do anything—even act as a friendly ear, just message me directly for any desired service. I'm running out of money for food **[website link]**

Pei Ran spent ten minutes reading through his friends' new Moments from the previous day. But ultimately, he couldn't resist clicking on that link.

It looked like a typical profile for a gaming companion. Yan Zhun's account seemed to be newly registered, as the number of clients served was a solid zero. His rate was 20 yuan per hour—the lowest on the platform.

Pei Ran checked it over and over before placing an order

for ten hours. He closed the webpage right after paying.

He was about to go to sleep with his phone on mute when a WeChat message popped up.

Yan Zhun:
Boss.

Yan Zhun:
When do we start?

Pei Ran widened his eyes and pondered for several seconds before typing.

Pei Ran:
What are you talking about

Yan Zhun:
You bought 10 hours of my gaming companion service.

Pei Ran:
... How did you know it was me?

Yan Zhun:
I saw your WeChat profile pic.

Pei Ran facepalmed. How could he forget about that?

So, the million-dollar question: would it be disrespectful if he admitted that he was only trying to support Yan Zhun with a bit of lunch money?

Yan Zhun:
?

Pei Ran:
Uh... it's too late for gaming today.

Yan Zhun:
Then tomorrow?

Pei Ran:
The next few days... I have a part-time job.

Yan Zhun:
Classes are on break next week. I'll play with you then.

Yan Zhun:
I don't like being in debt.

Well, if the conversation was steering that way...

Pei Ran:
Okay

Pei Ran:
I hung up too quickly earlier and didn't hear what you said at the end, sorry.

Yan Zhun:
Don't worry, it was nothing.

Pei Ran:
Alright then. By the way, could you please put a glass of water beside Luo Qingshan?

Yan Zhun:
You're my boss now.

Pei Ran:
?

Yan Zhun:
I'd pry open his mouth open and squirt water inside if you asked.

Pei Ran:
...

It took a while for people around Pei Ran and Luo Qingshan to learn about their breakup.

It wasn't Pei Ran who made the breakup public—he had never liked to talk about his feelings with others. It couldn't have been Luo Qingshan either. In his mind, this was only a hurdle in their relationship that they would eventually overcome.

One day, Pei Ran met Lin Kang on his way to school.

"Luo Qingshan doesn't even bring you to our dinner parties anymore. Anybody could see that there's something wrong between you two," Lin Kang said. "Someone mentioned it last night as a joke, but Luo Qingshan lost his temper on the spot. He would have made a scene had we not stopped him."

Pei Ran didn't know what face to make, so he answered

stiffly, "Is that so..."

Lin Kang gave him a strange look. "But why did you two break up?"

Pei Ran gave a well-rehearsed excuse, "Incompatibility."

"You were together for three years, and only now you realize that you're incompatible?" Lin Kang smirked. "Fine, I won't ask if you don't want to say. By the way, how are you getting home this afternoon? Wanna go together?"

The school's week-long holiday was about to start. Lin Kang and Pei Ran lived close to each other, so they would normally get off at the same bus stop.

"My family will pick me up," Pei Ran said, "Do you want a lift?"

That was precisely what Lin Kang wanted. The bus ride was always so shaky that it never failed to make him nauseated.

"When are we leaving? I won't be late, promise... I think my class ends ten minutes after yours—I can skip the end."

"Don't worry; just follow your schedule. Take your time; I'll wait for you."

Lin Kang thanked him, then felt his cell phone buzzing in his pocket. Mechanically, he took his phone out and checked his home screen—it turned out that one of his group chats was caught in a heated debate and was mentioning him nonstop.

"These idiots, they'd rather plan for activities instead of going home..." Lin Kang mumbled. "They have nothing better to do, don't they? Su Nian suggested that we all go on a trip—as if seven days would be enough for traveling... Will you go?"

Pei Ran stared at him, confused. "Go where?"

"On the trip, duh. Didn't you see the group chat?"

"I'm not in it," Pei Ran answered.

Taken aback, Lin Kang swiftly verified the list of group

chat members.

Indeed, Pei Ran was not in it.

It was Su Nian who had created the group a week ago. In his usual style, it had more than 30 people. Lin Kang hadn't known at first that Pei Ran and Luo Qingshan had broken up, so he'd assumed that Pei Ran was also in the group.

He and Pei Ran shared a lot of chat groups. Pei Ran seldom talked, only replying with a sentence or two when someone mentioned him. Therefore, even though he didn't see Pei Ran in the chat group for a few days, he had no idea that something was amiss.

"I thought someone added you... Well, Su Nian wants to go on a trip to Dali," Lin Kang fumbled.

How could Su Nian be so careless? He shouldn't have missed Pei Ran when Pei Ran had been friends with them for so long.

But now that he was up to date with the current situation, Lin Kang felt weird about adding Pei Ran to the group. After all, Luo Qingshan was quite active in it.

"It's alright." Pei Ran smiled.

Lin Kang wanted to change the subject as quickly as possible to not dwell on this uncomfortable topic. Before he could come up with something to say, he saw another friend coming their way.

Yan Zhun was wearing a plain black T-shirt. One of his hands dangled lazily over a basketball, pinning it to his thigh. He was walking and talking to the person beside him.

Lin Kang yelled out to him, "Yan Zhun!"

Yan Zhun glanced at him. His chest heaved slightly as sweat dripped from his chin.

Trying to break the ice, Lin Kang grinned and asked an

obvious question, "Just finished your game?"

Yan Zhun didn't answer and turned back to continue his conversation. Lin Kang felt even more embarrassed.

He laughed uncomfortably and was about to curse at Yan Zhun when the latter nodded to his friend, turned around, and walked towards them.

"You..." Yan Zhun said, then paused. "What are you two doing here?"

"Our classes just ended," Lin Kang replied. "What, you think I'd come here just for a walk?"

Yan Zhun stared at Pei Ran. Surprised, Lin Kang also shifted his gaze towards Pei Ran.

Pei Ran spoke casually. "I came to help the professor move some art supplies."

Lin Kang breathed a sigh of relief. Thank goodness they've moved past the awkward topic. "Yan Zhun, did you see the chat group? They want to plan a trip to Dali. Are you going?"

Yan Zhun, "I didn't check, and no."

Lin Kang nodded; he had already guessed the answer. "Why are you standing like a mile away?"

Yan Zhun, "I stink after my basketball game."

Lin Kang snickered. "I didn't know you were so fussy."

Pei Ran didn't pay much attention to their conversation. He lowered his gaze, which fell on Yan Zhun's hand.

Yan Zhun's fingers were long and slender. His nails were well-kept, and his skin was stained with dirt from the game. Pei Ran remembered how attractive his protruding knuckles had been when his hand clutched the mouse.

"Are you coming tonight?"

Pei Ran couldn't tear his eyes away and wondered if Yan Zhun could become a hand model.

Then he noticed Yan Zhun's curled index finger that gently tapped on the basketball twice.

"Are you coming tonight, Pei Ran?" Yan Zhun added.

At the sound of his name, Pei Ran looked up, startled. It took him a while to realize the meaning of Yan Zhun's words.

Yan Zhun was asking if his "job" would start tonight.

Remembering that Yan Zhun didn't like to owe favors, Pei Ran replied without hesitation, "Sure."

Yan Zhun nodded, and the hair on his forehead which was matted with sweat bobbed along. "Then I'll be waiting."

As Yan Zhun left with his friend, Lin Kang stared at his back for a few seconds, then turned to look at the person next to him, quite bemused.

"Are you coming tonight?"

Wasn't that the same question he always asked his girlfriend?

Lin Kang mentally slapped himself. Just what the hell was he thinking...

"I had no idea," Lin Kang remarked as he reined in his wild imagination, "that you and Yan Zhun were so close."

"Not really," answered Pei Ran.

"If you two are not that close, why would he ask you to join him tonight?" Lin Kang snickered. "What will you do, anyway?"

"Play video games."

Lin Kang was at a loss for words. "Fine. But playing with him is indeed quite a treat. Don't tell this to other people, but I know that Team TZG tried to recruit him for a handsome salary when he was in high school. That team has been hiring nothing less than the country's top players for the last few years and even won the national championship last year, yet he didn't sign with them.

"So you see, it took Luo Qingshan a long time to finally get to play a match with him. Haha..."

Pei Ran was a bit taken aback. "Is he that good?"

Then... was he paying Yan Zhun too little?

Much later, he did some research on his own. Even fledging gaming companions for mid-to-high ranked players would set their rate higher than a measly 20 yuan per hour—that wasn't even enough for a Starbucks.

Pei Ran suddenly felt he had taken advantage of Yan Zhun.

"Just kidding. He's a great gamer, but let's not exaggerate." Lin Kang patted him on the shoulder and chuckled. "Maybe he didn't like to play with Luo Qingshan because he was too loud for him."

In the afternoon, Lin Kang left his class early despite Pei Ran's words and instead waited with Pei Ran at the school gates for their ride.

A two-tone Maybach stopped in front of them. Lin Kang's eyes grew wide.

He turned his head, then held up his fingers, whispering, "Holy shit, this car is perfect. It must be worth at least this much!"

The driver's door opened, and out walked a middle-aged man in a white shirt and black pants. "Xiao-Ran, I hope I'm not late! Where are your bags? I'll help you put them in the trunk."

Pei Ran, "No need. We only have a couple of days off, so I didn't bother packing."

Lin Kang was speechless.

Lin Kang's expression twisted as his embarrassment faded away. "No wonder my dad beat me up for saying that I wanted to go into fine arts. I don't have your life."

Pei Ran was amused. "It's not that impressive."

Lin Kang was just about to get in the car when someone yanked on his coat, making him almost fall to the ground.

Startled, Lin Kang turned around and swore, "Who the fuck..."

Luo Qingshan pursed his lips, still clutching Lin Kang's jacket in his hand, his eyes darting between Lin Kang and Pei Ran.

Realizing that it was Luo Qingshan, Lin Kang became even more baffled and slapped his hand away. "Are you crazy? Is this how you greet people?"

Luo Qingshan's sight finally landed on Pei Ran.

Pei Ran's gaze was calm. He stared impassively into Luo Qingshan's eyes for a few seconds, then looked away.

"Did you hurt yourself?" Pei Ran asked.

"No, just a bump." Lin Kang looked at the car nervously. "I didn't scratch your car, right?"

"Don't worry about that." Pei Ran answered. "Get in the car. We can't park here for too long."

As soon as the words left his mouth, someone grabbed Lin Kang's coat again.

Confused, Lin Kang muttered, "Say what you want to say. Stop pulling my clothes!"

Luo Qingshan tightened his jaw, then snarled, "What are you going to do?"

Lin Kang said, "Go home."

"Together?"

Lin Kang was about to reply when he suddenly noticed something fishy about the question.

"Ah, no..." Lin Kang frowned. "Luo Qingshan, what do you

mean by this?"

Luo Qingshan said, "Why did you walk together this morning? Why did you put your hand on his shoulder? Oh, and you ate together, right?"

Lin Kang was so infuriated that he could only laugh. He spoke in a grave voice, "Luo Qingshan, are you crazy? I have a girlfriend!"

"You have a girlfriend, and you still stick to him?"

"Wow, your brain is amazing. Do you think the whole world is gay or what? And what's wrong with my relationship with Pei Ran? We took a walk and went home together, that's all." Unaware of what had happened, Lin Kang rambled on, "We're nowhere as close as you and Su Nian, so what are you mad about?"

Luo Qingshan's face suddenly turned pale, and his overbearing attitude dissipated.

He saw everything at noon, atop the stairs. Pei Ran didn't reply to his texts and didn't answer his calls, but he walked side by side with Lin Kang, talking and joking on their way. In the end, Lin Kang even put his arm around Pei Ran's shoulders.

"Luo Qingshan," Pei Ran said at length. "Let him go."

It was very dark outside by the time Pei Ran got home. All the houses in the neighborhood had their lights on; only his was pitch black inside.

After saying goodbye to the driver, he entered the house. The rooms were clean and tidy—he could tell that someone had been cleaning them every day. It was a shame that they were left vacant most of the time.

He took a shower and changed into silk pajamas. Light fell on him, bringing an air of gentleness about him.

However, Pei Ran was not feeling gentle at all.

In fact, he was annoyed.

As he picked up his phone, he saw that Luo Qingshan's messages had almost covered the lock screen.

Luo Qingshan:
I'm sorry

Luo Qingshan:
I'm sorry, babe. Please don't be mad at me

Luo Qingshan:
I rushed in without thinking, I didn't actually doubt you

...

Pei Ran didn't want to read anymore and cleared the screen.

After drying his hair, he went straight to the walk-in closet and began to inventory everything that Luo Qingshan had gifted him.

He had already worn out the shoes and backpack, so he couldn't return them as is. Instead, he researched their prices online and converted them into cash value. Some of the sneakers had been discontinued for a while, causing their prices to skyrocket, so Pei Ran had a hard time with his research.

By the time he managed to calculate a number, he had stayed up until the small hours in the morning.

He transferred money to Luo Qingshan's Alipay account, then left him a single message on WeChat: "Money sent."

As he exited the chat window, he inadvertently glanced at a particular icon.

The reason why the icon attracted his attention was that it was a picture of a rabbit.

The rabbit on the brand of White Rabbit milk candy.

Next to the rabbit were two large characters: "Yan Zhun."

Pei Ran's gaze fixated on the picture for a few seconds as if his brain had shut down before he abruptly brought himself back to reality.

Pei Ran:
I'm sorry!

Pei Ran:
I had something to do, so I forgot...

Pei Ran:
Apologies

Yan Zhun:
It's alright.

Pei Ran:
Go to sleep, I won't disturb you

Yan Zhun:
I'm not sleeping yet

Yan Zhun:
Still waiting for you

Pei Ran logged into the game, and immediately, Yan Zhun's invite message popped up.

Pei Ran quickly joined the team and turned on his mic. "I was just organizing some things, and I got so caught up that I forgot, sorry."

Yan Zhun replied, "It's okay; don't apologize."

Pei Ran had time to breathe a sigh of relief before the speaker icon next to the "111GOD" ID flashed again.

The other end stayed silent for two seconds. When Yan Zhun finally spoke, his tone was very soft as he murmured, "I thought you wouldn't come."

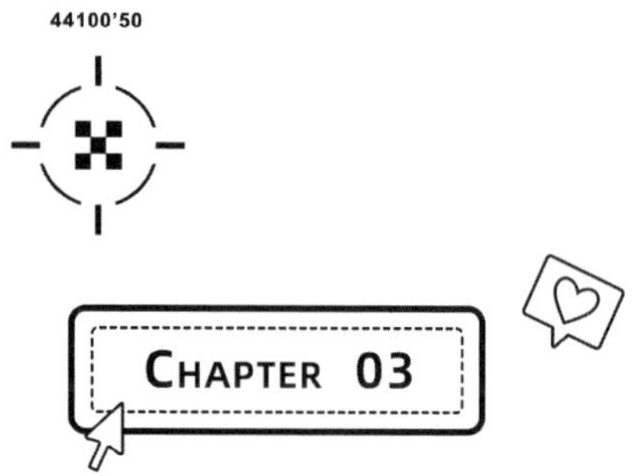

While Pei Ran had never hired a game companion before, his roommate was no stranger to such services.

His roommate had once hired a female companion. She kept addressing Pei Ran's roommate as "brother" in the sweet voice that girls tended use when flirting. Pei Ran could clearly hear her through the speaker.

It seemed like she could only play support. She kept close behind Pei Ran's roommate for the entire game, all the while exclaiming, "Help me, brother," "Don't die, brother," and "You're so good at this, brother," and it left Pei Ran's mind filled with the word "brother" for the entire night.

Just as Pei Ran recalled that memory, Yan Zhun leaped in from the window on his side. With a thud, a gun and two first-aid kits appeared on the ground.

"Pick them up."

Pei Ran asked, "What would you use then?"

"Yours. Just give me whatever."

Then, Yan Zhun picked up the Vector that Pei Ran dropped

to the ground and leaped out of the window again.

Yan Zhun led Pei Ran as they dropped into the wilderness. Yan Zhun was using his main account, so he had a hing ranking. As a result, they got matched with really good players for their team. Right from when they were still in the waiting area, their teammates had been yelling about dropping at the containers so that they could fight straightaway.

Yan Zhun was unaffected. When the plane was about to reach the end of the map, he leisurely marked a spot on the map and said, "Jump."

Since the team was split, the other two teammates were knocked down within a few minutes. Most people wouldn't be in their best moods at night, so the two teammates didn't quit the game even after elimination. Instead, they kept trash-talking into the team channel.

"I did log in with my main account, right? Why am I still matched with people who don't follow their teammates' parachutes?"

"King of Wilderness, that's what. Hide till endgame and steal the last kill for the chicken dinner."

"So annoying. Would you like to join me in the next game, bro?"

"Sure, I'll exit after I see them get killed."

The game progressed more or less how they'd expected: their teammates did scour the wild areas clean, going into the semi-finals without any kills. However, that was when things began to diverge from their expectations.

Once they entered the semi-finals, the teammate called "111GOD" was like a freaking god of war. With a Vector, he began to reap kills left and right. First, he finished off a full squad of four from behind. Then, he took out a lone wolf next door with a grenade.

His teammates weren't exactly elites, so when they saw the pop-up saying Yan Zhun had gotten a kill with his grenade, all they could manage was a dumbstruck "what the hell."

"Bro, bro, this body has an M416 in his loot crate. Why don't you swap the Vector out?" The teammate's voice had become much more cordial.

Pei Ran cautiously crept forward in a crouch and opened the loot box. There was indeed a fully decked M416 in it. He asked, "Wanna change guns?"

"No." Yan Zhun said, "I'll use the Vector."

Player 1 said, "Yeah, that's how all the pros play."

Player 2 said, "You're right. You can do it, bro!"

The safe area this time was nearby, so it wasn't that difficult to win. With only one enemy left, the two asked Yan Zhun if he wanted to join them for another game.

Yan Zhun said, "Ask Player 3."

Pei Ran looked down... He sure was Player 3.

"Are you two a team?" they asked. "Player 3, another game?"

Pei Ran said, "Nah."

After killing the last player on the battlefield, Yan Zhun stopped at the winner's screen for a while. He lowered his eyes and picked up the cigarette pack beside the keyboard.

"Player 4 is a gaming companion," Pei Ran continued. "If you want him to boost you, you'll have to pay."

Yan Zhun clutched the cigarette pack and chuckled softly.

Pei Ran's tone remained unchanged. He was serious about promoting Yan Zhun, "You can find him on XX app, he's not expensive. He's giving huge discounts since he's new, so you won't get such a good price later. His ID is..."

The teammates were caught a little off-guard and responded with a few affirmatives.

As soon as Yan Zhun returned to the game hall, his phone screen lit up. He unlocked it and glanced at the screen. Someone had placed an order, probably a teammate from the last game.

He put the cigarette back in place and rejected the order.

Pei Ran returned with a cup of coffee. He added milk to it, and as he stirred, the color gradually faded.

"Did they place an order?"

Yan Zhun's tone was regretful as he said, "No."

They entered another game, and before Pei Ran could look at the map, he heard the voice of an unfamiliar male player from his headphones—

"111, what a coincidence."

"Don't you know 111? He's the one who shot up the ranks of the Asian server a while back."

"111, are you there? Do you remember me? We added each other in the game."

Yan Zhun looked at his ID: "xktv197." From the name, Yan Zhun guessed that he was a game streamer.

It was just that he had added so many streamers that he couldn't remember exactly who he was.

Yan Zhun merely hummed, giving him a response of sorts.

Mr. 197 was obviously still streaming, as he kept interacting with his viewers. On the plane, 197 asked, "Where are you landing, 111? I'll follow."

Right after he asked, a yellow mark appeared in a small wild region on the map's far-right.

197 was confused.

197 asked, "Was that a misclick?"

Yan Zhun answered, "I entered as a duo."

197 looked at team IDs and understood immediately, "You mean Player 3? BabeRan? Oh... you're with your girlfriend?"

Pei Ran's account had been set up by Luo Qingshan, who'd also chosen his ID, which was one half of a matched set.

Pei Ran had also thought initially that the ID was too feminine, but it was too much trouble to change the account, so he had always left it as is. He finally felt a little embarrassed now that someone had read his ID out loud.

Pei Ran unmuted his microphone: "It doesn't matter. Don't mind me. Just play as you always do."

197 was a little surprised by the male voice, but he quickly answered, "Are you a newbie? All right, we'll land in the wild then. It's not like we got a large map, so we'll be meeting enemies soon enough."

Yan Zhun had chosen to play in random mode, and they'd gotten a small map of the rainforest.

Shortly after, Yan Zhun came to him with a fully decked M416.

Pei Ran looked at the gun on the ground and said, "I'm fine. This map has tons of weapons. I have an M416 on me as well."

Yan Zhun said nothing and just stood there for a long time. The gun remained on the ground.

Finally, Pei Ran squatted down and threw his bare M416 on the ground. Yan Zhun picked it up quickly and left through the door.

Pei Ran had no response.

Seeing everything, 197 joked, "111, what are you doing? Don't tell me there's a buff on BabeRan's gun?"

Yan Zhun said, "I fight better with my boss's gun."

A sudden realization overcame 197, "You're now a game companion too?"

Yan Zhun replied, "Sort of."

197 was right. This little map was crowded. The team had just looted two small wild areas when they hear gunshots nearby.

"From the east," 197 glanced at the map, "what the heck? Where are you going, 111?"

Pei Ran looked at the man close behind him, "...We're heading over now."

A gunfight had already broken out when they arrived. It was two versus four, so they were clearly at a disadvantage. One of their teammates had already been reduced to a loot box. 197 hid behind the stone with a precarious line of health. He kept squatting down to heal up, utterly panicked.

Pei Ran caught a glimpse of an enemy taking aim at someone with his back towards him, so he fired subconsciously. Fortunately, the gun was stable, and he managed to knock the enemy down.

Pei Ran seldom got kills in this game. Even one kill would be more than lucky for him. He didn't realize how hard his heart was beating until his opponent went down.

"Good job." Yan Zhun's voice was mingled with the hail of bullets.

Feeling bizarrely like he'd been praised by a primary school teacher, Pei Ran's cheeks began to heat up. He went behind a tree and reloaded his bullets.

197 used a first-aid kit and quickly reported the position of the enemy. Yan Zhun guzzled a bottle of painkillers and said, "I'll bomb them. You go approach them from the left, and I'll hit them in the front."

The two men rushed up to their enemies with their guns blazing. Yan Zhun claimed two lives with two shots, and 197 managed to steal a kill on his end.

"All dead, mine was killed with a headshot. We can loot them now." 197 dropped into a prone position on the grass, "Bro, you're good."

Yan Zhun didn't answer. He heard a silenced snipe in the distance, so he sneaked to his right and pulled up his scope.

Before he could find anyone, though, he heard several shots from behind.

197 went, "Fuck! There's someone behind us! There's another fucking team..."

Right as he said that, two kill alerts popped up on the upper right corner. 197 and Pei Ran were knocked down.

Yan Zhun reacted immediately. He pulled up his scope and turned around to eliminate an enemy, who landed two shots on Yan Zhun before he went down. Yan Zhun's health bar plunged into an instant pink.

Yan Zhun was in a good position, and 197 could feel his heart in his mouth. "There's one more. Don't be hasty and use some meds first. I think he went after BabeRan..."

Before he could finish, 197 saw Yan Zhun cancel his meds and then charged forward with his gun.

197 was utterly baffled.

Before Pei Ran could utter the word "Don't," Yan Zhun had already barged into his line of sight.

In those seconds when Yan Zhun was firing against the enemy, Pei Ran felt as though his chest would explode.

When Yan Zhun killed the opponent with minimal hp remaining, Pei Ran heaved a sigh of relief. He couldn't help leaning back into his chair. Only when he released the mouse did he find his palms already drenched in sweat.

...It was too exhilarating.

"Shit! Fuck! Others may be playing the game, but you, brother, are playing with our heartbeats!" 197 finally crawled to Yan Zhun with the utmost difficulty. After he got knocked down, he took two more shots from the enemy. His health bar was almost emptied, "Bro, hurry up and revive me."

As soon as he said that, 197 could only watch as Yan Zhun left him behind and ran straight to the slope, where BabeRan was crawling with a good half of his health bar left.

"Do you have any meds?" Yan Zhun asked.

Pei Ran snapped back into focus, "Yes."

"OK, go loot the crate. There are plenty of meds in there."

197 wailed, "It's over, it's over, I'm finished, I'm finished..."

Fortunately for him, Yan Zhun was not completely heartless. As the last drop of blood was about to drain from 197, he finally revived him.

"I was scared to death, bro." 197 was aggrieved, "I have crawled to your side, but you didn't revive me. What were you thinking, bro?"

Yan Zhun replied, "Thinking of my boss."

Pei Ran was speachless.

197 cried, "Your boss still has half his health bar!"

"That guy has got teammates. What if they killed my boss?" Yan Zhun reloaded his 98K, "If you died, I could try my best to give you a chicken dinner."

197, "?"

"If he died, I'd have to commit suicide."

197 fell silent for a moment, "Okay... I get that you are a top-notch game companion. Those who didn't know would reckon that you two are gay."

Yan Zhun saw the avatar in front of him stop in his tracks.

A few seconds later, BabeRan continued to run, and the

microphone icon in front of his ID began to flicker, "Well, it's not every day that you can find a game companion this good at only 20 yuan per hour. On XX platform..."

Yan Zhun burst out laughing and pressed down on the mouse, making his running avatar swing a heavy fist to the air.

They played until 4 AM.

Pei Ran was so engrossed in the game that he lost track of time. He didn't realize it had gotten so late until Yan Zhun suggested that they rest.

As soon as Pei Ran got in bed, he got a buzz on his phone.

Yan Zhun:
Was my service satisfactory?

Pei Ran:
Very good

Thinking that it might feel too patronizing, Pei Ran sent another message.

Pei Ran:
For real

Yan Zhun:
Yeah, this was my first time, so I had no experience

Pei Ran:
Have you gotten any new orders?

When Pei Ran's message popped on his screen, Yan Zhun had just opened the game companion app's dashboard.

He'd received more than 40 orders tonight.

He recalled how seriously Pei Ran tried to promote him during the games. Yan Zhun covered his face with his hand and could not help but smile.

Yan Zhun:
No, I don't seem too popular.

Pei Ran pondered for a while, holding his mobile phone. In the end, he could only type out a bare: "I believe in you."

But before he could send it, another message arrived

Yan Zhun:
Do you really think that I'm good at this game?

Pei Ran:
Absolutely.

Yan Zhun:
Would you like to purchase my service for a little longer?

Pei Ran paused.

Yan Zhun:
Huge discounts since I'm new. Place more orders, and I'll be yours for the whole holiday

Yan Zhun:
How does that sound?

Yan Zhun:
Boss Pei

The next day, Pei Ran was awakened by a ray of sunshine that just so happened to land on his eyelids.

It had been a long time since he last pulled an all-nighter. After turning off his computer last night, he was overcome by drowsiness so intense that he fell asleep immediately when his head touched the pillow. He didn't even close the curtains properly.

Pei Ran raised his hand to cover his eyes. He fumbled for his cell phone to check the time and was stunned by what he saw on the screen.

His screen remained on the page where he left off the night before. There was a line of bolded characters:

Dear pr123, you have successfully placed an order! Click here to view order details.

Pei Ran's mind went blank for a moment. He clicked on the invoice, only to realize that he had ordered 50 game hours from his game companion, who was named "Approved."

Pei Ran was at a loss.

Clearly, he was susceptible to late-night impulse-buys.

Switching to WeChat, he found that it had remained on the chat between him and Yang Zhun.

Yan Zhun:
Thank you, Boss Pei.

Yan Zhun:
Are you asleep? Good night

It seemed like the game companion industry was going through a slump, Pei Ran thought. Even Yan Zhun, with such amazing skills, had trouble getting orders. He even needed to convince a newbie customer like him to stay.

However, after last night, Pei Ran understood why so many people enjoyed playing with game companions. If even Yan Zhun could be nice to him online, he could only imagine how sweetly other companions might humor their customers.

Pei Ran:
I fell asleep...

Yan Zhun didn't reply. Pei Ran looked at the time. It wasn't even 10 AM yet; Yan Zhun was probably still asleep.

He went back to WeChat and began to read through his new messages.

Pei Ran immediately saw Su Nian's name.

Su Nian:
Are you there?

Su Nian:
Reply when you see this

Pei Ran frowned instinctively. He hesitated for a few seconds but still replied out of courtesy.

Pei Ran:
Yeah

Su Nian:
Are you from Mancheng?

Pei Ran:
Yeah

Su Nian:
Would you like to go on a trip to Dali together? The day after tomorrow. **[cat tilting its head emote]**

For a second, Pei Ran didn't know what to reply.

Even Lin Kang knew he had broken up with Luo Qingshan. Su Nian had no reason not to know.

Su Nian:
You there?

Su Nian:
We've created a smaller group chat, by the way. I think you know everyone inside, but I forgot to invite you. I'm sorry, should I add you now?

Pei Ran:
No thanks, and I'm not going to Dali. Have a good time.

Pei Ran went to wash up after sending that message. When he returned, his cell phone had been flooded by notifications.

Su Nian:
Why?

Su Nian:
Did you have a fight with Qingshan?

Su Nian:
Qingshan explained everything to me last night. Please don't be mad, Pei Ran. I was drunk that night and took Qingshan as my ex-boyfriend. We only exchanged a few kisses and nothing more

Su Nian:
Really

Su Nian:
If it makes you unhappy in any way, I apologize. You guys shouldn't quarrel because of me...

Su Nian did not receive any reply to his messages. After

some thought, he sent Pei Ran a custom emote of someone begging for mercy. Then, he received the prompt of him being blocked by the recipient.

When Pei Ran ate breakfast, his cutlery clanked noisily.

The housekeeper looked at him anxiously and asked if the eggs were overcooked.

Pei Ran shook his head, picked up the remainder of his egg with his fork, and finished his breakfast.

After the housekeeper left, Pei Ran moved the boxes he packed into storage.

The boxes contained everything Luo Qingshan gifted him. He would never use them again.

After returning to his room, Pei Ran realized that there was something else he needed to clean.

Pei Ran was browsing through the album when Lin Kang's messages arrived.

There was an album on Pei Ran's cell phone containing pictures of him and Luo Qingshan. Not many, just a dozen photos over the past three years.

Pei Ran was not keen on taking photos. Those were all taken by Luo Qingshan, who then sent them over one by one. Whenever Pei Ran changed over to a new phone, he would always transfer them to his new device. Not a single photo was lost.

Some of those pictures showed them in their school uniforms, and a photo was taken at the university's gate. The last photo showed a sleeping Pei Ran; Luo Qingshan had secretly taken a picture of him and had inserted his smiling self into the shot.

Pei Ran took a deep breath and, in the end, deleted the intimate photos they had. He left just one picture in the album, the one they took in front of the university gates.

After which, he switched back to play Lin Kang's voice message.

"Pei Ran, what are you doing? Are you free?"

Pei Ran:
Yeah. What's up?

"Ah, it's about Su Nian. He wanted me to ask if you were angry with him and why you deleted him without saying anything... What's going on between you both? He refused to tell me anything when I asked and simply told me to pass the message."

Lin Kang was genuinely curious.

People always had the impression that Pei Ran was calm and collected. He didn't tend to initiate conversations, but as long as a conversation started, he would respond placidly and politely. All in all, he seemed to be a man of no temper.

But there was no such thing as a human without a temper. Pei Ran just didn't think it was necessary. There was no need for him to get even with Luo Qingshan on his affair, which would have been time-consuming and meaningless. Su Nian, of everyone, had no business in this.

However, while he was willing to let them off the hook, it seemed like they were bent on disgusting him.

Pei Ran typed calmly.

Pei Ran:
Sorry to trouble you, but could you pass him a message?

"What?"

Pei Ran:
Tell him to get lost

Yan Zhun was awakened by his ringing cell late in the afternoon. He accepted the call, pressed his cell phone near his ear and then proceeded to stay silent.

From the other end of the call came the sound of someone furiously tapping away at the mouse and keyboard, "You're still sleeping?"

Yan Zhun could already guess who it was from that voice alone. He shut his eyes and said, "Spit it out."

"Well, it's understandable, considering you only slept at four in the morning." That boy clicked his tongue, "You got off the game later than a professional player like me."

Yan Zhun said, "Lin Xuhuan, got too much time on your hands? Why are you digging on me so early in the morning?"

"Early in the morning? Hell, it's already two PM."

Yan Zhun opened his eyes and glanced at the time.

As Lin Xuhuan spoke, he got killed with a headshot. He let out a curse and reported all four of his enemies. Then he picked up his cell phone and continued, "I hear you're a game companion now. What were you thinking? I can't believe you gave up the glorious career of professional gamer just to become a game companion!"

Yan Zhun minimized the call tab so that he could reply to his boss's message. "You got up this early?" he wrote.

"How did you find out?"

"The streamer you met is contracted with the same platform our team signed on with," said Lin Xuhuan. "He's quite popular. He recorded the game he matched up with you last night and posted it online. Think it got around two or three hundred thousand likes... Damn, why didn't you let me in first since you're doing it anyway?"

"It's not like I expected to meet him there." Yan Zhun said.

"But you are really something else. You're convincing no matter what you do. You sure have a way with your clients!

People are flooding the comments of that TikTok video, asking for your game companion ID." Lin Xuhuan leaned back into the chair, "Okay, back to the main topic. Did your family go bankrupt?"

Yan Zhun ruffled his hair, "Sorry to disappoint—not yet."

"Why are you working as a companion then?" Lin Xuhuan was speechless. "I thought I could finally trick you into TZG."

Yan Zhun scoffed. Just as he was about to reply, his cell phone buzzed.

Pei Ran:
Yeah. Are you up?

Pei Ran:
I'd like to game.

Pei Ran:
It's okay if you're not. I'll play solo for a while.

Lin Xuhuan asked, "By the way, aren't you on school break? Come to our base. A member of our second team applied for leave, so we're short on players. Those youth trainees are not good enough. Come join us for a customized training match."

"No."

"Dang, we'll pay you!" Lin Xuhuan clenched his teeth and said, "We'll pay you three times as much as your game companionship charges... Wait a minute, surely your fees don't exceed 200 yuan per hour?"

Yan Zhun stood up and said, "No, you guys can play the match yourselves. I'm hanging up."

"Ah, what's the hurry? Let's talk more."

"I've got something else to do."

"Like what?"

Yan Zhun threw on some clothes and said lazily, "Like serving my boss."

Li Xuhuan was left speechless.

A piece of bread in mouth, Yan Zhun got online. Seeing that Pei Ran was in the middle of a game, he thought that he might as well check his game record.

0 damage.

0 damage.

0 damage...

It was quite tragic.

Yan Zhun sent a WeChat to Pei Ran, telling him to wait for him when he's done. He then began to scroll through his unread messages.

Yan Zhun didn't have many close friends. Since he almost stepped into the door of competitive gaming, most of his friends were professional gamers. They were all forwarding that short video to tease him.

He scrolled down a little more and found a group chat that he hadn't opened for a long time.

Yan Zhun frowned upon seeing a particular phrase. He clicked into the chat and began to read the last two pages of chat records.

Lin Kang:
@Su Nian, what's up with you and Pei Ran? Why is he so mad?

Su Nian:
No idea

Su Nian:
Maybe he just doesn't think me worthy

Su Nian:
Wasn't Pei Ran always this way? Do any of you actually feel close to him?

Su Nian:
Rich ppl are all like that, I'm not good enough for him lol...

Su Nian:
@Everyone Trip to Dali, we're setting off the day after tomorrow! If you wanna participate, please sign up with me!!

Su Nian:
@Approved Bro, will you be coming?

Generally, Yan Zhun just ignored pings like this.

He swallowed his mouthful of bread, looked down, and began to type with an expressionless face.

Approved:
Are we that close? I'm not your bro.

Approved:
Who added me to this group? I'm deleting you. Don't just pull people into dumb groups like this in the future

Yan Zhun has got really swift hands, so before the group could recover from the shock of it, he had already sent the message, unfriended Su Nian, and left the group.

This time, Pei Ran still didn't survive for more than five minutes. He looked at the enemy bending down and looting his crate, then frowned.

Was the game supposed to be this hard?

He unlocked his cell phone and scanned his new messages.

Most of them were from Lin Kang, who sent him screenshots of Su Nian gossiping in the chat group.

Lin Kang:
[chat history], Shit, I always knew this kid was a bit of a pain, but I had no idea he such a blabbermouth.

Lin Kang:
What the heck did you do to him? Do you need me to add you to the group? Don't worry, I'll take your side.

Lin Kang:
If you're embarrassed, I can teach him a lesson for you. We are all friends; he didn't have to diss you like that

Pei Ran:
No, but thank you

Pei Ran:
And no need for screenshots. I owe you one—the bill's on me the next time we eat together

Pei Ran opened the chat history and reread it, his face devoid of emotions.

To be honest, Su Nian wasn't entirely wrong—Pei Ran did think that Su Nian wasn't worthy of his friendship.

Yan Zhun's game invite message popped up. Pei Ran set his phone aside and accepted the invitation.

"Boss." Yan Zhun's voice sounded a little hoarse, as if he had just woken up.

Pei Ran replied reflexively, "Hmm?"

Then he added, "You don't have to call me that..."

Yan Zhun removed his character's outfit and reverted to the default look like Pei Ran's character.

He pondered for a moment and decided to change the gender of his character to female.

"Want to play something different today?" asked Yan Zhun.

Pei Ran, "Play what?"

"Duo-queue in Sanhok," explained Yan Zhun. "Kill-fest."

Pei Ran curled his lips. Although they had played quite a few rounds yesterday, he often ended the match with no kills.

Even if he depended on his teammates to win, at least he was having fun.

He responded, "All right."

Soon, he understood what Yan Zhun meant by "kill-fest."

As soon as they entered the game, Yan Zhun immediately marked the Bootcamp on the map.

The Bootcamp, also known as "Despair City" for players,

was a spot where people vying for loot crate outnumbered the crates themselves. Dropping in there meant that one could spare no effort if they wanted to survive.

"Jump." Yan Zhun reminded him.

Pei Ran quickly pressed the "F" key and dropped down following the parachuting tips Yan Zhun taught him yesterday.

As they almost reached the Bootcamp, Pei Ran looked back and saw a crowd behind him.

Pei Ran was a bit at a loss.

"Go to Camp Charlie, follow me."

As soon as he landed, the sound of gunshots blasted from Pei Ran's earphones, reminding him of a symphony concert he had attended some time ago.

He scrambled to pick up his rifle. By the time he loaded it, Yan Zhun had already killed two people.

Just as Pei Ran readied himself to follow Yan Zhun, he heard the sound of a door opening behind him, then someone swiftly knocked him to the ground. The enemy mercilessly made sure that he was dead before rapidly absconding.

This player came from a distance, so Yan Zhun didn't notice him when he parachuted. He shot down two teams, then asked, "What clothes did the guy who killed you wear?"

Pei Ran seemed taken aback. "I think... the default ones. Don't worry about it."

"Wait and watch me," said Yan Zhun while looting the crates. "I'll be done soon."

Ten minutes later, Yan Zhun had killed every player wearing the default skin within the Bootcamp, armed with nothing but a rifle.

Only one team remained. Yan Zhun struck down one of its members, then turned on his mic. "What clothes does your teammate wear?"

The player sounded thoroughly confused as he obediently answered, "A black coat, the really expensive one. Do you want it? I'll ask him to take it off and give it to you."

Then, before the ardent gaze of that player, Yan Zhun blew himself up with a grenade.

Pei Ran was stupefied. "You didn't need to kill yourself. I'm fine watching you play."

"I'm not playing without you," Yan Zhun replied. "Click 'Ready.' We're starting the next round."

After three parachuting sessions, Pei Ran finally got a kill.

"Yan Zhun, I killed someone!" Pei Ran felt his palms blazing hot and blurted out, "And... it's a double kill!"

Having said that, Pei Ran was suddenly overcome by embarrassment. He only managed two kills in three matches. Any random teammate would've done better than him.

"I saw it," Yan Zhun carried the conversation naturally. "It was amazing."

Pei Ran's heart was pounding, and he felt his nervousness spike—even more so than during an exam.

Now that he was in the zone, Pei Ran killed another player. After a few minutes, the Despair City became quiet.

"Yan Zhun," Pei Ran whispered, asking for confirmation. "I don't think there's anyone left?"

Yan Zhun chuckled out of amusement. "Well, you did kill all of them... You don't need to keep your voice down. I'm the only one who can hear you."

Pei Ran also felt rather silly. He squatted down and began to look for crates inside the house when Yan Zhun suddenly leaped in through the window. Since last night, Pei Ran had developed a conditioned response to this move: he automatically dropped the pistol in his hand on the ground.

Yan Zhun's in-game character hesitated for a moment. Then, he said with a smile, "I just wanted to see if there were any extra scopes in this crate."

Pei Ran didn't respond, then immediately picked up the pistol again. He thought he had never been this fast before.

Yan Zhun, "But I still want to use your gun."

Yan Zhun squatted next to him and let go of his weapon. "Seriously though... Give me another chance to get a buff."

Pei Ran turned around and walked away. "Never mind, I don't want to switch."

Yan Zhun rose up abruptly and chased him across the entire Bootcamp. When Pei Ran stopped to pick up an item, Yan Zhun's character kneeled down in front of him and bowed deeply.

Pei Ran returned the bow.

Yan Zhun bowed again.

The two of them bowed back and forth like idiots. In the end, Pei Ran gave in and handed his pistol to Yan Zhun.

"No more bowing? We just needed one more." Yan Zhun was talking the three sets of bows usually required for traditional wedding rites.

However, Pei Ran was confused. "One more of what?"

"Nothing."

Yan Zhun set his character on auto-run, then muted his mic. He lit up a cigarette as he considered the idea that had they bowed one more time, they would be settled to enter the bridal chamber.

They played two more rounds. Just as Pei Ran was getting the hang of the game, he heard Yan Zhun say, "Let's land somewhere else this time. It's raining hard outside; I can't hear footsteps."

Only then did Pei Ran notice the sound of raindrops hitting the window.

"It's raining here, too."

Yan Zhun continued. "We live in the same area. My home is near Mancheng High School."

Pei Ran blurted out, "I was in Mancheng High School for senior high."

"I know," Yan Zhun replied, "we were schoolmates."

Pei Ran was astonished. He had no memory of meeting Yan Zhun in high school.

Noticing Pei Ran's silence, Yan Zhun said, "Don't overthink it. We were on different floors; that's why we never met."

Pei Ran hummed in response. There was something about Yan Zhun's answer that bothered him, but he had no time to figure out what it was before Yan Zhun interrupted his train of thought.

"Jump, I'll play seriously and carry us to victory."

The two played duo-queued for the whole night. When he logged out, Pei Ran suddenly remembered that he had already made other plans for his break beforehand.

"Come play with me tomorrow," Yan Zhun said lazily, "boss."

Well, plans are meant to be broken anyway, Pei Ran thought.

Before going to bed, Pei Ran opened WeChat to check his messages by habit. When he saw the 23 unread messages sent from Luo Qingshan, he finally recalled his incredibly revolting encounter of the day.

The night he spent in Despair City had been so thrilling that he almost wiped that incident from his mind.

Luo Qingshan's messages were nothing more than excuses: he didn't see the group chat; he had no idea what went down between Su Nian and him; he'll make sure to keep his distance from Su Nian, so please don't misunderstand...

Once Pei Ran had finished reading, he cleared the chat history and shut his eyes.

The holiday went by quickly. When Pei Ran received a call from his mother, it suddenly dawned on him that his break would be ending the next day.

His mother wanted to check on him, feeling sorry for being abroad and not spending time with him. She also asked what he did during the break.

Pei Ran blinked rapidly and blurted out a clumsy lie, "I drew stuff."

In reality, he had become addicted to gaming, to the point that he'd begun to adapt to his guns' recoil patterns.

He hung up the phone. After a moment of hesitation, Pei Ran ultimately decided to cancel today's gaming session.

As soon as he opened WeChat, he received a voice message.

"Boss Pei, they just released a new vehicle—the helicopter. Whoever's in the copilot seat gets to shoot," Yan Zhun said. "When will you be on? I'm taking you on a helicopter ride."

Pei Ran bit his lower lip and typed.

"Not today."

Then he deleted it.

"Later."

Then he deleted it.

Yan Zhun sucked on a White Rabbit candy as he stared eagerly at the word "Typing..." in his chat with his boss.

Finally, after a long wait...

Pei Ran:
OK

Yan Zhun smirked subconciously and swallowed his candy.

With a guilty conscience, Pei Ran opened his computer and logged onto PUBG. Instantly, a team invitation popped up on the right side of the screen, which he accepted instinctively.

Once he joined the team, he saw that the player beside him was dressed in outlandish clothes—limited edition skins from head to toe.

Yet before Pei Ran could react, the room host started the round. Since the host had activated duo mode, they were paired up as a team of two.

"Pei Ran..." Luo Qingshan's faint voice came through the earphones, sounding deeply hurt. He muttered, "You're finally willing to talk to me."

Yan Zhun had just logged on and was about to send a team invite to Pei Ran when he saw that "BabeRan" was already in a match.

He lowered his gaze—"LoveBabeRan" was also in a match.

Yan Zhun squinted for a good while before finally picking up his phone to send a message.

Yan Zhun:
?

Pei Ran:
It was an accident

Pei Ran:
You can play on your own for a bit

And so Yan Zhun leaned back in this chair, smoking a cigarette as he stared at Pei Ran's ID.

His phone suddenly pinged. Someone had added him into a new chat group, but it wasn't Su Nian this time.

Lin Kang:
Let's talk here from now on

Lin Kang:
Should I add Pei Ran? **@Luoqingshan**

Lin Kang:
Hello? **@Luoqingshan**

Luo Qingshan:
Not yet

Luo Qingshan:
And stop pinging me, I'm in a duo with my wife

Lin Kang:
?? You guys are back together?

Luo Qingshan:
I finally got him to stop ignoring me... ttyl

Yan Zhun closed the group chat and raised his hand to stub out the cigarette. His finger accidentally grazed the ash and became soiled.

He ignored the stain and immediately called Lin Xuhuan on WeChat.

Lin Xuhuan picked up almost instantly. "What's up? I'm streaming right now."

"Got a spot on your team? Invite me."

Lin Xuhuan paused. "What, you wanna force me to buy your service?"

"It's free," replied Yan Zhun in a low voice. "Your team is highly ranked; the kills feel better."

Lin Xuhuan chuckled. "Cranky, are we? All right, invite sent... You're not with your boss today?"

Yan Zhun let out a dry laugh. "Nope, the boss doesn't need me today."

When he recognized Luo Qingshan's voice, Pei Ran's first thought was to exit the game.

A few seconds later, he canceled his attempt to exit, opened his map, and marked a random location.

Luo Qingshan was so nervous that it took him a while to figure out what to say. "I've been... at home for days; couldn't go anywhere. My mom told me there's a really good Japanese restaurant that just opened nearby. Do you wanna..."

Calmly, Pei Ran said, "Did you check over what I sent you?"

Luo Qingshan was stunned. In the last few days, Pei Ran had only sent him one thing: the entire list of gifts he had given to Pei Ran while they were still dating.

"No," Luo Qingshan muttered. "I bought you a lot of stuff just out of impulse. There's no way I can remember all of them after so long."

Pei Ran landed in the wilderness and began to search the area. "I'm pretty sure I listed everything. I couldn't find the prices for two pairs of limited-edition shoes, but that's about it."

"Babe..." Luo Qingshan choked up, then reconsidered his words. "Pei Ran, do you have to do this?"

Pei Ran replied, "I didn't want this to happen."

"I know. I already said it was my fault," Luo Qingshan said. "But there was nothing going on between Su Nian and me. At least, I don't have feelings for him at all. You know me, right? I've always seen him as just a bro. I just didn't think—"

Pei Ran stood still in the room for a few seconds, then bent down to pick up an item. "Enough."

"You won't even give me a chance to explain myself?" asked Luo Qingshan in a brittle voice. "Pei Ran, I've been thinking for a while. Do you even care about what happened? Why aren't you angry with me? You just kept silent and gave me the cold shoulder. You're ignoring me and pretending that I don't exist—same as when I pursued you back in high school."

How could he try to explain himself? And what's considered "angry" by him? Pei Ran wondered.

Did Luo Qingshan expect Pei Ran to lash out at him? Fire questions like "How many times did Su Nian and you kiss?" or "Did you actually delete Su Nian from your contacts?"

Or did he want Pei Ran to quarrel with Su Nian in front of everyone else and air their dirty laundry?

Pei Ran remained silent for so long that Luo Qingshan thought he might have muted his mic or quit the game.

"I just don't want an ugly end." Pei Ran said softly.

This was the first time Luo Qingshan has heard Pei Ran sound so disappointed since the incident.

Pei Ran only spoke a few words, but Luo Qingshan seemed to have understood everything from them.

Both of Pei Ran's parents were artists. Naturally, Pei Ran had been born with an artist's pride, seeking nothing less than perfection and romance. This was also what Luo Qingshan liked most about him.

Luo Qingshan felt a sting in his eyes. "I'm sorry."

He rubbed his eyes as he realized how much he missed Pei Ran. Much later, he finally asked, "Can we still be friends, though?"

Pei Ran said nothing.

"I'm begging you, please don't say no," Luo Qingshan pleaded. "At least give me some time."

Pei Ran's instinct was to refuse. If he hadn't needed to settle the gifts, he might have blocked Luo Qingshan a while ago.

Luo Qingshan bit his lip and forced out a laugh. It was his chance to play his trump card. "By the way... The weather has been getting chilly. My fingers are constantly in pain—Do you think it's possible to get arthritis in your fingers? You should make sure to dress warmly, or you'll catch a cold again."

Like always, Pei Ran fell for it. Luo Qingshan was disgusted with himself, but he also felt immensely grateful.

Just as expected, Pei Ran became quiet for a moment, then asked, "Did you get it checked at the hospital?"

"Nah, it doesn't hurt that much." Seeing that Pei Ran's attitude had softened, Luo Qingshan discreetly breathed a sigh of relief and immediately changed the subject. "Have you found a weapon yet? Don't move; I'll toss you an M24 with a 6x scope equipped."

Pei Ran walked past Luo Qingshan without halting. "Thank you, but I don't snipe."

"Someone's coming from the north. Boss Biscuit, thank you so much for the donation. Kiss kiss..." Lin Xuhuan was interacting playfully with his stream viewers. Yet when he noticed where his teammate was heading, he promptly sat bolt upright in his chair. "Shit, calm down Player 2, wait for me! Player 2... Yan Zhun, hold the fuck up; there are four people over there!!!"

Yan Zhun was riding a motorcycle. Even with four more wheels, Lin Xuhuan couldn't possibly catch up to him in his pathetic pickup truck, so he had no choice but to watch Yan Zhun rush toward the enemies.

"Fuck, playing duo in four-player squad mode is hard enough without you feeding them on purpose!" Lin Xuhuan's temper was at its limit. "Now I get why you suddenly decided to play with me; you're trying to bring down my rank..."

111GOD knocked out **TIKERX** with an **AKM**.

111GOD knocked out **HUMI2B** with an **AKM**.

111GOD knocked out **JEONG** with a **Frag Grenade**.

111GOD eliminated **MRxu** with a **Frag Grenade**.

"All gone," said Yan Zhun.

"Haha, I knew it! Bro, I trusted that you knew what you were doing when you ran into them." Lin Xuhuan smiled. "Guys, what did you think of my bro's epic gameplay? If you enjoyed it, be sure to send me all your donations."

As he looted the crates, Lin Xuhuan asked, "What's the matter with you, bro? You don't seem to be in a good mood."

Yan Zhun retorted, "I wouldn't play with you if I was."

"Wow." Lin Xuhuan snickered. "Fine, then why don't you tell me what's going on and let me help out?"

"You can't." Yan Zhun snatched up an attachment he needed and leaped on the roof, preparing to aim. "Be quiet; I can't hear the footsteps."

Lin Xuhuan was long used to Yan Zhun's temperament, so he turned his attention to the live chat. "No no no, he doesn't use cheats... How do I know? We've played together IRL more times than I can count. If I get the chance later, I'll show you the play from his POV; then you'll see he's the real deal."

"He's not a trainee on our team. If we had a trainee with his skills, then I would retire right here and now."

"I'm well-aware of what I can do, but he really is that good. If you don't believe me, go ask any other PUBG pro streamer if they've heard of 111GOD."

Yan Zhun listened to Yan Xuhuan's flattery with a poker face, thinking that he should've chosen to play solo.

At the end of the round, Yan Zhun successfully brought home the Chicken Dinner with 21 kills.

"Damn, you're like a warrior of old." Lin Xuhuan exclaimed.

Taken aback by his choice of words, Yan Zhun lit up a cigarette and stopped paying attention to him.

He looked down at the phone placed in front of his keyboard, then clicked in and out of the chat pinned on top of the list over and over.

"Bro, everyone in my livestream is asking where they can hire you as a gaming companion. Tell me your platform, I'll advertise it for you." Lin Xuhuan added, "I guarantee you'll be overloaded with orders; go raise your rate while you still can."

Yan Zhun puffed out a cloud of smoke. "No, I quit."

Lin Xuhuan was speechless for a moment, his expression shifting in uncertainty. "You're giving up way too quickly. Someone your age should have more perseverance than this."

Yan Zhun replied, "Well, I tried."

Lin Xuhuan turned his mic back on and spoke to his livestream audience. "Stop asking, you guys; he's not taking orders anymore. Why? Because he can. Expert players are fickle like that... Bro, wait a sec. Some idiots in my team just woke up and said they want to play together as a squad of 4."

Yan Zhun didn't answer. He was about to shake off the cigarette ash on his fingers when his phone on the table suddenly vibrated. He lowered his eyes and almost dropped his cigarette into the ashtray.

Pei Ran:
I'm done. Are you still playing?

Lin Xuhuan's squad assembled in less than two minutes. He was at the point of starting the match when the game notified him that one of his teammates was not ready.

He took a second look. The checkmark next to 111GOD had vanished.

"I'm leaving; you guys continue." Yan Zhun said.

"Fuck!" a male voice shouted—it was the entry fragger. "I crawled out of bed to play with you, and now you're telling me that you're leaving? To do what?"

Yan Zhun shot back, "Accompanying my boss. What else?"

Yan Zhun exited the stream, leaving behind strings of question marks in the live chat. Fans pressed along with their questions—didn't you say that he wouldn't take any more orders? Are you freaking kidding me?

Lin Xuhuan seemed unfazed. "I told you; expert players are fickle like that."

Pei Ran just sent out his message when he remembered that Yan Zhun was still in the middle of a game, so he fired off another text.

Pei Ran:
Don't mind me if you're in a match

Yan Zhun:
Invite me

Pei Ran had never been a team leader, so he struggled to send the invite. 111GOD joined him soon enough.

"Which map?"

"You're solo?"

The two of them spoke at the same time.

Pei Ran was taken aback. "Yeah, I'm on my own. Need me to invite someone else?"

"No," Yan Zhun paused. "I saw you were in a duo earlier."

Pei Ran explained, "I joined the wrong team. I didn't check the ID on the invite and thought it was you."

Yan Zhun raised an eyebrow. "Oh, you thought it was me."

Not noticing the hint of joy in his voice, Pei Ran replied with a hum of affirmation before asking, "So, which map?"

"Erangel," Yan Zhun confirmed. "I promised I'd take you on a helicopter ride."

During their match, Pei Ran's phone kept ringing nonstop.

He glanced at the voice messages from Luo Qingshan. On the one hand, he didn't particularly want to listen to them; on the other, he worried that his hand was paining him. In the end, he pressed on the shortest message.

"What time are you going to school tomorrow? Wanna go together? I can pick you up—"

Pei Ran tapped out before the audio finished playing. He took a minute to record his answer, "No thanks."

Yan Zhun looked at the date. The feeling of irritation that dissipated moments ago returned in full force, so much so that he wanted a smoke.

Suddenly, he heard a faint sound from his earphones—the rustle of a candy wrapper being torn.

He resisted the urge, took out a White Rabbit milk candy from his drawer, then sucked on it to curb his craving.

Playing with Pei Ran costed him quite a few candies.

Their last round lasted far into the night. As Pei Ran stared at the black computer screen, something popped into his mind. He opened the gaming companion software and transferred the money to Yan Zhun.

This software required the customer to place their order first. Once the gaming companion played enough hours, the customer would complete the transaction on the back end. Only then would the companion receive payment.

The maximum number of hours per order was 50. Additionally, the companion must complete the order within one month before it became void.

Yan Zhun:
?

Pei Ran:
I probably won't have time to play once school restarts, so

I'll pay right now

Pei Ran:
I'll come back if I get the chance.

Pei Ran didn't realize how much his last sentence sounded like a veiled apology. "I'll come back if I get the chance" could easily be interpreted as "I'll never come back."

Yan Zhun could no longer hold himself back. He walked to the balcony and lit a cigarette, but didn't smoke it. Instead, his gaze rested on that final message.

It took him awhile to move again.

Yan Zhun:
[money transfer: ¥1200]

Confused, Pei Ran reflexively sent out a question mark.

A voice message arrived almost immediately. Pei Ran held his phone close to his ear and listened.

"Did you really think I'm just a gaming companion?"

Pei Ran considered sending another question mark, but it felt rather impolite to him. Hence, he tapped on the voice button and replied dumbfoundedly, "Yeah..."

In voice messages that ensued, Yan Zhun's chuckles sounded muffled and low, as if he couldn't help it:

"Gaming companions at my level of play would charge at least 200 yuan per hour.

"I'm not currently short of money.

"I tricked you into placing an order so that you would play games with me."

Pei Ran listened to all three messages. His ear was warming up having pressed closely to the phone.

He paused for a moment before asking, "You like playing with newbies or something?"

Yan Zhun's self-restraint was coming to an end. He stubbed

out his cigarette and chuckled with his head hung low for a very long time. Only then did he give his reply in earnest.

"No, I just like playing with you."

"To be exact, I like doing anything with you."

"What I mean is, I like you. Do you understand? It has nothing to do with whether you're a newbie or not."

As if somebody pressed the pause button on Pei Ran, he froze on the spot holding his cell.

He even held his breath for a few seconds, listening to his own heartbeats resounding in his head. They reverberated in his temples, pounding like drumbeats.

When he put his phone down, he accidentally tapped on the voice again. Yan Zhun's voice rang out:

"What I mean is, I like you—"

Pei Ran fumbled to turn the sound off. He blinked rapidly, then darted to the window and slammed it shut.

It must be the rain getting too loud tonight, he thought.

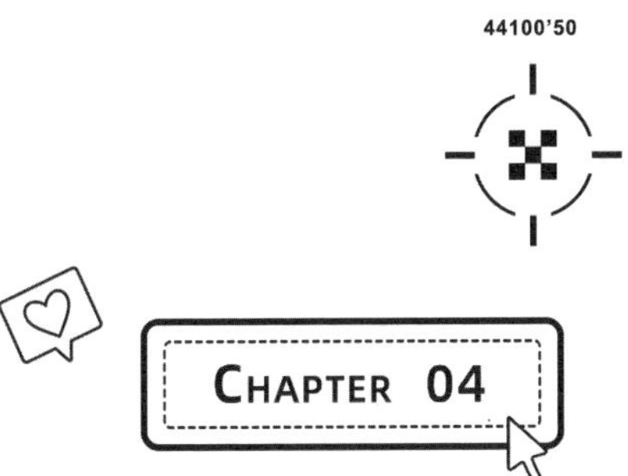

Pei Ran stood by the window for a long time. The window was shut, yet those sounds still echoed in his head.

It wasn't until he turned on the bathroom light and saw himself in the mirror that he realized his face and ears were flushed.

He washed his face, left the bathroom with the back of his hand pressing against his cheeks, then picked up his phone again.

Pei Ran had received many love confessions in the past. He'd been given his first in primary school: The fifth-grade girl had worn her hair in a ponytail, and her smile had been refreshing like the scent of lemon. With her blushing cheeks, she had shoved her confession letter into his hands and asked him to read it only when he reached home.

He hadn't even blinked twice before he'd politely pushed the letter back and replied with a "Thank you, but sorry."

Luo Qingshan had also received the same apology before.

He took a sip of water and thought that he was probably

reacting this way due to shock.

Why would Yan Zhun like him? They never crossed paths before the break. They didn't share an intimate bond or even exchanged more than a couple of words.

Pei Ran unlocked his phone. The screen remained on his conversation with Yan Zhun.

In the dark, the phone vibrated once again, sending tingles in his palm.

Yan Zhun:
I was just explaining myself, not confessing. You don't need to respond to me right away

Pei Ran was stunned speechless.

So that wasn't a confession?

Words of rejection ended up stuck in his throat, leaving him with nothing to say.

Yan Zhun:
But from now on, I won't call you boss anymore.

The rain was easing off. Yan Zhun went to the balcony to feel the breeze. After that last message, he finally pressed the back button to check the avalanche of notifications.

It was the group of streamers from before, pressing him to log back in and continue his killing spree.

They couldn't even wait for Yan Zhun to text back before starting a voice call. When Yan Zhun declined, they called him once more. In the end, he yielded and picked up with a frown on his face.

"Bro, what are you doing? Why did you hang up my call?" asked Lin Xuhuan.

"Was busy."

"What could keep you busy so late at night?"

"Waiting for a message."

Lin Xuhuan was dumbfounded. "Huh?"

Yan Zhun didn't bother to explain. "What do you want?"

"You to log back in and play, duh. Lao-He and the guys all woke up; we're waiting for you." He could overhear a rough male voice in the background, calling out his name.

Yan Zhun refused, "I'm a student; I have classes tomorrow."

"Heh, Lao-He wants you to skip school and come party at the base for a couple of days."

"Not a chance, bye."

Lin Xuhuan halted him. "Wait, stay on the line! My audience wants to hear your voice; don't hang up so soon."

"I'm in a hurry," said Yan Zhun.

"In a hurry to do what?"

Yan Zhun grasped his phone, his voice mingling with the howling wind. "To find you an in-law, and myself a wife."

The other end of the line fell silent for a few seconds; Lin Xuhuan was a bit confused before coming to his senses.

"Shit! Are you serious? You took an interest in women? "

Yan Zhun's tone was flat. "I like men."

"Hahaha..." Lin Xuhuan burst out laughing, thinking that Yan Zhun was being sarcastic. "Just kidding, no offense. I assumed you'd stay single all your life... So who's the extraordinary lady who managed to catch your oh-so demanding eyes?"

"Extraordinary, that sounds about right." Yan Zhun continued, "Anything else you want to say?"

For once, Lin Xuhuan read between the lines. "You wanna call my sister-in-law?"

"Don't say that; we're not together yet," said Yan Zhun, gazing at the moon. "I'm waiting for a reply."

Unfortunately, even after the call had ended, he didn't receive any new messages.

Yan Zhun had a hunch that he might not get his answer for

the night, so he shut the balcony window, tossed his phone next to the pillow, and prepared to sleep.

He stared at the ceiling for God knows how long when all of a sudden, the phone's screen lit up.

Pei Ran:
OK

Forty minutes have passed since the last message.

Yan Zhun curled his lips and, despite his drowsiness, managed to bring up the keyboard and type a short reply.

Yan Zhun:
I'm off to sleep, Pei Ran

The next day, Pei Ran refused to have the driver pick him up and returned to school on his own by bus.

By the time Pei Ran reached his dorm, his roommate had just finished a game. He took off his headset and turned toward Pei Ran. "You didn't see the class group chat?"

Pei Ran bent down to unpack his bag. "No, what's wrong?"

"It's about the sports festival. We don't have many guys in our class, so the counselor required all of us to sign up. Registration is happening right now." His roommate then asked, "Which activity do you want to sign up for? I suggest the 100-meter sprint. The ranking doesn't matter; you only need to finish the race."

Pei Ran considered his options. "I'll do the three km."

The roommate mumbled an "Oh," then calmly texted his girlfriend back. Seconds later, he jerked his head around, eyes wide with astonishment. "HUH?"

The roommate's strong reaction was justified. Although Pei Ran was tall, his physique would strike people as rather frail and vulnerable. His roommate once suspected that he was thinner than most girls in their class.

But since Pei Ran never undressed in front of his roommate—he would even bring spare clothes to the bathroom so he could change inside directly after showering—his roommate only had a vague idea of Pei Ran's figure.

Pei Ran signed up for the race under his roomie's questioning eyes. He lifted his head to meet his roommate's gaze and let out a chuckle. "I really can finish the run; don't worry."

As soon as he finished sorting out his luggage, Pei Ran received a text from Lin Kang, asking if they could eat dinner together.

Recalling his promise to treat him to a meal, Pei Ran agreed right away. The two arranged to meet at a Western-style restaurant near the school.

"I wanted to invite you to come to school together, but it was too late after my basketball game." Lin Kang sipped on his lemonade, then whispered, "Isn't this restaurant too expensive? We can always go for spicy hotpot. I'm not picky."

Pei Ran, "Don't worry. Since I have a membership card, I can get discounts."

So even someone who sat in a Maybach knew how to use discounts.

How familiar. Lin Kang felt that the gap between Pei Ran and him had shortened ever so slightly.

As they were chatting, Lin Kang suddenly received a call from Luo Qingshan. He shot an awkward glance at Pei Ran and saw him focused on the menu, not disturbed in the slightest.

After hanging up, Lin Kang gave a little cough. "He asked me where the basketball was."

Pei Ran nodded and looked away from the menu. "How

about we order the combo?"

Lin Kang agreed without hesitation.

They sat still for a while, but Lin Kang's curiosity eventually got the better of him. "Um, Pei Ran, I'm not gossiping or anything, but I wonder... is it true that you and Luo Qingshan broke up because you guys weren't compatible?"

Pei Ran returned the question, "What do you think?"

"I have no idea what to guess..." Yet, despite these words, Lin Kang still hazarded a guess. "Don't tell me it was because of Su Nian?"

Pei Ran stopped short of flipping over the menu page, not uttering a single sound.

Lin Kang was the kind of straight guy who couldn't notice that his girlfriend was angry until many hours later. If his friend hadn't mentioned Su Nian last night, he wouldn't have spared a thought for him.

But now that he had time to muse about the issue, those two... were indeed pretty damn strange.

"So it was him? Well, shit. No wonder Su Nian was acting weird in the chat group that day..." Lin Kang recalled. "Do you need help or something? Let me know if you need anything. I absolutely cannot stand this kinda stuff."

"It's all right; we already broke up." Pei Ran didn't really want to pursue the topic.

Yet Lin Kang didn't pick up the hint. "Don't be shy. I might be close with Luo Qingshan, but I won't stay loyal to someone for no good reason. Need me to scold him for you?"

The conversation was on the verge of spinning out of control. Pei Ran pondered for a moment and spoke thoughtfully, "I don't need your help for that, but there's something I want to ask you."

"What's it?" replied Lin Kang.

"Did Yan Zhun attend Mancheng High School?"

"Erm... yeah?" Lin Kang was confused.

"I don't remember seeing him back then," said Pei Ran.

"No way!" Lin Kang didn't even notice the abrupt switch of topic. "He was super famous in high school. We were in the same class, but our homeroom was on the first floor, a few floors below yours. By the way, he also won the PUBG competition at a cybercafe. You've never heard of that?"

That was when PUBG was at the peak of its popularity. A high school student winning a gaming tournament was considered more news-worthy than if they had scored first on the regional exams.

Pei Ran subconsciously gripped his glass and shook his head.

"Then you must've been... quite focused on your studies," Lin Kang noted. "Back then, his fame spread far beyond our school. Someone once posted a photo of him in the tournament online. It only showed his profile, yet it still garnered more than twenty thousand reposts. Pretty crazy."

Hearing this, Pei Ran finally remembered.

Not about Yan Zhun, but about that Weibo post.

At first, his attention had been caught by the keyword "Mancheng." He'd even tapped on the photo to make it bigger. But before he could take a good look at it, the phone screen had been covered by Luo Qingshan, who laughed as he joked that he wouldn't let Pei Ran look at other boys.

Pei Ran murmured, "I think... I have some idea of him."

"What do you remember about me?" A familiar voice came from behind the two of them.

Both were startled, especially Pei Ran, whose eyes widened

abruptly as his expression betrayed the panic and embarrassment of someone getting caught.

He turned around stiffly, and his gaze crossed over the fake greenery to meet Yan Zhun's.

Pei Ran rarely made such a face. Yan Zhun examined him for a couple of seconds before glancing over to Lin Kang and explained himself, "I didn't eavesdrop; I've been sitting here for a while."

Every table in the restaurant was separated with a tabletop divider, so it was difficult to identify other guests without paying close attention. Lin Kang came to his senses. "I didn't notice you at all... You're eating on your own?"

"I was stood up." Yan Zhun eyed the people standing in line outside and continued, "How about we share a table? There are a lot of people waiting outside."

As soon as Yan Zhun sat down, Pei Ran felt that their dining table for four suddenly became a bit crowded.

He had never talked about someone else behind their back before. This was his first time... and he got caught.

Pei Ran clutched his phone with his head hung low, and stayed silent, trying his hardest to make himself invisible.

"What did you two talk about?" He heard Yan Zhun ask in a lazy tone.

"When you won the tournament back in senior high," Lin Kang replied. "Pei Ran had no idea that you two went to the same school."

Yan Zhun made no attempt at modesty. "He was on the honor roll. It makes sense that he wouldn't pay attention to gaming news."

Lin Kang looked down at his phone and grumbled, "Why is the class group chat so busy? It's just the sports festival. They can pick anything as long as we can make up the numbers! Anyway, what did you guys sign up for?"

"Nothing yet," said Yan Zhun.

Sensing two pairs of eyes upon him, Pei Ran answered honestly, "The three kilometer run."

"Impressive. Guess I'll just slack off when it's my turn," said Lin Kang, as he stood up with his phone in hand. "I'm going to the bathroom; then I'll give the counselor a call."

After Lin Kang left, the table became completely quiet.

Pei Ran instinctively pursed his lips, searching in his mind for an excuse to walk away.

If he couldn't ease the awkwardness, then the second-best option was to escape it.

Just as he managed to invent a good pretext, Yan Zhun suddenly spoke again. "So what did you remember about me, Pei Ran?"

Like a student who wanted to skip class but was called on by the teacher, Pei Ran resigned himself to admit the truth. "I remembered the Weibo post that Lin Kang mentioned."

Yan Zhun jogged his memory. That photo of his profile was very blurry, but at least it wasn't ugly.

"People gave me too much credit. I'm not that great."

Pei Ran hummed noncommittally. The dining table wasn't large. When Pei Ran lowered his head, he could see that Yan Zhun had casually crossed his legs underneath. The sneakers he was wearing were a limited-edition model from the current season.

How did he get fooled by Yan Zhun when he said he had to work as a gaming companion for money for food?

Wrapped up in his thoughts, Pei Ran only belatedly noticed that one of Yan Zhun's shoes had turned and was now brushing against his own foot.

Yan Zhun looked down and compared their shoes for a while, then concluded, "You've got quite small feet."

Pei Ran wanted to argue back, but when he compared his shoes with Yan Zhun's, he had to concede that his feet were indeed slightly smaller.

He didn't say a word and quietly pulled his feet back.

Yan Zhun smirked, but he didn't tease Pei Ran further. Instead, he took out his phone to check the messages.

Lin Xuhuan:
:(((((bro wait for me, I'll be outside right after I change! Fuck, I didn't stream for nearly enough hours, so my coach caught me and railed at me for hours... I'm paying for today's dinner!

Yan Zhun:
Wait, don't change yet

Lin Xuhuan:
?

Yan Zhun:
How much does it cost to send your stream a rocket?

Lin Xuhuan:
2000, why?

Yan Zhun:
[money transfer: ¥2000]

Lin Xuhuan:
?

Yan Zhun:
Something came up at the last minute, you'll have to hang out with yourself.

Lin Kang returned soon enough. Being a chatterbox, he couldn't eat quietly without prattling after every other bite.

"It was raining for the whole seven-day break. I couldn't go anywhere and just rotted away at home." Lin Kang wiped his mouth. "Where did you go during the break?"

The question was addressed at Yan Zhun. Pei Ran seemed so engrossed in his meal that Lin Kang didn't have the heart to disturb him.

"Nowhere." Yan Zhun replied. "I was busy making money."

Lin Kang asked, "Making money? You got a part-time job?"

"Kind of," Yan Zhun brushed over the subject. "Worked as a game companion for a couple of days."

Lin Kang was so astonished that he didn't notice that the other person beside him momentarily froze, then resumed chewing at a much slower pace.

"You... as a gaming companion?" said Lin Kang. "Like those on Bixin?"

"Pretty much, but on another platform," Yan Zhun said.

Lin Kang had mixed feelings about this. Whenever he and his friends played together, they would always hire a gaming companion. One could say he was well-versed in the way of gaming companions. It didn't matter if they sucked or played dirty, but they needed to have a pleasant voice and know how to cheer people up.

After all, the purpose of playing video games was to have fun. If someone solely wanted to climb up the ranks, hiring a booster to play in their place would save both time and effort.

But Yan Zhun... He didn't even pay attention to people most of the time, let alone cheer them up.

Lin Kang chose his words carefully. "Well, how did it go?"

"Not bad." Yan Zhun glanced at Pei Ran, whether intentionally or not. "I only accepted orders from one person."

Pei Ran was at a loss for word.

He had prepared a response beforehand. If Lin Kang were to question him later, he would answer truthfully that he spent the break playing video games. After all, there was nothing unusual about two guys gaming together.

But in just a few words, Yan Zhun made the whole experience sound almost shady.

Sure enough, Lin Kang had to pause for a couple of seconds before asking, "Only one? How many hours did you sell?"

"Sixty." Yan Zhun said.

Lin Kang took a deep breath and began to calculate. "Sixty hours... I assume you charge at least a hundred an hour? That's six thousand yuan in total. If your boss was willing to blow that much on you in just one week... You've got yourself a sugar mommy!"

Pei Ran choked and broke into a coughing fit, causing both people beside him to stare in his direction at once.

Sensing two pairs of eyes on him, Pei Ran uttered emotionlessly, "It's just a transaction... I wouldn't call that having a sugar mommy."

Yan Zhun leaned back in his chair and smiled lazily.

Not noticing the subtle tension between the two of them, Lin Kang explained to Pei Ran in earnest, "You probably don't understand since you've never hired a gaming companion. When people like us need one, we'd usually pay right after each game. But it's different for big spenders—they would store the money in the gaming companion's account and let the companion deduct their pay directly from the balance. Even if they sometimes withdrew too much, the big spenders wouldn't mind."

Then, he turned toward Yan Zhun. "Did you finish your sixty hours?"

"No, my boss was worried that I wouldn't get the money, so I was paid in advance." Yan Zhun then asked in return with amused interest, "What do you think my boss was thinking? Not the least bit worried that I might run away with the money?"

"This shows that she wants to become your long-term boss; she'll definitely hire you again!" Lin Kang asserted confidently. "She must have a thing for you!"

Silence fell across the table.

A while later, Yan Zhun gave a short laugh. "Is that so? But my boss is a guy."

Lin Kang was stunned speechless.

Yan Zhun's "long-term boss" calmly sipped on coffee and finished his meal.

When it came time to pay the bills, Yan Zhun whipped out his WeChat Pay QR code before anyone else. He stated naturally, "Let me treat you with what I earned from my part-time job."

After dinner, the three of them left the restaurant together. They walked together for a while before Lin Kang headed to the nearby supermarket to buy cigarettes.

After much hesitation, Pei Ran finally opened his mouth. "I didn't mean to act like a sugar daddy. I was just worried that you might not get paid on time if I become too busy to play after we're back to school. If it offended you... I apologize.

Yan Zhun wanted to tell him to keep offending him, but decided not to tease him any further. "It's OK."

Pei Ran breathed a sigh of relief and took out his phone. "How much was dinner? I'll pay you back."

That Western-style restaurant was quite expensive. One combo meal cost at least 200 to 300 yuan.

Yan Zhun stuffed his hands in his pockets. "No need."

"But you didn't make any actual money," Pei Ran insisted.

"Can I transfer the amount via WeChat?"

Pei Ran barely opened the WeChat app when he received a call from his roommate. The other young man explained that he was moving in with his girlfriend and would be leaving tonight. He needed Pei Ran to be back at the dorm to discuss what to do with the bigger appliances that they had brought together.

Meanwhile, Lin Kang came out of the supermarket. Seeing that Pei Ran was on the phone, Lin Kang didn't interrupt him and instead pointed toward their campus. "Yan Zhun and I will get going. You should take this path when you head back; it's a shortcut."

Although they attended the same university, they lived on different campuses separated by a street in-between. Walking from one place to another takes ten minutes.

Pei Ran wanted to stop them, but his roommate on the other end of the line kept asking, "Can you hear me? Are you free to come to the dorm right now?"

Pei Ran had no choice but to agree, "Yeah, I'm on my way..."

All of a sudden, Yan Zhun stepped toward Pei Ran. He took out something from his own pocket, then gently placed it inside the pocket of Pei Ran's hoodie.

When Yan Zhun's figure faded into the night, the roommate finally hung up.

Pei Ran locked his phone and turned away. After taking a few steps, he reached inside his pocket...

...and pulled out a few candies.

On the day of the sports festival, Yan Zhun was woken up at noon by the class president's call, who reminded him of the 1000-meter race that would take place in the afternoon.

Yan Zhun answered nonchalantly and hung up as soon as he could. He laid under his blanket for a while before sitting up sluggishly.

As he put on his sneakers, Luo Qingshan said, "I was just about to rouse you. Wanna go for a run together as a warm-up?"

Yan Zhun refused. After a brief pause, he asked, "What did you sign up for?"

"The three-K." Luo Qingshan's tone gave away his excitement. "I asked someone to find out Pei Ran's event—he'll also run the three-K. Wish me luck, bro."

Yan Zhun frowned, but quickly smoothed out his expression. He retrieved his phone from underneath his pillow and didn't respond.

Since the day he stood Lin Xuhuan up, it was as if Lin Xuhuan had tasted blood. From then on, Lin Xuhuan would try to invite him to dinner every single day.

Lin Xuhuan:
Bro, wanna eat out tonight? The bill's on me. If you're busy, feel free to flake.

Yan Zhun sneered.

Now he's tricking money from his friend instead of his fans. How shameless.

As he was thinking, another message from Lin Xuhuan popped up.

It was a block of text, evidently a funny copypasta shared across chat groups.

Yan Zhun skimmed it and was about to close the app when he suddenly had an idea. With a smirk, he tapped and held the message, then forwarded it to another chat.

At this time, Pei Ran was sitting in the canteen. In front of him were only two vegetable dishes.

He had a long-distance race to run later that afternoon. Overeating would upset his stomach.

His phone dinged quietly.

Yan Zhun:
Onii-chan, it's the end of the season, but I haven't reached 6K points yet QAQ I'm not very good, but I'll always tag behind my onii-chan o(" \' ∇ \' ")o fragging and rushing are too scawwy for me ;w; I don't wanna kill, I just wanna follow you around with my handy dandy healing kits!

Pei Ran was baffled.

He widened his eyes ever so slightly to confirm he was looking at the right ID.

Pei Ran:
Did you send this to the wrong person?

Pei Ran:
I'm Pei Ran.

Yan Zhun:
Yeah, my mistake

Yan Zhun:
When's the 3K race?

Pei Ran:
3 PM

Yan Zhun:
Stop if you can't finish it, the Faculty of Arts doesn't require you to do well at the sports festival

Pei Ran:
...

Pei Ran:
I'll finish it.

That afternoon, Pei Ran and his roommate arrived at the playing field together.

His roommate signed up for the 1000-meter race as the easy option. The sports festival had not yet begun, so the two sat in the stands and waited for registration.

His roommate was chatting on the phone when he suddenly cracked a smile. "My girlfriend will be running the relay. I have to go cheer her on."

Pei Ran nodded. "Sounds good."

"What about you?" asked the roommate. "Luo Qingshan isn't here to root for you?"

Pei Ran replied, "We broke up."

"Huh?" His roommate froze his typing, then turned around in shock. "When did that happen? But I met him on the first day of the break. He told me that you two didn't make any plans, so you were gonna stay at home..."

Pei Ran had no idea about this. His lips twitched. "We broke up before the break."

The roommate wasn't as gossipy as Lin Kang, so he ended the conversation after expressing his surprise. He patted Pei Ran on the shoulder, "Enough about that, it's my time to race. Come on, go to the finish line so you can cheer me on."

When he noticed Yan Zhun on the starting line, Pei Ran stopped short.

Yan Zhun was very tall. His start position was as proper as the two student-athletes beside him. Although the student-athletes were quite fit, Yan Zhun's broad shoulders and long legs easily attracted the audience's attention.

Pei Ran even overheard two girls discuss how they'll bring water to Yan Zhun later.

As the starter pistol fired, Yan Zhun darted from the starting line like an arrow shot from a bow.

The 1000-meter run wasn't too challenging for young men. The two student-athletes sprinted forward, followed by Yan Zhun. As for his roommate... he was trailing at the tail-end alongside a Computer Science student.

Pei Ran watched as Yan Zhun got closer and closer, ultimately crossing the finish line in third place, then heading straight toward him.

After the sprint, he needed to jog over a short distance to slow himself down. Pei Ran had a hunch that Yan Zhun might collide with him, so his body drew back subconsciously.

Steadily, Yan Zhun stopped in his tracks.

His chest rose and fell as he struggled to regain his breath. After a while, he panted, "Don't worry, I won't hit you."

Pei Ran blinked rapidly, then said drily, "Congrats on the third place."

"Third place is nothing to write home about." Yan Zhun looked down at the two bottles of water in Pei Ran's hands. "For me?"

Pei Ran thought for a moment, then instinctively raised the bottle in his right hand. "This one—"

As soon as he spoke, Yan Zhun snatched the bottle, untwisted the cap, and took a swig of water.

As the ice-cold water reached his throat, a refreshing feeling pervaded his being.

He drank most of the bottle in one swift gulp. When he finished it, he saw the person in front stare back at him, eyes wide with shock and dismay.

Pei Ran had been about to say that he'd already drunk from that bottle and that the other bottle was reserved for his roommate.

Yan Zhun raised an eyebrow and was about to ask when someone came up to remind him to report his time.

"I'll go report in." He was so close to Pei Ran that Pei Ran could feel his breath. "Don't sweat it. Worse comes to worst, I'll buy you another bottle."

When his roommate crossed the finish line, gasping for air like a fish out of water, Pei Ran rushed to hand him a bottle of water.

His roommate bent over with his hands on his knees to recover his breath. After a long time, he finally looked up and burst into laughter. "I won! I outdid that guy in comp sci!"

"Good job," replied Pei Ran.

The roommate was so delighted that he nearly forgot to ask, "What's my ranking?"

"Second to last."

The roommate paused, scowling, but then he changed his mind. "Whatever, at least I didn't lose to the comp sci guy."

After the roommate reported his time, he suddenly remembered something he meant to ask, "You're pretty close to Yan Zhun, aren't you? I just saw you two chatting near the finish line."

"He's Luo Qingshan's roommate," Pei Ran explained.

The roommate had an epiphany. "I see; he wants you to give that guy a second chance."

Pei Ran hesitated, wondering if he should correct him, but decided not to.

The roommate soon left Pei Ran to cheer for his girlfriend, so Pei Ran found himself a quiet spot to warm up before the 3-kilometer race.

The 3k race wasn't difficult, but the boys in their class lacked exercise. Some flat-out refused to participate in the sports festival. Most were hesitant or unwilling. A few even tried to dissuade Pei Ran when he signed up.

He did a few leg stretches with his gaze fixated on the

ground while his mind wandered elsewhere.

Since his father had been away from home for two weeks, he didn't go for morning jogs as often. When he tested himself yesterday, he managed to finish the run, but his speed was a tad slow.

He'd try to run faster today.

When Luo Qingshan found Pei Ran, he was doing high-knees.

His movements were careful. The contours of his tensely bent legs were smooth and pleasing to the eye.

Luo Qingshan gawked at him for a long time before mustering the confidence to call his name, "Pei Ran."

Pei Ran stopped. He turned back to face Luo Qingshan, then slowly brought his leg down. "Do you need anything?"

"So you're taking part in the sports festival, too?" Pei Ran's formality stung him, but Luo Qingshan tried hard to keep his tone casual. "Which event did you sign up for?"

"The three-K."

"What a coincidence, so did I." Luo Qingshan licked his lips nervously. "Wanna warm up together? I'll massage your legs."

Pei Ran shook his head. "No need, I'm almost done."

Pei Ran's eyes lowered and fell on Luo Qingshan's right hand dangling at his side.

Feeling his gaze, Luo Qingshan quickly lifted his hand and extended his fingers for Pei Ran to see. "Didn't you see the text I sent you? My finger has recovered; it doesn't hurt anymore."

Luo Qingshan's right ring finger differed from his other fingers. It could move without any problems, but upon close inspection, one could discern a thin, jagged scar across it.

Before, Pei Ran would often hold Luo Qingshan's finger

while being lost in his thoughts. His strokes were always incredibly gentle, as though he were caressing Luo Qingshan's heart. Therefore, as Luo Qingshan spoke, his hand subconsciously reached toward Pei Ran.

Pei Ran didn't touch him.

"That's good to hear." Pei Ran then stared into his eyes. "If you feel any aftereffects or general discomfort, you must call me. I'll take full responsibility."

Luo Qingshan suddenly felt a lump in his throat. He withdrew his hand and smiled wryly. "All right."

It was not until Pei Ran turned around and left that Luo Qingshan realized that he didn't even say a word of encouragement to him.

He tousled his hair in frustration and flopped down on a nearby stone bench to play with his phone. He had already finished warming up before he sought out Pei Ran; what he said before was but an excuse to strike up a conversation.

After their brief chat, Luo Qingshan became even more certain of his goal—he had to win Pei Ran back.

This task was more complicated than expected. With hesitation, Luo Qingshan tapped on the topmost conversation in his chats list. Su Nian had sent him several messages in a row, asking for the time of his race so he could come to cheer him on.

Luo Qingshan pressed on Su Nian's profile. His finger hovered back and forth over the "Block" button.

But then he reconsidered, why did it matter whether he blocked Su Nian or not? He wasn't interested in him. Even if he kept Su Nian in his friends list, he had no desire to cheat with him.

Besides, Su Nian... was really nice to him. Blocking him

while not being blocked back seemed rather uncharitable.

Luo Qingshan:
Don't come. If Pei Ran sees us together, he'll get the wrong idea again.

Su Nian:
...

Su Nian:
Fine, good luck with your race. If you meet Pei Ran, tell him sorry on my behalf

Su Nian:
Text me whenever you need me, I'm always available :D

The phone vibrated again. Luo Qingshan pressed the back button to check his new message—surprisingly, it was from Pei Ran.

He instantly perked up and leaped to his feet.

Babe:
My number is the same, 134xxxxx. Call me whenever you need help

Luo Qingshan was so emotional that he made a couple of typos.

Babe:
What's wrong? I never forgot your number

He reread the message twice before pressing "Send".

!
Pei Ran has enabled friend confirmation. Send a friend request to chat.

Luo Qingshan was stunned by the red exclamation mark.

His eyes widened in shock. After sending a few punctuation marks in succession to confirm his suspicion, he had no choice but to face the reality that...

Pei Ran had blocked him.

Pei Ran was the last one to register. By the time he finished, everyone else had already lined up at the starting line.

Standing on Lane 5, Luo Qingshan eyed him nervously. When he saw Pei Ran approaching, he automatically stepped toward him, yet halted when someone nearby tugged on his shirt.

"Hey, the race is about to start. Don't leave now."

Pei Ran squatted down and tied his shoelaces again.

A crowd had gathered around the running track, most of whom were sneaking glances at Pei Ran.

He was quite well-known throughout the school, the first reason being his outstanding track record, which professors frequently touted as an inspiration. The second reason was that everyone was aware he had a boyfriend.

Nowadays, most young people have become accepting towards homosexuality. They didn't look at Pei Ran with disgust or repulsion, but with interest and curiosity.

Even so, Pei Ran never felt comfortable with it.

The starting pistol interrupted Pei Ran's thoughts. As he sprinted from the starting line, the cool breeze blowing toward him finally brought him some much-needed relief.

The 3k race lasted nearly eight laps, and Pei Ran counted them as he ran. Halfway through the fifth lap, his breathing was still steady, but his ranking fell slightly behind.

Pei Ran couldn't resist peeking behind him. Good, he wasn't in the last place.

When he turned back around, he heard the people around him shout, "Watch out—!"

Before Pei Ran could react, someone had crashed into him.

Pei Ran occupied the leftmost lane. Somehow, a student in the audience ended up on the running track and collided head-on with him. Since he maintained a certain speed, the impact sent him tumbling to the ground. His eyes were seeing stars and his arms stung painfully as if they were on fire.

Pei Ran winced, but quickly propped himself up into a sitting position.

"Sorry sorry sorry sorry!!!" The other student was caught by her friend in the nick of time, which softened her fall. She apologized profusely, "Somebody just pushed me. Sorry again! Are you injured? Where does it hurt?"

"Don't worry." Pei Ran bent his arm to examine it. There was a cut still seeping blood—apparently a superficial wound.

He glanced at the petite female student in front of him. "Did I hurt you?"

The girl panicked, shook her head, then nodded. "Not at all. Are y-you all right though? What should I do? Did you get wounded?"

Seeing her getting flustered, Pei Ran wanted to reassure her.

But he soon found out that his arm wasn't the only body part with injuries—he had also sprained his ankle, and a dull pain radiated from his lower leg.

He took a deep breath and pushed on the floor in a strenuous attempt to stand up.

"Don't move."

Pei Ran raised his head and met Yan Zhun's gaze.

Yan Zhun squatted down, held his arm to inspect it, then asked, "Did you hurt your waist?"

Pei Ran answered, "I don't think so."

"Can you walk?" Yan Zhun continued. "Let me carry you."

Yan Zhun practically picked him up.

Putting an arm around Pei Ran's shoulder, he cradled his waist and effortlessly lifted him to his feet.

They were very close, so much so that Pei Ran could feel Yan Zhun's warmth spreading through his thin clothes.

Once he got up, Pei Ran was ready to let go of Yan Zhun when he heard the other boy ask quietly, "Are you sure you can walk to the school clinic by yourself?"

Pei Ran paused for two seconds. "Thank you for your help."

Since the sports festival was in full swing, the school clinic was packed. The school doctor cast his eye over Pei Ran's injuries, then handed him a bottle of iodine and an ice pack before ordering the two of them to treat his wounds in the resting room next door.

Pei Ran sat on a bed in the resting room and carefully rolled his pants up to his knees. A large, red bruise covered his lower leg.

Yan Zhun arrived with the medicine. His gaze lingered on Pei Ran's bruise for a moment before he turned around to leave.

"Where are you going?" Pei Ran blurted out when he saw the antiseptic in Yan Zhun's hand.

"To the doctor, so I can ask her to prescribe more medicine," Yan Zhun answered.

"Don't!" In the heat of the moment, Pei Ran grabbed Yan Zhun's shirt. "It's just a scratch. Disinfecting it will be enough."

Yan Zhun frowned.

"Really."

Thirty seconds later, Yan Zhun dragged a chair in front of Pei Ran and sat down.

Pei Ran heaved a sigh of relief. Just as he prepared to thank Yan Zhun one more time, he heard him say, "Put your leg up here."

Pei Ran was somewhat confused. "Where?"

He watched as Yan Zhun unscrewed the bottle of iodine when suddenly, he understood his intention. "It's fine; I can do it myself."

Yan Zhun didn't respond. Instead, he bent down and held his ankle, then laid it on his thigh.

Pei Ran still wore his shoes. When he recovered from his bewilderment, he immediately tried to pull his leg back, but to no avail.

"My shoes are dirty," Pei Ran protested.

"So don't move." Yan Zhun pinched a cotton swab stained red by the antiseptic while his eyes fixated on the bruise across Pei Ran's leg.

Before Pei Ran could refuse, the cotton swab had been pressed on his leg.

Pei Ran's legs were very straight, and his skin was paler than most other boys. The iodine liquid spreading on it appeared like paint which accidentally spotted a blank canvas.

Yan Zhun wore short sleeves today, so his arm would occasionally graze Pei Ran's leg, causing Pei Ran to furrow his brows subconsciously. Each time it happened, his frown would deepen.

The position they were in was much too strange.

"Does it hurt?" asked Yan Zhun.

Pei Ran replied right away, "Not anymore."

In reality, the skin still prickled, but that sensation was well within his level of tolerance.

Yan Zhun glanced at the injury quietly for a while, then suddenly lowered his head again.

Pei Ran felt a cool breeze brush against his wound, sending waves of itchiness from his lower leg to the rest of the body...

Yan Zhun was blowing on his injury.

Pei Ran held his breath, then sucked in a lungful of air as subtly as he could. He could feel the thumping of his own heart.

Just as he was about to draw his leg back, the resting room's door swung open.

Luo Qingshan stood outside, still panting heavily. As he came to grips with the situation inside the room, his body froze as his eyes slowly widened.

A momentary stillness fell over the resting room.

Luo Qingshan's eyes darted back and forth between the two of them. When he finally found his voice again, it was filled with shock and confusion.

"Yan Zhun?"

Luo Qingshan only found out about Pei Ran's fall after he completed the run.

As Luo Qingshan was quite athletic, he quickly left Pei Ran behind once they started running. When he finally crossed the finish line and turned around, Pei Ran was already gone.

Upon hearing what happened from the students nearby, he rushed over without reporting his time.

Pei Ran stopped mid-track, clearly surprised that he would come. A sudden chill applied to his ankle then pulled him back to reality.

Yan Zhun glanced at Luo Qingshan and merely hummed a small affirmation. He then put the ice pack on Pei Ran's sprained ankle, asking, "Is it here?"

Pei Ran reflectively answered, "Around there."

Luo Qingshan steadied his breath and quickly entered the resting room. "Pei Ran, Pei Ran, where did you get hurt? Do your bones hurt?"

Seeing Pei Ran's leg injury, he inhaled sharply and picked up his phone. "I'm calling a cab. We're going to the hospital."

"No need," Pei Ran said. "It's not that serious. Disinfecting the wound is more than enough."

"No, you should still take an X-ray. What if there's a fracture?" Luo Qingshan insisted.

"My bones are fine. It's just a sprain." Seeing that he had opened a ride-hailing app, Pei Ran could only reply, "I won't get in the car even if you called one."

Luo Qingshan froze for a second, uncertain what to say, then closed the app uneasily.

He shot an awkward glance at Yan Zhun. Yan Zhun was helping Pei Ran to apply the ice pack and didn't even raise his head.

"Yan Zhun, why are you here?" He changed the topic and gave a forced smile, "Done with your 1000-meter race?"

Yan Zhun replied, "Yeah."

"How did you do?"

"So-so, I guess."

"It's okay. The ranking doesn't matter; it's not like you're expected to win," Luo Qingshan said casually. "You gamers don't really exercise, after all."

Pei Ran went quiet for two seconds. Seeing how Yan Zhun remained silent, as if in tacit admisision that Luo Qingshan was right, he couldn't help but defend Yan Zhun's honor before Luo Qingshan could say anything else. "He took third place. The first and second places were both students from the athlete track."

Yan Zhun's expression melted a little. He smirked as he lifted the ice pack and wiped away the condensation on Pei

Ran's ankle with his hands, then reapplied the pack.

Pei Ran felt scalded by his warm palm.

Luo Qingshan was slightly stunned. "Huh? Well... congrats."

There were a lot of questions on his mind, which one could quickly tell from his frown. He wiped his sweat with a tissue and extended a hand to Yan Zhun. "Thanks for taking Pei Ran here. I'll take the ice pack. Just leave the rest to me."

Yan Zhun finally looked up, but that was all he did. He stared at Luo Qingshan, sounding surprised. "Didn't you two break up?"

Once these words came out, the mood in the room became tense again.

Luo Qingshan ran through an erratic array of expressions. After a while, he smiled and pretended not to mind. "That's why I need a chance to prove myself."

Yan Zhun retorted, "And why should I give you this chance?"

Luo Qingshan was confused.

All this talk was too much for Pei Ran. Pulling his leg back, he said, "I won't trouble you guys any further. It's just a minor injury; I can deal with it myself."

Luo Qingshan was still staring at Yan Zhun with a mixture of emotions in his eyes. Just as he opened his mouth to ask, his cell phone rang.

It was their class president, telling him to get back to the field to sign the check-in list. Without a check-in signature, his run would be considered invalid, and his score nullified on the spot.

Luo Qingshan asked a few more questions before he left. Even when he was leaving, he turned to look back at almost every step, his face filled with worry.

The ice pack was too cold to hold. Pei Ran casually put it on his ankle and sincerely thanked the person beside him. "Thank you for today."

Yan Zhun hummed in acceptance, then suddenly said, "You stepped on my feet several times on our way here."

It was tough to walk on one foot, especially right after he got injured. Both of his legs were hurting, so he was really wobbly.

Pei Ran stared in his eyes for two seconds, then looked down at Yan Zhun's shoes.

One could see a footprint across a pair of white limited-edition sneakers. That was some damning evidence.

"I'm sorry," Pei Ran said. "Let me wash them for you."

In a rare show of surprise, Yan Zhun raised his eyebrows. "You're gonna wash them for me?"

Pei Ran added, "I'll send it to a laundry shop. They do shoe-cleaning over there too."

Yan Zhun's interest dissipated. "No."

He looked at Pei Ran's hands, which he found to be quite breathtaking. It was ideal for drawing, ideal for playing the piano, and ideal for Pei Ran.

Yan Zhun thought that even if Pei Ran wanted to wash his shoes with his own two hands, he would not have the heart to ruin them.

Pei Ran asked, "Then I'll wipe them with a wet tissue?"

"No." Yan Zhun retracted his gaze. "Consider this a favor you owe me."

Pei Ran frowned ever so slightly, but his tone was firm, "I'll buy you a new pair. What's your size?"

Feeling the subtle shift in Pei Ran's attitude, Yan Zhun looked at him for a long time, then sighed.

He turned to grab a tissue from the nearby table. With Pei Ran's wrist in his grasp, Yan Zhun wetted the tissue by rubbing it on the ice pack's wet surface and haphazardly wiped his shoes clean.

"It's all clean now. You now owe nothing."

Just as his voice fell, Yan Zhun's cell phone rang several times.

Reading the messages, Yan Zhun remembered his promise to Lin Xuhuan. He was supposed to play a couple of practice matches with them at the gaming house.

Yan Zhun stood up and said, "Let's go."

Pei Ran looked up at him. "Where to?"

"I'll take you back to the dorm," Yan Zhun replied. Before Pei Ran could answer, he held Pei Ran's hand and placed it around his neck. "Hold tight."

Pei Ran's room was spotless. He wiped the place down after his roommate moved out, and there was a faint fruity scent lingering in the air.

Yan Zhun put him down and left without closing the dorm door.

Pei Ran wasn't worried. As he opened the black plastic bag on the table, he thought he should've asked Yan Zhun if he wanted to have some fruit.

Pei Ran walked to the sink with great difficulty and carefully peeled the peach. He was about to take the first bite when he noticed a slight stir at the door.

Yan Zhun returned, a black plastic bag in hand. "Take it."

Pei Ran asked, "What's this?"

"Ice cream," Yan Zhun replied. "Put it on your ankle."

Pei Ran chuckled.

Yan Zhun didn't know what he did that tickled Pei Ran

so much. He stared at Pei Ran long and hard. "Why are you laughing?"

Pei Ran laughed and shook his head. He took the bag and said, "Thank you. Would you like some fruit?"

"Sure." Yan Zhun peered at his hand. "Peaches?"

Pei Ran nodded. He hesitated, but still decided to give him his peach. "I've washed my hands. It's clean."

Right as Pei Ran said that, Yan Zhun swooped in and bit down on the peach, lifting it from Pei Ran's hand.

He swallowed a big mouthful of peach flesh as Pei Ran looked at him in shock.

"It's sweet," said Yan Zhun.

After several practice matches, TZG's coach found his WeChat bombarded with messages.

"They're all asking if I had tricked you into joining the team, and they call me cunning for keeping it under wraps." The coach sneered. "What a joke. If I had truly snagged you, don't you think I'd be the first to grab a megaphone and blast the news at the house?"

Yan Zhun leaned back in the gaming chair as he engaged in a shootout with another player. Three seconds later, he managed to kill his enemy with a headshot.

"Bravo!" The coach reclined against the chair. "So what do you think? Will you give me the chance to announce the good news?"

Yan Zhun snickered. How come everyone wanted him to give them a chance today?

"No," Yan Zhun replied. "If you nag me again, I'm going home."

"Don't; we've already prepped the room for you. You're

sleeping here tonight." The coach had long gotten used to this. "Then could you come over more often to train them?"

Lin Xuhuan wailed, "Please no, he'll just kick my ass."

The coach retorted, "That's precisely why he's here, to make you get off your high horse. Your streams have become daily gloating sessions. You must think your paycheck is too big."

"What does this have to do with that..." Lin Xuhuan grumbled. "Bro, how many people are in that building?"

After the practice matches, all but two players left for a kebab restaurant. Lin Xuhuan was suffering from canker sores and couldn't eat greasy food, so he stayed behind and begged Yan Zhun to play with him in a duo.

"Full squad of four ahead. I'll take down three." Yan Zhun switched to a rifle. "Clear the building."

Near the end of the round, they were sniped down by an aimbot and only made second place.

Yan Zhun felt annoyed. This game was getting overrun by cheaters. He was about to exit the game when he noticed a friend who logged in out of the corner of his eye.

He immediately sent him an invitation.

"Bro, you're leaving?" Lin Xuhuan asked, seeing that his character still wasn't ready.

Yan Zhun replied, "I don't know."

Lin Xuhuan pressed on, "What do you mean, 'I don't know'?"

Yan Zhun lit a cigarette. "Depends on if he ignores me or not."

Before Lin Xuhuan could ask another question, another player's character avatar suddenly popped up on the game interface. He wore the default white T-shirt—a clear sign that he was a newbie.

"Who is this?" The coach stepped forward with a wary look. "Someone from another team?"

He couldn't think of anyone who could make Yan Zhun say something so passive.

The coach's words reached Pei Ran's ears through the microphone that Lin Xuhuan left permanently turned on. From the sound of it, Yan Zhun was not at his dorm.

Pei Ran didn't know why he had wanted to log on to this game in the middle of the night, but when he saw Yan Zhun's invitation, he had accepted without a second thought.

Pei Ran examined the player beside him sporting strange ID and even stranger clothes, then asked, "Did you invite the wrong person?"

"No, no, he didn't," Lin Xuhuan answered in a hurry.

He had seen this man, BabeRan—Yan Zhun's boss—in one of 197's livestream replays.

"Get ready, BabeRan. We'll start the game soon and carry you to victory."

As they loaded into the waiting lobby, Lin Xuhuan turned off his mic. "Bro, that's your boss, right?"

Yan Zhun replied with a hum of confirmation, then stubbed out his cigarette after taking only a few puffs.

Lin Xuhuan's character walked up to Pei Ran's. "But if you ask me... I don't see him as a big spender. He's not even wearing a skin."

Yan Zhun didn't bother to respond and turned his mic to ask a question. "Does your foot still hurt?"

Pei Ran answered, "Not anymore."

"Mhm. Avoid walking. Skip classes that aren't important."

Lin Xuhuan, "Bro, you're being a bad influence on your boss!"

"You think everyone is like you?" Pei Ran could overhear Yan Zhun reply to the person beside him in his lazy voice. "My boss is well-behaved; he can't be corrupted."

Light from the computer screen reflected Pei Ran's face. In his image, he could see the tip of his ears tinged with light pink.

Pei Ran pursed his lips and took a sip of water.

When Lin Xuhuan and the others first learned that Yan Zhun worked as a gaming companion, they were collectively astounded.

They secretly discussed how much money Yan Zhun charged. The entry fragger remarked that even though Yan Zhun was phenomenally skilled, his personality left much to be desired. Not that he had a nasty temper, but he was untalkative and aloof. For that reason, his rate should not exceed 100 per hour.

Lin Xuhuan made the highest guess at 200 per hour—although he reckoned Yan Zhun's boss might want to report and block him afterward.

After two rounds, Lin Xuhuan's opinion did a 180.

He witnessed with his own eyes Yan Zhun drop a fully equipped gun in front of BabeRan. "Pei Ran, here's a buff."

On the hill, the volley of gunfire sounded like firecrackers. The one who would usually escape faster than anyone upon hearing a gunshot was now following BabeRan and looting in an open area.

"We'll leave after he finishes searching the house."

But the most mind-blowing part was...

After BabeRan died, Yan Zhun wiped out the squad that killed him, then took out a frag grenade...

And blew himself up.

Blew Himself up.

Blew Himself up...

Lin Xuhuan's jaw dropped as he stared at the two loot boxes lying side by side.

After a long time, he turned his head and asked pensively, "Bro... how much money do you owe that guy?"

Their school was hosting a two-day sports festival. After the sun went down, students flooded the night market's street food stalls.

Luo Qingshan sat on a bench with his legs crossed, taking no part in the conversation at the table.

Someone beside him tapped on his glass. "What are you staring at?"

Luo Qingshan raised his chin and took a sip from his glass. "Nothing. What are we talking about again?"

"He's been like this ever since his breakup." A friend poured him a bottle of beer. "Here, drink up. You'll feel better after you get wasted a couple of times."

"Stop pouring him drinks. Who's gonna carry him home once he's drunk?"

"Su Nian, duh."

Su Nian sat opposite Luo Qingshan. Upon hearing this, he couldn't stop himself from sneaking a glance at Luo Qingshan.

Luo Qingshan didn't even look in his direction and simply

shook his head. "I don't need anyone's help. It's just beer; I won't get drunk."

After a while, Luo Qingshan suddenly exclaimed, "Yan Zhun didn't come?"

The students at the table—all of them belonged to the same faculty as Luo Qingshan—froze at his question.

"Did you get plastered already?" His friend looked at him with a questioning gaze. "When does Yan Zhun ever come? Except for that one time on your birthday."

"I did invite him." Lin Kang poured himself a drink. "He said he was busy and couldn't come."

"Holy shit," Luo Qingshan's friend cried out when he noticed a particular Weibo post as he casually browsed his feed. He flipped his phone to show it to everyone else. "Isn't this Yan Zhun?"

The post was made by TZG's entry fragger with the caption "getting skewers after practice". The right side of the photo happened to include the figure of a young man slumped against the gaming chair. The outline of his face looked quite charming.

One of the top comments asked who he was.

The entry fragger replied: My bro, not a new trainee, don't try to guess.

TZG was arguably the most prominent e-sports team in the country, especially in the past two years, as it excelled in both PUBG and *League of Legends*. Thanks to its extremely strong online presence, it had become a household name for male gamers of all kinds.

"It really is him..." Lin Kang looked away and shook his head while clicking his tongue. "For a member of TZG to call him 'bro,' Yan Zhun must be quite something."

"Yeah. If I were him, I'd drop out and make a killing from e-sports. With his looks, he'd have fangirls throwing money at him even if he sucked." The friend remembered something and poked Luo Qingshan's arm. "Hey, you played with Yan Zhun, right? Is he good?"

Luo Qingshan didn't particularly feel like answering him.

He scrutinized the photo, sipped on his drink, and smiled. "He's good at video games, so what?"

"Bro, it's 2020 and you still believe that? Do you know how much signed gamers are paid each year? How much prize money they get for winning a championship? How much they can earn from a sponsorship deal?" Lin Kang was amused. "If Yan Zhun had decided to go pro, he certainly would've made a name for himself."

"What, you can predict the future now?" Luo Qingshan sneered. "There's no shortage of extraordinary players. Yan Zhun might never have a chance to show off."

"You don't understand. Back then, TZG's coach came to our school to corner him. I saw him many times..." Lin Kang hesitated. "What's the matter with you today? You don't sound like yourself."

Luo Qingshan lowered his head and fell silent for a moment, then shook his head. "It's nothing."

Halfway through the get-together, Luo Qingshan grew bored and left early.

He found an excuse to decline Su Nian's company and returned to his dorm alone. On his way back, he couldn't resist the urge to whip out his phone and send a text to Pei Ran, yet only after he finished typing did he remember that Pei Ran had already blocked him.

The dorm room was dark and empty, so Luo Qingshan

turned on the light and glanced toward Yan Zhun's bed.

Aside from a computer and a pair of headphones, the table was otherwise empty. It appeared as dull and uninteresting as its owner.

As he plopped down in his chair, Luo Qingshan turned on his computer.

He sat, lost in thought, as his mind kept flashing back to what he witnessed in the resting room: Pei Ran, resting on a bed, subconsciously clutching the bedsheet out of pain; and Yan Zhun, supporting Pei Ran's knee with one hand, bending his head to blow on Pei Ran's wound.

From a distance, it had looked like Yan Zhun was kissing Pei Ran's leg.

A message notification interrupted Luo Qingshan's train of thought. A friend he met on PUBG asked if he wanted to play since his squad of four was waiting for one more player.

Unable to fall asleep, Luo Qingshan logged onto Steam. As he casually opened his friends list, he immediately noticed that "BabeRan" was online.

Luo Qingshan frowned.

Pei Ran didn't like PUBG very much because the matches ended too quickly for him to enjoy the experience. In the past, it took Luo Qingshan a lot of coaxing to convince Pei Ran to log in just once.

But lately, Pei Ran seemed to be playing much more often.

Luo Qingshan pondered for a moment, then disregarded the invitation popping up on the right side of his screen. Instead, he closed the game to check Pei Ran's stats.

He discovered that Pei Ran had indeed been very active recently, logging in every day during their week-long break.

Plus, his stats were good—too good to be true.

Pei Ran's kill count almost always amounted to zero. Occasionally he would knock down an enemy or two, but his overall damage was never high.

However, scanning his list of recent matches revealed that he somehow made it into the "Top 10" or emerged as the "Winner Winner" more often than not.

Luo Qingshan gulped, then clicked on a match report to see Pei Ran's teammate's ID.

Almost every match included a certain "111GOD".

The only game without 111GOD was the one time he teamed up with Pei Ran a while ago. Afterward, 111GOD showed himself again.

Luo Qingshan couldn't believe his eyes, so he clicked open each match report one by one for confirmation...

...all the way to the game Pei Ran played with Yan Zhun, Su Nian, and himself.

Luo Qingshan had been gritting his teeth to the point his cheeks became sore, forcing him to unclench slowly.

He sat still for a while, then grabbed the phone from his desk and searched through his WeChat contacts list to find his roommate.

Luo Qingshan:
You're playing PUBG too? With who? Invite me.

After what seemed like ages, he finally received a reply.

Yan Zhun:
No

Luo Qingshan:
No way, are you really that mean?

On the other side, Lin Xuhuan's shouts resounded through the gaming house. "BabeRan! BabeRan, run! You've got a crowd behind you! JUMP WHILE YOU RUN!! Hurry, come over here! I'll protect y—Wait no, why are you heading toward

Yan Zhun?!"

Yan Zhun looked at the person running in his direction, smirked, then wiped out the opposing squad. Only then did he take out his phone to type an answer.

Yan Zhun:
Yeah, no place for you

Yan Zhun ended up staying at TZG's gaming house for a few days in a row.

Like junkies who couldn't get enough, the team insisted that he coach them for a couple more days. Considering that the room they prepared for him was large and quiet enough, Yan Zhun reluctantly nodded.

On his day off, Lin Xuhuan took Yan Zhun out to dinner.

TZG's base was just across the street from Yan Zhun's school. Standalone houses were cheap in the area, and there weren't many entertainment venues nearby that could distract the players—it was the ideal location.

When they passed a computer store, Yan Zhun took a cursory glance inside, then stopped dead in his tracks.

"How much will it cost to repair this?" Pei Ran asked as he looked at his laptop.

The owner stroked his chin. "Not much, around... three or four thousand."

Pei Ran nodded. Just as he was about to pay the deposit, he heard a voice from behind, "What's wrong with your laptop."

Pei Ran turned around and noticed Yan Zhun.

Beneath the brim of his hat, Yan Zhun's eyes looked down nonchalantly. "Busted?"

Pei Ran replied, "Mm-hmm. I dropped it by accident and broke the keyboard."

"BabeRan?!" The moment Pei Ran finished his sentence, Lin Xuhuan's eyes grew round.

Startled by the shout, Pei Ran froze and stared back at him.

"It's me! Me! Y'know... your daddy Huan!"

Lin Xuhuan's in-game ID was "yourdaddyhuan".

Pei Ran's voice was easy to recognize—his tone was neither subdued nor shrill and had a soothing quality to it. As soon as he heard it, Lin Xuhuan knew that it had to be him.

Yan Zhun stared at the owner. "How much did you say you charge for a keyboard replacement? Four thousand?"

His face was devoid of emotions, yet the owner felt his heart skip a beat.

"Four thousand?!" Lin Xuhuan exploded before the owner could answer. "What kinda keyboard are you selling to him? Cherry MX Black switches? Custom keycaps? Or maybe you're designing an exclusive ID for it?"

Pei Ran gaped at Lin Xuhuan as he snatched his laptop away from the owner's hands while cursing under his breath, then walked out of the store muttering about how this place was a complete rip-off.

"Don't come here anymore." Yan Zhun's voice brought him back to reality. "He's cheating you."

The owner stood right in front of them, quite speechless.

Pei Ran nodded gently. "Oh, ok."

"Now come," Yan Zhun said smoothly. "Let's have lunch together."

By the time they arrived at the restaurant, Lin Xuhuan had not yet ceased to rail about the store.

"You just look like an easy target," Lin Xuhuan said. "Don't tell me you were actually going to pay?"

"I don't know much about the cost for this sort of thing,"

Pei Ran replied.

Lin Xuhuan shook his head and tutted.

Well, it made sense. If Pei Ran could afford Yan Zhun as his gaming companion, then this amount must be chump change for him.

However, Pei Ran's appearance did take him by surprise. Before they met, he thought of Pei Ran as an average nerd with a pleasant voice who liked video games and spent money like water.

But from the moment he laid eyes on Pei Ran, he knew that boy was special... but why, exactly?

As someone who'd dropped out of junior high to focus on his e-sports career, Lin Xuhuan was at a loss for words.

He turned toward Pei Ran and saw him with his head bent down, carefully disinfecting the bowls and utensils with hot water.

His delicate, pale fingers stood out against the garish, old-fashioned patterns on the ceramic spoons.

Lin Xuhuan suddenly had an epiphany: Pei Ran's exceptional physique and straight back reminded him of a crane standing quietly by itself. The elegance he exuded had even lent a touch of class to the disorganized repair store.

Lin Xuhuan had never met someone like this before. Driven by curiosity, he couldn't resist moving his chair closer to Pei Ran.

"BabeRan, what's your real name?"

Pei Ran responded with his full name.

"I like how it sounds!" Lin Xuhuan then asked again, "So you're in the same university as my bro right here? Since you're schoolmates, did he give you a discount on your order?"

Pei Ran pondered for a second. "Yes."

Probably.

"How big was it? How much money did you save?" Lin Xuhuan pressed on.

"None of your business." Yan Zhun interrupted their conversation.

He took off his hat, so his hair was slightly ruffled. That, coupled with his cool expression, made him seem weirdly adorable.

Pei Ran's gaze subconsciously drifted to the few strands of hair that stuck out; then he locked eyes with Yan Zhun, who happened to glance over.

"Is your leg better?" asked Yan Zhun.

Pei Ran replied, "Mm-hmm, it already fully recovered a few days ago."

Yan Zhun continued, "Let me check."

Pei Ran didn't respond.

Faced with Pei Ran's silence, Yan Zhun raised an eyebrow.

Pei Ran's eyes first glanced at Lin Xuhuan, then subconsciously landed on Yan Zhun's thigh. Just as he was about to refuse, he saw Yan Zhun purse his lips and smile.

"I wanted to ask you to roll up your pants," Yan Zhun said, "not to put your legs on top of my thighs."

Lin Xuhuan propped up his hands on the table and leaned over after hearing Yan Zhun's words, "What happened to your leg?"

Pei Ran shook his head, "It's nothing. I fell during the Sports Festival."

Although the leg injury was almost recovered, in order to avoid irritating the scabs and potentially causing inflammation, Pei Ran had been wearing loose Capris these days.

Yan Zhun looked down at the scabs on Pei Ran's leg.

After a few seconds, Pei Ran tried to put down his trouser awkwardly.

"It scabbed." Yan Zhun said.

"Well," said Pei Ran, "it happens. It will be fine in no time."

Yan Zhun didn't say anything, but after tearing his gaze away from Pei Ran's wound, the image was still lingering in his head.

Lin Xuhuan was kind of a public figure and even had more followers on Weibo than many celebrities, so he was wearing both a mask and a hat when he came out. Before going out, the coach made fun of him, reassuring him that he looked like an assistant when standing next to Yan Zhun.

But to be on the safe side, the coach had booked a private room for him. Although there was a no-smoking sign outside the restaurant, no one would care what they do in the room. Lin Xuhuan took out a cigarette and handed it to Pei Ran, "BabeRan, have one."

Pei Ran said, "No thank you. I don't smoke."

"True, smoking is too vulgar, it doesn't suit you." Lin Xuhuan flattered casually, turned to Yan Zhun and handed it to him, "Bro, here." Yan Zhun skillfully took the cigarette and spread out his palm towards Lin Xuhuan.

Lin Xuhuan was shocked and gave the whole cigarette packet to him, "Bro, is your addiction back? Smoking a whole packet at a time?"

Yan Zhun took it, put the cigarette in his hand back to the case, covered it and threw it aside.

"Your coach asked me to look after you." Yan Zhun didn't even lift his eyelids. "Stop smoking, it's harmful to your health." Lin Xuhuan's expression changed rapidly. There were regulations in their base. If they smoked, they would be fined.

He didn't expect that after finally managing to sneak out, he still couldn't touch a cigarette.

And—

"Well, bro, if others educate me, that's fine. But you out of all people?" Lin Xuhuan said, "When you were in high school, it was me who took out the ashtrays for you. Now you realize it's harmful to your health?"

"You're talking too much." Yan Zhun said, "Pay the fine and you'll get one cigarette."

Lin Xu Huan was so angry that he could only hold up his hands in surrender. "Forget it, forget it." The waiter knocked on the door and handed them a menu. Yan Zhun's cell phone rang at this time. He looked at the caller and got up, "I'm gonna take this call outside, you guys go ahead and order."

"What would you like to eat?" Asked Lin Xuhuan.

"Don't mind me." Yan Zhun looked at Pei Ran's leg and said, "No seafood." When the door closed, Lin Xuhuan opened the menu, "BabeRan, what would you like?" They had played games together for several nights in a row now, and Pei Ran had gotten used to being addressed like that.

"I'm fine with anything." Pei Ran took out Yan Zhun's chopsticks from the plastic bag and put them in hot water.

"Chicken with green pepper is our specialty." Said the waiter.

Lin Xuhuan shook his head, "No, he's injured. He can't eat spicy food..."

"I'm fine. I can eat other dishes. You don't have to worry about me." Pei Ran said hurriedly.

"No," Lin Xuhuan said with a smile. "My bro can't eat spicy food either, not at all. He has a bad stomach."

After they've finished ordering, the waiter left the room.

Pei Ran pursed his lips several times. After chatting with Lin Xuhuan for a few words, he turned and asked, "Does Yan Zhun have some sort of stomach issues?"

Lin Xuhuan wiped his hands with a hot towel, "Yeah, been a while. He used to go to the hospital all the time."

Pei Ran asked, "Why? Didn't he eat properly?"

Lin Xuhuan thought that this question was funny. When he turned around and saw Pei Ran's serious expression, he wanted to laugh even more. This was not a secret. Most people in the base knew it.

And his intuition was that his brother treated Pei Ran differently. They had been playing games together for several days, and he had never seen Yan Zhun taking care of anyone like this.

Lin Xuhuan thought about it, and threw out the question, "How much did my brother charge you for playing with him?"

Pei Ran answered truthfully, "Twenty."

Lin Xuhuan was stunned.

Pei Ran blinked, "Is it too little?"

Lin Xuhuan took a sip of tea to calm himself down.

How should he tell Pei Ran that his coach offered Yan Zhun an 8-figure annual salary last year—8 figures post-tax, and it didn't even include the shares from competitions, activities and endorsements. Lin Xuhuan had an idea of what's going on now. He put down his teacup and said, "He didn't eat well. My brother used to be a youth trainee for a period of time. It was summer vacation, and he joined the team with me."

"At that time, he often ate one meal a day only, saying that if he was too full, he would be sleepy, which affected his performance... Of course, that wouldn't work. It barely took a month before he started having problems. He couldn't eat and would vomit when he did. At that time, we didn't pay attention to it, because in this industry we stay up all night that it is normal for us to have some minor issues. He didn't want to go to the hospital, so he took some stomach medicine casually."

"One day, he couldn't walk because of the pain. At last, he was carried to the emergency room. Later, his parents came, and they made a scene... In the end, he wasn't allowed to play e-sports anymore."

Lin Xuhuan sighed and smiled to shift the mood, "I still remember what his father said to him."

Reason told Pei Ran not to pry into others' privacy.

He tried to hold in the question but failed, and then asked, "What did him say?"

"He said, 'What's the future of this industry? Even our garden at home is more spacious than your competition venue.'" Lin Xuhuan was amused by what he said, "Damn."

Pei Ran wasn't sure how to respond.

Yan Zhun came back from his call with his family and heard this sentence as soon as he pushed the door.

"What are you gossiping about?" He passed behind Lin Xuhuan and tapped him on the head with the cigarette case.

"I didn't!" Lin Xuhuan immediately pretended to protect his head. "It was BabeRan, he asked me how your stomach got this bad." Yan Zhun paused, then pulled out the chair and sat down. Pei Ran was caught on the spot the second time when he was talking about others behind their back.

By the same person.

"Not as bad as he said." Yan Zhun said.

Pei Ran looked at him, "Huh?"

"It's just a stomachache. I won't die. The garden is not

bigger than the venue either." Yan Zhun remained rather expressionless. He asked, "Have you finished washing them?"

Pei Ran was taken aback, "What?"

"My chopsticks." Yan Zhun reminded him, "You've soaked them three times." Pei Ran handed him the chopsticks and calmly explained, "The chopsticks in the restaurant are very dirty."

"Well." Yan Zhun glanced at his crimson ears and casually responded, "Germophobe, understandable."

After dinner, Lin Xuhuan walked out of the restaurant holding Pei Ran's laptop. "I'll take it back to our base and ask the repairman to change the keyboard for you. When it's fixed, I'll give it back to you."

Pei Ran replied, "Don't bother, I can go to another repair shop."

"Will other repair shops be as good as ours?" Lin Xuhuan asked. "Don't worry, I'll get you a good one."

Pei Ran hesitated, then said, "Thank you. Can you tell me the cost via WeChat?"

Lin Xuhuan waved his hand, "It's nothing. We have sponsors."

"No." Pei Ran insisted, "I still need to pay."

Lin Xuhuan was about to argue with him further when Yan Zhun took over the conversation, "Well, I'll send you the price then."

"Okay," said Pei Ran said.

Yan Zhun put on his hat and looked up, "Going back to the dorm?"

"Yes." Pei Ran thought of something. "My computer password is 'feiyi.'"

Lin Xuhuan wrote it down in the memo. "What does it

signify? Your girlfriend's name?"

"No, I don't have a girlfriend." Pei Ran looked at his watch, "I'm going back now. I have to catch up with my homework."

"OK, let's chat via WeChat when we have the time." Lin Xuhuan smiled. As soon as Pei Ran turned around, his clothes were pulled by someone. "Wait." Yan Zhun glanced around and then said to him, "Stand here and wait for me." A few minutes later, Yan Zhun came out of the drugstore with a bag.

He put the bag into Pei Ran's arms, "Three times a day, do not scratch." Pei Ran opened the bag, which was full of the same ointment, five of them to be exact.

Pei Ran was stunned. He looked at the ointment and looked up at Yan Zhun. He looked adorable when dumbfounded. Yan Zhun looked back at him and didn't say a word. After a long time, he said, "Boys don't look good with scars."

Not until Pei Ran got back to his dorm did he realize that something's a bit off with that statement.

Wasn't it normal for a man to have some scars? Girls are the ones that should worry about that. He frowned as he thought about it and slowly changed out of his clothes. After washing an apple for post-dinner snack, he sat on the chair, bent his legs, and applied the ointment Yan Zhun had just bought for him.

Yan Zhun didn't go back to the base with Lin Xuhuan. He had something to get from the dormitory, and it would be too late to go back to the base again. He decided to stay at school for one night. When the door opened, Yan Zhun had just removed the keyboard from his computer. The equipment in the base was not easy for him to use. There would be a game next month, and Yan Zhun promised to help them play training matches for the next couple of days, so of course he needed to maintain the best condition.

Luo Qingshan was stunned when he saw Yan Zhun. He quickly returned to his senses and threw the basketball around the corner. Neither of them spoke. The dormitory was silent as usual. Yan Zhun didn't speak much, and Luo Qingshan didn't usually chat with him before. This kind of silence was normal.

Today, however, it was slightly different. "Yan Zhun." His roommate's voice came from behind after a long time, "Do you know if there is a laundry near the school? I want to get my shoes cleaned. I've been practice running all this time. The shoes are getting dirty."

Yan Zhun didn't even turn around, "I don't know."

"Ugh, they sure are dirty." Luo Qingshan sat with his legs crossed. He looked at Yan Zhun and looked down at his shoes, "If Pei Ran saw this, he would think I didn't cherish what he gave me. That would be terrible." Yan Zhun skillfully wrapped the connecting wire around the keyboard, stuffed it into the bag, and finally glanced back.

Black and white shoes, classic with no complicated design. They're certainly ones that Pei Ran would choose.

"There is one on the right when you exit the back gate of our school." Yan Zhun said.

"Sure, thanks." Luo Qingshan smiled, "This pair was a limited edition two years ago. Pei Ran was just going abroad and bought it for me after queuing up all night outside the store."

Yan Zhun lowered his gaze and zipped up his backpack.

"Then he had a cold and was sick for several days when he came back" Luo Qingshan said, "Oh, this pair might have been his one-year-anniversary gift to me."

Yan Zhun put the hat in the wardrobe and took out a black one again.

"Do you think artists especially care about special dates? He prepared gifts for me in advance for every anniversary."

Yan Zhun tucked his hat into the side of the backpack.

That was when the mobile phone on the desk vibrated.

Pei Ran:
You can drink a glass of milk in the morning to help calm your stomach

Pei Ran:
Thank you for the medicine.

The tight curve of Yan Zhun's mouth relaxed instantly. He picked up his cell phone, pulled off his towel and walked to the bathroom. He stopped to look at the person around him after two steps, as if he just realized that he was talking.

He asked, "I remember Pei Ran discounted all the things he received and gave them back to you in cash?" He heard Luo Qingshan saying that once when he got too drunk.

Interrupted so suddenly, Luo Qingshan was left speechless with his mouth open.

Yan Zhun's face was expressionless, but Luo Qingshan somehow felt he was sneering at him. He blinked twice fast and was about to say something, but then—

"In that case, what he gave you should also be returned." Yan Zhun gave him a smile with no emotion. "Of course, it's just my suggestion."

It was deep into the night when Pei Ran finally finished his homework. He got up and washed his coffee cup. Before going to bed, he casually checked the updates on Weibo.

He hadn't been on Weibo for a long time. There were hundreds of unread direct messages on it, many of which were commissions for his artwork. When Pei Ran had been in high school, he had made several commercial sketches. He liked to try different things, and that's when he got a taste of the rigor of creating for a customer. After a few pieces, his fans rose to 60k, but he didn't take any order after college.

He glanced at his DMs briefly, and was just about to make a statement that he will no longer accept commissions when the preview of a private message caught his attention.

TZGisthebest:
Hi, do you accept private coms? I want art of Lin Xuhuan...

It was from a fan of Lin Xuhuan. Before the message, there were some photos of Lin Xuhuan playing games. His hair was so short that it must have been from some time ago.

P&EI:
What are the requirements?

The other side replied immediately.

TZGisthebest:
!!! Ahhhhhhh!

TZGisthebest:
None! No requirements!! It's just, what's the pricing? QAQ

P&EI:
How much do you usually pay?

TZGisthebest:
The last one was about 800 yuan...

TZGisthebest:
Ah, I didn't mean to offer 800 for your work! I know your paintings are very expensive! It's just that, I'm currently a student QAQ, I can't afford something super expensive. Please name your price, I'll make an order if it's alright, or I'll just continue being your fan quietly. I genuinely really like your paintings so very much!

Pei Ran's paintings were indeed really expensive. His last commercially commissioned piece had been over 10k yuan.

Pei Ran saved the pictures into his phone.

P&EI:

Thank you. Then it's 800. Could you give me your email?

After taking down the client's email address, Pei Ran closed his DMs, made a post saying that he won't take any future orders, shut down the phone and went to sleep.

It was the weekend when Lin Xuhuan called again.

"BabeRan, your computer has been repaired." Said Lin Xuhuan, "When will you be free to come and get it? Or I'll ask someone to send it to you?"

"I'll come get it myself." Pei Ran took out his pen and paper and held his phone at his shoulder, "Would you mind giving me the address? Or you can put it in the security room?"

"No, you can come to the training base directly and hang out with me." There was noise on the other end of the call. Lin Xuhuan said in a hurry, "Alright. I'm going to order take-out. I'll send the address to your WeChat." When Pei Ran finished breakfast, Lin Xuhuan still hadn't sent the address.

Maybe he was too busy training and forgot about it? Pei Ran thought about it. Just as he was about to open WeChat to text Lin Xuhuan, the message came. It was a voice message.

"BabeRan, wait, my bro will pick you up later." The moment the voice message ended, Yan Zhun's voice call came in.

Pei Ran tapped twice before he could answer it. "Have you had breakfast?" Yan Zhun's voice was a little husky. It sounded like he just got up.

"Yes." Pei Ran asked, "What about you?"

"I'll eat in a bit. Are you busy this morning?"

"No, today's the weekend, I'm free all day." Pei Ran looked at the time, "Or you can get some more sleep?"

There was a brief "beep" on the street. Yan Zhun said, "I'm

almost at the gates of campus. Come out when you're ready."

After hanging up the phone, Yan Zhun put his hands in his pocket, lowered his lids and continued to read the messages in the WeChat group. TZG's active members were all boys in their teens and early twenties. They were always chatty and energetic. When they didn't have to train, the unread messages in their group could easily reach three digits. Today's topic in the group was Pei Ran.

Lin Xuhuan found out that Yan Zhun was only paid 20 yuan per hour and now everyone in the base knew about it, within two hours after Lin got back to the base.

YourRaiderDad:
@Yan Zhun, I will give you 50 yuan, I want your fully equipped M4 too.

YourSniperDad:
@Yan Zhun, I'll give you 80, and I don't need you to do anything. Just stay still and let me kill you a few times.

OneShotInSistersHeart:
@yourfatherlinxuhuan Are you sure his boss is not a beautiful sister?

yourfatherlinxuhuan:
Not a beautiful sister, but a beautiful brother.

Yan Zhun sneered and typed.

Yan Zhun:
@TZGCoachYong, Their cigarettes are hidden in a vase in the hallway on the first floor. Go and confiscate them

TZGcoachYONG:
.

The chat group was instantly swamped by question marks.

yourfatherlinxuhuan:
Bruh! I trusted you! This is how you treat me? Bro???

Yan Zhun:
Do you know what day it is today?

yourfatherlinxuhuan:
?

Yan Zhun:
The annual no-smoking day in the TZG base

yourfatherlinxuhuan:
How come I didn't effing know of such a festival!

Yan Zhun:
Just set it up today

yourfatherlinxuhuan:
……

Yan Zhun put the phone in his pocket and saw Pei Ran as soon as he looked up. Pei Ran was in a hurry. There was some distance between the campus gate and his dormitory. He was slightly out of breath, "Waiting for long?"

"Just got here." Yan Zhun turned around. "Let's go. It's not far." Pei Ran followed him and took out the thing in his pocket and handed it to Yan Zhun. "I didn't know if there's any milk in their base," said Pei Ran. "So I took one with me, and you can have it with breakfast later."

TZG base had just gotten noisy and now everyone was sitting around the living room for breakfast. When the gate opened, everyone looked up, and saw Yan Zhun walking in slowly. His face was as cold as ever, and he was holding a cup of milk in his hand.

Yan Zhun was followed by another boy, wearing a white T-shirt with a gentle face. The boy nodded to them, "Excuse my intrusion."

"Shit." Sitting on the right side of the sofa, the commando collected his wits and whispered, "Indeed a beautiful brother."

"BabeRan!" Lin Xuhuan immediately waved to him, "Come and have breakfast!"

Pei Ran said quickly, "I've already had it."

Lin Xuhuan said, "Then you sit and wait for a bit? I'll give you the computer when I'm done." As a noble team in the e-sports industry, TZG's base was very luxurious, and the sofa in the living room was large and comfortable. The team members liked to use the sofa as a table.

Both sides of the armchairs were occupied, and Yan Zhun walked towards Lin Xuhuan, "Scoot."

Lin Xuhuan made room for him. Yan Zhun sat down, looked up at Pei Ran, then pointed at the space beside him. Pei Ran sat down slowly, keeping quietly to himself.

The man sitting on the left picked up the glass filled with boiled water and made a toast to Yan Zhun, "I just seized their four packs of cigarettes and fined 20,000. I will transfer the reporting prize to you later."

"Who cares." Yan Zhun chuckled. "Save it. I've got nothing to answer your toast with."

"Didn't you bring a bottle of milk?" Then the coach frowned and wondered aloud, "Did you get kidnapped by aliens? Didn't you hate milk?"

Pei Ran stuck his back to the sofa, surprised at the words.

Yan Zhun poked a straw into the packet of milk and answered the toast. "Well, it's said to be good for the stomach."

Pei Ran had no words.

He realized that, here at the base, Yan Zhun was very relaxed and he spoke more. Yan Zhun seemed to be close with the team members. They all called him "bro," and sometimes bantered with him when talking. Yan Zhun let it all go.

"Is this my brother's legendary boss?"

Suddenly mentioned, Pei Ran sat up straight subconsciously. "No, I am not his boss, we are schoolmates."

The player nodded and pointed to Yan Zhun, "Weren't you

who gave him that strange buff?"

Pei Ran said, "It was me."

Another asked, "Wasn't it you he went with to wander around the small houses in the wild area with?"

Pei Ran said, "It was me."

"Wasn't it you who made him kill himself with a grenade?"

Pei Ran paused, then said, "It was me."

Someone suddenly stood up and reached out to Pei Ran, "Boss, boss, let's shake hands... Excuse me for asking, but how many hours did you buy? Is there any time left? I'll buy it five times the price, please, boss?"

Before he reached Pei Ran, Yan Zhun slapped his hand and said, "Go away." The man smiled broadly, "BabeRan, let's discuss this in WeChat later. I'll find you with Lin Xuhuan's account in the evening."

"No way. I'm going to interact with female fans tonight." Lin Xuhuan said, "Of course, you can transfer me some rent..."

"Well, I'll expose your private Weibo and let them see that the world champion chases female idols on Weibo every day."

"Fuck... Then I will expose that your screensaver is a female streamer!" The two began squabbling and finally decided to battle in Speed Linkup one versus one.

"Go! Come here!" Lin Xuhuan was furious. "If I don't blow your head off, you don't know what the king of linkup is!"

"Who cares? First of all, three wins in five games, loser has to post ugly photos on Weibo!" The training room was on the first floor, surrounded by transparent glass. It was only when they started the first round of Speed Linkup that Pei Ran remembered that he forgot to ask Lin Xuhuan for his computer

Other players also slowly returned to their positions, and the coach stood up. "Yan Zhun, come upstairs with me, I need to discuss something with you."

The coach's expression was serious. It was obvious that he wanted to talk about some personal matters. Yan Zhun said, "Can't you say it here?"

"No." The coach said simply. Pei Ran just wanted to tell Yan Zhun not to worry about him when Yan Zhun got up from the sofa. "Go to the training room to find Lin Xuhuan and let him give you a computer to play with first." Yan Zhun was tall enough to be able to naturally raise his hand and touch Pei Ran's head. He did so before quickly moving away. "Wait for me to come down."

When Pei Ran walked into the training room, the "king of linkup" Lin Xuhuan had just lost a round. "Shit, come again." Having caught sight of Pei Ran, Lin Xuhuan pulled a chair beside him. "BabeRan, come on, sit and watch me abuse him."

Pei Ran sat down obediently.

Lin Xuhuan's was not as fast as the others', but his voice was loud. Pei Ran watched them play silently, but eventually he couldn't help but raised his hand to rub his ears.

Yan Zhun's touch had been subtle, his warm fingertips brushing over Pei Ran's ear.

The linkup match ended in the third round. Lin Xuhuan lost three rounds in a row. "King of linkup? Shame!" The commando sneered, "Hurry up and post ugly photos."

Lin Xuhuan was angry, but he admitted defeat. He picked up his phone and said, "Who cares? Wait for me to take one..." He pressed his cell phone's power button. Then he did it again. The screen still didn't light up—there was no power.

"You did it on purpose! We have to play the training match when the coach come down later. I think you want to delay the time and wait until late night when the traffic is quiet."

"Bullshit! My WeChat and Weibo are all online on the computer. Wait for me." Lin Xuhuan rolled his eyes and then said, "BabeRan, take a picture of me with your mobile phone, and send it to my WeChat. My mobile phone won't turn on for a while." Pei Ran turned on the camera, and Lin Xuhuan made a weird face, "Take some more, I'll pick one."

"Ok." Pei Ran said. After taking the pictures, Pei Ran handed Lin Xuhuan his cell phone and heard the noise behind him. Two people came down the stairs.

The coach was still saying something to Yan Zhun, which couldn't be heard clearly. Pei Ran looked back and found that Yan Zhun's lips were lightly pursed but that he didn't speak.

Meanwhile, Lin Xuhuan inadvertently swiped the screen of the mobile phone. It wasn't until he was close to the lounge that Yan Zhun finally opened his mouth, "I haven't thought about it for the time being, and later..." "Holy shit!!!"

Lin Xuhuan suddenly shouted and interrupted Yan Zhun.

Everyone looked at him subconsciously. Lin Xuhuan blinked, excitedly picked up Pei Ran's mobile phone, and turned the screen to him in both shock and delight, "BabeRan! You have saved so many pictures of me!!! Are you my fan? Why didn't you say that before? I can't even find such ancient photos myself. You still have it saved... Have you been my fan for a long time?" Yan Zhun, who just walked into the training room, paused.

Pei Ran went blank. He had forgotten about this.

Lin Xuhuan tried to collect his memory, then took a deep breath looked touched, "This was like when I just finished the youth training and was still a substitute... BabeRan, you hid yourself well."

Pei Ran said, "No..."

Before he could finish speaking, his shoulders were lightly brushed by someone.

Yan Zhun went to Lin Xuhuan and pulled out the mobile phone in his hands, "Don't dig around others' phones."

"I didn't mean to. I don't know how many photos he took for me. I swiped it by accident." Lin Xuhuan felt wronged.

Yan Zhun ignored him and handed Pei Ran his cell phone.

Pei Ran reached for it, but felt the resistance from the other side. He couldn't get it at first.

Yan Zhun lowered his lids and looked at the photos again before letting go.

Knowing that Pei Ran was his number one fan, Lin Xuhuan couldn't help straightening his back, he lifted his hand and styled his hair slightly, "BabeRan, don't play with my brother in the future, come to me directly, I will accompany you for free, and I will bring you on live stream."

Pei Ran thought about how to explain this situation. It was a secret that he did commercial paintings on the Internet. He never told anyone, and that Weibo account was a secret.

"All right." The coach suddenly said, "Go to the training match first. The room over there has already been set up. Hurry up. Today it will be customized games. I have made an appointment with several teams."

"If there are other teams, then I'll sit out," said Yan Zhun.

"No, our youth team is included. I've reserved a place for you." The coach came up to him and put his hand on Yan Zhun's shoulder. "I think highly of those three boys. Help me out and check how they're doing."

Yan Zhun said, "I haven't played training games for a long time. Can't do that."

"Don't fool me like that. I know you're capable. Come on, do me a favor. I told them you were coming, so they all trained for two hours more last night..." The coach picked up his cell phone and said, "They're all calling me. Hurry up. Don't let other teams wait for you."

Lin Xuhuan left Pei Ran a message before he rushed to the match: "BabeRan, I'll send you a set of signed equipment later." He was pushed away by the teammates before Pei Ran could answer.

Yan Zhun was being ushered forward by the coach when he suddenly turned around. "Can you wait for me?"

Pei Ran originally wanted to take the computer back to his dormitory, then watch a movie. He already knew what film he wanted to watch—a recent release that was highly acclaimed.

Yan Zhun paused, then said, "It won't be long."

Pei Ran canceled the movie plan in his mind and put his mobile phone back in his pocket. "Okay. Good luck on your training match."

The coach was definitely confused by the situation and bent his arm around Yan Zhun's shoulders. After walking away for a while, he asked, "What's going on? Is he your relative?"

"No," Yan Zhun said. "Help me look after him."

"I see. He won't get away under my watch." Just outside the match room, the coach patted his shoulder. "Play well."

Pei Ran was taken to the lounge. There was a big screen in the room, which could be used for data analysis and also for viewing. Several bottles of different drinks and snacks were put in front of him.

The coach smiled and said, "I don't know what you like to eat, so I got several kinds. These boys all like to drink soda."

Pei Ran thanked him and took a bottle of mineral water.

The coach held the remote control for a while and lit up the screen, showing the game screen of PUBG.

After two teams of TZG team parachuted, the coach took out his notebook and was ready to pick out the faults of the team members at any time. There were two match rooms in the base, one of which was very noisy and lively. If the room was not soundproofed, it could be heard by the other team of youth trainees next door even with earphones.

"Where will you land, bro?" asked Lin Xuhuan cheerfully.

"Who knows, but the youth training teams are generally conservative, maybe in the scattered wild areas." Good players usually like to jump to places full of enemies. But matches are different. There would be teams in wild areas in the middle of the circle, so you could easily run into your rivals.

Lin Xuhuan looked at the map and was ready to parachute to the little wild area marked by the commando when a prompt popped up on the interface.

TZGmoxie knocked out **XPP-hot** with an **AKM**.

TZGmoxie knocked out **XPP-youxiang** via headshot with an **AKM**.

TZGmoxie knocked out **secret _happy** via headshot with an **AKM**.

The match room was silent for a while. After landing, the teammate asked, "The moxie account is played by?"

"Well... It's Yan Zhun." Lin Xuhuan frowned and searched the wild area. "Shit, my bro is crazy. He ran into two teams before I landed... They must have jumped at the airport."

By the time Lin Xuhuan finished searching a wild area, Yan Zhun had eliminated six players, and almost the entire two teams in the airport were destroyed by him alone.

"Macho, really macho." Lin Xuhuan sighed, "The one and only brother." In the semi-finals, there were only six teams left, specifically five teams and one person.

The three youth team members had already been killed, leaving Yan Zhun by himself. He found a house area and crouched in the corner, healing himself.

"Bro! Bro? Is that you, my brother?" Lin Xu Huan turned on the microphone for everyone, and the voice reached Yan Zhun's headphones. Lin Xuhuan saw Yan Zhun entering the wild area. There was only one person wearing moxie's outfit, easily recognized by Lin Xuhuan.

Lin Xuhuan sniped a few shots and didn't knock him down, so he just took his teammates down to block Yan Zhun. Yan Zhun ignored him and started looking for their location. There were only two people on Lin Xuhuan's side, and the other two were in the wild area behind. "Shall we wait for them to attack the building?" Teammate said.

"It's okay." said Lin Xuhuan. "It's two-on-one. We can beat him. Besides, my bro and I are tight, he'll go easy on me."

Two minutes later, both of them were knocked down outside the building by Yan Zhun, who then immediately killed them. He turned around to leave.

"Bro." Since he was dead, Lin Xuhuan was free to talk to him through the microphone, "You killed your little fan who has liked you for so many years. So cruel, so fierce. I love it—"

Before Lin Xuhuan finished, a grenade bounced on the ground and rolled to his "corpse" which had yet to disappear.

Bang! The avatar lying flat on the ground was blown up.

Lin Xuhuan was shocked speechless.

His teammate joked, "You sure are on good terms, any closer he would battle with you one-on-one in person."

In the second round, the teammates wanted to be more stimulated and jumped to the airport. Lin Xuhuan was knocked down by Yan Zhun just two minutes after landing. Yan Zhun didn't end his life but threw a grenade on his face and turned to leave without a second glance at the explosion behind him. In the third round, Lin Xuhuan was knocked down by other teams. He quickly climbed to the back of the house and was about to be rescued by his teammates. With a bang, Yan Zhun took his head off in one with a 98K from the distance. The fourth round... The fifth round...

At the end of training, Lin Xuhuan took off his headphones and rushed to the next room. "Bro, why are you targeting me! You even shot my corpse! You came to screw me over even if I was with two teammates!!!"

The most irritating thing was that the three of them together couldn't take Yan Zhun, with two of them killed by one grenade only. Yan Zhun took off the earphone and got up receiving the youth trainees' nervous and adoring look.

"Fashion," he said.

Lin Xuhuan was confused.

"The outfit you were wearing was too ugly."

Lin Xuhuan was speechless.

Yan Zhun ignored him and headed for the replay room. It was Pei Ran's first time watching a PUBG competition.

The training match was much more casual and exciting than the formal match. The coach had been observing from Yan Zhun's perspective most of the time. The door was pushed open, and Yan Zhun walked in with a calm face. "Zero error today, bravo." The coach gave a generous compliment.

"Why are you looking at my perspective, and not those of your own players?" Yan Zhun sat down beside Pei Ran.

"I wanted to see them, but those youth trainees died too fast." The coach whispered, "It's still not good enough..."

Yan Zhun didn't answer. He lowered his lids and saw Pei Ran holding a bottle of mineral water in his hands.

Feeling his gaze, Pei Ran held it up. "Want some? It hasn't been opened yet."

Yan Zhun took it but didn't hurry to unscrew it. "Did you watch the training match?" he asked.

"Yes." Pei Ran paused. "You're amazing."

The insincere praise obviously didn't satisfy Yan Zhun. He pursed his lips and took a sip of water. The rest of the team continued to walk into the lounge to prepare for the replay. Soon the room was full of people.

As soon as Pei Ran was discomfited, Yan Zhun spoke: "Take your time. We'll stop intruding on you now. See you all."

"You're no intrusion." The coach wanted him to stay.

Yan Zhun said, "Let's go, Pei Ran."

"Oh, wait." Lin Xuhuan said quickly, "BabeRan, I didn't get you the equipment yet. I'll go get it out of storage."

But Pei Ran stopped Lin Xuhuan before he went upstairs.

"What's the matter? Don't be shy; the equipment was sent by a sponsor. We get sent several sets of equipment every holiday, more than we need for sure." Pei Ran didn't want to expose his online alter ego, but he couldn't pretend to be the fan with so much love and enthusiasm for Lin Xuhuan.

"The pictures were sent to me by someone else." He explained, "It's your fan who asked me for a painting and wanted me to draw you."

At first, Lin Xuhuan was still in a daze, but then he began praising Pei Ran: "Are you an art student? Ah, I knew as soon as I saw you that you must be a fine arts major. Have you gotten many commissions? Are you often asked to draw me?"

Pei Ran said, "Only this once."

Lin Xuhuan didn't know how to respond to that. The team members in the lounge all laughed called him shameless.

"You know nothing, one can easily tell that BabeRan draws very well. His paintings must be expensive! Besides, my fans are all little girls. How can they have money for this?" After that, Lin Xuhuan coughed and asked Pei Ran, "BabeRan, since we're so close, you have to give my fans a discount... How much did you get for the painting?" Pei Ran wanted to talk but stopped himself. Lin Xuhuan said, "You can rest assured that it's ok if it's too high. I'm worthy of that price."

Pei Ran said, "Eight hundred."

Lin Xuhuan was again speechless. When the team assistant came in, Lin Xuhuan was fighting with others while murmuring things like: "You're cheap," "You look down on 800 yuan," and "Your fans don't want art of you even if you pay for it."

"What are you laughing at?" The assistant put the box in his hand on the table. "The sponsor's gifts are here."

Lin Xuhuan stopped. "What is it?" "Merchandise." The assistant opened the box and hung a pendant on his hand. The pendant was a pair of pink sneakers as big as a thumb, a miniature model of the sponsor's new shoes. "So small and pink." Lin Xuhuan frowned, "I don't want it."

"There are different colors. You can choose whatever. They are good for backpacks, or you can send it to your girlfriend."

The assistant turned around and said, "Yan Zhun, are you leaving? I also brought one for you. What color do you want?"

Lin Xuhuan laughed. "Come on, these don't interest my bro."

"White," Yan Zhun said in a low voice, "Do you have any?"

They left the base and walked for a long time without anyone speaking. Pei Ran didn't know what to say. Yan Zhun walked slowly. He was probably a little tired from the training match, so he didn't speak. Pei Ran felt something chilly on his cheeks, and he looked up in a daze.

The drizzle came down gently and softly. This kind of rain didn't affect normal traffic. The pedestrians on the street were walking as usual. At most, they just hastened their steps. Pei Ran was looking at the rain in the air attentively. Suddenly, he felt something covering his head, and a hat brim blocked most of his sight. He reached up automatically and caught hold of Yan Zhun's black baseball cap.

Yan Zhun lowered his gaze, only looking into his eyes for a moment before reaching out to help him adjust the position of the hat.

The baseball cap had Yan Zhun's scent, like the floating rain, cold but gentle. Pei Ran came back to himself. "It's OK, it's not raining heavily."

Yan Zhun said, "Wear it."

Pei Ran didn't know how to respond.

As they walked in the rain, Pei Ran's view was blocked by the brim of that hat. In order to get a better view, he tilted his chin slightly subconsciously.

He didn't notice the person beside him looking down at him this whole time. A few training games wouldn't make Yan Zhun tired. He didn't speak because he was not calm inside.

When he'd seen Lin Xuhuan's pictures in Pei Ran's cell phone, Yan Zhun had returned to a summer back in high school. That day, he'd come out of the supermarket with two bags of milk candy. When he'd passed by an alcove, he'd seen Pei Ran leaning against the wall, head hung, quietly letting Luo Qingshan hold his hand.

When they got to the intersection where they would

normally part, Pei Ran stopped, "Thank you for taking me to the base today—"

"Pei Ran." Yan Zhun interrupted him.

Pei Ran looked at him, "Yes?" Yan Zhun was taller than Pei Ran. Because of the brim of his hat, Pei Ran had to raise his head to talk to him.

Yan Zhun raised his hand and flipped the brim up a little. "The part where I said I like you. Do you remember?"

Pei Ran suddenly became silent, slowly widening his eyes to reveal his confusion. He even wanted to press the brim back down.

Realizing Yan Zhun was waiting for his answer, Pei Ran remained quiet for a long time before he said, "Yes."

Yan Zhun hummed in response.

Feelings were not meaningless items that could simply be collected into a suitcase and thrown away, so he had always planned to give Pei Ran some time, but now he suddenly didn't want to wait.

If Pei Ran had hangups over his ex's infidelity, Yan Zhun would clean it up.

If Pei Ran still had feelings for Luo Qingshan, Yan Zhun would destroy them.

"Hand," Yan Zhun said.

Pei Ran was still a little bit confused. Almost instinctively, he held out his hand. A white little sneaker appeared in his palm—the pendant that could be sent to one's girlfriend, as the assistant had said just moments ago.

Yan Zhun said, "Pei Ran, I have started to court you."

The rain cloaked the Magnolia trees on both sides with a thin layer of tulle. There were not many people on the campus path. Pei Ran slowly walked on the road with the computer in his right hand, gently holding the small pendant he just received. The phone rang in a hurry.

Yan Zhun:
Walk faster.

Pei Ran was shocked. Subconsciously, he turned to find two couples holding umbrellas side by side.

Pei Ran:
Are you still there?

Yan Zhun replied with a voice message. Pei Ran put his phone up next to his ear and listened: "I guessed. You usually walk very slowly."

Pei Ran pursed his lips and silently put his phone into the computer bag.

His heart was beating like crazy. He barely calmed down after walking away for such a long while, it would only become worse if he listened to it more times.

Pei Ran hadn't accepted Yan Zhun's pursuit. As always, he had wanted to say sorry first, but when he'd opened his mouth, he'd found his voice trembling.

Yan Zhun had waited quietly, but Pei Ran had become more nervous in the face of his patience. He'd finally said, "I don't want to be in a relationship for the moment." He'd stuttered out that sentence with very little confidence.

Yan Zhun had nodded quietly and responded, "I know, but I still want to court you." Then, he'd also asked, "May I?"

Pei Ran had stayed silent, afraid that he'd stutter again.

Finally, Yan Zhun had pressed the brim of Pei Ran's hat back down and said, "I see, I will continue courting you then."

"Pei Ran?"

Pei Ran turned around and saw Su Nian.

Su Nian was standing next to another boy. The two of them looked intimate. Su Nian took a look and asked, "It's raining; don't you have an umbrella? And your face, why is it so red?"

Pei Ran's face was red, but his tone was as calm as ever when he replied, "What's up?"

"Oh, nothing. Just wanted to say hello." Su Nian paused and said, "By the way, I made you unhappy previously. Now that we're meeting in person, I want to apologize again—"

"That won't be necessary," Pei Ran said, then asked, "Didn't Lin Kang send you a message for me?"

Su Nian smiled. "Sure, but I knew you were angry at that time. I didn't mind. As long as you are fine now."

Pei Ran frowned, not wanting to talk to him anymore. He turned around to leave.

"Oh, wait." Su Nian stopped him, "Take my umbrella. Don't

catch a cold."

Pei Ran refused, "No, thank you."

"No," Su Nian smiled, "This umbrella was given to me by Qingshan. I always forgot to return it. Now that you're here, you can help me return it after you use it."

"I've broken up with him. Since you borrowed it, you should return it." Pei Ran walked away, and let the rest of the words float in the rain. Su Nian stood in the same place and looked at his back without moving.

The boy beside him bumped his shoulder, "Listen to what you just said. Bitchy much?"

Su Nian smiled and said, "This is how one should talk with Pei Ran. If it's too subtle, he wouldn't understand."

"They've already broken up. Why are you still trying to antagonize him?"

Su Nian's smile remained. They had indeed broken up, but, deep down, Luo Qingshan still cared about him.

He couldn't solve Luo Qingshan's problem, so he turned to Pei Ran. As long as Pei Ran didn't get back together with him, Luo Qingshan had no way back.

Seeing Su Nian's silence, his friend couldn't help frown at him. After a long moment, he asked, "Why? I don't think Luo Qingshan is any good. Handsome boys are everywhere. Let me introduce some to you?"

"No." Su Nian took out his phone and glanced at it. He sent more than ten messages to Luo Qingshan, but he didn't receive anything. He looked up at the rain, "Let's go."

Pei Ran got back to the dorm, took off his hat, changed his clothes and took his hat to the bathroom.

He took a new toothbrush and gently cleaned the hat while

gazing down at it. Pei Ran loved washing things. Doing simple repetitive actions allowed him to space out. But now he couldn't clear his mind at all. His mind was full of Yan Zhun.

He heard that voice saying, "I like you." Then, it said, "I'm courting you," and now it asked, "May I?" Before parting, Yan Zhun had patted his head through the hat for barely two seconds before he moved his hand back and asked Pei Ran to go home, saying that the rain was getting heavier.

A sharp sound brought Pei Ran back to reality. As soon as he turned, he saw a rain drop splattering into the room and a puddle forming on the ground under the windowsill. Pei Ran closed the window, went back to his desk, and saw multiple message notifications on his phone.

Unknown:
I lent the umbrella to him a long time ago...

Unknown:
Did you get wet today? Remember to drink some hot water to keep out the cold.

Unknown:
Call me next time this happens; I'll pick you up

Unknown:
I miss you very much. Would you please text me back

It was useless to block the WeChat and phone number. Luo Qingshan was still everywhere.

Pei Ran looked at the time. It was less than half an hour after meeting Su Nian and Luo Qingshan already knew about it. Pei Ran didn't reply. He backed out of the chat to read the other messages he received on WeChat.

Yan Zhun:
.

Pei Ran:
?

Yan Zhun:
Seeing if I'm still there.

Pei Ran:
Where?

Yan Zhun:
Your contact list.

Pei Ran took a deep breath and felt that his ears were a little hot. He held onto his phone for a long time before typing a series of ellipses, which he hadn't had the chance to send yet.

Yan Zhun:
You've been typing for five minutes. What type of essay are you drafting here?

Pei Ran:
...

Pei Ran:
I was busy with something else. I forgot to close the dialogue box.

Yan Zhun:
What is it

Pei Ran:
...Something private.

After sending the last sentence, Pei Ran flipped his mobile phone and set it on the table. Then, he got up and went back to the washstand to wash Yan Zhun's hat.

It was late autumn, and it rained intermittently for two days. After his roommate moved out, the dorm became quieter than before, and Pei Ran felt more comfortable drawing.

He was just starting to draw when his phone rang.

"BabeRan, what are you doing?" It was Lin Xuhuan. It was a rare case of no typing sound on his end.

"Drawing." Pei Ran asked. "What's the matter?"

"Drawing? Me?" Lin Xuhuan's voice was a little louder, "Let me have a look!"

"I've barely started. There's not even a sketch." Pei Ran asked again, "Anything important?"

Lin Xuhuan didn't answer immediately. There seemed to be others around him, and his voice became a little distant: "Bro, BabeRan seems to be drawing me. This kind of thing requires concentration. Maybe let's not disturb him?"

Pei Ran instantly knew who the person around him was. He grabbed the phone a little harder. Before he realized, he had already put down his pen, turned the speaker off, and put his phone up to his ear.

Lin Xuhuan came back soon enough. "Nothing... We were planning to play basketball at your school court today. You can come."

When Lin Xuhuan hung up the phone, the person sitting by the sofa asked, "What did he say?"

"Of course he said yes." Lin Xuhuan wondered, "Why didn't you ask him yourself? Why make me call him?"

What else could the reason be? Of course it was because he was afraid that he couldn't get him to come out.

Lin Xuhuan had helped Pei Ran previously. As long as he asked, Pei Ran would show up.

Yan Zhun got up and patted Lin Xuhuan's shoulder, saying, "An army trains for a thousand days for one hour's battle."

It had been rainy recently. The ground was wet, so all the players had moved to the indoor stadium.

Most people went out of campus for Saturday, so there was no one on the court. They didn't even have to fight for a place. When Pei Ran arrived, he saw Yan Zhun effortlessly jumping up to land a mid-range shot. One corner of his jersey lifted. His tight abs were covered with a thin layer of sweat.

"BabeRan." Lin Xuhuan could barely breathe after playing. "How you were so slow? Let's play three-v-three."

Not expecting to play against others, Pei Ran hesitated. Then he started taking off his coat, saying, "I'm not good..."

"It's okay; we're all the same. You even took part in the sports festival. Meanwhile we're too lazy to walk on a daily basis. Join us," said Lin Xuhuan.

Pei Ran paused and was about to nod when his half-off coat was suddenly pulled up by someone and put back on him.

"He won't play." Yan Zhun stood behind him. He panted a bit, and his voice was deeper than usual. "He has a leg injury."

Pei Ran's shoulders were stiff. He didn't reach for his coat even though it was hanging a little loose.

"Oh, yes." Lin Xuhuan was confused for a while, then asked, "You knew he couldn't play but still let me call him over?"

"None of your business. Go play. Don't be lazy."

Lin Xuhuan didn't realize what was wrong at all. He said, "Come quickly." Only two of them were left.

Pei Ran calmed his breathing, then turned around slowly. They had been playing for a while, and Yan Zhun's hair was clumping together by sweat, his eyes as dark as ever.

Yan Zhun looked much more lively than usual at this time, maybe because he had just exercised. He still had sweat under his eyes. The room was filled with masculine hormones. Pei Ran took out the baseball cap from his coat pocket. It was a little wrinkled, but, fortunately, the brim of the cap was fine.

He smoothed it out and gave it to Yan Zhun, "Thank you."

Yan Zhun smelled the faint fragrance. He asked, "Did you wash it for me?"

Of course he'd washed it; it had gotten drenched in rain. Pei Ran found Yan Zhun's question a bit odd.

"Well, it should be clean," siad Pei Ran.

Others were calling for Yan Zhun, who answered them casually, then said to Pei Ran, "Help me hold onto it first."

The sound of basketball hitting the ground was too loud that Pei Ran didn't hear it clearly, so he asked, "Huh?"

"Hold onto it for me for a bit," Yan Zhun said. "My hands are dirty and I stink. I'll get it dirty." He was talking about the hat, but he stared at Pei Ran's eyes all that time.

Pei Ran put the hat on his leg and sat in the audience to watch them play. His coat, a water bottle, and other random things were strewn about him. Everyone else was panting with their hands on their hips, looking like standard gamer nerds.

Except Yan Zhun.

Yan Zhun ran very fast and didn't stop much, so others mostly passed the ball to him. Half way through the game, Lin Xuhuan seemed too tired to run. He stood in the same place and waved his hand to ask for a rest. Yan Zhun threw the ball into the hoop, not rushing to pick it up but standing in place and raising the corner of his shirt to wipe his sweat.

Lin Xuhuan stood beside him and took off his shirt. He didn't seem fat, but evidently the meals at the TZG base weren't half bad—judging from his chubby figure.

When the two of them stood side by side, the contrast was somewhat tragic. Right there and then, Yan Zhun glanced at Pei Ran's direction.

Pei Ran paused and pretended to look away calmly. Lin Xuhuan was so tired that he wanted to collapse. He couldn't help but walk to Yan Zhun and rest his elbow on him. Because he wasn't tall enough, though he had to raise his hand to reach Yan Zhun. The posture was rather hilarious.

"Bro, are you tired?"

Yan Zhun said, "I'm okay."

Lin Xuhuan coughed softly, "I know the coach told you to watch us exercise, but I think we've been playing for half an hour, and everyone is tired..."

"Aren't we resting now?" Yan Zhun asked.

Lin Xuhuan wanted to tell him not to use his standards to measure the rest of them gamers, but he soon realized that Yan Zhun was also a gamer, a better gamer than him, even.

He looked up and wanted to say something else when he found that Yan Zhun's attention was focused elsewhere. Lin Xuhuan followed his gaze and saw Pei Ran sitting in the audience. Pei Ran sat upright and looked very proper, a clear standout among the other guys sitting with their legs crossed.

Lin Xuhuan tutted, "You called BabeRan here, just to let him help us keep an eye on our belongings?"

"He doesn't have a name?" Yan Zhun asked.

"But BabeRan is more intimate, and it's his ID." Speaking of this, Lin Xuhuan wondered, "But he doesn't look like the kind of person who would use this ID."

Yan Zhun didn't answer him. The basketball was thrown at him, and he easily caught it, bouncing it in place.

Lin Xuhuan looked at Pei Ran and suddenly realized something, "Bro, that hat BabeRan is holding, is it yours?"

It was a limited-edition hat, and he had asked Yan Zhun for it once, but he'd been refused.

The ball hit the ground and bounced, Yan Zhun caught it in one hand and threw the ball to him. "Let's grab dinner in ten."

After playing, the five of them went up the steps, sweating profusely. Pei Ran offered them all tissues, and Lin Xuhuan took a sheet. "BabeRan, you even brought tissues with you."

"Force of habit." Pei Ran pulled out another one and handed it out in front of Yan Zhun. "Do you want it?"

"Thank you." Yan Zhun picked it up, and their fingertips touched. Having just finished playing basketball, Yan Zhun's fingertips were hot, and Pei Ran felt almost scalded.

Quickly, he handed out the tissues among the others.

"Pei Ran." The sound came from Pei Ran's right. He turned his head and saw Luo Qingshan standing there.

Luo Qingshan had a crew cut now, and he looked very fresh. He dressed himself neatly, clearly not here for sports. He walked towards them, giving Yan Zhun a weighted glance.

Then, he looked at Pei Ran again, "I heard that you were here, so I came to find you."

After a pause, Pei Ran asked, "Is something wrong?"

"Yes." Luo Qingshan stopped and suddenly chuckled, "It was actually Yan Zhun who reminded me."

The atmosphere was somehow tense, and the others all looked at Yan Zhun in question.

Yan Zhun lowered his head to wipe the sweat of his neck, and his expression was as indifferent as usual.

Luo Qingshan continued, "He said that after we broke up, you gave me everything back, and that I should also return them to you. I thought about it, and he's right. No matter if we ever get back together, those things should be returned."

As soon as he said this, everyone became uncomfortable, and atmosphere suddenly turned very awkward. They all stopped wiping their sweat to look at each other, breathing as quietly as possible.

Lin Xuhuan stared at Pei Ran, who was tense and still.

"After we broke up"? "Get back together"?

If he understood the words correctly, then BabeRan and

this man... were once in that kind of relationship?

Luo Qingshan obviously didn't come here to return things, or he wouldn't have come empty handed. He just wanted to find a chance to be with Pei Ran alone. And knowing Pei Ran, of course he wouldn't be allowed too return the items.

Seeing other people's expressions of utter surprise, Luo Qingshan felt oddly satisfied. He had done it intentionally; he wanted to let these people know that he and Pei Ran's relationship was complicated, that it was not so easy for them to disassociated from each other.

"I don't remember a lot." Pei Ran calmly broke the silence.

"What?" asked Luo Qingshan

"I can't remember what I gave you very clearly. Do you?" Pei Ran looked up at him with no emotion in his eyes.

Luo Qingshan didn't see his own sexual orientation as a matter of privacy; Pei Ran had long been used to it. He'd felt awkward at first, and he'd talked to Luo Qingshan about it, but Luo Qingshan had said that he didn't want to be a secret, that he wanted to be in love like "normal people."

Pei Ran hadn't known what to say, so he'd just let it go.

He never expected it would be like this after the break-up.

"I... You gave me so much, how can I remember..." Not getting the expected answer, Luo Qingshan's tone was a little flustered.

Pei Ran nodded, "Just count what you remember and convert it into cash."

Luo Qingshan panicked, licking his lips. "I'm afraid that I'll get it wrong. Let's go have a dinner and figure it out together."

Seeing this kind of scene, Lin Xuhuan was a little embarrassed. He and his teammates looked at each other, trying to find an excuse to run away and leave these two alone.

Lin Xuhuan coughed softly. "Then we—"

"We've booked a restaurant," Yan Zhun finished for him. Then, to Pei Ran he added, "You're included."

Lin Xuhuan was baffled, and he tried to indicate to Yan Zhun with his eyes: *Why are you trying to involve us, bro?*

Yan Zhun didn't seem to see it, eyes still fixed on Pei Ran.

Luo Qingshan frowned, "Yan Zhun, you..."

"Oh, yes, BabeRan, we have a reservation for you!" Now that his bro had spoken, Lin Xuhuan of course had to help. He cut in and said, "Japanese, almost two thousand yuan per seat! Our coach is reimbursing it, but there's no refund if you don't go, so it'd be such a waste of money!"

"BabeRan? Why do you call him BabeRan?" Luo Qingshan squinted. "Wait, are you TZG's? Who allowed you to play in our school? Were you brought in by Yan Zhun?"

"Luo Qingshan." Pei Ran frowned and interrupted him, "Forget the dinner. You can calculate the amount and transfer the money to me. Don't bother with any lists."

"We have other things to do. We're leaving." Pei Ran turned around and walked away.

Lin Xuhuan was upset by Luo Qingshan's attitude, wanting to say something in response, but then Yan Zhun touched him on the shoulder, indicating for him to follow along.

When they left the gymnasium, only Luo Qingshan was still standing on the steps with a gloomy expression.

Lin Xuhuan hadn't lied. The coach did book them Japanese food. They arrived at the restaurant just as they finished changing in the car.

The awkwardness still lingered in the air, but Pei Ran stayed calm. Once they got to the restaurant, he said, "Sorry for the trouble."

On the way over, Lin Xuhuan had already calmed down, and so did the others. The TZG captain said, "We didn't mean to overhear. It's all good as long as you're okay."

Lin Xuhuan tried to hold it in, but couldn't help it at last, "That man, is he really your ex-boyfriend?"

As soon as the words were said, he was knocked on the head by the captain.

"Ouch..." Lin Xuhuan curled his mouth, "I'm just curious. BabeRan and I are so close, it doesn't matter if I ask."

"Yes." Pei Ran admitted it very simply.

The group of straight men nodded as one, trying to act natural. A small dish of salmon was put in front of Pei Ran.

Yan Zhun picked up the mustard tube next to him and squeezed a little, "Eat."

Their arms contacted gently; Pei Ran looked down at the plate. "Thank you."

Lin Xuhuan got energetic after eating two mouthfuls, and began to talk nonsense again. "BabeRan, don't worry about it. We don't mind. Love is love." He pointed to the raider of their team and said, "He used to simp for a female streamer with a private account. In the end, he spent over a hundred thousand and got nothing. Even then we didn't look down on him."

The accused raider swore, "Fuck you! That has nothing to do with Pei Ran's affairs!"

"Both are about relationships. What's the difference?"

The raider sneered and counterattacked: "Well, as you said, our captain handed a love letter to someone in junior high school and the letter was handed over to the teacher. He was punished to read it word by word in front of everyone. As his classmate, I didn't dislike him."

The more that was said, the more the topics changed, and

the awkwardness dissipated.

Then, someone suddenly said, "What else is new? You're all better than Yan Zhun, the supreme VIP gold bachelor." The person of interest was indifferent and picked up the empty cup for some tea. Everyone chatted noisily, and no one found that he was holding Pei Ran' cup.

"He's not a bachelor." Lin Xuhuan said, "My brother will be taken real soon."

Everyone was shocked. Pei Ran also paused for a moment and quietly slowed down chewing.

"Taken? Who?" The raider's curiosity was piqued, and he immediately put down his chopsticks and stopped eating.

It wasn't that they thought Yan Zhun couldn't find a girlfriend—it would be too easy for him to find a girlfriend—but he had always been single, so their reactions were extreme.

"I don't know." Lin Xuhuan thought for a moment. "Last time he told me he was about to find me a sister-in-law, and that he was waiting for a reply."

Yan Zhun wiped his hands with a towel and threw out a single word, "Yep."

Pei Ran looked down to hide his face.

"Damn it... Really? I thought he was talking nonsense..." The raider was shocked. "Where's she from? Real life or online?"

"Schoolmate." Yan Zhun said.

"Why didn't you bring her here?" The captain asked. "What's her name? How old? Let us see the pictures."

Yan Zhun put down his chopsticks and leaned back in his chair. "Stop asking. Not mine yet."

"It's been such a long time, haven't you succeeded?" Lin Xuhuan was shocked. "What kind of girl is so hard to get? BabeRan, have you met her?"

Suddenly mentioned, Pei Ran looked up from his plate. His face was fine, but his ears were flushed. "Not yet."

"Wow, you don't even know." Seeing him acting so calm, Lin Xuhuan asked, "Are you not curious?"

Pei Ran said, "I am." The tone was not convincing at all.

"Then you should pay more attention to it. It must be a girl from his social circle! Tell me at once when you find her!"

Pei Ran pursed his lips. "Then... I'll start paying attention."

This topic was very intriguing for TZG members. They began to speculate wildly about this girl. Soon, the scope narrowed down to "long hair," "big eyes," and "thin waist."

Yan Zhun played on his cell phone and ignored them all.

Pei Ran drank a cup of tea, feeling secretly relieved. But then his phone suddenly buzzed.

Yan Zhun:
If you're curious, you can try turning on the front camera

Pei Ran locked the screen of his phone and put it away. The dining table was not that big, and the light was sufficient.

Lin Xuhuan's gaze roamed as he chatted, settling on Pei Ran. He looked for a few seconds, then asked, "BabeRan, why is you face so red? Are you hot?"

Pei Ran waved his chopsticks and said, "Wasabi, too spicy."

Fed and watered, the gamers were picked up by the car their coach sent, and Pei Ran hitched a ride with them. Yan Zhun didn't go back to campus, so Pei Ran handed his hat to him before getting off the car.

Yan Zhun took it and said, "Exchange."

Before Pei Ran could understand, his fingers were gently pried open, and Yan Zhun gave him two pieces of milk candy. The car was dark, and everyone was sleepy after eating, so no one saw even them.

Back at the base, Lin Xuhuan took a shower. When he came out, he saw Yan Zhun sitting on the sofa in the hall, wearing his hat and playing a card game on his phone. He dried his hair with a towel and was about to go up for a chat when he stopped. Yan Zhun had evidently lost the game, for he threw his mobile phone to aside and slouched into the sofa.

But then, he took off his hat, put it next to his nose and closed his eyes—as if sniffing it.

Two days before the TZG competition, Yan Zhun packed his belongings and got ready to leave. The coach sat next to him and tried to convince him, "Didn't you like living here? Why do you have to go back?"

Yan Zhun didn't even look up. "I'm distrupting training."

The coach said, "Not true, you can help me watch them."

"I have an exam coming up, so I don't have time to practice with them." Yan Zhun said cooly.

The coach accused him of having no conscience, closed the door and asked, "Are you really set on not coming back?"

Yan Zhun looked down to hide his emotions. He zipped his bag. "Not planing to."

Yan Zhun walked out of the room with his bag on one shoulder, then saw Lin Xuhuan lying on the sofa, looking at his baseball cap before holding it closer for a sniff.

Yan Zhun took his hat from Lin Xuhuan's hand, frowning. "What are you doing?"

Lin Xuhuan widened his eyes and said innocently, "It's out of production, so I just want to take a look. Oh, what's that fragrance on your hat? Smells good. No wonder you held it for so long that day."

Others lazing about the room looked at them strangely.

The raider put down his chicken wings. "Come and let me smell. Did you use perfume?"

Yan Zhun didn't want to answer him. He put on his hat, saying, "Leaving now."

"Wait a minute." The coach stopped him and gave him something—a pair of internal tickets. "Take these. The seats are near the front. You can also come backstage if you want."

Yan Zhun looked at the TZG logo printed on the tickets and accepted them. "Thank you."

Back in his dorm, Yan Zhun set his backpack on the table, got his phone, and sent a photo of the tickets to Pei Ran.

Pei Ran:
Huh?

Yan Zhun:
This Saturday, downtown, twenty minutes by taxi

Pei Ran:
OK, I'll help you post in Moments

Yan Zhun:
?

Yan Zhun:
What post?

Pei Ran:
Don't you want to sell the tickets?

Yan Zhun stared at that message for a few seconds and started a voice call.

It rang several times before the other side answered. "Do I look like a scalper?" Yan Zhun asked.

Pei Ran was confused. "I just saw Lin Xuhuan's post. He wanted to sell two tickets. Aren't these his tickets?"

Yan Zhun was speechless. What was wrong with Lin Xuhuan? Why sell tickets when his salary was in the millions?

"I'm not trying to sell the tickets," Yan Zhun said. "I wanted to ask if you wanted to watch the game together."

Pei Ran was coloring his painting. The tip of his pen paused when he heard Yan Zhun, and then he blinked rapidly.

"There's no class on the weekend. I can pick you up. We don't need to line up with these tickets, and I'll explain the game to you if you don't understand," Yan Zhun offered. "Will you come?" It was very quiet on the other side of the phone. Yan Zhun didn't speak, silently waiting for him to answer.

After a long moment of no response, Yan Zhun folded the ticket to put them back in his backpack. "I see."

Pei Ran's tone was very soft. "I'm not a girl, so you don't have to pick me up. Can we meet at the bus stop?"

This was Pei Ran's first time at a live gaming event. They entered through the back door, and there weren't many people there when they arrived.

Knowing that they were coming, Lin Xuhuan arranged in advance for them to be allowed backstage. Other players were serious as hell, but TZG members were relaxed. They were used to international competitions, and their mentality had already been trained out of nerves. When Pei Ran went in, he even saw the raider playing Linkup on his mobile phone.

"You can go grab some water. The sponsors provide it for free." Then, the coach looked at Pei Ran smiled, saying, "Yan Zhun, do you know why you haven't gotten the person you like to accept you?"

Both of them paused when they heard this. Pei Ran even stopped opening the water bottle. Yan Zhun was calm. "Why?"

"I gave you two tickets to invite the girl here, but you... you brought Pei Ran." The coach laughed. "Of course, not that he isn't welcome. You could have asked me for another ticket."

"Leave them for Lin Xuhuan to sell," Yan Zhun deadpanned.

Lin Xuhuan swore. "That ticket had been for a friend, but he couldn't make it, so he asked me to help sell it!"

The coach scolded him. "Then you shouldn't sell it on your main account! It was screenshotted and posted on Weibo, where you became a trending topic—by getting criticized!"

After chitchat, the team began to discuss the game.

Their strategy had been set for a long time; now they were only discussing the details. Yan Zhun sat next to the coach and spoke when prompted, and also gave an opinion or two from at times, his tone carefree, but his expression serious.

After staying in the lounge for a while, Yan Zhun got up, "The organizers are going to shoot the video soon. I'm taking him out." There were 16 teams in this competition. The lounge was densely packed, leaving only a narrow corridor open.

On their way out, Pei Ran asked, "Have you ever taken part in a competition before?"

"No." Yan Zhun said casually, "I left the team two days before the big game."

Pei Ran pursed his lips and didn't press.

They were in the fourth row, and they could see the screen without looking up. The surrounding seats were all full.

All the players took their seats, and the host began to introduce them one by one. When introducing the team of TZG, the cheers and applause were the loudest. When the camera focused on the team members of TZG, Lin Xuhuan even winked. At the beginning of the game, Yan Zhun turned his head slightly and lowered his voice, "They want to occupy the lower right field area and block the bridge."

Pei Ran paused and then realized Yan Zhun was explaining to him, "Will they also block the bridge in a competition?"

"Sometimes. It depends on the circle. You can also move around in the wild area. It's all the same." Yan Zhun looked at the other team players who were about to meet with Lin Xuhuan and said, "TZG is going to get scores." In ten seconds, the screen jumped out with an announcement that Lin Xuhuan killed his opponent.

"You have a lot of confidence in him." Pei Ran said.

"He practiced this terrain for a couple nights just a few days ago," Yan Zhun said. "Even pigs would become better."

Pei Ran wasn't sure how to respond. He heard the girl next to Yan Zhun chuckle.

Yan Zhun also heard her, and his voice became lower. TZG played well in this first round, and the lower right field was taken by them. Unfortunately, their position was not good in the latter half, and they ended up ranking third.

With Yan Zhun's help, Pei Ran miraculously understood the whole game. He frowned and was about to speak when—

"Well..." a gentle female voice whispered, "I heard you explaining. Are you an up and coming commentator? Wanna add my WeChat? Maybe later... we can play games together."

It was the girl on the other side of Yan Zhun. Pei Ran stayed silent leaned back in his seat. Yan Zhun said, "I can't."

"Huh? Why?" asked the girl.

"The person I like is here. It's not good for us to be seen."

Pei Ran was speechless.

The girl was also taken aback. "Sorry about that," she said.

In the third game, the camera gave a main perspective of a player from another team. The commentators talked about him for nearly a minute, praising him as a rare all-around player and saying that he was about to catch up with TZG's Lin Xuhuan.

That player also lived up to the expectations. Under the enthusiastic gaze of the commentators, he fought against two players and won by a narrow margin.

"His reactions are very fast," Yan Zhun said. "He's good, but not as good as Lin Xuhuan."

Pei Ran said, "Not as good as you."

Yan Zhun was stunned. After a few seconds, he asked, "Who's better, me or Lin Xuhuan?"

Pei Ran was focused on the game. Without thinking, he answered, "You."

"Why?"

Pei Ran paused, "I don't know, I just think... it's you."

Yan Zhun hummed, propping his hands on the armrest. He covered his mouth, and smiled in the dark.

By the end of this round, TZG's total score ranked second.

Pei Ran was not satisfied yet. He got up with other people in the field and was ready to leave the venue.

After walking for a few steps, he heard an exclamation from the side, a girl called out a name with a surprise.

Pei Ran was shocked. He had heard that name before, so it was probably that of a male celebrity. Pei Ran didn't pay much attention to entertainment news, so if even he knew a name... then that person must really be famous.

For example, as soon as this one was discovered, there was a big stir in the field. The people in the back row all crowded over. Even those who had already left the venue turned back, and the situation became uncontrollable. Pei Ran was pushed around by the crowd.

The girl behind him had even started a live broadcast, screaming at her phone: "Ah ah!!! It's him! It's him! He came to watch the game!!"

Twice, Pei Ran said "Excuse me," but his voice was overwhelmed by the screeching, which made his head buzz. One hand held him steadily in the crowd.

First, it held his wrist, then moved down to hold his hand.

Feeling its strength, Pei Ran clutched the hand too. Then, he looked up to find the owner of the hand—Yan Zhun.

Yan Zhun didn't look back and led him forward. Pei Ran could only see the back of his head. His hand suddenly began to burn, Pei Ran relaxed a bit, but Yan Zhun tightened his grip in response.

The shrieks in his ears were almost overwhelmed by the sound of his heartbeat. They got all the way to the side door of the ticket booth before Pei Ran felt the cold wind outside and tried to take back his hand.

It didn't work. But this move let him realize something very embarrassing—his palms were sweating.

Pei Ran's palms never sweat no matter how long he held the pen, but now, after just a few minutes...

"Yan Zhun." Pei Ran said, "We have already come out."

"Well." Yan Zhun's eyes were on the ticket booth.

Pei Ran also wanted to say something, but then Yan Zhun raised an eyebrow and got a tissue from the box on the table Then, he loooked down and held Pei Ran's hands, help him wipe his hands clean of sweat.

The place where their fingers touched and pressed seemed to be on fire and burned all the way to Pei Ran's ears. It took him a long time to remember to pull his hand back.

His phone rang. It was his roommate. Pei Ran quickly picked up, thankful that he'd been saved from the moment.

"Hello." Pei Ran held the phone and looked away, "Left in the dorm? In a hurry... Now? I see. Wait a minute. I'll be back in twenty minutes." As soon as he hung up the phone, Yan Zhun had already raised his hand to call a taxi.

"Let's go."

Back on campus, Yan Zhun lowered his head to reply to Lin Xuhuan's messages and opened the door to his dorm room.

His roommate was sitting in a chair, arms crossed, staring motionlessly at the computer. Weibo was open on it, showing the interface of a finished video. There was no response to the sound of the door opening.

Yan Zhun took off his hat and put it on the table.

"Yan Zhun." Luo Qingshan cut through the silence and asked, "What is the relationship between you and Pei Ran?

"I saw it. You went to the TZG game together." Luo Qingshan tried to stay calm. "There was an streamer filming the celebrity, and you were in it."

Yan Zhun opened his game for updates, not paying attention to him. The sound of a lighter came from behind him, and smoke slowly filled the whole dorm.

Luo Qingshan asked, "Are you in a relationship? When did it happen? Recently... or before he broke up with me?"

"Not together yet." Yan Zhun said softly.

Luo Qingshan's clenched fist relaxed a little bit.

Yan Zhun said, "I am pursuing him."

Luo Qingshan bit his tongue and stubbed out half of his cigarette on the paper, leaving a singed hole.

"Yan Zhun, that's not how you treat a brother, you son of a bitch." Luo Qingshan gnashed his teeth.

Yan Zhun raised his eyebrows, "You and me, since when did we become brothers?"

Luo Qingshan cursed and stared at Yan Zhun. "Who do you

think you are? Do you think you can get Pei Ran? That he'll like you? Just because you played a few games with him?

"Listen, Pei Ran and I quarrel occasionally. It's out of affection. I can be at odds with him, but it's impossible for others to come between us." Luo Qingshan's words were fierce, and his voice was loud. Only he knew how flustered he was now.

What he said was only half true. Pei Ran was pursued by many people, both men and women. Luo Qingshan was always at ease about this. Pei Ran never gave anyone hope, and his refusal was always straightforward and absolute.

But this time was different.

Pei Ran treated Yan Zhun differently from everyone else.

This was also the reason why Luo Qingshan was angry.

"Finished?" Yan Zhun asked. "Can you shut your mouth?"

Luo Qingshan was now enraged, the coldness and contempt in Yan Zhun's tone made lose his cool completely. As if remembering something, Luo Qingshan sneered, "You're really something. You dare to challenge me just because you held his hand. When he lay on my bed—"

The chair screeched against the floor.

Before Luo Qingshan could finish his words, his collar was suddenly gripped by a hand strong that he almost fell down.

Yan Zhun stared down at him from above, his eyes as cold as ever, vicious and cruel. Luo Qingshan was not afraid of him normally, but at this moment, somehow, his body seemed to be out of his control and he couldn't move.

"If I hear that again," Yan Zhun warned, one word at a time, "then say goodbye to your mouth."

It wasn't until the dorm door was slammed shut that Luo Qingshan returned to his senses, gasping in shock and anger.

It was cold in November. Yan Zhun went downstairs and

walked into the supermarket around the corner. He bought a pack of cigarettes and sat on an empty bench.

The lighter flashed for a moment in the dark. He threw the lighter aside and dropped his hands, holding the cigarette with his teeth. After a while, he pulled out his cell phone to make a call. When the call was picked up, Pei Ran gave a soft greeting. Yan Zhun put his phone closely next to his ear and quietly listened to the sound of Pei Ran's breathing.

After a while, Pei Ran put down his pen. "Yan Zhun, what's wrong?"

"I left too fast today and forgot to grab the competition merchandise." Yan Zhun kept his voice from showing emotion.

Pei Ran paused, then asked, "Did they offer merchandise?"

"Yep," Yan Zhun said, "keyboards, models, team logo keychains and the like. Did you want any? I'll ask Lin Xuhuan to get a set."

Pei Ran shook his head, "No, I don't need a keyboard. Keychain... I have one, already." Yan Zhun breathed out softly. Pei Ran paused, "Are you smoking?"

"Occasionally," Yan Zhun said. "No more smoking in the future." Then, Yan Zhun closed his eyes.

They were not in a relationship, and Pei Ran wouldn't want to control his smoking habits. Sure enough, there was silence on the other end of the phone.

Yan Zhun stubbed out his jealousy along with the cigarette.

"Okay."

Yan Zhun's movement paused lightly, and his drooping eyelashes trembled. "What?"

Pei Ran opened his window and reached outside to feel the temperature. "Smoking is bad for you. You should smoke less... Are you still outside?"

Yan Zhun said, "The dorm manager keeps a close watch on us at night, so I came out to smoke."

"Then... will you go back soon?"

"All right."

After hanging up the call, Pei Ran stared at the screen for a long time before closing the window to continue his painting.

He absentmindedly sketched for a while. Then, his nose suddenly itched, and he couldn't help but turn his head and sneeze, twice in succession. Looking back again, after seeing his painting clearly, Pei Ran's pen paused, and his eyes widened slightly. He seemed to be at a loss. He'd only sketched a rough draft, thinking to show the client before refining it.

In the sketch, there were gaming chairs, computers and TZG uniforms. These were all correct. But the facial features of the man in the sketch... It was Yan Zhun.

The Yan Zhun he remembered with headphones and a TZG team uniform, sitting on the site of the competition.

The next day, Pei Ran went to class wearing a mask.

After class, the professor stopped him and asked, "What's the matter? Have you got a cold?"

"A little bit." It was stuffy behind the mask, and his voice sounded heavier.

This professor had always liked him. Seeing the dark bruises under his eyes, the professor scolded, "Young man, you must have stayed up late."

Pei Ran said, "Busy with a commission." It was normal for college students to have part-time jobs, but the professor hadn't expected that someone of Pei Ran's family background would also accept business orders.

"There's no need to damage your health for that little

money. Resting well is important," the professor said.

Pei Ran nodded. "Okay. Thank you, professor."

After a full day of class, Pei Ran went back to the dorm and took some cold medication. Just after swallowing the pills, he got some messages from the girl who commissioned him.

TZGisthebest:
Hiii! I'd like to check the progress QAQ **[carefully emote]**

P&EI:
Sorry, I haven't started painting yet.

TZGisthebest:
Great!! Well, I wanted you to include this trophy in it, is it OK? I can add money!! **[image]**

P&EI:
Sure. No extra fee.

The girl was so pleased that she sent a bunch of stickers.

Pei Ran looked at these custom emotes and thought of that commission that had gotten sidetracked. He felt a little embarrassed. After working on it for two hours, Pei Ran got up for a break. Just after making a cup of coffee, a WeChat notification from Lin Kang showed up on his computer.

It was a video attachment. The preview was a little fuzzy, and the content couldn't be seen clearly. There was loud music once Pei Ran clicked open the video. The scene was dim and ambiguous, and the human figure in it was blurry. Then the chaos dissipated a bit, and Pei Ran finally saw who it was.

It was Luo Qingshan. He was holding a small glass of alcohol and thoroughly engrossed in drinking. When he chugged the whole glass, people around him immediately screamed and applauded. After a few seconds, the video ended.

P&EI:
?

Lin Kang:
Distilled liquor. So terrifying.

Luo Qingshan liked to play around back in high school. Almost every night he would hang out in bars, so his alcohol tolerance was good.

P&EI:
Oh, have fun.

When Lin Kang saw this message, he was really worried.

He looked at the liquor bottle on the table. How is this drinking? It was playing with fire. Luo Qingshan's face already turned red. He picked up the dice and said to the person next to him, "I finished. Dare to continue?"

Yan Zhun didn't even look at him. "Yep."

A friend couldn't help but tap Lin Kang's shoulder, saying, "These two people... What are they doing?"

"I also would like to know." Lin Kang said. It was a friend's birthday tonight, and he'd invited some guys out to drink. Then these two had started quarrelling out of the blue. By the time the others had realized, the waiter had already brought out the hard liquor.

Lin Kang looked at them in confusion.

Luo Qingshan had always liked to play. It was not strange for him to try to find someone for a drinking game. What was strange was that Yan Zhun had joined in. They drank back and forth for another ten minutes, and Luo Qingshan got wasted and started babbling. Meanwhile, Yan Zhun slouched into the sofa and watched him with a cool gaze.

"I have a headache. Damn it... Psst." Luo Qingshan bumped into Lin Kang's leg and said, "Help me... Call Pei Ran for me."

Lin Kang replied patiently, "You two already broke up. Why do you want to call him?"

"Do as I ask," Luo Qingshan said. "He will come, he will come... He doesn't have the heart to leave me."

Lin Kang was annoyed. He really couldn't let Luo Qingshan drink any more. But still, he picked up his phone and made a video call directly to Pei Ran.

Luo Qingshan smiled. He turned his head and asked tauntingly, "Do you think he will come?"

Yan Zhun sat quietly and stayed silent.

"I, I can call him when I'm drunk because... we have love, even if we broke up, our feelings are still, still there..." Then, Luo Qingshan asked, "What about you? You're drunk. Do you dare to look for him? You are... not worth it for him. He won't clean up your mess..."

Lin Kang raised his phone and sent a picture of the scene to Pei Ran. "See, he's been shouting for you. I really can't help it... Can you come here?"

"People all over the world know about my relationship with him." Luo Qingshan stared at Yan Zhun. "You are nothing."

Lin Kang hung up the video call and put their glasses further away, "Pei Ran said he would come here now. Calm down, Luo Qingshan." Luo Qingshan closed his eyes and gave a winning smile.

Pei Ran seldom came to such places.

He passed through the crowded booths and walked towards the rooms. He took out his mobile phone and took a look at the room number sent by Lin Kang again. His shoulder was bumped by someone, and the waiter quickly apologized, "I'm sorry, did I hurt you? I'm really sorry."

"It's alright. Could you tell me where room 103..."

Seeing the customer suddenly stop talking, the waiter prompted, "Room 103? Shall I show you?"

Pei Ran had been momentarily stunned. Now, looking

back, he said, "No, I saw my friend. Thank you."

After the waiter left, Pei Ran looked up again. Yan Zhun was standing behind where the waiter had been. He had just washed his face, and his cheeks were dotted with water. It was hard to tell the expression in his eyes.

Yan Zhun was also looking at Pei Ran.

Pei Ran wore a gray sweater. His hair was a little messy, and he still had on a face mask. It was evident that he had come in a hurry. The mask added a touch of fragility to him, and he looked comfortable and warm. As soon as Pei Ran approached Yan Zhun, he got a whiff of smoke and alcohol.

He frowned and said, "Luo Qingshan, he..."

Before he finished speaking, he was caught by the wrist. Yan Zhun's grip was so strong that it almost hurt.

Pei Ran was caught by surprise and was taken into the empty room next to him. He did not have time to respond before he was pushed to the sofa. The door was closed automatically, and the room was dark safe from the light that spilled faintly through the window in the door.

Pei Ran could barely see Yan Zhun's face.

Because of the alcohol, Yan Zhun's eyes were glassy. He put his hands on the sofa and locked Pei Ran between him and the sofa. Pei Ran felt that he was surrounded by Yan Zhun's smell, and his heart beat uncontrollably again.

Yan Zhun looked down at him. After a long time, he asked, "Why did you come?" Yan Zhun's voice was very husky from the alcohol, and it heated up Pei Ran's ears. Pei Ran's Adam's apple bobbed slightly.

Just as Pei Ran was about to respond, Yan Zhun suddenly bent down—

—and bit his lips. It was a real bite with very little force, and there was a layer of mask between them, so Pei Ran didn't feel much pain. He widened his eyes slowly, too shocked to speak. Outside, the music was deafening, mixed with the ambiguous murmurings of grown men and women.

Inside, there was no sound except for their heartbeat and their breaths. Yan Zhun saw Pei Ran's panicked expression and wanted even more to continue being mean.

He wanted to go back to high school and capture Pei Ran, no matter if they loved each other, no matter if they were happy. He wanted to keep him in his room and not let anyone touch him. He wanted to kiss him. Yan Zhun raised his hand to lift up the hair on Pei Ran's forehead and lowered his head again. Pei Ran used all his strength to lift his hand and pressed it against Yan Zhun's chin.

Pei Ran's palms were hot and burning, and there was even a slight fragrance to his fingers. He had probably just washed his hand with hand soap.

Pei Ran's voice was very soft and it was a little shaky, "The mask... It's dirty."

Yan Zhun hummed in reply, then lowered his head to hold one of Pei Ran's fingers in his mouth.

Then, Yan Zhun pulled off his mask, bent down, and kissed anew.

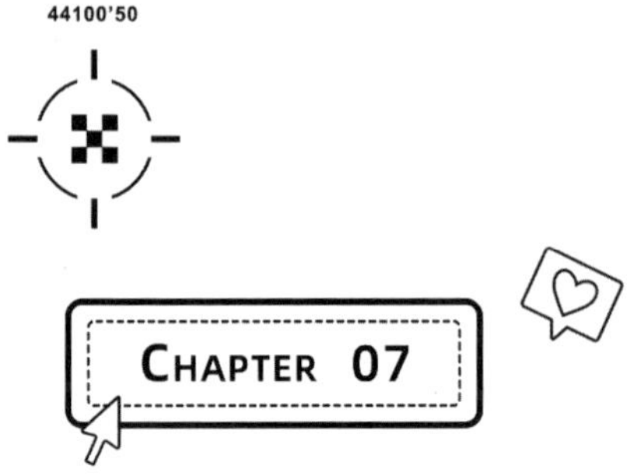

Yan Zhun had been drinking. His lips were cold, and his tongue was a little bitter. Pei Ran didn't think about much else. His neck, ears and cheeks were too hot and his head was about to explode.

He had never felt like this. He was holding his breath, eyes half closed, gazing absentmindedly at Yan Zhun's eyelashes. His back was pressed to the sofa, and he did not dare to move.

His heart was about to jump out of his chest.

Finally, Yan Zhun looked down and bit his lips patiently.

When Pei Ran opened his mouth, his breathing pattern was off, "How much... did you drink?"

Yan Zhun stopped and looked up at him. His eyes were inflamed by alcohol, "I'm not drunk."

Pei Ran asked, "Why did you challenge him to drink?"

The alcohol content of hard liquor was so high that Yan Zhun had been suffering from a headache. Hearing those words, he grimaced a little.

They hadn't been simply having an drinking contest. Seeing

Luo Qingshan's expression in the room, he'd almost bashed his head with a bottle.

Suddenly, a phone pinged. They moved too much and too abruptly just then, causing the phone to fall out from Pei Ran's pocket and was now lying on the sofa.

Lin Kang had sent messages asking Pei Ran where he was and whether he needed to be picked up.

Yan Zhun stiffened his spine, showing no sign of emotions.

He could smash the phone and lock him up, Yan Zhun thought. Then, a warmth on his stomach interrupted his thoughts, and his body froze.

Pei Ran's palm covered his abdomen, and Pei Ran was looking down. "How's your stomach feeling?"

That was when Yan Zhun felt everything, and the pain surged up in waves. He had never complained to anyone ever since he'd been a kid. During that period of training, he hadn't even spoken up when he was tired. If he hadn't suddenly collapsed in front of the computer, no one would have known that his condition was so serious.

His throat bobbed, then he said, hoarsely, "It hurts."

Pei Ran frowned. His face was still red, but his expression was more serious, "I'll call a car. Let's go to the hospital first." Not getting a response, Pei Ran looked up in confusion, only to find that Yan Zhun had been staring at him all that time.

His eyes seemed to be asking for confirmation. "Hospital?"

"Well," Pei Ran said, "unless you brough medication?"

Yan Zhun asked, "You're not picking him up?"

"Who..." Pei Ran was confused for a moment, and then he realized, "Luo Qingshan? He's got lots of friends here. I don't have to pick him up..."

Yan Zhun stayed silent for a moment, and his deep voice

changed a little, "Who did you come to pick up?"

Pei Ran didn't reply.

"Who's it?" Yan Zhun asked again, "Me?"

Pei Ran removed his hand from his abdomen and pursed his lips. Finally, he murmured, "Does it still hurt here..."

Before Pei Ran could finish his sentence, Yan Zhun suddenly leaned his entire body over Pei Ran. With his loose sweater, Pei Ran's shoulder and collarbone were partly exposed. Yan Zhun buried his face in Pei Ran's shoulder and closed his eyes.

Their posture was like a hug, but it wasn't a hug. Pei Ran could feel Yan Zhun's temperature and heartbeat, which were not much better than his own. Pei Ran got scared, thinking that Yan Zhun had passed out. He patted his back. "Yan Zhun? Is it too much to bear? Hold on, I'll call an ambulance..."

"Don't." Yan Zhun's breath was next to Pei Ran's ear.

Pei Ran's right ear became numb and he couldn't move.

"Let me smell for a while." Yan Zhun had relaxed, and his tone was lazy.

Pei Ran blinked twice, then finally said, "I'm not a cat."

Pei Ran had a fresh and cooling scent, like a shower gel.

Yan Zhun thought that if Pei Ran was a cat, he would hold back his arms and legs and bury himself face first in his belly for the entire night. Yan Zhun didn't stay collapsed for a long time. His head was too heavy, and his stomach really did hurt. He even staggered when he got up.

Worried about him falling, Pei Ran reached out to help.

Yan Zhun raised his hand and pulled Pei Ran's mask back up. Then he wiped the back of his hand over where he had bitten it. "There's a drugstore outside. I'll buy you a new one."

"No, I have more in my dorm. Let's go back to campus."

Across the corridor, room 103 was still bustling. Luo Qingshan had been lying on the sofa for a long time. He turned his head, frowned, then asked, "Why hasn't Pei Ran come?"

"I don't know. He isn't replying to my messages." Lin Kang said, chewing sunflower seeds.

"Call him," Luo Qingshan said. "Hurry up... Call him."

Lin Kang put down his snack, left with no choice but to say, "Okay, okay, I'll call him... Where are you going?"

"Nature calls," Luo Qingshan said.

"I'll go with you if you can't go alone."

"No, I haven't drunk that much." Luo Qingshan waved his hand, "You call Pei Ran now." Luo Qingshan stumbled out of the room, leaning against the wall to step falteringly towards the restroom. Then, hearing a ringtone, he looked up.

He saw two boys walking side by side. The shorter one was holding the person beside him. The walked close together. No one paid attention to the phone, no matter how loud it rang. After a few steps, they disappeared around the corner.

On Luo Qingshan's way out of the restroom, he washed his face. He put his hands on the washstand and lowered his head in silence. After a pause, he got out his phone and made a call.

Soon, the call was picked up. "Qingshan, what's wrong?"

Luo Qingshan's throat was dry. "Su Nian, come pick me up, I'm drunk."

On the ride back to school, Pei Ran bowed his head to reply to the messages and told Lin Kang that he wasn't coming.

Lin Kang:
You just asked me about the room number...?

Pei Ran:
I came to pick up someone else.

Lin Kang:
???

It was dim in the taxi, with only the streetlights shining in.

Yan Zhun was leaning on the window to rest. When he heard the constant WeChat pings, he sat up and looked down at the person next to him, "I didn't bring my dorm key."

Pei Ran was preoccupied with typing. "Huh?"

Yan Zhun was shoulder to shoulder with him, "Take me in."

Back at the dorm, Pei Ran put him on the chair and went into the bathroom.

Yan Zhun endured the pain and lifted his eyes to study the objects on Pei Ran's table one by one. It was very tidy and clean, and the computer's standby light was on. A digital board was next to it, along with a gray thermos bottle.

Yan Zhun stared at it for a while, and suddenly found something. He raised his hand and turned the cup.

On the other side of the thermos bottle, there was the charm. The small white sneaker swung in the air. The sound of water in the bathroom stopped. Yan Zhun put the bottle back in place. A hot towel was put on his face, warm and cozy. Pei Ran's touch was very gentle. After wiping his face, he took Yan Zhun's hand. Yan Zhun was languid, letting the towel wipe down his fingers one by one. Pei Ran rolled up his clothes to the elbow. The inside of his arm was dazzling white. One could tell that he'd been well taken care of growing up.

"Why did you come to pick me up?" Yan Zhun broke the silence. Pei Ran paused, then continued. He stared at his hand and said, "Your stomach is not good."

"You worry about me?" Yan Zhun asked.

"Yep."

Yan Zhun asked again, "You like me?"

Pei Ran didn't speak. Yan Zhun felt Pei Ran added a bit more force to his movements. After a long time, Pei Ran said,

"I don't know."

He didn't know what "like" was.

Once, he thought he liked Luo Qingshan. He wanted to be nice to Luo Qingshan. He didn't dislike being with Luo Qingshan, and sometimes he felt happy because of Luo Qingshan.

But, upon finding out that Luo Qingshan had cheated, he hadn't actually been that sad.

His fingers were suddenly hooked by Yan Zhun's, Pei Ran reactively raised his head, and their gazes met.

"Don't think about it." Yan Zhun's voice was very low, and his eyelids were half closed. "Try to like me a bit."

Pei Ran stared, at a loss for words. His fingers burned.

Yan Zhun waited until his stomach began to ache.

"Okay." Pei Ran quickly said when he saw Yan Zhun frown.

Then, before Yan Zhun could react, he let go of his hand and turned to open the closet.

"Do you want to change? I'll get you pajamas. They haven't been worn." Yan Zhun's eyelids were so heavy. His head had been dizzy that whole time. He stayed dumb for a few seconds, then said, "It's okay if they're worn."

For the sake of comfort, Pei Ran bought his pajamas two sizes larger than needed, which was just right for Yan Zhun.

After, Pei Ran took out a small crate from somewhere. It was full of medication. "What kind of stomach meds do you usually take?" Pei Ran looked at the instructions on a carton.

Yan Zhun asked, "Does your family run drugstores?"

Pei Ran smiled. His mother was very conscious of health, and they put a medicine box in every house.

Yan Zhun did actually find the medication he usually used. He took two with hot water. It brought warmth to his belly, and he finally felt the drowsiness from the alcohol.

There was only one bed in the dorm. The other three bunks were barely more than a few pieces of wood, which were impossible for them to sleep on. The single bed was suffused with Pei Ran's scent. Yan Zhun buried half of his face in the pillow for a moment, then pulled out his head to ask the person out of bed, "When are you going to sleep?"

Pei Ran's heart jumped, but he calmly responded, "I have a cold, and I don't want to get you sick. Go ahead and sleep. I'll stay up and draw," he lied. The subject of his sketch was now sleeping on his bed. He couldn't draw at all.

"If you could infect me, it's too late to worry about it now." Yan Zhun's voice was a little hoarse, "Come up to sleep."

Pei Ran hesitated. Dormitory beds weren't big, so it would be a little crowded for two boys to sleep together.

Pei Ran slept on his side with Yan Zhun behind him. He was listening to his heartbeat. He felt that he might be sick; cardiac arrhythmia or something, it had to be.

There was no movement behind him. Yan Zhun had probably fallen asleep. Pei Ran thought he would stay awake the whole night, but the effects of the cold medication were too strong, and soon he closed his eyes and his breaths evened out.

Late at night, Yan Zhun opened his eyes in the dark.

The person in front of him had changed his posture. Pei Ran had turned over and put his hand gently on Yan Zhun. The warmth from the back of his hand softly passed through the pajamas. Pei Ran hand moved constantly, as if trying to find a comfortable position. Yan Zhun pressed and held his hand, entwining their fingers. He closed his eyes and fell asleep after he was sure that Pei Ran was still.

Pei Ran had a dreamless night of sound sleep, so when he woke up and saw Yan Zhun, he was a little confused.

They were very close, if either of them moved forward, their bodies would touch each other. Pei Ran was only stupefied for a few seconds before he immediately woke up.

Yan Zhun's eyes were bleary and tired. Seeing him awake, he began to speak lazily. His voice was hoarse. "Morning."

Then, hearing his own voice, Yan Zhun raised an eyebrow and said slowly, "Seems like I got infected."

Pei Ran was at a loss for words.

Pei Ran looked away first. His right fist clenched, and he felt his palm heating up, not knowing if it was just in his head. Yan Zhun's phone rang several times repeatedly on the table. It seemed extremely urgent.

"I'll go down and have a look." Yan Zhun said. Pei Ran nodded and did not understand why Yan Zhun asked for his permission before getting out of bed.

He soon found out the reason. Yan Zhun lifted the blanket and climbed over him.

The small shabby bed creaked, and Yan Zhun's supporting hands were planted beside Pei Ran's face, nearly touching him. He could even feel the heat from his arms. Pei Ran tried to breath as lightly as possible, and he became fully awake.

When Pei Ran was getting ready, he discovered that there were a couple of unread messages on his phone.

Lin Kang:
Pei Ran, who did you come to pick up last night?

Lin Kang:
...Su Nian took Luo Qingshan away.

Pei Ran:
That's good.

Lin Kang:
???

Yan Zhun had already gotten dressed. He sat in Pei Ran's chair, played with his phone and looking tired.

A call came in. Seeing the caller, Yan Zhun couldn't help but look at the time.

"Bro!" Lin Xuhuan's voice was especially energetic.

Yan Zhun asked lazily, "Didn't you sleep?"

Lin Xuhuan was one of those pro gamers who practiced day and night. He usually got up at two or three o'clock in the afternoon and didn't sleep until dawn. He was confused for a moment, then said slowly, "I played for two days then got too tired, so I went to bed early yesterday, and I've been up for over an hour... Bro, what's wrong with your voice? It sounds like a broken gong." Lin Xuhuan was exaggerating a bit, but Yan Zhun's voice really was hoarse.

"Cold," said Yan Zhun. "What's up?"

"Yeah." Lin Xuhuan said, "I got up alone in the base. The housekeeper asked for a day off today. It's boring to eat breakfast by myself. Can I go visit you, bro? Let's have breakfast together." From the front came the sound of footsteps. Yan Zhun's eyes followed Pei Ran's movement, watching him reopen the medicine box from last night, rummaging for a long time before finally digging out a bag of lozenges.

Yan Zhun put his phone away, and then tugged at Pei Ran's clothes lightly, "Let's go out for breakfast?"

Pei Ran paused, then said, "Okay."

After hanging up, Lin Xuhuan had sent over the restaurant address, which was a very famous Cantonese dim sum place.

Pei Ran tore open the package of lozenges and squeezed out one to Yan Zhun. "Do you feel awful?"

Yan Zhun leaned over took the minty lozenge in his mouth.

"No." He got up from Pei Ran's chair, raised his hand and

pressed down a piece of Pei Ran's hair that was unruly. "I'll go out and make a phone call. Take your time."

Yan Zhun's palm was big and warm. Pei Ran thought of its warmth on his forehead last night. He was dazed for a long time before regaining his composure. He lowered his gaze and slowly folded the wrapper, tucking it inside his pocket.

Yan Zhun didn't have any call to make. He leaned on the wall of the dormitory corridor and opened WeChat to read the messages he'd gotten last night. There were more than 20, all of them from Luo Qingshan. All were questions or insults, and many didn't make much grammatical sense.

There were even a few voice messages that were more than ten seconds long. Yan Zhun had no interest in knowing what they contained.

The latest one had been sent half an hour ago.

Luo Qingshan:
Where did you sleep last night

Yan Zhun blocked him.

When Yan Zhun and Pei Ran appeared together at the restaurant, Lin Xuhuan was shocked.

"Did you two sleep together last night?"

Pei Ran almost choked on his tea.

Lin Xuhuan had heard another person's voice on the phone, but he'd thought that person was Yan Zhun's roommate.

Lin Xuhuan inched closer to Yan Zhun and sniffed, "Full of BabeRan's scent! Didn't you go back to your dorm last night?"

Pei Ran took off his mask, put the back of his hand to his nose, and sniffed. What did he smell like? He couldn't tell.

"Are you a dog?" Yan Zhun spoke curtly. "I was drunk. I only slept over."

"Drunk? Did you drink? Heavens... Do you want to stay at the hospital for half a month again? And you caught a cold from drinking?" Glancing at Pei Ran, who had also worn a mask, Lin Xuhuan said, "You slept over at his place even with a cold. BabeRan was infected by you."

"I passed it on to him." Pei Ran said honestly.

Lin Xuhuan was silent, then asked, "Should I stay away from you?" He pretended to lean back in fear.

Yan Zhun poured tea for Pei Ran without looking at Lin Xuhuan, "You can't be infected so far away."

Pei Ran was speechless.

Straight as a ruler, Lin Xuhuan automatically overlooked the tense atmosphere and got himself a piece of shumai. "You call this far away? I'm almost in your face."

After breakfast, Lin Xuhuan was wiping his mouth when he saw Pei Ran take out a box of medicine from his pocket. Pei Ran squeezed out a pill and whispered, "Hand."

Yan Zhun sat in a relaxed posture and spread out his palm to get a tablet of cold medication.

Pei Ran squeezed one out for himself, and they took it with warm water together. Lin Xuhuan's open mouth closed slowly.

It was normal to take medicine when someone was ill, but why did he think that something... well... seemed weird...

"When is the next game?" Yan Zhun asked.

"Next week." Lin Xuhuan recalled, "It was supposed to be the day after tomorrow, but something happened... There is a team accusing the organizers with fraudulent activities so now both sides are collecting evidence."

Yan Zhun raised his eyebrows, "Fraud?"

"Strange, huh?" Lin Xuhuan continued, "A team landed with good equipment and superb locations several times in a row, so it was reported, hahaha." The topic changed rapidly. Lin Xuhuan was always energetic when he told amusing anecdotes from playing games. After hearing him brag for a while, Yan Zhun finally got sick of it. He asked for the bill.

Before leaving the restaurant, Yan Zhun and Pei Ran put on their masks together. Lin Xuhuan frowned in a puzzled way. He somehow felt left out. Lin Xuhuan didn't plan to go back to the base so early. His lazy teammates wouldn't wake up until the afternoon. It was boring to train alone.

Passing an arcade, he couldn't help but stop. "Bro, let's go in and check it out."

Yan Zhun ignored him, looking instead to Pei Ran.

Pei Ran said, "I'll go buy coins." Pei Ran had rarely visited such places since he was a child. His parents loved art and would rather take him to galleries whenever he was free.

He looked around, and it appeared that only the hoops and the claw machines were within his ability. Lin Xuhuan was the polar opposite. He'd enjoyed a carefree childhood. As soon as they went inside, he asked Yan Zhun to race cars with him and play games. Pei Ran stood by and looked silently on.

Yan Zhun was definitely gifted at games—Lin Xuhuan never won a single game against him. "Bro, can't you cut me some slack?" Lin Xuhuan yelled.

Yan Zhun said, "You're so bad. I can't help myself."

Lin Xuhuan said, "Shit, I think you're great at doing that when playing PUBG with BabeRan! Just treat me like him!"

Yan Zhun held the steering wheel of the racing game in his hands and said, "Impossible."

Pei Ran pursed his lips behind the mask. His eyes did not show his emotion, but his heart was beating rapidly.

At the end of the game, Lin Xuhuan looked at the "defeat"

on the screen and said, "I don't want to play this, bro. Let's go for a motorcycle run."

"Play by yourself." Yan Zhun stood up.

"Where are you going?" Lin Xuhuan was confused.

"The coins are purchased by my boss," Yan Zhun held Pei Ran's wrist and pulled him away. "I'll play with my boss."

Pei Ran was dragged to a large machine surrounded by black curtains to give them space. The screen showed zombies.

Pei Ran collected his wits, "I don't know how to play."

Yan Zhun put the gun in his hand and held it up to point at the screen, and instructed him, "When you see something, hit it. If it gets close to you, run to me."

After playing for two minutes, Pei Ran sighed. Video games nowadays focused on more immersive experiences; the zombies seemed so close to his face.

Scared by the zombies running by, Pei Ran dodged to the side, accidentally bumping into the person beside him.

Yan Zhun was still. After killing the zombie in front of him, he turned to clean up the road in front of Pei Ran. At the end of the game, Pei Ran had 112 points, and Yan Zhun had 1419, breaking the single player killing record of the machine.

If Pei Ran scored over 800, they could have broken the dual-player record too. Pei Ran took off the headphones. His palms were hot after playing. "I'm not good at this. You can go get Lin Xuhuan."

Yan Zhun said, "I want to play with you."

Pei Ran paused, then realized how childish their conversation was. He was taken to the motorbike, and he sat down, only to find that this was the last game machine left empty.

Pei Ran didn't want to play alone. He wanted to get up. But then he heard the person behind him say, "Sit, I'll teach you."

How? Pei Ran was about to ask, but the game had begun. He sped out from the starting line, bumped into an NPC, and was about to run off track when he felt warmth at his back.

It was Yan Zhun's palm. Yan Zhun's hand was on his back, pushing him to go down one runway after another. By the end of the game, Pei Ran's back was sweating.

"Why are you playing this?" Lin Xuhuan came over with three cups of cold drinks. "Is it hot? BabeRan's face is red. Come on, have a cup of watermelon juice and take a rest."

Pei Ran took the drink, thanked him, and took a sip.

"I just broke a Star Wars record and left a selfie in the machine," Lin Xuhuan said triumphantly.

Yan Zhun said, "I'll take a picture and send it to coach."

Lin Xuhuan was confused.

But then, a phone pinged. The three of them had the same ringtones, so they all looked up at the sound.

Mom:
Xiao-Luo just sent me a message. Did you two break up?

It was Pei Ran's phone.

Pei Ran paused for a moment and picked up the phone to type a reply. Seeing the content clearly, Lin Xuhuan felt a little awkward. He looked at Yan Zhun and wanted to share the embarrassment with his brother, but he saw Yan Zhun drinking his juice without even meeting his gaze.

Lin Xuhuan cleared his throat and said, "BabeRan, you've even brought that guy to meet your parents?"

"Yes," said Pei Ran.

Lin Xuhuan, an innocent baby pretended to be mature, said, "You youngsters are always impulsive. Since he's met your parents, now you have to explain your breakup to them. Isn't it very troublesome?"

Pei Ran stopped for a moment. "Not at all."

The cold drink in Yan Zhun's hand had begun to pain him.

On the way back, Yan Zhun didn't speak again. Pei Ran replied to his mother's messages, and Lin Xuhuan chattered.

At an intersection, Yan Zhun stopped. "Tell me when you arrive at your dorm."

Pei Ran hesitated, then said, "Sure."

He could feel that Yan Zhun wasn't very happy, but he couldn't think of any solutions. After Lin Xuhuan got a taxi, Yan Zhun pulled on his mask and turned to leave.

But then his arm was gently pulled. Pei Ran walked quickly, and with a mask on, he could not help but pant.

He looked up at Yan Zhun after he quieted his breathing.

"My parents have many gay friends, so they're usually more perceptive. When Luo Qingshan was hospitalized, they realized on their own." Pei Ran paused. "I didn't take him home."

Yan Zhun paused, stunned, then finally asked, "Are you trying to sweet-talk me?"

Pei Ran didn't know how to sweet-talk others.

He just wanted to catch up and explain, so he did. He hesitated for a moment, then took out a milk candy and put it into Yan Zhun's pocket, just as back when they'd been outside that café. "Thank you for teaching me how to play games."

Yan Zhun felt butterflies in his stomach. He regretted that he'd only cared about teaching him how to play games under those black curtains.

After a bit, he reached out to ruffle Pei Ran's hair, and his eyes slowly showed a little smile. He said, "Pei Ran, you seem to like me a little bit now."

Just as Luo Qingshan received the reply from Pei Ran's

mother, Su Nian came out of the bathroom with a hot towel.

Su Nian spread out the towel on his hand and tried to help Luo Qingshan wipe his face. Luo Qingshan stopped him and said, "I'll do it myself."

Su Nian paused, then gave him the towel. Luo Qingshan absentmindedly wiped his face, keeping his gaze on his phone.

Luo Qingshan:
Auntie, I went travelling a while back and brought you some specialty products. Ran-Ran and I have been having some minor issues recently, so I can't ask him to be the messenger. When are you free?

Pei Ran's Mom:
Don't worry. Gifts aren't necessary. I don't need anything. Besides, we've been abroad of late. Thank you.

Luo Qingshan rubbed his sore temples and stood up.

Su Nian made room for him and grabbed his elbow, "Is everything okay? Can you walk?"

"Yes." Luo Qingshan's voice was hoarse. He patted Su Nian on the shoulder when he passed by. "Thanks for yesterday."

Su Nian's smile froze. It wasn't until the bathroom door closed that he came back to his senses.

He was very sensitive towards physical contacts between guys, and the pats that Luo Qingshan had just done? They merely showed his gratitude towards a bro, nothing else.

Su Nian ordered breakfast, and Luo Qingshan came out just as the delivery arrived.

"I bought soy milk and fried dough sticks. You'd better have some since you drank so much yesterday. An empty stomach is gonna cause you pain." Su Nian put the food on the table. "You look awful, not feeling well?"

Luo Qingshan looked very upset, not looking much better than last night. "Pei Ran came yesterday." He took two bites of the dough sticks, and couldn't help but start venting.

Su Nian asked, "And then? Did you two fight?"

Luo Qingshan drank a mouthful of soymilk, "Then he took Yan Zhun away."

Su Nian raised an eyebrow, his expression unreadable.

Luo Qingshan couldn't hold back. He was so angry, he had been keeping his temper in check since last night. If it wasn't for his friend's birthday, he would have smashed the bar.

Worried that he would make a scene, he had asked someone to take him away first.

"Yan Zhun..." Su Nian deliberated. "No wonder."

Luo Qingshan asked, "No wonder what?"

"Nothing. I just remember... we seemed at odds with each other," Su Nian said with a smile. "I was chatting in the group before and he insulted me for seemingly no reason. Did you forget?" Luo Qingshan certainly didn't. Su Nian continued. "But I remember that, back then, you and Pei Ran had only broken up for few days, right? That sure was fast... Didn't you find anything wrong with Pei Ran before?"

Luo Qingshan couldn't have his breakfast anymore. He put down the dough sticks and turned to take his coat.

Su Nian grabbed him quickly, "Where are you going?"

"The dorm," Luo Qingshan said. "Thank you for helping me last night." But he was stopped by Su Nian at the door.

Su Nian was frowning. He seldom had such an expression. After a while, he managed to say, "Qingshan, Pei Ran had cheated on you. You still want to find him?"

Luo Qingshan said, "It was Yan Zhun's fault."

Su Nian had other questions for him, but Luo Qingshan was too strong for him to stop, so he could only ask the one question he wanted to ask the most, "Bro, what am I to you?"

"A good friend." Luo Qingshan threw out these three simple

words. Then, he reached out and rubbed Su Nian's neck. His tone was as careless as his movements. "Go and get some rest. When I go down, I'll extend your stay for a night. Bye."

Late at night, Pei Ran sent the final draft of his work to his client and prepared to shut down the computer and go to bed. However, not ten seconds after sending out the message, DM notifications started to bombard him.

TZGisthebest:
Ah

TZGisthebest:
Ahhhhhh what kind of deity are you

TZGisthebest:
You are sooooo good! You are so great! What have I done to deserve your art!!!

P&EI:
... You've done a great job providing me with the information and photos.

TZGisthebest:
Great, excellent!!

TZGisthebest:
Can I post on Weibo, please? Can I print it out and take it to the competition site as a poster? **[praying]**

P&EI:
Yes, but the price I quoted is for private use. If you're going to make profit from it, you'll need to discuss the price with me further.

TZGisthebest:
Got it! You're so beautiful and kind-hearted!

P&EI:
...

This was not the first time Pei Ran had been praised like that. Fans online seemed to think of him as a girl all the time.

After handing in the manuscript, Pei Ran breathed a sigh of relief and shut down Weibo.

His sight fell on the last file on the desktop. After a few seconds, he double-clicked to open it. The boy in the picture looked distant, the TZG team uniform loosely draped over his shoulders. His fingers were on the keyboard casually. Behind him was a slightly messy training room with several empty gaming chairs and clothes of other teammates strewn about.

Yan Zhun perfectly blended into this environment, as if he was a professional e-sports player. Pei Ran quietly looked at it for a while, until the new message notification arrived.

Yan Zhun:
Lin Xuhuan will celebrate his birthday the day after tomorrow. Would you like to go to the base together?

Pei Ran:
No, he didn't invite me. It's bad to show up without leave.

Yan Zhun:
He was going to ask you but I volunteered for the job.

Pei Ran:
...

Yan Zhun:
I'll see you in the evening the day after tomorrow?

Pei Ran:
OK

Yan Zhun:
Go to bed early

Pei Ran replied, "You too," and exited the chat. Then, he blurred out the TZG team logo in the image, transferred it to his phone, and posted it on Weibo.

After washing up, there were hundreds of comments under that post. Pei Ran seldom commented back, but he felt particularly keen tonight, lying on one side of the bed with his phone and browsing through the comments one by one.

> Ahhh, it's a handsome E-sports player! Beautiful! I see a lot of differences from your previous art style. Is it a draft for a commercial commission?

> I feel like it's fanart?

P&EI:
Not a commercial commission nor fanart.

> An OC? Is there a follow-up? Want to see more!

P&EI:
It's someone from irl.

> There's such a handsome guy irl?! I don't believe it! It must have been edited!

P&EI:
Yes, there is.

> Wait a minute. This background, as a fan of e-sports, I don't know why but it looks familiar?

> So I'm not alone! Is this an E-sports player? It doesn't make sense. I should have remembered if someone was this handsome.

P&EI:
Not a player.

After sending out that reply, Pei Ran thought about it and added more seriously:

P&EI:
But he's also very good at video games.

Later, he intermittently responded to a few more comments. He didn't close Weibo until he felt sleepy and didn't think of it again after waking up. Posting his art on Weibo was just a way to save or commemorate pictures for him. He didn't do it for the feedback.

On Lin Xuhuan's birthday, Pei Ran had no classes. He went out early in the afternoon to buy a present. When he came back, he saw Yan Zhun standing outside campus, wearing a black baseball cap, a white sweater, and a mask, holding two cups of room temperature milk tea in his hand.

He had a great physique, garnering much attention from

the passersby, both from men and women. Yan Zhun turned around and met his eyes.

Yan Zhun walked up to him and handed him the milk tea, then lowered his gaze and asked, "What did you buy?"

Pei Ran said, "A very small massage gadget for the neck and shoulder."

Very small?

Yan Zhun looked at the sizeable bag and raised an eyebrow, but he didn't comment. Since they were still in the middle of a tournament, Lin Xuhuan's birthday was celebrated at the base. When they arrived, a small feast was served with plenty to drink. The room was bustling.

When Lin Xuhuan opened Pei Ran's gift, he held it in his hand and yelled, "Hey, look! Now that's a proper gift! Won't you be ashamed of the shit you sent me..."

"What did they send you?" the coach asked.

"Free socks from buying shoes, umbrella from a bank's charity event with the fucking logo on it... Am I a garbage can?" Lin Xuhuan was furious. He pointed at the raider and said, "This fool even sent me 5 GB of porn!"

With great righteousness, the raider said. "You think I wanted to? If it wasn't for the tight budget, I wouldn't have sent that. What kind of disaster is this month? Why do I feel like everyone around me has a birthday this month?"

"Well," Lin Xuhuan said, "if I hadn't seen you spending twenty thousand yuan for a female streamer last night, I would have believed it."

Pei Ran was a bit at a loss.

Lin Xuhuan had enough fun. He took a picture of the food to share it with his fans on Weibo.

Lin Xuhuan always liked to talk about his fans, which

he did have a lot of. The number of Weibo fans he had was among the top three in the e-sports circle. He was most definitely one of the advertisers' favorites.

As such, as soon as he logged in his Weibo, he was overwhelmed by the enthusiasm of his fans.

Most of them wished him a happy birthday. Some of them directly sent him money, and a small portion sent special birthday gifts. Lin Xuhuan's smile widened as he looked at it all. When he saw a private commission sent by one of his fans, he couldn't help but let out an excited swear.

It was sent by a fan named "TZGisthebest." In the picture, he looked cool and handsome, with a trophy in his hand. Lin Xuhuan kept looking at it, then he couldn't help but reply:

> You're such a good artist.

Within a few seconds, the person at the other end went crazy, and sent several "ahhhhh" in succession to calm down.

TZGisthebest:
No, no, no, wait! It's not my work, it is from **@P&EI!**

Curious, Lin Xuhuan entered that person's homepage.

Pei Ran was always quiet when eating. Even in such a noisy environment, he seldom opened his mouth. He only laughed when he heard something funny.

Having spent so much time together, they were all pretty close friends. So, when the raider poured alcohol for himself and noticed the empty cup in front of Pei Ran, he automatically went to top him off. "Pei Ran, you can have some—"

Yan Zhun covered the cup with his hand, "He doesn't drink."

The Raider was confused and then said with a smile, "Why are you acting like his dad? Just a little bit is fine."

They were in the middle of a competition, so the coach only allowed them two small glasses of cold beer each, and only after a lot of pleading.

Yan Zhun looked at Pei Ran.

Realizing that Yan Zhun was asking for his opinion, Pei Ran said, "It doesn't matter. I can drink it."

The raider laughed, "See—"

"Shit!" Lin Xuhuan shouted, "Shit! Bro!"

He was so loud that Yan Zhun frowned. "What's wrong?"

Lin Xuhuan raised his mobile phone and turned around. "Look at the person in this picture! Don't you think it looks like you?"

Yan Zhun raised his eyes and glanced at it. Before he could look very carefully, the person beside him coughed violently.

Pei Ran was rarely flustered. He widened his eyes slightly, at a loss for what to do.

Lin Xuhuan was showing his art.

To be exact, it was his art of Yan Zhun. But... how? He didn't have that many followers on Weibo. This wasn't some commercial commission, so it had no external publicity. How could Lin Xuhuan have found it?!

Yan Zhun's voice floated from his side, "Let me see."

When he saw himself in the painting, Yan Zhun was stunned. Then, he opened the picture and studied it carefully.

After a while, he went to look at the ID of the blogger.

"P&EI".

"Damn. It really looks like you." The coach leaned over to look at it and said, surprised, "Isn't this you?"

Yan Zhun glanced at the person beside him. Pei Ran was looking down, playing with the vermicelli one by one.

He found it funny, and said calmly, "Who knows."

"What's more, I read the blogger's reply. They said that it's a real person who's good at playing games..." Lin Xuhuan said.

"Such a coincidence!"

The coach looked at it again, "Don't you think that even this background looks similar to our training room?"

Pei Ran ate without tasting the food, thinking that he shouldn't have been so lazy, directly referrencing the TZG training room like that.

"Wait a minute, bro. Is that possible?" Lin Xuhuan stroked his non-existent beard. "Could this person be a fan of yours from youth training? Although you have been away for many years, she has always kept you in her heart..."

"No." Yan Zhun said, "My hair wasn't this before."

Lin Xuhuan looked at it again and agreed, "True."

The raider clicked his tongue and said, "The more I look, the more it looks like you. It must be you... Are you being chased by a girl artist?"

Pei Ran froze. He felt like he was being called on in class. His heart was beating as fast as a drum.

"No." Yan Zhun said, "I don't know many artists."

The people on the table discussed the painting for a long time. Yan Zhun listened quietly until the person next to him was so embarrassed that he tried to bury his head in the bowl.

Then he said, "Enough, it's just a coincidence. Do you all want to play a training match when you are full?"

Although it was Lin Xuhuan's birthday, there was a competition the day after tomorrow, so they still had to train.

He didn't manage to eat any cake on his birthday last year since it all got wasted getting smeared on his face. This year, Lin Xuhuan simply didn't order a cake. Full of booze and food, they stretched and moved to the competition room.

As always, the coach arranged the audience seat for Pei

Ran. He walked at the end, shoulder to shoulder with Yan Zhun. When he came to the fork between the training room and the lounge, Yan Zhun pulled his finger. Pei Ran stopped automatically, but Yan Zhun didn't.

He brushed past Pei Ran and said, voice lowered. "It's beautiful. Thank you, Teacher Pei."

Pei Ran had been called "teacher" many times. Some of the people online who liked his art called him "Teacher P." When he participated in exhibitions before, the staff had also called him "Teacher Pei."

At first, he'd been a little embarrassed. Later on, though, he'd gotten used to it. Pei Ran walked into the lounge in silence. After adjusting the perspective for the viewing screen, the coach got up and said, "You can change the angle here. I have to go there and keep my eyes on them, you..." He paused. "Why are you blushing?"

Pei Ran was pale, so his flush was usually quite obvious.

He was used to hearing "teacher," but being addressed like that by Yan Zhun felt a little different. Pei Ran dropped his gaze, and he touched the place on his hand where Yan Zhun had made contact earlier. "I'm fine," he said. "Just had a drink."

The coach cast his mind back to dinner. Pei Ran had only had... a sip or two? Yan Zhun had blocked his cup afterwards, not letting anyone else give Pei Ran more alcohol.

"I'll open the window for a bit of fresh air then, to help wake you up. Should I ask the housekeeper for a glass of warm milk for you?" asked the coach.

"Don't bother. I'll be fine soon," Pei Ran said. "Thank you."

Then, once the coach left the lounge, Pei Ran changed the perspective so that it focused on Yan Zhun's character.

How Yan Zhun played in training matches was totally different from how he played with Pei Ran. His teammates were very good, so there was nothing holding him back. Thus, Yan Zhun's every move had a superior precision that was tangible even through the viewing screen.

Yan Zhun played the second ranger of the home team today. Although they didn't train together normally, they'd all known each other for a long time, so they had a good understanding of each other's abilities. They soon destroyed two teams and went to a small house in the wilderness to rest.

Yan Zhun was healing himself and studying the map, contemplating their next destination when he heard a thump.

Closing the map, he saw Lin Xuhuan crouched beside him. Dropped on the ground between them was a SCAR-L.

"Bro," Lin Xuhuan said in a saccharine voice, "I also wanted to give you a buff!"

He wanted to exchange it for Yan Zhun's fully kitted M4.

Lazily, Yan Zhun said, "Take your small shabby gun and scram. The enemies can see you through the window."

Lin Xuhuan swore. "Can't you just pretend I'm BabeRan?! I can pay for your company. I'll book five hundred hours!"

"I can't."

"Why?"

"You're not as cute as him," Yan Zhun said.

With that, the entire call fell silent.

Not just Lin Xuhuan, but their other two teammates also couldn't help but give him a confused look.

In terms of appearances or talent, Pei Ran was indeed superior to most ordinary people. He was pretty quiet, but he was a good guy—this, they all readily admitted.

But, "cute"???

"Bro, I'm not bragging, but if BabeRan's is cute, then I'm the world's biggest sweetheart." Lin Xuhuan was shameless with his words. "The type where you could harvest honey just by pinching my cheeks."

The other two chuckled, and Yan Zhun also smiled, but his was faint and mocking. "Then you should get this guy beside you to simp after you instead of those e-girl streamers."

The guy in question sneered. "I'd just as well start throwing money into water to hear the lovely splash."

Lin Xuhuan pinched him. "Asshole. Apologise to me."

The coach laughed as he took notes at the back, feeling suddenly nostalgic for back when they'd all been youth trainees and he'd also been new to coaching. They'd all been squeezed into the same little training room, bickering. Back then, Yan Zhun hadn't been as stoic as he was now, and he'd even swear sometimes. His hair had been cut very short then, and it had made him seem full of youthful vigor.

Yan Zhun didn't usually do training matches with the main team. Today was because their other ranger had a wrist problem, and the team manager had taken him to do acupuncture. They wouldn't be back for another couple hours.

Two hours later, Yan Zhun's attention was obviously straying. At the end of another round, he checked the time. "Hasn't him come back yet?"

"He's still receiving treatment right now. It's almost over." The coach looked at the date. "I thought you didn't have class today; what's the hurry? Why don't you just finish today's training matches? The doctor already told me, even when he comes back, he's not allowed to move his hands for the time being. He has to rest for a day."

"No," Yan Zhun said. "Someone is waiting."

The coach just remembered that there was a guest sitting outside. He thought and said, "Then I'll send him back first?"

Yan Zhun pressed the "ready" key, then said, "Last round."

It was a rejection. The coach considered it, then figured that it was a bit impolite to make a guest sit outside alone for so long. He compromised: "Okay, then I'll go and ask the ranger of the second team to fill in. When did you want to pack up and move over here?"

Yan Zhun no longer intended to live in the dorms; it wasn't a good environment, and the roommate was too annoying.

He'd wanted to rent at first, but the coach had found out and had badgered him into moving here to the base.

"Tomorrow," Yan Zhun said.

Once finished with training, Yan Zhun stretched and went into the lounge. Pei Ran looked up at the sound of the door.

"Finished?" Pei Ran was a little surprised.

"Yep," Yan Zhun said. "Tired of waiting?"

"No," Pei Ran said. "I like watching."

Yan Zhun walked closer to the screen and noticed his own game stats. He raised his eyebrows, "Have you been watching from my perspective this whole time?"

Pei Ran nodded honestly.

The coach's assistant came in with her phone. "They're all clamoring for a midnight snack. We're ordering from that seafood barbecue place. What about you two?"

"Nothing." Yan Zhun said. "He'll be turning in when he gets home, and he won't be able to sleep if he's too full."

They left the base side by side. Back from seeing them off, the assistant stood in the foyer, still on her cell phone.

Coming out of the restroom, Lin Xuhuan sent her a puzzled look. "What are you doing? Have you ordered the takeout yet? I'm starving."

"Yes," said the assistant. She followed him to the training room, then suddenly asked, "Xiao-Huan, do you think there's something going on between BabeRan and Yan Zhun?"

"What's do you mean?"

"I can't put my finger on it, but I just always feel like Yan Zhun is pretty considerate."

Lin Xuhuan looked at her with mixed feelings. After a while, he patted her on the shoulder. "You're overthinking it. I've known my bro for so many years, the only thing he has ever been considerate of is his keyboard babe."

Meanwhile, the inconsiderate Yan Zhun stayed with Pei Ran until the campus gates. "Time to go back, Teacher Pei."

Pei Ran's drowsiness from the ride vanished in an instant. He hummed in acknowledgement, then handed Yan Zhun the package in his hand. It was a massage gadget, just like the birthday gift he'd given Lin Xuhuan. No wonder the bag had been so big—there'd been two of them.

Yan Zhun asked, "You picked it up along with the gift?"

"No." Pei Ran dropped his gaze and said, "I've been eyeing it for a while." This meant Lin Xuhuan's gift had been the one that got "picked up" along with this.

The night breeze blew by, tickling at his heart. Yan Zhun's eyes seemed to smile as he said, "Thank you, Teacher Pei."

With all the "Teacher Pei", Pei Ran dreamed of being an art teacher that night.

Fortunately, before he could fret too much over his students, he was woken up by a call.

It was from Lin Kang. Pei Ran squinted at the time. It was 2 AM, he had only been asleep for half an hour.

Pei Ran cleared his throat, then picked up. "Hello?"

Anxiously, Lin Kang asked a pointless question: "Pei Ran, were you asleep?"

Pei Ran rubbed his eyes. "No. Is something wrong?"

"Yes, there is!" Lin Kang said. "The car just left. You should head over to the hospital, the City Hospital!"

Pei Ran was still confused. "For what?"

"You don't know yet?" Lin Kang asked. "Yan Zhun and Luo Qingshan got into a fight with each other!"

It was the middle of the night, and Lin Xuhuan was still live streaming when Yan Zhun called. He didn't even manage a proper goodbye to the stream when he left abruptly. The coach too was worried enough that he didn't even bother calling their driver; he got into the driver's seat himself.

"Which hospital?" Asked the coach.

"The City Hospital, on Xiansan Street." Lin Xuhuan said, "Bro, there isn't even a fly on the road. Drive faster!"

"I'm almost speeding!" The coach said. He glanced at the sidewalk, then suddenly stepped on the brakes.

Pei Ran was standing at the bus stop waiting for the bus. At this hour, taxis were usually queuing in front of entertainment establishments, making them very difficult to hail. The rideshare app was also currently having issues; he'd been waiting for a long time without getting a ride.

Guessing that Pei Ran was looking for Yan Zhun, the coach pulled over and opened his window to say, "BabeRan, you—"

"Could you please take me to the City Hospital?" Pei Ran interjected. "Thanks."

The coach was taken aback. "We're headed there, too. But don't you have class tomorrow? You should rest..."

Before he could finish speaking, Pei Ran opened the door

and got in the car.

The coach was speechless.

The whole way there, Pei Ran stared quietly out the window.

Lin Xuhuan kept glancing at him. Finally, he said, "BabeRan, don't worry, my bro has never lost a single fight."

"Has he ever had a fight before?" Pei Ran asked.

"Of course!" Lin Xuhuan got excited in reminiscence. "There was a youth trainee who had stolen his things. After getting caught, he got angry and damaged my bro's keyboard. Then, because he wanted to get substituted in, he even tried to add laxatives into our water. My bro caught him and knocked him down right then and there."

The coach looked at them in the rear-view mirror and said, "They're old stories, not worth dwelling on."

Lin Xuhuan shrugged and turned, asking, "By the way, BabeRan, how did you know where he is? He called you?"

"My friend told me."

Lin Xuhuan nodded. Fiddling with his hands, he said, "I wonder who the other guy was. My bro is usually pretty laid back; dunno what dumbass could annoy him into violence."

Pei Ran hesitated. Then, "His roommate," he said.

"His roommate? Luo something?" Lin Xuhuan paused, suddenly remembering something. He stared at Pei Ran. Finally, he said, "Isn't he..."

Pei Ran finished for him, "Yeah, my ex-boyfriend."

The hospital corridor smelled of disinfectant.

As they searched for the emergency room, Lin Xuhuan glanced anxiously at Pei Ran. *It's over*, he thought, *BabeRan might not have come for my bro, but instead for that ex of his.*

Pei Ran wasn't wearing much, just a thin long sleeve top

and a pair of jeans. His hair was a little messy, and the corners of his eyes were a bit red, as if he'd recently been woken up.

Lin Xuhuan swallowed. Would they quarrel later? That would be very messy. Lin Xuhan was much better at quarreling than at preventing quarrels. Deeply troubled by all these thoughts, Lin Xuhuan found the emergency room.

It was the middle of the night, so the place was pretty empty. His bro was sitting alone on the bench outside the emergency room. He was slouching in a rather relaxed way. His arms and face were covered with bandages, and he was gazing fixedly down at the ground, seemingly spacing out.

Hearing approaching footsteps, Yan Zhun turned his head slightly, and meeting the gazes of the newcomers.

Lin Xuhuan rushed up with a vigorous step and stood in front of them.

"Bro, damn, how did you get so badly injured? Does it hurt? That son of a bitch... Where is the kid? Don't tell me you lost! If you wanted to teach someone a lesson why didn't you call me in advance..."

The babbling annoyed Yan Zhun to the point of headache.

He raised his hand and waved it at Lin Xuhuan.

Lin Xuhuan breathed in. "What does that mean? Does your hand hurt? I'll go get the doctor!"

Hoarsely, Yan Zhun said, "Get out of the way. You're blocking me."

Lin Xuhuan was speechless.

Finally, he got out of the way, gaze wavering warily between these two men, internally preparing himself to get in between them and try to persuade for peace.

Pei Ran had been frowning this whole time. His gaze was lowered, studying the bandages near Yan Zhun's wrist.

Yan Zhun merely let him take in the sight, waiting a bit before making his move.

He reached out with a leg. Then, under Lin Xuhuan's nervous gaze, he lightly made contact with Pei Ran's shoe.

"I started it," Yan Zhun confessed. His voice low, he added, "Don't be mad... Teacher Pei. "

Chapter 08

Lin Xuhuan swallowed back down all the peacemaking words he had spent so long racking his brain for.

The last time Yan Zhun had gotten into a fight, his expression had been particularly frightening. Lin Xuhuan had been worried that Pei Ran would get scared, but now...

Lin Xuhuan had never seen his bro looking like this. Yan Zhun's eyes and eyebrows both drooped, and he exuded an air of downtroddenness that seemed at odds with his character.

Wait a minute. Downtrodden?

"Shit, bro." Lin Xuhuan inhaled deeply. "Did you win? You can't have lost, right? How many were you up against? Why did you pick a fight? That's not very nice at all!"

Yan Zhun's pretense of victimhood wavered.

If this had been in a game, he'd have shot his teammate.

Pei Ran's lips were a bit dry. He'd been in such a hurry to get here that he hadn't drunk any water yet. "Does your hand hurt? What did the doctor say?"

"It's okay, the injury is external." Yan Zhun paused for a

moment. "It hurts."

Lin Xuhuan became anxious. "It's still hurting? Let me take you to the doctor again. Hand injuries are no joke!"

Yan Zhun said nothing.

Pei Ran's tight shoulders relaxed slightly. He glanced at the vending machine not far away and stepped back, "I'll go to buy some drinks. What would you like?"

Even as Pei Ran walked off, Lin Xuhuan kept talking: "Come on, let's go to the doctor again while there's no one else here."

Yan Zhun leaned back. Calmly, he said, "It no longer hurts."

Lin Xuhuan was baffled.

Yan Zhun glanced at the figure before the vending machine and frowned. "Why did you bring him?"

Lin Xuhuan felt wronged. "I didn't bring him. We met on the way here."

"On the way?"

"Yes. Coach drove me, and BabeRan was standing by the gates of your campus." Lin Xuhuan's tone was casual. "I didn't even say you were injured. He came for his ex-boyfriend."

Yan Zhun, who'd been rolling his wrist, paused.

Lin Xuhuan continued, "But why did you fight him? Even though your roommate does seem a little... But still, he's BabeRan's ex-boyfriend. Couldn't you just put up with it a little more? You have no idea how awkward it was in the car on our way here..." Lin Xuhuan kept babbling. He'd always been a chatterbox. Even his fans, despite continuing to support him, always complained that he talked too much on stream.

When Pei Ran came back with a few bottles of water, and the sound of footsteps echoed in the corridor, Yan Zhun said to him, "Shut up."

Pei Ran had bought five bottles of water. He handed Lin

Xuhuan three of them and said, "One is for the coach."

Then he looked down and asked, "Where's Luo Qingshan?"

Yan Zhun looked up, Pei Ran's figure reflecting in his eyes.

There was a long pause before he rasped, "Level seven."

The elevator next door just opened, and two policemen came out and went straight to Yan Zhun.

"We've talked to the other guy, and he seems determined," said one of them. "But we still advise that you two try to reconcile. After all, it's not a big conflict, and you're both still young. A man should know when to yield and when to stand his ground. You started the fight, so just apologize."

The coach came from parking the car to heard the end of that speech. He rushed in front of Yan Zhun and said, "Yes, yes, all trivial matters. Thank you both for your hard work tonight. This is my kid, and you know how youths are often high-tempered... But anyways, what happened?"

The policemen looked at him, a bit confused.

The coach lowered his voice, saying, "He never tells us adults the truth."

The policemen seemed to understand. "No big deal. It was just a domestic quarrel, then the other one broke some of his stuff—nothing very valuable, just some massage gadget..."

Lin Xuhuan also got up to join the conversation, leaving Pei Ran and Yan Zhun alone, one standing, one sitting. Pei Ran listened in silence for a moment until his finger was hooked.

"Pei Ran."

Pei Ran hummed. Then he said, "I'm going up."

Yan Zhun kept hold of him. They stayed like that for a while, but then Pei Ran pulled his hand back, picked up a bottle of water, and opened it.

"Drink some water," Pei Ran said. "I'll be back soon."

The elevator door shut, and Lin Xuhuan returned, having gotten bored again. "Did BabeRan go look for his ex?"

Yan Zhun took a sip of water, turned, then asked in a low voice, "Do you know what 'ex-boyfriend' means?"

Lin Xuhuan was taken aback. "Yes..."

"If you know, then don't bring it up again. There is no such person," Yan Zhun said, "understand?"

There was barely anyone in the hospital so late at night. Pei Ran saw Luo Qingshan instantly; he was sitting on a bench and making a phone call.

"It's okay. Don't come here. I didn't get hurt... Of course I'll make him pay..." Hearing the sound, Luo Qingshan looked up and was stunned. Then he said, "I'm busy now, gotta go."

Luo Qingshan's injuries were obviously much more severe than Yan Zhun's. On his face were bruises and two large patches of gauze. His mouth was still blue, and he had various injuries on the rest of his body too.

Eyes alight, he straightened his posture and said, "Babe..."

"Don't call me that." Pei Ran handed him the water.

Luo Qingshan paused, took the bottle, gulped a mouthful, and pursed his lips. "Why did you come over?"

"Lin Kang called me."

"Is he insane to call you this late?" Luo Qingshan scolded, and then snuck a look at Pei Ran.

Pei Ran sat beside him. There was some space between them, but he could smell Pei Ran's fragrance. "He must have woken you up."

"No," Pei Ran said.

After Luo Qingshan capped the water, Pei Ran asked, "What would make you agree to make a settlement?"

Luo Qingshan froze, his gentle expression fading away.

He met Pei Ran's gaze, eyes filled with sadness and powerlessness. After a long time, he said with great difficulty, "Pei Ran, why did you become this way?

"How is Yan Zhun better than me?" he couldn't help but complain. "Is it worth breaking up with me for him? I used to be good to you. The years we've been together have meant nothing to you, right?" He continued, "You don't have to deny it. That massage gadget must have been from you. I can tell at a glance that the brand is niche and hard to find. No one would use it except you."

"Yes, I bought it," Pei Ran said calmly. "But he is not Su Nian, and I am not you."

Luo Qingshan's throat tightened. He couldn't speak.

Pei Ran was wearing a look that he knew too well. He had always been like this back when Luo Qingshan had been courting him incessantly. No matter how hard he'd tried, Pei Ran wouldn't respond. But Luo Qingshan felt guilty and ashamed. He refused to admit to being in the wrong, as if pushing away the fault could lessen his own responsibility.

"Pei Ran," Luo Qingshan couldn't help but ask again, "have you ever liked me?"

The hospital had resumed its peace and quiet, with only the clock ticking overhead. Luo Qingshan lowered his head and laughed bitterly. He was about to say, "Forget it," but then—

"Yes," Pei Ran said.

Some time ago, Pei Ran had stayed up late thinking about this question. It hadn't been until he'd almost fallen asleep that he'd remembered when he'd experienced such feelings.

In high school, Pei Ran's homosexuality had been discovered by his classmates through a computer search record. Some of the boys in his class hadn't been able to accept it, and that had been Pei Ran's first experience of schoolyard violence.

Textbooks had been torn; school uniforms had been cut during breaks; stationery had disappeared, and even insults had been written behind his back.

Then Luo Qingshan had confessed his feelings to him, and new textbooks, new uniforms, and new stationery had appeared in his desk. It had been at point that he'd begun to pay attention to Luo Qingshan.

The door of the doctor's office suddenly opened, breaking the silence between them. The doctor passed by with a cup of water and looked at them suspiciously. He didn't understand why the patients were staying in the hospital so late at night.

Pei Ran looked down when his phone pinged.

Yan Zhun:
Teacher Pei

It showed that the other side was typing for a while, but then an irrelevant message popped up.

Yan Zhun:
Lin Xuhuan is so noisy

Pei Ran locked his phone and went back to the conversation. "This incident is pretty trivial, you know this. We still have hope of coming to a private settlement. Just tell me your conditions. I'll unblock you, just message me what you want."

Pei Ran got up, hesitated, then said, "You should rest soon."

Luo Qingshan clenched his jaw, silent.

This whole time, Pei Ran never asked him whether he still hurt, whether he was comfortable.

Pei Ran was two steps away when he heard from behind him: "Pei Ran, is it really over between us?"

Pei Ran turned back, then solemnly said. "Yes. Goodbye."

Back on the first floor, Pei Ran stepped out of the elevator. Beside Yan Zhun stood two middle-aged people, a couple.

Before he could get a proper look, he was pulled aside by Lin Xuhuan. "BabeRan, you back already? Don't go over yet. It's awkward still." Lin Xuhuan stepped closer and whispered, "His parents."

The man looked grim when talking to the doctor, and the woman looked anxiously at her son, who was sitting before them and typing on his cell phone.

As soon as the message was sent, there was a ping nearby. Yan Zhun raised his head and met Pei Ran's eyes.

Yan Zhun's father just finished talking to the doctor, and he saw him off as his wife went to help her son stand. Only, Yan Zhun avoided her hand. "I can walk by myself, Mom."

His mother paused, then nodded, "Fine, fine. Then be careful." When the family of three walked closer, Lin Xuhuan automatically stepped back.

Maybe it was the past words of Yan Zhun's father that held swaying power, or maybe his bearing now was just that stern, but Pei Ran felt an inexplicable sense of awe and respect.

Yan Zhun's father stopped in front of them. The corridor fell into silence.

After a stretch of time, he said, "It must have been troublesome for you to have come so late at night."

One short sentence—spoken as if to underlings.

"Not at all. We're all friends," said the coach.

His father nodded and turned away. Yan Zhun walked to Pei Ran and stopped.

They were very close. "I asked them give you a lift back."

Pei Ran gave his assent.

Yan Zhun remained standing there. He lowered his voice,

then said, "Teacher Pei."

Pei Ran hummed a response.

Yan Zhun looked down. "The massage gadget you gave me. I accidentally broke it."

"I know."

"I liked it a lot," Yan Zhun said. "I wanted to hide it."

"You'll have a new one, tomorrow." Pei Ran raised his hand, curled his index finger, and touched the gauze on Yan Zhun's wrist very lightly. "Sleep well tonight. Careful of your hand."

There was dead silence in the car all the way back.

Yan Zhun's mom sat in the front passenger seat. She first looked at his sullen husband and then looked back at her son.

Yan Zhun slouched lazily in the car, expression relaxed, and looked down at his phone.

"Xiao-Zhun, it's easy to get carsick if you play on your phone in the car," Yan Zhun's mother reminded gently.

His father snorted coldly. "If he listened to you, he wouldn't have made you rush to the hospital for a talk with the police so late at night." His voice was as cold as ever. So was his expression. He glanced in the rear-view mirror and said, "Only your mother is willing to take care of you."

"You came too," Yan Zhun said.

Yan Zhun's father was speechless for a moment. Then, he said, "I'm here to drive her, not to see you."

Despite his harsh words, Yan Zhun knew that his father did care about him, so he just nodded and agreed without arguing.

Yan Zhun's mother clutched her purse and asked, "Xiao-Zhun, those boys just now, are they friends from when you play games?"

Yan Zhun gave a placid hum.

His mother continued, "The one who was speaking with you earlier, is he a new member?"

"No, he isn't," Yan Zhun said.

His mother nodded and said, "They came here for you at night. Next time, you should remember to thank them."

Yan Zhun agreed.

"So, why did you get into a fight with that person tonight?" Yan Zhun's father was silent for a long pause before asking, "Were you bullied?"

"No," Yan Zhun said. "I bully others."

His father frowned and glared at him from the rear-view mirror. "What did that boy break? Was it worth a fight?"

Yan Zhun stared out the window, saying, "Yes."

"Come on, it's all over. Don't be so tough on your son." His mother turned back and said, "Xiao-Zhun, was it a very valuable item? Mom can get someone to buy you another one."

The phone in his hand vibrated. Yan Zhun looked down.

Pei Ran:

Just got to my dorm. Are you home? Pay attention to the wound. Stay away from water.

Yan Zhun tapped on his phone. "No need."

Once they got home, Yan Zhun went straight to his room.

Yan's father was not a chatty person. After a few words in the car, this incident had finished. He went back to his room after his ablutions and saw his wife sitting at their bedside, spacing out with a worried expression.

"What's the matter?" He sat next to his wife.

"Nothing." Yan Zhun's mother fell silent for a moment, then suddenly said, "I haven't seen xiao-Zhun playing with friends for a long time."

She had attended a parent-teacher conference for Yan

Zhun in his third year of senior high. From the school gates to the classroom, then for nearly two hours of the meeting, Yan Zhun had just stood there, leaning on the railing of the walkway and not speaking to anyone.

At the end of his first year of university, she had gone on a whim to pick him up. The other students had all been joking around in groups. He alone had sat on a bench in the gardens. Then he'd seen her, and he'd simply said a quiet, "Let's go."

Yan Zhun's father frowned. "Wasn't he always like this?"

"But before, he'd at least been willing to socialize with his friends," said Yan Zhun's mother.

Yan Zhun's parents hadn't actually been opposed to Yan Zhun playing games at first, not until Yan Zhun almost had to get a gastrectomy. It was only when Yan Zhun's mother had fainted from crying, when both mother and son had gone on an extended hospital stay that Yan Zhun's father had strictly prohibited him from e-sports.

Yan Zhun had been stubborn at first, but then he'd seen his mother lying on the hospital bed, so many of her hairs seeming to have turned white overnight.

Without saying another word, he'd left the base with his luggage, stoic as ever. After that, Yan Zhun had become even more indifferent.

Yan Zhun's father was silent for a long time. Then he said, "Don't overthink it. Go to sleep."

The next day, Pei Ran bought the massage gadget after class. On his way back, he got a WeChat from Lin Xuhuan.

Lin Xuhuan:
BabeRan, we're having dinner near your school. Would you like to join us?

Pei Ran:
Is Yan Zhun there?

Lin Xuhuan:
No, he's not in school. Isn't he coming back the day after tomorrow?

Lin Xuhuan:
We're here. Come following your GPS. **[location pin]**

Pei Ran hesitated for a moment.

Pei Ran:
I still have work to finish, so I can't go. Enjoy.

Lin Xuhuan:
? So you won't come if my bro isn't here?

Pei Ran's eyelids twitched, and he prepared to explain.

Lin Xuhuan:
Wait a minute. Are you finishing my fans' commission? Fine, hurry back and draw carefully. Make me look cooler. It must be more handsome than the one on Weibo!

Pei Ran:
... Sure.

After getting out of the car, Pei Ran went to the studio.

He hadn't lied to Lin Xuhuan. He really did have homework to do, but the professor had given him plenty of time.

The studio was empty, and the whole world went silent after the door closed. Time passed without Pei Ran paying attention. He held the brush and pursed his lips, studying the work before him. Art was impossible without serenity.

He'd just torn off the top sheet of his sketchbook and had scrunched it into a ball when his phone rang.

Pei Ran got up to wash his hands and picked up the call just a few seconds before its last ring.

Pei Ran didn't get a response after his "Hello," so he asked, "Yan Zhun?"

Yan Zhun hummed quietly.

"What's the matter?"

There was a pause. Then, Yan Zhun suddenly asked, "Why didn't you keep your promise?"

Pei Ran froze. "What?" A few seconds passed, then Pei Ran saw the box beside him and realized what Yan Zhun had meant. "I bought it, but you're not at school."

Yan Zhun hummed again, still not very cheered.

Pei Ran hesitated, then asked, "Do you feel better?"

Having already lied once, Yan Zhun felt little embarrassment this second time around: "It hurts. I didn't sleep well."

Pei Ran frowned. He wanted to say something else, but the studio door opened just then.

Seeing him, the professor was not surprised. He just raised his eyebrows, "Pei Ran, you're here? Just in time, I wanted to see you for something. Come with me."

Pei Ran said, "Okay, please wait—"

"Go ahead," Yan Zhun said. "I'll hang up."

Pei Ran listened to the busy tone for a few seconds, then put the phone into his pocket. Holding the box of the massage gadget, he kept pace with the professor.

The professor didn't have anything significant for him. He just wanted Pei Ran to take part in a competition. Pei Ran came out of the office with the application form and took out his phone. The screen was empty of any new messages.

Pei Ran went to the convenience store next door, bought a bottle of water, put it on the box, then took out his phone.

Pei Ran:
Or I'll send it to you?

Two seconds passed, and Pei Ran typed, "Is it convenient," but before he could send it, the phone vibrated again.

Yan Zhun:
[location pin]

Yan Zhun:
I'll call a ride for you. Wait at the station.

After getting on the car, Pei Ran carefully stowed the application form. He was about to tell Yan Zhun that he was on the car when he noticed a few unread messages in WeChat.

Lin Kang:
Pei Ran, are you there?

Lin Kang:
Well, I don't know... Take a look yourself.

Lin Kang sent a few screenshots of a group chat.

It started with someone in the group saying that Yan Zhun and Luo Qingshan had gotten into a fight.

> OMG... what did Luo Qingshan do? To make Yan Zhun fight him?

> Who knows, but Yan Zhun is weird.

> It must have been Luo Qingshan who provoked him. With Luo's temper, he could creat conflict out of a game of basketball.

There were a few more texts before an "insider" appeared.

Su Nian:
You sure are something. The basketball thing was because the other guy had fouled. How is that Qingshan's fault? And this time it was Yan Zhun who got physical first. Don't blame the victim here, OK?

> Then why did Yan Zhun hit him? For fun?

Moon:
Fine, if you want to know. Last time on Zai's birthday, Yan Zhun disappeared halfway through, do y'all remember? It was Pei Ran who picked him up. They were duo-queuing for video games together almost daily at one point. Also, Pei Ran had sent gifts to Yan Zhun.

Pei Ran zoomed in on the icon of the person named "Moon." The photo was a selfie; he vaguely remembered the girl as Luo Qingshan's classmate. She'd sat pretty close to Su Nian at the party before.

Moon:
Yan Zhun made a move on his bro's wife. He was the homewrecker, understand? Luo Qingshan was pretty civil when he only spoke to him, but who could have known that Yan Zhun would respond with violence?

After that were all surprised reactions and harsh insults. Pei Ran didn't want to read them all, so he backed out of the schreenshot. Lin Kang was also very conflicted. He didn't understand why he sent those screenshots to Pei Ran. He just felt that neither Pei Ran nor Yan Zhun would do such things.

He hesitated, then tried to withdraw the messages he sent, but the system said that it had been more than two minutes, so they couldn't be taken back.

Pei Ran:
Is this group chat still there?

Lin Kang:
... Yes. It's for organising casual basketball games. There are almost a hundred people in it. Yan Zhun is also in it, but he seems to have muted the notifications. Either way, he hasn't spoken in it yet.

Pei Ran:
Can you pull me in?

Lin Kang:
Not the best idea... This topic is still being discussed

Pei Ran:
It doesn't matter. I just want to say a few words.

Pei Ran:
Please.

Lin Kang hesitated, then finally acquiesced.

Moon:
Forget it. As the saying goes, a mistress will always need to fear a successor; those who cheat will get cheated on in turn. It's better to find them out early on. I just feel bad for

all the money Luo Qingshan spent on Pei Ran. I heard Nian-Nian say that it was at least six-figures.

Pei Ran:
@Moon You don't have to feel bad. It's all been returned. If I missed anything, just tell Luo Qingshan to let me know.

The group chat immediately went silent. Sensing drama, they all held their breaths.

Moon:
... wtf, who added him to this chat? Lin Kang? Why would you do this?

Pei Ran didn't pay any more attention to her. He opened the list of members and looked through. All the names looked familiar, and most of them were from the same major as Luo Qingshan and Yan Zhun.

Pei Ran had always been passive. Whenever he was misunderstood or misinterpreted, he rarely tried to explain himself. It was both troublesome and unnecessary. Even when other people took advantage of him, he rarely tried to get even with them. Now, however, he typed quickly.

Pei Ran:
The reason why Luo Qingshan and I broke up was because he cheated on me with **@Su Nian**, so we reached an agreement to break up peacefully.

Pei Ran:
This matter has nothing to do with Yan Zhun.

Pei Ran:
And **@Moon**, I'm a man, not Luo Qingshan's wife.

The onlookers were utterly shocked. Pei Ran wasn't too close with anyone. Although he was soft-spoken and polite, he seemed distant. No one had expected him to openly tell everyone that he'd been cheated on, much less directly ping the homewrecker. Some of the onlookers couldn't help but send a few rows of question marks.

Pei Ran:
Excuse my intrusion. Please continue as you were.

With that, Pei Ran left the group chat.

Following suit, Su Nian and Moon also quickly left it.

The group was in an uproar, and many asked Lin Kang to pull them back.

However, Pei Ran didn't know about this; the car had arrived at the destination, and he opened the door to get off.

Yan Zhun was standing at the gate of the park, looking down to read the chat history on his phone.

Hearing the sound of the closing door, Yan Zhun raised his head and saw Pei Ran come out of the car with a small package. He frowned slightly.

As soon as Pei Ran reached him, he plucked the box out of his grasp and stuffed a piece of candy in its place.

Yan Zhun said, "Teacher Pei, calm your temper."

Thinking that his expression had given him away, Pei Ran pursed his lips and said, "I am calm."

Yan Zhun was about to say something when his phone rang. It was a WeChat call from Lin Kang, who no longer felt any guilt from having been the informant. Now, he just wanted the tea, and he wanted Yan Zhun to read the WeChat messages. Besides, most of the people involved had already left the group, so there wouldn't be any open conflicts.

Yan Zhun answered the call on speaker mode.

Calmly, Yan Zhun said, "Yeah I saw."

Lin Kang was taken aback. "I meant that you should scroll back up a bit further. They were really spamming the chat. Anyways, Pei Ran just entered the group..."

"I know," Yan Zhun said. "And? Anything else?"

Lin Kang was left speechless. After a long pause, he said, "No, nothing else. I'll just... hang up now?"

Yan Zhun hummed and hung up in advance.

Pei Ran hadn't expected that Yan Zhun would look at the group chat. He frowned as he listened to the call finish up.

After a long pause, he said, "I'm sorry, I handled it poorly."

He didn't expect things to get so twisted.

Yan Zhun held the gift box in one hand and put the other hand in the pocket. "It doesn't matter."

It was a matter of reputation, and Yan Zhun had also been forced out of the closet. Pei Ran rather thought it did matter. "I'll talk to him later. This won't happen again."

"You don't have to, really." Yan Zhun paused for a moment, "Didn't you stand up for me?"

It had only been a few words.

Thinking back, Pei Ran realized how angry he'd gotten. He seldom acted so impulsively, but he had no regrets at all.

Pei Ran wasn't often expressive with emotions, so his anger had been especially obvious to Yan Zhun, who looked at him again and ruffled his hair. "Have you eaten yet?"

They went to a noodle shop. Yan Zhun wasn't picky; as a trainee, he'd been used to only two meals a day, one of which had often been pot noodles. It wasn't that the club had been too poor to properly feed them—it'd just been to save time.

They luckily occupied the last empty table at the restaurant. It was dinner time, and there was only one couple working away in the small bustling shop. Seeing that several bowls of noodles had been left at the pick-up window, Yan Zhun got up to go grab their meals on his own. Turning back for the table, Yan Zhun saw Pei Ran sitting quietly in the corner. He was staring at the empty jar of chopsticks in front of him, contrasting drastically against the mottled wall behind him.

Yan Zhun set the noodles down before him, pulled out a pair of chopsticks, and split it apart. Then, he put it across Pei Ran's bowl. Pei Ran ate the noodles carefully and slowly. When broth got on his lips, he soon licked them clean.

"Does your hand still hurt?" Pei Ran looked at Yan Zhun's wrist, "Do you need to go to the hospital again?"

In truth, Yan Zhun hadn't been seriously injured. His wounds were all superficial, bandaged for fear of infection.

"A little bit, not too bad." Yan Zhun ate very quickly. When he finished eating, Pei Ran was only half done.

Pei Ran took a bite of noodles. He looked at Yan Zhun, then at Yan Zhun's empty bowl.

When Pei Ran started to eat more quickly, Yan Zhun said, "Slow down."

Pei Ran swallowed a mouthful and said, "Almost done."

Yan Zhun was amused to see his cheek bulging. "I'm used to it," he said.

Pei Ran looked up, "Huh?"

"When I first trained to be a pro, we couldn't arrange training matches because we were so new, so we had to substitute for other teams. I was often called away in the middle of a meal," Yan Zhun said. "Later, I took all my meals at the computer, and most of them were noodles."

Pei Ran seldom heard Yan Zhun talk about these things. He hesitated, then asked, "Back then... Was the salary bad?"

"A few hundred to a thousand per month," Yan Zhun said. "I was fine. Many people didn't get paid when they first joined the team; they only got meals and accommodations."

It was a whole new world to Pei Ran. He raised a eyebrow, surprised and intrigued, and stopped eating so quickly.

6 or 7 PM was peak rush hour. When they walked out of the noodle restaurant, an impatient horn honked on the road.

"It's difficult to get a taxi at this time," Yan Zhun said.

Pei Ran nodded and was about to say that he could take the subway, but then—

"Would you like to see a movie?" Yan Zhun asked.

At the cinema, there were only two films available. One was an formulaic urban romance, and the other was horror film that couldn't even frighten elementary school children.

They looked at each other and walked out of the cinema. They then went to the nearby arcade. It was Friday night, so it was full of students. Almost all the machines had queues.

Meanwhile, the basketball court next to it was empty.

Leaving the court, Pei Ran somehow felt amused. Those emotions he had been bottling had already disappeared.

They had nowhere to go, so they walked aimlessly for a while, but neither of them asked to leave. It was winter, and wind blew harshly into their faces. Pei Ran sniffled.

Yan Zhun suddenly stopped and grabbed the corner of his coat, "Do you have your ID card?"

Pei Ran was confused. He looked back at him and then at the hotel nearby. His head went blank for a moment. After a long time, he said in a hoarse voice, "Yes."

And then he was taken away by Yan Zhun.

Every entertainment place has its down time during the day. There was only one place that made itself an exception.

At the internet café, boys sat side by side. The room was filled with words like, "Wow you really fucking suck," or "Do you have the super rare drops called 'bullets of healing'?" or "Fight with us, fight with us! What were you up to, hanging in the back? Did you think you were watching a cockfight?"

Yan Zhun pushed open the glass door, then noticed the person behind him slowing down. He gently raised his eyebrows. "You don't want to play?"

Pei Ran hesitated, then said, "I do."

Yan Zhun and the café owner were acquaintances. The pricing here wasn't cheap, but it was clean, disinfected and soundproof. Their guests enjoyed this type of atmosphere.

Yan Zhun easily got a two-person room. The chairs inside were spacious and soft, very comfortable to sit on. Yan Zhun took out his phone to read his messages. It had been vibrating constantly back in the noodle restaurant.

He gave a question mark to Lin Xuhuan, and the other party immediately called in response: "Bro, games?"

Yan Zhun entered the password to turn on the computer. "You don't have to train?"

"Friday today. I'm off," Lin Xuhuan said. "Come over? We just finished eating hot pot. We're on our way back to base."

Yan Zhun asked, "How many people?"

"Two, just me and a-Yu. The other two went to their girlfriends..." Lin Xuhuan paused for a moment. "What's up, bro, is there someone with you?" Yan Zhun didn't answer him. He held his phone aside to ask, "They wanna game. Are you in?"

Pei Ran asked, "Can you play with your hands?"

"It doesn't matter."

"Then sure," said Pei Ran. Lin Xuhuan asked a few more questions, Yan Zhun answered him half-heartedly. When he turned to see Pei Ran, Pei Ran had already logged on and had started a round on the training mode.

He hung up and asked, "Why are you using this mode?"

Pei Ran was staring at the targets on the screen. "I'm bad at the game... Just wanted to practice."

Although it was just a game, he couldn't always be slowing down his teammates. After watching for a bit, Yan Zhun suggested, "Try a light grip."

Pei Ran, "Huh?"

"Replace the muzzle to a compensator." The chair's wheels rolled across the floor, and Yan Zhun stood up. "I'll teach you."

Pei Ran was wearing headphones and focused on shooting. After a round of bullets, he asked, "How—"

Pei Ran stiffened before he could finish, immediately freezing in place. Yan Zhun had encircled him. His voice came from just behind Pei Ran: "What range did you want to practice first?"

They'd both taken off their coats after they'd come in, so they both only had a thin shirt on. The posture made Pei Ran's shoulder and back inevitably close to Yan Zhun. Heat exuded through the soft cloth. Pei Ran held his breath.

Yan Zhun hummed in question.

"...I don't mind, " Pei Ran said. "Teach as you please."

Yan Zhun picked a midrange target. "Try this one first."

Pei Ran obediently shot. After 40 shots, there were only a few bullet holes on the stationary target. If it had been a moving enemy, there wouldn't have been even one hit.

Pei Ran paused. He tried to explain: "Performance anxiety."

Yan Zhun laughed very softly, and his breath ghosted over Pei Ran's ear. Pei Ran became silent instantly.

"I see." Yan Zhun said, "Load."

Pei Ran loaded the gun and wanted to try again, but the back of his hand had been covered by another. Yan Zhun's palm was very hot, holding Pei Ran's hand.

"Each gun has its own recoil force. The M4 doesn't shake as much. You don't need to press as hard..."

Pei Ran was manipulated into moving the mouse. Bullets exited the chamber, and the target was instantly full of holes.

"If you still can't manage it, you can crouch or fall prone, and the recoil will lessen. Try it," Yan Zhun said, extending his other hand to hit the crouch command on Pei Ran's keyboard. His arm made contact with Pei Ran's neck. It was boiling hot. "Turn your head aside when pressing. It also reduces recoil. When you shoot, try to aim at your enemy's head."

As those words sounded lowly, Pei Ran held his breath and let himself be led. The gun was loaded again and again.

"See?"

Pei Ran paused, then said, "I think I get it."

Think so? Yan Zhun raised his eyebrows, wanting to ask. Then the phone suddenly rang. It was Lin Xuhuan.

Yan Zhun let go to answer the phone. "What's up?"

Lin Xuhuan said, "Bro, we're home. Get online now."

Yan Zhun said, "We're already online. Can't you see?"

"But I invited you and you didn't respond. BabeRan is also in a game."

Yan Zhun glanced at the screen and saw the invitation message, "I was teaching him to hold the gun. Wait a minute."

Pei Ran breathed a sigh of relief and quietly let go of the mouse while Yan Zhun was speaking on the phone.

His fingers were numb, and his palms were sweating. The back of his hand had been held for too long; he could feel the subtle coolness of the lack of body heat. The palm of his hand still tremored with someone else's pulse.

His headphones soon filled with Lin Xuhuan's chatter: "Come on, BabeRan, come here and shoot the tree." Lin Xuhuan joked, "Let me see the results of my bro's teaching. If he's good, I'll also go to him for a class."

Pei Ran could only shoot a clip of bullets into the tree.

The holes zigzagged and drifted off-center.

Lin Xuhuan had no response. He stepped forward and examined them. "BabeRan, what did my bro teach you..."

Pei Ran choked on his words, unsure of how to reply. Then put away his gun to go find Yan Zhun.

Yan Zhun had actually been a very precise teacher, but Pei Ran just couldn't remember anything. His only thought then had been that his heart had been beating faster than the gun.

"Bro, you'd better not mislead your students in the future. BabeRan, when you come to the base, I'll teach you how to press. Let's look at the longer run and learn how to control an AK with a quadruple sighting telescope directly."

Before Pei Ran had time to refuse, Yan Zhun interrupted: "Shut up. It's not your place."

Lin Xuhuan was in the middle of streaming. He was lazy in everything he did except for live stream. After all, as a chatterbox, he lived for the real-time feedback.

His viewers laughed at him, saying he himself could barely control an AK equipped with a quadruple sighting telescope, let alone teach others. Some asked who he was talking to.

"Who said I can't control an AK? Except for my bro, I have never seen anyone play with an AK better than me. If you don't believe me, go outside and shout and see who dares to respond," Lin Xuhuan said. "It was my bro who talked just then. Yes, that game companion before. Nice voice, right? ... Oh, he doesn't take orders anymore... Is he handsome? Are you kidding me? He's a real heartbreaker..."

"Are you finished?" Yan Zhun asked.

"Yup, I'm finished," Lin Xuhuan joked. "Where are you?"

Yan Zhun ignored him.

Pei Ran turned on the microphone: "Cybercafe."

Lin Xuhuan was surprised. "Why did you go there? You can come to our base directly. I'll cover your taxi fare! Which one are you at? I'll come to you."

As soon as he said that, several shots were taken at Lin Xuhuan's feet. He nearly jumped and screamed. "Shit, someone is nearby! I didn't even hear him! Damn scripter!"

He jumped up and down several times and looked back in horror. Yan Zhun had raised his gun and was aiming at him. The muzzle faced him directly.

Lin Xuhuan foze, then bit out, "Okay bro, I'll shut up."

Pei Ran laughed silently. Every time he played games with these guys, Pei Ran felt especially relaxed. After a game, even if he ended with a zero score, he'd still be in a good mood.

After searching the small wild area, he found that Yan Zhun and Lin Xuhuan had bumped into the enemies. Hearing the sound of gunfire, Pei Ran was trying to see if there was anything he could do to help when the person next to him suddenly reached out. Yan Zhun pressed the key for Pei Ran's inventory and took a quick glance at his gun and add-ons.

Pei Ran tightened his grip on his mouse. "What's wrong?"

Yan Zhun had shot down the enemy in two seconds and was on his way to loot. "Just seeing what you're missing."

Then Pei Ran opened the door to a new world.

He didn't even see what was in the enemy's loot box clearly, with how quickly Yan Zhun looted it. Lin Xuhuan and the other teammate hadn't even approached yet.

"Here," said Yan Zhun, glancing at the sad looking gun on Lin Xuhuan's back, "secretly."

Lin Xuhuan was puzzled, muttering to his viewers, "I just

saw a muzzle there... My bro wouldn't take it; I saw that he already had one... Am I blind?"

Then he turned around and saw his other teammates.

"Shit, bro, you're so fuckin' biased!"

Yan Zhung realized that he'd been found out. "Yep."

"It's not fair!" Lin Xuhuan yelled. "Put it back. I'll compete with BabeRan. It should go to whoever picks it up first!"

Pei Ran hadn't participated in the skirmish just now, and it was just a muzzle—he didn't care about it because of how his performance varied. He turned around, intending to acquiesce to Lin Xuhuan's demands.

"It was me who killed both of them, and also me who looted them. Whatever I get is his. How is it unfair?"

Lin Xuhuan didn't notice the strange logic in Yan Zhun's words. His gun was only missing this one last attachment before being fully equipped.

Seeing that there was no way out with Yan Zhun, he tried another tactic: "BabeRan, come on, give me this one first, and I'll give you the next one I find from killing enemies."

Pei Ran turned to Lin Xuhuan at first, then turned back with a few words from Yan Zhun.

Instead, Pei Ran said, "Maybe try searching the house?"

Lin Xuhuan shook his head, speechless. Pei Ran had really been led astray by his bro—he'd always been willing to share attachments before.

He glanced at the chat and noticed the strange atmosphere. He couldn't understand some the comments, but he did see one sentence: "Does Player 1 fancy Player 2?"

Lin Xuhuan double checked the numbers. Player 1 was his bro, and Player 2 was Pei Ran.

Xuxu:

My gaydar is blaring. There's something between them.

He hurriedly turned off his microphone and spoke to his stream: "Don't gossip. We're all bros! Ah, and the one called 'Xuxu,' turn off your gaydar. Nonsense!"

Although this was what he said to the viewers, Lin Xuhuan did feel slightly awkward in light of their comments.

"Is there a light grip?" Yan Zhun asked.

"Yes, I just got one," said Peir Ran. "I'll give it to you later."

Lin Xuhuan went in a random house, saw a light grip on the floor, and looked at the map. He was closer to Yan Zhun.

"Bro, I found one here. I'll give it to you," Lin Xuhuan said as he went to Yan Zhun.

But Yan Zhun brushed right by him and went to Pei Ran.

"Throw it to me."

Lin Xuhuan stood foolishly in place, holding the light grip in his inventory, and gazed at the two people in the distance. He blinked twice, dumfounded.

"Well." Lin Xuhuan dropped the light grip and cleared his throat. "Is the girl named 'Xuxu' still there... Please DM me. No, nothing important, just to chat."

They played in a team of four until 11 pm. Back at the café, Yan Zhun glanced at the time and turned on his microphone, "Let's call it a day." With that, he took off his headset, unheeding of Lin Xuhuan's response.

"Going back?" he turned and asked.

Pei Ran said "Yes," then sent a "Goodnight," to Lin Xuhuan before quit the game. Yan Zhun had already put on his coat when Pei Ran shut down the computer.

They left the room. The café was still full of patrons, but it wasn't as noisy as it had been during the day. They walked side by side, shoulders brushing one another. Pei Ran could smell the cool fragrance of Yan Zhun's winter coat.

A few noisy boys came in front of them. Pei Ran automatically turned aside, bumping into Yan Zhun's arm, who thought that he'd stumbled and grabbed his wrist.

Pei Ran froze. Before he could respond, those boys suddenly stopped before him. One of them raised his eyebrows.

"Pei Ran?" he asked. "Why are you here?"

Pei Ran looked at him. The boy had a familiar face, but he couldn't remember where they'd met.

"To go on the internet," Pei Ran said.

Hearing this, the other boy realized how dumb his question had been and laughed at himself. "Just you? Where's Luo Qingshan?"

Pei Ran remembered: this was a friend of Luo Qingshan's. He had gone to a different senior high, but they'd gotten dinner together just after high school graduation.

The other boy obviously also knew Luo Qingshan. He raised his eyebrows and asked quietly, "Who's this?"

"Pei Ran," the boy said, "Luo Qingshan's boyfriend, the one he's been with for several years."

The boy widened his eyes, it all clicked in his head, and said to Pei Ran with a smile, "Oh, oh, I've been hearing about you for a long time. Luo Qingshan used to tell us about you in the group every day. So annoying."

"Yeah, he's always going babe this and babe that. Super whipped."

"There's more, too!" When it came to embarrassing tales of a good bro, these boys didn't keep their mouths shut. "Do you remember that time when he got drunk in Soho? He kept bragging about having successfully proposed to Pei Ran, saying that they'd go abroad together after uni graduation to get a marriage certificate..."

Pei Ran felt the pressure on his wrist lifting; Yan Zhun had let go of him. Yan Zhun looked down, his expression unchanged. "I'll wait for you at the front."

Pei Ran was silent for a moment, then agreed.

These boys clearly had a good relationship with Luo Qingshan. Just his name alone seemed to be a topic of interest to them. Pei Ran listened a while before someone finally asked, "Didn't he come with you?"

"We've broken up already," Pei Ran said.

The atmosphere quieted down immediately.

These boys were stunned at first. Then they awkwardly looked at each other. In truth, they couldn't be blamed for the social misstep. After all, Luo Qingshan had mentioned Pei Ran in the group just last month, saying that he'd bring Pei Ran to a renunion dinner with them when he was free.

"Well, I see." The first boy ruffled his own hair, ill-at-ease.

"Well," Pei Ran asked, "anything else?"

"No..."

Pei Ran nodded, "Goodbye then."

Yan Zhun leaned on the front desk, doing something on his phone. The café owner spoke to him for a second but stopped when he realized that Yan Zhun wasn't very interested.

Yan Zhun wasn't doing anything specifically. He swiped around in his phone but didn't read anything. Luo Qingshan used to like showing off. He'd often call Pei Ran in the dorm, not bothering to avoid Yan Zhun. Yan Zhun had overheard countless calls, whether he wanted or not. At first he would go out for a smoke to give them privacy, but later on he'd gotten used to it, and he would just quietly listen to them.

Time passed, perhaps just a few minutes, perhaps longer. Yan Zhun could no longer stand still. He tapped the counter and asked the café owner, "Can I get a pack of cigarettes?"

"The brand you like is sold out." The owner took out his own box. "I opened the last one. You can take one, but you have to go outside. Can't smoke in here."

Yan Zhun took it and put it in his mouth.

"I'm ready, shall we go?"

The owner was about to give Yan Zhun a lighter when Yan Zhun suddenly took the cigarette out of his mouth.

Then he looked back with a casual expression and said to the person behind him, "Sure."

When the two people left the internet café, the owner was still pondering what had just happened. It had felt inexplicably familiar.

It was like...

Like his own reaction when he got out a cigarette and his wife suddenly appeared.

The night air was chilly. Other shops on the street had already closed. Only a few barbecue shops were still open.

They walked silently. The taxis were all headed to the street over, which had a bunch of nightclubs. It was a one-way street here, and all the cars that drove past were showing "Occupied."

Pei Ran looked down, thinking of what to say.

Yan Zhun seemed a little upset.

When the rain first started, a drop fell onto the tip of Pei Ran's nose. It was freezing.

The winter rain was unexpected, and it had come without any warning. With the heavy rain coming, the guests sitting on the street enjoying barbecue were all shocked. Then, they got up to hide in the restaurant.

Pei Ran was about to raise his hand to block the rain when someone wrapped an arm around his waist.

Yan Zhun pulled him to the nearby convenience store.

They didn't go inside. The building's overhang left them a dry strip to stand in. The store had also put out a bench here, probably so patrons could sit and eat sugarcane in the summer or oden in the winter.

The space wasn't big. Both of them had to sit with their legs held back to avoid the rain.

Although they had only been in the rain for a short time, Pei Ran had still gotten wet, and his hair was in spiky streaks.

Yan Zhun went into the store, bought a package of tissue, and pulled one out, "Come here."

Pei Ran wanted to say that he could do it on his own. After some thought, he leaned in as he was told.

Pei Ran's hair was very soft. Yan Zhun's movements were a little stiff at first, but they eventually softened.

They were very close to each other. The smell of Pei Ran got into his nose. The sound of rain blocked out all the unnecessary and unwanted noises. At this moment, the outside world seemed to have disappeared; it was just Pei Ran and him. In the dark, all those difficult-to-articulate notions which had been tucked away deep inside his heart reemerged.

He held his breath for a moment and let go of Pei Ran's soft black hair.

"Okay."

Pei Ran raised his head and looked at him.

The emotions in Yan Zhun's eyes were deep and heavy. He looked at Pei Ran in silence. After a long time, he said in a hoarse voice, "Don't look at me like that."

"Why?" asked Pei Ran.

Yan Zhun's sight fixed on a space below his nose. Then he said, "Or I will do something bad."

With that, Yan Zhun looked away. He scrunched his half-wet tissue into a ball, and then spread it back out.

He could feel that Pei Ran was still looking at him, gentle and appealing.

Yan Zhun's throat bobbed gently. He was about to say something when his shoulder was suddenly held, and something touched the corner of his mouth very lightly.

Pei Ran's heart was thumping loud, but he was already used to this strange and wonderful physiological reaction.

Yan Zhun's mouth was cool, just like the rain around them.

The short kiss had only gone on for maybe half a second before he blushed and wanted to retreat. But then his neck was suddenly held by a hand, pressing him from behind.

Yan Zhun refused to let him retreat. Turning his face slightly, he bit down on Pei Ran's lips.

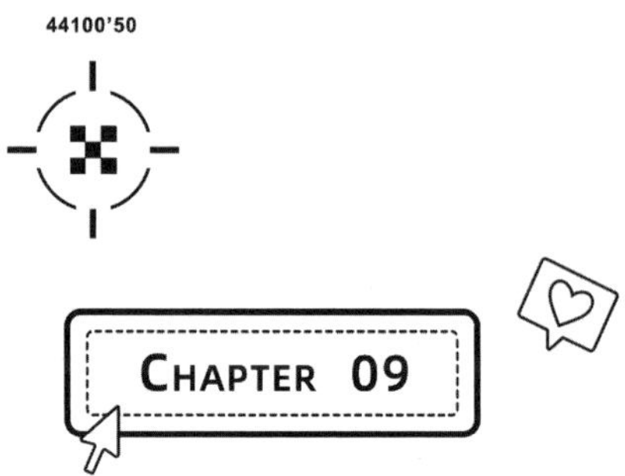

Unlike the last kiss they'd had, the one where his mask had separated them, Pei Ran could clearly feel Yan Zhun's bite. It was neither too heavy nor too light. Just when he started to feel the slightest bit of pain, Yan Zhun let go.

Thinking it was over, Pei Ran was about to relax his tight shoulders, but the strong hand on his neck remained.

Yan Zhun rubbed the back of his neck very gently. Then, he deepened the kiss with gentle and soothing care.

Pei Ran could no longer hear the raindrops. He was getting incredibly dizzy, to the point of feeling slightly anoxic. He held tightly on to Yan Zhun's clothes. When Yan Zhun pried open his lips, he instinctively responded.

Pei Ran gently licked the tip of Yan Zhun's tongue.

Yan Zhun felt a soft tug at his heartstirngs.

There were few pedestrians on the street, and all of them were in a hurry under their umbrellas; no one noticed them.

Their breath was hot and entangled in the rainy night. On the inside of the convenience store window was a spread of miscellany that blocked the view inside. Only light leaked through the gaps.

When Yan Zhun let go, Pei Ran's face and ears were a deep red. Pei Ran could barely swallow without feeling embarrassed. He released Yan Zhun's clothes and blinked rapidly.

Just as he was about to speak, Yan Zhun raised the back of his hand to help him wipe his lips.

Yan Zhun looked down and asked in a hoarse voice, "What did that kiss mean, Teacher Pei?"

Pei Ran realized just then that he'd been the initiator.

His face heated. Then, after a long time, he said, "Just wanted to. Sorry."

His tone was as placid as usual, and Yan Zhun almost couldn't stand it. H swallowed several times before he could say, "You can kiss me whenever you want. I'm all yours."

Yan Zhun looked down and straightened out his wrinkled coat. "Is this jaket comfortable to grip? I can change to a different one next time if it's not."

Pei Ran closed his eyes for a moment and decided to fuck it. "Pretty... comfortable."

The rain was gradually getting lighter. Many people were walking into it, and the shops had set up umbrellas outside.

Yan Zhun had already sat up straight. Their thighs were brushing each other's through their clothes, but neither of them moved away. A phone suddenly pinged. Pei Ran automatically pulled it out his pocket, but his elbow bumped against the table, and his phone thudded to the ground.

Pei Ran was about to pick it up when Yan Zhun bent over.

"It's dirty. Wait." Yan Zhun picked up the phone, pulled out a piece of tissue and wiped down the screen.

More messages came in. Yan Zhun glanced at the preview

on the lock screen, then quickly looked away. He handed the phone back to Pei Ran.

Luo Qingshan:
I heard xiao-Yang say they bumped into you at a cybercafe. I didn't have time to tell them, I'm sorry

Luo Qingshan:
I was playing basketball just now. I didn't know what happened in the group chat

Luo Qingshan:
Sorry

Luo Qingshan:
Can we still be friends?

Pei Ran had just finished reading the messages when the person next to him suddenly stood up.

"I'm going to buy an umbrella." Before Pei Ran realized, he'd already grabbed Yan Zhun's hand.

Yan Zhun stopped and looked down at him, "Anything you want to buy?"

Pei Ran looked at Yan Zhun's hand. It had a faint medicinal smell. After a long time, he raised his head and asked, "Can I be friends with him?"

For once, Yan Zhun was stunned to silence. He looked into Pei Ran's eyes, and seemed to sense something, "It's up to me?"

"Yes."

"Why?"

Pei Ran tried to control his expression, but he was blushing so hard that he felt he might start bleeding.

Just as Yan Zhun opened his mouth to speak, Pei Ran quietly said, "You're allowed... to make the decision for me.."

The person in front of him became silent.

Pei Ran regretted his words immediately after he spoke them aloud. He had never said such things before. Shyness and shame almost overwhelmed him. He started to let go.

Yan Zhun gripped him in return. "Pei Ran," he said, "I don't want you to be friends with him, and I don't want you to contact him, because I like you.

"You asked me what I wanted, allow me to make decision for you..."

"Because I do, too," Pei Ran answered.

Yan Zhun pursed his lips. With those words, his heart had silently exploded. He released Pei Ran's hand to ruffle his hair.

"Teacher Pei."

After a pause, Pei Ran responded with a questioning hum.

"Will you be in a relationship with me?"

Pei Ran's eyelashes trembled slightly. First, he hummed in acceptance. Then, a few seconds later, he said, "Yes."

Yan Zhun's hand twisted in his hair. He tried to hold himself back, then failed. "Raise your head a little, just slightly."

Pei Ran knew what was about to happen. His heart hadn't stopped pounding since they got to this convenience store.

He raised his head and got his second kiss of the night.

They finally went into the store together. The way the clerk looked at them was a little odd, as if she'd seen something.

Although they bought two umbrellas, they held the same one all the way to the car.

"I'll go back to campus tomorrow," Yan Zhun said.

"It's the weekend tomorrow. No classes."

Yan Zhun hummed agreeably. "It's to see my boyfriend."

After closing the door, Pei Ran told the driver the address, then looked out the window.

It was late. There were barely any cars on the road. The driver was on the verge of speeding, and the streetlights flashed past one by one. Pei Ran looked at it quietly for a while, then raised his hands and covered his face. His palms cupped his cheeks, and he couldn't tell which was warmer.

Pei Ran took a shower after getting back to his dorm. When he picked up the towel, he remembered the feeling of Yan Zhun drying his hair.

He slowly rubbed his hair and picked up his phone to read the unread messages. After he'd messaged that group earlier, he'd received a lot of direct messages and even some friend requests. He hadn't opened them yet.

Pei Ran had the good habit of almost always replying to the messages he got. After reading them, a new one came in.

Yan Zhun:
I forgot to say thanks for Teacher Pei's new gift.

Pei Ran dreamed all night of rain, convenience stores, and Yan Zhun. When he woke up, he was still a little dazed, staring at the ceiling for a long time. After his morning ablutions, he made himself a cup of coffee with biscuits for breakfast.

It was not until Luo Qingshan sent another WeChat message that Pei Ran remembered: he still hadn't replied to him after the convenience store last night.

He'd unblocked Luo Qingshan after that night at the hospital, mostly for Yan Zhun's sake, but also because he'd remembered a few more things that he hadn't returned.

Pei Ran couldn't remember how much the high school uniform cost, nor those textbooks, so he straight up transferred him 1000 yuan.

Luo Qingshan:
?

Pei Ran:
The cost for school uniforms and textbooks in high school. Thank you for the past.

Luo Qingshan:
?

Luo Qingshan:
What uniforms and textbooks?

Pei Ran:
The ones you put in my drawer.

Luo Qingshan:
Did you remember wrong?

Luo Qingshan:
I've never put uniforms or textbooks in your drawer.

Luo Qingshan:
I don't even know where to buy those things.

Luo Qingshan:
There's no class today. Why did you wake up so early?

Pei Ran held his phone and was slightly distracted.

Thinking back, Pei Ran hadn't actually verified the matter. Luo Qingshan had been the only one to show overt kindness to him back then, so he'd subconsciously attributed it to him.

Pei Ran's palm tingled from the notification vibrations of Luo Qingshan's messages; he'd spaced out for a while. Luo Qingshan seemed to have realized that something was up, and he'd asked a lot of follow-up questions.

Pei Ran:
Never mind. And no.

Luo Qingshan:
No what?

Pei Ran cleaned up the remains of his breakfast as he typed.

Pei Ran:
No, let's not be friends.

Luo Qingshan didn't send any more messages.

Pei Ran typically went to the studio when he had nothing to do on the weekends. Today, a classmate had requested that he go to the studio. He refused, then started a movie to while away the time. Two lines into the film, he looked down at his mobile phone.

The icon of the White Rabbit candy lay quietly in the list. The latest message had been from 2 AM. He glanced at it a few more times, then continued to scroll down, finding the group chat for his high school class.

The group chat was pretty dead. People only chatted in it every week or two. Pei Ran looked through the group members one by one, trying and failing to figure out who'd put those things in his drawer. At the end of the 90-minute movie, Pei Ran didn't even know what the plot had been. Too lazy to watch it again, he browsed idly for a new one.

His phone suddenly vibrated, and he looked down.

Yan Zhun:
Are you awake

Pei Ran:
Yep

Yan Zhun:
I'm at the campus gates.

Pei Ran put on his coat and went out the door. Yan Zhun was tall and slender, and he was wearing his hat so low that when he lowered his gaze, the brim of hat blocked out his eyes. Standing at the gates, he was very eye-catching.

When Pei Ran approached, Yan Zhun was facing away.

"I'm busy today." Yan Zhun said into his phone.

On the other end of the call, the coach said, "Just two training matches, they won't take long... What are you doing?"

Annoyed, Yan Zhun said straightforwardly, "Date."

The coach had initially prepared a whole speech, which now stuck in his throat. It took a long time before he could squeeze out a question: "Huh?"

A few seconds later, he asked, "Date... You? With whom?

Someone from your school?" He had known Yan Zhun for so many years. Dating aside, at one point he'd even thought that Yan Zhun had gone to an all-boys high school and university.

The coach suddenly remembered that when Yan Zhun had been a youth trainee, PUBG had been at its height of popularity. Even though e-sports hadn't been properly popularized then, the young trainees had gotten plenty of attention. Yan Zhun had been the most popular among his teammates.

At the time, there'd even been a small influencer who'd asked for Yan Zhun's number, but Yan Zhun had refused without even asking after the person's name or appearance.

Yan Zhun interrupted the coach's thoughts with a hum.

"Well, then you... go and have a good date." The coach wanted to tell him to be kind to the girl, but, on second thought, maybe she liked how aloof Yan Zhun was. "Why don't you bring her to our base?"

Yan Zhun was about respond when a passerby glanced behind him. Sensing something, Yan Zhun turned around. He saw the person standing behind him and lifted an eyebrow.

Though it was winter, it was still sunny at noon, so Pei Ran hadn't buttoned up his coat. He wore a white shirt inside. He'd dressed in a hurry, so the collar was crooked. He was looking down at Yan Zhun's luggage.

Yan Zhun was surprised for merely a second. He took off his hat and put it on Pei Ran.

He adjusted the hat as he continued the call. "No," he said.

By the sound on the other end, there were probably others nearby the coach, among whom Lin Xuhuan stood out the most. Vaguely, Yan Zhun heard, "I don't believe it."

Yan Zhun said, "I'm hanging up now if there's nothing else."

"Wait, there is," the coach said. "Are you coming tonight?"

"Yep."

The coach responded with an "Oh," then asked nosily, "Not spending the night outside?"

Yan Zhun hung up the phone.

To block out the sun, Yan Zhun had pressed the brim of his hat very low. Pei Ran had to raise his head to meet his eyes, "Have you been waiting for long?"

"Just got here," Yan Zhun said. "Is it cold?"

Pei Ran shook his head and looked at the bag beside his leg again. Yan Zhun glanced at him and explained, "I can't get used to living in dorms. I'm moving to the base tonight."

In truth, it wasn't a matter of being used to living in dorms. He could no longer be roommates with Luo Qingshan.

Pei Ran understood immediately. He looked down and kept silent. Before he could say anything, Yan Zhun stretched out and touched the back of his hand. It was icy cold.

"But they have an interview this afternoon. I'll go later this evening." Yan Zhun said, "Before then, can you take me in?"

In TZG base, the coach hung up the phone under everyone's intense gaze.

Because he was holding a cigarette in one hand, he'd been calling on speaker the whole time.

Three seconds of silence, then—

"I never expected"—The assistant lit up a cigarette—"that Yan Zhun would find someone before I did..."

The raider chimed in: "I don't want to train any more. I want to go to his school and be a stalker."

"What does his girlfriend look like?"

"I don't know, but she's got to be divine to tempt that stubborn monk."

"It's just, I'm really curious. What kind of girl does he like?

Cute? Sexy? Smart?"

"Male or female?" Lin Xuhuan had been pondering for a long time before suddenly asking that.

The others stayed quiet for a moment. The raider picked up the tissues on the table and threw it at him, "Why don't you say dead or alive?"

Lin Xuhuan was also surprised by what he'd blurted out. He picked up the box and threw it back, laughing and cursing.

"But for sure this was a bit unexpected," the assistant said. "There was no sign."

"What if it was love at first sight?"

The coach put out his cigarette and said, "Stop talking nonsense. You still have training match. I'll ask the boy from the second team to take his place."

Lin Xuhuan walked behind them. He wrinkled his nose. The comment from his stream last night floated in his mind.

In the end, he couldn't help it. He took out his phone to send a message as they waited for the substitute to arrive.

Lin Xuhuan:
BabeRan, where are you?

A few minutes later, the reply came back.

Pei Ran:
Dorms. What's up?

Ugh. That girl who'd sent the comment must've been messing with him. He too was pretty ridiculous for believing that so-called "Xuxu."

Lin Xuhuan:
Not much, I was just thinking of you. Come to the base to play with me when you're free. I'm going to teach you how to control a gun with a quadruple sighting telescope.

When Lin Xuhuan's message had come, Pei Ran's phone just so happened to have been in Yan Zhun's hand.

Pei Ran was washing the grapes. "Anything urgent?"

Yan Zhun sat on Pei Ran's chair. "No, he's just bored. Can I reply for you?"

"Sure," said Pei Ran.

Pei Ran:
No need

Lin Xuhuan:
Why, don't you like wiping out the enemies

Pei Ran:
I have Yan Zhun

Lin Xuhuan:
Well, my bro won't have time to teach you anymore

Pei Ran:
?

Lin Xuhuan:
He's in a relationship now, didn't you know? A man in love has no bros.

Yan Zhun had been about to stop texting when that last message came in. Seeing those words, he started typing again.

Pei Ran:
You're right.

Lin Xuhuan sent several more texts after that. He wanted to get some clues from Pei Ran. The phone kept pinging.

Pei Ran put down an extra chair and sat down beside Yan Zhun. "Are you still texting?"

"He's probing you."

Pei Ran was surprised. "For what?"

"My boyfriend."

Pei Ran paused in eating his grapes to glance at the screen.

Lin Xuhuan had asked many questions. Almost the entire chat history was just his messages, asking "hot or not," "from what year of uni," and "any pictures."

Yan Zhun had only responded with a "hot."

Pei Ran slowed down with his grapes. From this side of things... it seemed as if he was bragging about himself.

Yan Zhun told Lin Xuhuan he was busy. He put Pei Ran's phone back on the desk and accidentally touched the mouse. The computer had been in standby, so it lit up instantly.

Yan Zhun glanced at the screen. There were several games, some drawing software he didn't recognize, and some drafts saved on the desktop.

The last document caught his attention. He could tell from the preview that it was the one that Lin Xuhuan had found on P&EI's Weibo blog. On Weibo, P&EI had only added the default caption of "sharing an image." But in private, in Pei Ran computer, the file name was "Yan Zhun."

Pei Ran was still reading the conversation with Lin Xuhuan. "Would it be inconvenient for you to live in the base?"

"No, I'm used to it," Yan Zhun said.

"Last time in the dorm... Did the RA say anything?"

The person next to him was quiet for a while before suddenly saying, "Pei Ran."

Pei Ran looked up. "Hmm?"

Yan Zhun slouched into the chair and asked, "Have you ever drawn anyone other than me?"

Pei Ran blinked and said, "Yes, a lot."

Yan Zhun was silent.

"I've got a few nude models in my WeChat. All of them are very professional," Pei Ran said. "I've also taken private orders. I've drawn celebrities, and also e-sports pros."

Realizing that his question had been a bit stupid, Yan Zhun couldn't help but smile, "I meant... Besides these, have you ever painted anyone else privately, for yourself?"

Pei Ran's gaze softened. "No." Then he added, "Only you."

Yan Zhun looked at him for a few seconds and suddenly dropped his gaze. "Are the grapes sweet?"

"Yes. Here, have one."

Yan Zhun hummed in acceptance, leaning over. Then he lowered his head and licked Pei Ran's lips.

Pei Ran stiffened instantly, and his hand stayed frozen midair, where he'd been grabbing another grape.

Yan Zhun moved back slightly after he got a taste of the gentle sweetness in his mouth, but he didn't move back to his original position. The tips of their noses were still touching. If either of them moved forward, the slight distance between them would vanish.

"How much does Teacher Pei usually charge?"

Pei Ran didn't know why Yan Zhun asked this. His heart was pounding as he reported a number, his lips tightly pursed.

"It's too expensive for me," Yan Zhun said. "How's this, don't hire anyone else next time. I'll be your nude model."

Pei Ran had sketched a lot of bodies. His former tutor had valued classical beauty; all his models had been amazingly fit.

But for Pei Ran, learning had been simply that: learning. He had remained calm when looking at models, his mind clear. But right now...

He thought of Yan Zhun's smooth collar bones, his prominent Adam's apple, and his strong, slender fingers.

After a long time, Pei Ran said, "You can't."

"Why."

"I won't be able to draw..." Pei Ran said honestly. "With you nude, I won't be able to calm down or concentrate."

Even his honest answers felt like seduction.

Yan Zhun showed a faint smile. Before Pei Ran could see it clearly, he was kissed again. There was no one else in the dorm room, and it had stopped raining. When he heard the sounds he made with Yan Zhun, Pei Ran's ears burned.

Yan Zhun put one hand lazily on his waist. Pei Ran's waist was very obviously thin and trim. It was evident even through his clothes that there was not an ounce of extra fat.

When Yan Zhun reached inside, Pei Ran felt his head turning numb, even though this hand didn't wander anywhere, just stayed where it had been.

The furnace had turned on just now, and the temperature inside slowly rose. Pei Ran could barely breathe, yet there was a strange sense of comfort in that.

Until he let out a light, soft groan.

Pei Ran was shocked. He couldn't believe that he'd made that sound. Yan Zhun also paused. Half a second later, he let Pei Ran go. Pei Ran saw it clearly this time. Yan Zhun was indeed smiling.

"Thank you for your approval, Teacher Pei," he said.

The others were still training when Yan Zhun returned to the base. This morning, the PUBG competition organizer had announced that the competition would officially resume next Wednesday. Yan Zhun hadn't wanted to live here at first. Mostly, he didn't want to disturb their training, but also the base was a little farther than convenient, and renting a place would have been better.

The coach had asked several times before he'd accepted.

"Bro!" Lin Xuhuan saw him through the window and waved to him. "Come here!"

Yan Zhun put his bag on the sofa and went into the training room.

It was nearly ten o'clock in the evening; the training match had ended a while ago. The others were practicing in training mode. Lin Xuhuan and the ranger were playing in two-player mode. Now they were in the final round. He sat on the chair behind Lin Xuhuan and looked down to text. The win screen jumped out when Lin Xuhuan killed that last enemy.

Triumphantly, he said, "I told you, my AKM is invincible."

With that, he took out his phone and took a photo of the computer screen.

"Are you a noob?" the raider asked in disgust. "You're taking a picture of a single win?"

"I'm showing it to my new apprentice." Lin Xuhuan said.

"Who's the unlucky guy?"

"My BabeRan, of course."

As soon as Lin Xuhuan's voice fell, somebody hit him over the head.

Confused, he turned his head. "Bro, what was that for?"

"He has a name." Yan Zhun then glanced at the screen and scoffed, "You only got four kills. So this is your AK?"

As Lin Xuhuan started trying to defend himself, the coach came in with a midnight snack.

"Have some first." He lifted his chin and said to Yan Zhun, "I let them pack yours separately, no spice."

"I've already eaten," said Yan Zhun.

The barbecue smelled amazing. As soon as it entered the room, the other players immediately turned off their game and swarmed the table.

"Bro, did you come back after a midnight snack with your girlfriend?" the raider asked. "What did you have?"

"Noodles."

"In a restaurant?"

Yan Zhun didn't look up from his phone when he retorted,

"What are you, paparazzi?"

The raider grinned and resumed to focus on his food.

Waiting for messages, Yan Zhun licked his lips.

They'd had scallion oil noodles at the ten-year-old shop right outside campus. Surprisingly, they hadn't needed to line up tonight. But all he could taste right now was the lingering flavor of the milk candy from Pei Ran's mouth.

The others spoke of the competition. After a rest from competitions, teams tended to change their tactics. The coach was predicting the parachuting locations of several top teams.

Someone suddenly stood up while chatting, the others couldn't help but looked at him. It was the sniper who was also the team leader, the oldest of them all. He picked up the lighter on the table and said, "I'm going out for a smoke."

Lin Xuhuan looked at the table in front of him. There were only two empty skewers. "Wei, bro, that's all you had?"

"Yeah, I'm good," Wei said. "Take your time."

When he passed Yan Zhun, Yan Zhun looked up and saw his hand shaking as he took out his cigarette.

Yan Zhun thought of something and called out. Wei put his hand back in his pocket. "What's the matter?"

Yan Zhun stared at him for two seconds and said, "Don't smoke so much."

On Wednesday, the competition officially resumed. Many top teams were gathered at the competition, so the venue was packed to the brim, and the official live stream also climbed to the top of the listings. That day, Pei Ran was stopped by the professor right after school, who spoke to him a little. He didn't leave until pretty much every one else had already left.

Pei Ran went out and found Yan Zhun standing with his

back against the classroom door, only wearing one earbud and looking down at the live stream on his phone.

Sensing someone's gaze, he glanced over. He relaxed and asked, "You were held back?"

"Sort of." Pei Ran looked down. "Is it TZG's turn? Are things not going well?"

It wasn't simply "not well."

This was the third round, and TZG hadn't even made it to the top five yet. Yan Zhun picked up the other earbud, "Do you want to listen?"

"Sure." As soon as Pei Ran finished speaking, Yan Zhun had put the earbud in for him. Worried that it would be uncomfortable, he adjusted the earbud several times. His finger gently brushing Pei Ran's ear. Yan Zhun had been standing outside for a while, and his hands were a little cold. In the earbuds, the commentator was speaking:

"TZG seems to be in poor condition. Have they gone lax with training lately?"

"He got outsniped again. What's wrong with TZG's sniper? It seems that things have been going wrong... He's out."

"TZG is now playing three against four. Unfortunately, a team on their right has heard the gunshots and is approaching. TZG is going to be surrounded!"

"TZG has been team-wiped, achieving... sixth place."

Yan Zhun took out the earbud.

He was about to say something when his hand was held by the person next to him.

Pei Ran had spent the whole afternoon in the studio, so his hands were warm. Yan Zhun held him tight, and when he was just about to speak, he heard the door behind him. The professor walked out of the studio while speaking on the phone and saw the two people standing outside the door. She looked down and saw they were holding hands, then paused mid-sentence, stunned.

Yan Zhun let go.

But Pei Ran held on to him. "Goodbye, prof," Pei Ran said.

The professor regained her composure and nodded to them, "Take care."

After the professor left, Pei Ran asked, "Have you been waiting for a long time?"

Yan Zhun had come quite early. There was a window in the back door to the studio, through which he could see Pei Ran and his paintings perfectly.

However, he didn't look for a long, since he also had to tune in on the live stream.

What he saw a few days ago had left a deep impression on him. He felt uneasy, not knowing the truth.

"Not at all," he said.

Pei Ran looked down at the phone in his hand which was still playing the game, "You're not watching it?"

"It's still the half-time. Let's go have dinner first."

Pei Ran agreed. He took two steps, then said, "Their total ranking has always been very high. If they play the next round well, they can still make it back to the top three."

Yan Zhun stayed silent for a bit. "They can't."

"What?"

"There's something wrong with Wei's hand. They won't make it," Yan Zhun said. He'd gotten a hint during training, and it'd become more obvious during the competition.

Wei opened the sighting-scope more slowly, barely hit moving targets and couldn't even pick up things as quickly as usual. It made the sniper the most noticeable target on the team.

Pei Ran was astonished. Wei didn't show up for the last round. Instead, a substitute fought in his place. In this game, Lin Xuhuan performed very well and managed to reach the third place after three teammates were killed.

As soon as they came out after dinner, Yan Zhun's phone rang. The coach spoke in a serious tone and asked him to go back to base.

"Off you go. I can go back to the dorm by myself."

Before Pei Ran turned around, Yan Zhun reached out and grabbed the string hanging from his backpack.

"Are there classes tomorrow?" Yan Zhun asked as if he didn't know the answer.

"No."

"Would you like to visit your boyfriend's room?"

After losing the competition, TZG acted as usual, some of them went back to training, and some returned to the room to have a bath and rest.

Having played for so long, their moral was strong.

There were some differences though. When Lin Xuhuan and the ranger played together, they looked at Wei's closed door frequently. When Yan Zhun arrived, they both happened to be lying dead on the sofa in the living room. Seeing Yan Zhun come in, Lin Xuhuan sat up and said, "Bro... BabeRan!"

Yan Zhun put a box on the table, "Desserts bought by Pei Ran. Where's the coach?"

"Replay room. It's been two hours." Lin Xuhuan opened the dessert box and said something even sweeter than the pastries. "It looks so good. BabeRan is the best."

Yan Zhun gave up on correcting the nickname. He turned

back, "You go up first? It's the first room on the third floor. You can use anything you like."

Pei Ran shook his head, "I'll wait for you."

When Yan Zhun opened the door of the replay room, the big screen was on, showing the last game from earlier today.

He closed the door, sat next to the coach and watched with him. "Too slow." After the camera focused on the substitute who came on stage today, the coach said, "He kept going to the wrong positions."

Yan Zhun agreed and said lazily, "He must have practiced sniping for a long time in private. His weakness in close combat is too obvious."

"Can't keep up with the pace of the team."

"But he can handle instant sniping... Took one enemy down," said Yan Zhun.

"There are four enemies in a team. It's useless to knock down one without elimination." As the substitute was killed, the coach lifted his hand and paused the video.

"Finished?"

"You should come back."

They'd spoken at the same time, and the room fell silent.

Yan Zhun sneered, "Are you crazy?"

The coach sipped his tea and said, "No."

"Wei's hand has been like this for quite some time now. He took a temporary shot to minimise the effects because he wanted to finish the competition. But judging by his current state... he won't make it. During this period, I contacted a lot of people. This year, I trained three groups of youth trainees with painstaking efforts. None of them can compete right away. The raider of the second team was fine... But I don't need a raider right now."

Yan Zhun's smile faded and said, "I'm also a raider."

"You're different." The coach said, "You can be a freeman."

Freeman was the fourth role of a team. It challenged a player's overall skillset the most. This role not only required superb skills, but also needed the player to judge the position of the team while killing enemies and preventing sneak attacks. The player had to do everything he could, and get unthinkable tasks accomplished on top of that. In many teams, the freeman was also the in game leader. In recent years, TZG had been the only top team without a freeman.

Yan Zhun was silent for a moment, then said, "I haven't played in a competition for so long. There are so many brilliant young players. You don't need to recruit a reject—"

The coach interrupted, "I'm the coach, I know better than you whether you're capable or not."

"I know it's hard for you to give up your studies. Maybe your parents won't agree." The coach was obviously prepared. He opened the folder on the desk, "But I have to try."

"The annual salary is not as high as the rest of the tem for now, but it's definitely the best price for a new player you'll find. It's got full benefit coverage, with two free trips per year. Sponsorships and live stream income will be separately counted, but room and board are included. Everything is included. If you want, we'll even help with your wedding.

"There are physiotherapists, massage therapists, dietitians in the team... Every game is accompanied by a doctor. Wrist problems cannot be avoided, but we will do our best to protect our players. Other problems, like your stomach problems, will also be treated.

"As for your studies... You still need training, but the base is close to your campus. If you can handle both, I won't ask you to drop out.

"Yan Zhun." The coach closed the document and pushed it before him. "I sincerely invite you to join TZG. I hope you will consider it."

Yan Zhun looked down and pressed his finger so firmly into the document that his fingernail turned white.

In the end, he moved the document closer to himself.

"I'll think about it."

The coach breathed a sigh of relief and said, "If there is anything else... We can discuss again."

Before Yan Zhun went out, he looked back and asked, "What is Wei going to do?"

"Step behind the scene and become an assistant coach."

Yan Zhun nodded and closed the door of the replay room.

Although usually the two TZG raiders wouldn't be easily affected by much, their mood was still somewhat down from losing the competition, not to mention the injury of their teammate. After casually chatting with Pei Ran for a bit, they quieted down. Pei Ran went back to sitting on the sofa playing with his phone.

He was usually quite the introvert. He wouldn't initiate a conversation if there was no one speaking. But it would seem quite awkward if he just sat there, so he had to get something to do. There were two trends about TZG on the search list. Pei Ran checked the tags and browsed for a while and thumbed up some positive posts. Then the phone suddenly vibrated.

Lin Kang:
Pei Ran, are you free?

Pei Ran:
What's the matter?

Lin Kang:
Need to show you a post, my gf is making me forward it

Lin Kang:
[Mancheng University Forums Breaking News: Mancheng University Electronic Engineering major Su Nian has been on booty calls with my boyfriend every weekend, receipts and images included]

Lin Kang:
She also asked me to pass on a message: Don't be sad over scum. Hope all cheaters get hit by a truck and die.

Pei Ran:
...

Pei Ran originally thought that "receipt and photos" referred to chat records or something like that, but, to his utter shock, it was Su Nian's nudes. His lower body was covered by a quilt, and his face was blurred out, but It was obviously Su Nian himself being caught in the act. Pei Ran closed the photo with flagging interest.

Yan Zhun came out of the replay room. When Lin Xuhuan heard the sound, he immediately opened his eyes, raised his head and asked again stubbornly, "Bro, do you want to play a couple of rounds with me?"

"Not now." As soon as Yan Zhun's voice fell, a door on the second floor opened. They all looked up. Wei came out of the room with a cup in his hand and raised his eyebrow. "Why y'all staring at me? Glad to see you here, xiao-Zhun."

Wei was the eldest in the team. He was almost 25—the only one other than the coach old enough to call Yan Zhun "xiao-Zhun," which meant "little Zhun."

Yan Zhun said, "Yep, are you getting coffee?"

"No, just want a glass of water." Wei's tone was more relaxed than others. He went down to the break room and said, "You got time for a quick chat?" Neither of them was talkative, so it was a quick chat indeed.

Before Lin Xuhuan could gossip about it, Yan Zhun already came out from the room. Lin Xuhuan asked, "Bro, you sure you don't want to play? I'm tired of solo- and duo-queue."

"I don't." Yan Zhun went to Pei Ran and picked up his backpack with one hand. "We're going up."

TZG was a renowned domestic team, a dream team that all trainees and newcomers wanted to be admitted into. The PUBG training base alone was a five-floor mansion, including a warehouse full of computer accessory parts, a gym, a pool room, a movie room and so on.

Yan Zhun's room was next door to Lin Xuhuan's. It had the same layout and setup as other team members, with an en suite bathroom, a TV, and a computer. The windows were open, and the curtain stirred in the evening wind. The black hat he often wore was hung on the chair. The bed hadn't been made, but it wasn't too messy.

Tidy and clean, there was no other smell, but Pei Ran could feel Yan Zhun everywhere. Yan Zhun put the backpack on the chair, turned around and asked, "Are you going back tonight?"

Pei Ran opened his mouth in surprise.

A few seconds later, he said, "Will it bother you... if I stay?"

Yan Zhun said, "No, the bed is big enough."

Pei Ran stayed silent.

Yan Zhun checked the time and said, "I'm afraid the RA won't let you enter this late."

Pei Ran thought that he'd read too much into it; Yan Zhun looked natural, as if he was just asking a friend to sleepover.

So he nodded as naturally as he could. "Alright."

They had dinner at a Szechuan restaurant, so their clothes were stained with its smell. Yan Zhun gave Pei Ran a set of lounge wear. He'd bought a loose set for comfort, and it seemed too oversized on Pei Ran. The collar hung open, revealing a large area of skin, dazzlingly white under the light.

Yan Zhun genuinely hadn't thought too much when he'd asked Pei Ran to stay, but when he came out of the bathroom with Yan Zhun's clothes on, Yan Zhun became bit flustered.

"Is it too big?"

Pei Ran stood with his side to Yan Zhun, drying his hair with a towel. "A little bit, but it's quite comfortable."

The sleeve of the T-shirt was so big that Yan Zhun could easily see into it. Yan Zhun glanced without meaning to, then suddenly got up and grabbed a random pile of clothes.

"I'll take a shower."

The bathroom had just been used and was full of steam. Yan Zhun closed his eyes and stood under the shower head for a while. Then he raised his hand and lowered the water temperature. When he came out of the shower, Pei Ran was lying on the right side of the bed with his eyes closed.

So he had fallen asleep...

Yan Zhun took a deep breath. He slowed down, gently stepped forward, and pulled the covers up over Pei Ran's stomach. It was warm inside, so it would be too hot if he were properly tucked in. Yan Zhun had washed his hair, but now he couldn't use the hair dryer.

His phone vibrated; the coach had sent a message to him, saying that the physiotherapists signed on with the team were on their way and asking if he needed a wrist massage.

Yan Zhun turned down the offer, opened the drawer and took out a pack of unopened cigarettes. Planning to go to the balcony to let his hair air dry, he turned off the lights and left.

Yan Zhun became much calmer as the night wind blew on.

He had stayed away from cigarettes for a while. He took one puff and stopped. Leaning on the railing, he looked down at the streetlight downstairs. Wei hadn't really said anything in the break room. He said he first encountered e-sports when he was 15. He used to play CS: GO, and now he played PUBG. In the past decade, he had been praised and reviled, had gone from the bottom to the top. He had no regrets and was satisfied. Then he'd asked Yan Zhun, "How about you?"

Are you satisfied?

Yan Zhun left the cigarette alone until it burnt to its end.

He lit another. When Pei Ran opened his eyes, it was just as the spark lit on the balcony.

He didn't know how and when he'd fallen asleep. Maybe he'd stayed up too late painting last night, and then the entire day of classes had tired him out. Just earlier, he'd almost fallen asleep in the living room.

Waking up fully, Pei Ran got out of bed.

He didn't make any sound walking barefoot. Yan Zhun didn't look back until he opened the balcony door. Seeing him, Yan Zhun raised an eyebrow and put out the cigarette.

Thinking that he'd woken Pei Ran up, Yan Zhun asked, "Did the smoke waft through the door?"

"No," Pei Ran said. "Why are you standing outside? Did I... take up the entire bed?"

Yan Zhun smiled. "No, I just wanted to get some air."

Pei Ran looked at his hair. "With wet hair?"

"For a windswept look." Yan Zhun put the ashtray a little further away. "Go inside, it's cold out."

"And you?"

"I'll wait a bit so I don't reek of smoke."

It was true that Pei Ran disliked the smell of smoke. Most

people who didn't smoke disliked the smell of it.

However, Pei Ran didn't think Yan Zhun's cigarettes were that bad, maybe the brand was special. The smoke and night breeze mingled, seeming to form a different scent.

He stepped out towards the balcony and closed the door. Yan Zhun paused. He lowered his head and saw Pei Ran's bare feet on the dark balcony floor.

"No slippers?"

"It's too dark. I can't find them."

Yan Zhun took off his slippers. "Here."

Pei Ran stepped into them obediently, then suddenly remembered how Yan Zhun had compared their shoe sizes previously. He couldn't help taking two steps forward, extending a foot to compare with Yan Zhun's.

Pei Ran looked at their feet carefully for a while, "Yours aren't much bigger than mine."

As soon as Pei Ran stepped closer, Yan Zhun smelled it: his own shower gel. More intense after getting trapped in by the covers.

Yan Zhun looked down and saw Pei Ran's fair collarbones.

Yan Zhun looked away, then back again. Pei Ran was still studying the size of their feet.

A few more repeats, and Yan Zhun put his elbow on the railing. Teasing, he asked, "Looks like you're seducing me."

Pei Ran paused and looked up at him.

Yan Zhun's silhouette was hidden in the dark. He looked kind of aloof when not smiling. There seemed to be a crescent moon shining in his eyes.

Pei Ran had just woken up and had no energy to overthink, and they were also so close to each other. He was quiet for a while, then said, "Can't I?"

Yan Zhun couldn't tell whether he asked on purpose or he was genuinely confused.

But it didn't matter.

"Pei Ran," Yan Zhun said after a long while. Voice deep and slightly hoarse, he said, "Come closer."

Pei Ran moved forward, and they almost glued together.

Yan Zhun said, wheedling, "Give me a kiss."

Pei Ran was very glad that the light was dim, so no one could see his glowing cheeks. He held back his nerves and hummed a very calm assent. Then he raised his head and kissed Yan Zhun. It landed off-center.

He smelled the smoke. The scent was light, rather tempting.

Pei Ran felt around for Yan Zhun's lips in the dark.

Creak!

The crisp sound of a sliding door rudely cut them off.

They were both stunned for a few seconds. Then, they separated and turned together to look to the source of the sound.

Each room in TZG base had an independent balcony, so there was only a short distance between the balconies. It was easy to chat with each other while staying on inidividual balconies.

Lin Xuhuan was standing on the balcony next door. He was topless with only a bath towel wrapped around his waist. He was holding his red underwear in his hand and was about to hang it on the clothesline. He was frozen in place, looking at them stupidly.

His red underwear was fluttering in the cold wind. For a moment, no one spoke or did anything. Yan Zhun was the first to react. He raised his hand and covered Pei Ran's eyes.

Lin Xuhuan was confused.

Seeing that he still hadn't moved, Yan Zhun asked coldly,

"Are you going hold onto it until it dries?"

Lin Xuhuan was speechless. Trembling, he slowly hung up his underwear.

Then, he stayed in place. The two of them kept looking at each other.

Then, Yan Zhun asked, "Are you trying to enjoy the view?"

There was a pause, then Lin Xuhuan finally found his voice again. "No."

"Go inside."

"On it, bro!"

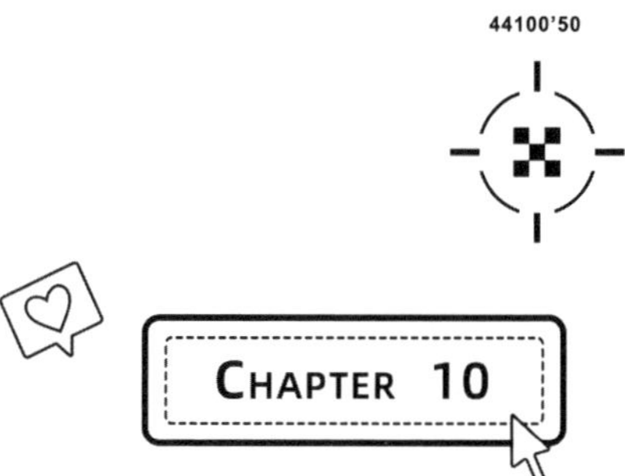

Chapter 10

Pei Ran's senses became hyperalert with his eyes blindfolded.

He could even hear the rustle of the leaves and Yan Zhun's heartbeat. Not until the door was closed and the curtain was drawn did the hand over Pei Ran's eyes move away. The warmth lingered on his eyelids.

After staying silent for a while, Yan Zhun suddenly said, "He's too young. He won't be able to keep it a secret."

Pei Ran's head was slightly tilted, still maintaining the angle it had been in for kissing. He hadn't processed what he'd heard. "Huh?"

"He won't keep it to himself unless he's clearly instructed." Yan Zhun asked, "Do you want to keep it a secret?"

Yan Zhun had a beautiful jawline. Pei Ran stared at it for a few seconds, then looked up at his eyes. "We can keep it a secret if you want to keep it a secret."

The conversation sounded like a tongue twister. Yan Zhun gave a silent laugh. His voice was quiet in the night: "I don't want to. Never did."

When Lin Xuhuan entered the room, he was still holding his bath towel tightly.

The raider was sitting on his sofa scrolling through Weibo. He looked up and asked, "Who were you talking to—were there fans out there? Why are you clutching that towel so tightly?" The address of their base was not a secret. Fans often swung by to take pictures outside the base.

Lin Xuhuan walked over and sat down. "Quick, slap me."

A loud and clear smack followed suit as the raider immediately slapped him. He showed no emotion while doing so.

Although it hadn't hurt, Lin Xuhuan was still shocked. "Shit, why did you actually do that?"

"We're bros. Of course I'll satisfy such a minor request," the raider said. "What's the matter?"

Lin Xuhuan joined TZG before he'd turned 15. Every member of the team, Yan Zhun included, was like family to him.

He nervously told his second bro about what he just saw, as if he'd accidentally found out about his big brother's relationship. The raider was also shocked upon hearing it.

After a long time, he raised his hand. "How about another slap. I don't think you're thinking straight."

"Try it. See if I won't hit back this time."

The raider wore a conflicted expression. "Are you sure you saw clearly?"

Lin Xuhuan felt indignant. "Screw you, my dynamic visual acuity is the best—not to mention they didn't move at all!"

They looked at each other in silence for a while. Then, they simultaneously lit cigarettes. "Well... I don't know why, but I'm not too surprised that it was with Pei Ran," said the raider.

"Me neither." Lin Xuhuan paused, "But is my bro really into men? I used to sit next to him topless playing video games at the base every day. Maybe I shouldn't have done that?"

The raider got up and patted him on the shoulder, "Don't worry. He probably never saw you as a human being at all."

Then, before Lin Xuhuan could process what he'd just said, the raider put on his slippers and rushed out the door.

It was too loud to not be heard from next door. Yan Zhun's room was dark and he heard Lin Xuhuan shouting and cursing. He frowned and opened his eyes. Automatically, he reached out to cover the ears of the person next to him.

Pei Ran slept on one side. He slept peacefully and didn't move. Even though Lin Xuhuan's voice was so loud, his eyelids barely trembled before his breathing evened out again.

Yan Zhun used his other hand to grab the phone and quickly typed out a sentence.

Approved:
Go downstairs if you want to fight

Lin Xuhuan:
No more fighting, bro. I'll tape myself to the bed right now

Yan Zhun was too lazy to joke with him. He was just about to put his phone away when he received another text.

Lin Xuhuan:
Umm... Bro, I couldn't help but tell that idiot about it just now, is that ok? Should I silence him? Do you want this kept quiet?

Approved:
Do whatever

Yan Zhun underestimated Lin Xuhuan's skills in information propagation.

The next morning, he quietly got out of bed to wash up and go out for a morning run. When he got downstairs, several members of TZG were eating noodles around the dining table. They'd just finished an all-nighter, and the coach was telling them not to stay up all night before competitions, but he stopped talking when he saw Yan Zhun coming downstairs.

The coach coughed softly, then asked, "Up so early?"

Yan Zhun bent down to tie his shoelaces. "Yeah."

Everyone looked a bit funny, muttering things like, "Did you sleep well?" or "Was the heating okay?"

Then, the raider asked, "did our training disturb you?" and Yan Zhun finally frowned.

"That's it, stop talking and go to bed after you finish eating." The coach drank a mouthful of milk and looked at Yan Zhun again, "Morning run?"

Yan Zhun humed and went to open the front door.

"Oh, wait a minute." The coach stopped him again. "It's just... Do you want a bigger bed in your room?"

Yan Zhun was confused.

Others were going crazy trying to hide their smiles. The coach pursed his lips and couldn't hold back his smile either.

"I'm just saying, the bed is only six feet. I don't want you two to feel cramped. If you didn't sleep well, I'll have someone change it in the afternoon."

Silently, Yan Zhun looked towards Lin Xuhuan.

Many thought that Yan Zhun would scold Lin Xuhuan. Even Lin Xuhuan himself thought so. He lowered his head, trying to pretend to be deaf and dumb.

Yan Zhun, however, paused for two seconds, then took out his earphones from his pocket and put one of them into his ear. "Don't bother. It's big enough."

On the morning run, Yan Zhun got a call from his family.

He stopped at the bridge and waited for his breath to calm down before picking up. "Mom."

"Xiao-Zhun. Have you moved off campus?"

Since the conflict had been with his roommate, after

returning home from the hospital, Yan Zhun's mother had asked him to request a room transfer or move off campus.

"Yes."

"Good, where did you move to?"

Yan Zhun looked at the riverside scenery for a moment, then said, "I moved to the base."

After a moment, his mother realized what "base" meant. Yan Zhun thought that she would express reticence, but, to his surprise, he heard her ask, "Are you comfortable there?"

Yan Zhun gripped the phone more tightly, "Yes."

"Good, since you've moved there, you should still pay some rent. Try not to bother the others if there's nothing urgent." She paused, then said, "Remember to eat on time and take care of yourself."

When Yan Zhun returned to the base, Pei Ran was already awake. As soon as he opened the door, he saw Pei Ran come out of the bathroom smelling refreshingly minty. Since he'd slept in the same position the whole night, half his hair was pressed up slightly. The T-shirt he was wearing was too big, giving him an air of coziness. "You're up?" Yan Zhun asked.

"Yeah." Pei Ran looked up at the sweat on his forehead. "Did you go running?" His voice was still a little sleepy.

"For a bit." Yan Zhun lifted his hand, wanting to help him smooth down his hair, then remembered that his palms were sweaty and put it down. "I'll take a shower. Wait for me."

When Yan Zhun came out of the bathroom, Pei Ran was sitting on his chair making a phone call. "Mr. Yun... Yes, it's been a long time." Pei Ran looked down when he spoke, like he often did in class, "I'm doing great, how about you? ... Class group chat? I read it occasionally, but sometimes it's too late and they've finished chatting, so I don't talk much."

Upon hearing "Mr. Yun," Yan Zhun raised his eyebrows and stood in front of Pei Ran in silence, helping him press down his unruly hair. "Yun" wasn't very common of a family name. He remembered that Pei Ran's homeroom teacher in grade 11 had had that name. If he remembered correctly, it was also this teacher who had fought for two major punishments to be given to the student who'd hurt Luo Qingshan. At that time, it had been a hot topic that even students in other classes had heard about it.

Pei Ran let Yan Zhun play with his hair, not moving away.

After nearly ten minutes, Pei Ran finally hung up.

"You hungry?" Yan Zhun asked.

Pei Ran said, "A little bit."

"The housekeeper left," Yan Zhun said. "I'll make some for you. There are noodles and dumplings in the refrigerator. What would you like?"

Pei Ran said, "Whatever you're having."

Yan Zhun was inexplicably put at ease hearing his answer. He said, "Well, your boyfriend will give you a bonus, an extra fried egg." Yan Zhun turned around and his hand was caught by Pei Ran.

"On the seventh of next month, I'm going to my high school class reunion." Pei Ran said. High school class reunion.

It meant there would be teachers, classmates and Luo Qingshan. Yan Zhun looked at the ground and answered after a long time, "Sure."

Then he asked, "Where would it be?"

"I don't know. I haven't read the messages in the group chat. The teacher said it was a local hot spring hotel." Pei Ran said, "It's far away. Maybe we would have to spend the night."

Yan Zhun hummed noncommittally.

Pei Ran waited, but Yan Zhun didn't speak any more, so he pursed his lips and asked, "Are you available?"

Yan Zhun was confused. "What?"

"I won't ask any classmates to share a hotel room; I'll book my own." Pei Ran paused. "I asked. I can bring a plus-one. Of course, if you don't have time, I can also go myself."

The day of the reunion was overcast, threatening rain.

The class president had organized it. They decided to meet at the gates of their high school and go to the destination by rented buses. The reason they'd decided to hold the reunion was that because their teacher was about to retire and move out-of-province, so there were quite a lot of students coming.

Even before the agreed time, more than 20 people had already gathered at the school gates. As soon as Luo Qingshan arrived, he was stopped by a classmate and the two chatted away. He said something absentmindedly and began to search through the people. The classmate thought that he was looking for those who fought with him in the past and said, "Don't worry, we didn't invite those idiots."

The three boys who'd taken the lead in bullying hadn't stayed in touch with them after graduation. Naturally, no one had invited them this time.

"That's good. What about our teacher?"

"The president asked him and his wife to wait in the bus because it might rain," the classmate said, then looked over his shoulder. "Didn't Pei Ran come with you?"

"No." Luo Qingshan paused and took out his cell phone awkwardly. "Well, I can call him and ask..."

"I just called.' The president walked up behind them and said, "He said he would be here soon."

Then, suddenly, the rain poured down in a rush.

Everyone was caught by surprise. They all raised their bags to block the rain, then ran as one to the bus.

"It's raining hard. Let's get on the bus and wait."

"You go first." Luo Qingshan took out an umbrella and said, "I'll wait for Pei Ran at the station. I'm afraid he didn't bring an umbrella."

"I doubt it," the class president said, "He's coming with his plus-one. Your umbrella can't cover three people."

Luo Qingshan paused. "Plus-one? Whose plus-one?"

"Pei Ran's. He DMed me and booked a separate room."

Just then, someone suddenly shouted, "Pei Ran is here!"

Luo Qingshan looked back slowly.

In the rain, Pei Ran and Yan Zhun walked side by side with an umbrella. The gray umbrella was held a little low, covering their eyes. Their expression couldn't be seen clearly, but they were very close under the umbrella.

Only one of them was carrying a bag.

Their luggage had been packed together.

Though it was pouring rain outside, it was lively in the bus.

It hadn't been too long since graduation, so everyone was still close, with endless topics to chat about. Unfortunately most people couldn't help take a quick peep towards the seats in the second-to-last row while chatting. Almost everyone knew the person Pei Ran brought.

Yan Zhun of Mancheng High School had also been their schoolmate of the same grade. Guys knew him for being good at video games, while girls knew him for being attractive.

Halfway through the mountain road, the bus was shaking viciously. The friend sitting beside Luo Qingshan couldn't help whispering, "You and Pei Ran... Did you break up?"

Luo Qingshan had been casually chewing gum when he felt his heart getting suddenly stabbed by someone. "Yeah."

"At first when the president said that Pei Ran wanted to bring a plus-one, I thought it was a relative," said the friend.

Hearing the word "plus-one," Luo Qingshan's mood became sour. He turned his head and looked out the window. When they arrived at the hotel, the rain had just stopped, and the air in the mountains was refreshing. After getting off the bus, the president quickly communicated with the hotel and distributed the key cards to everyone.

It was not dinner time yet. A group of people immediately discussed going to the hot springs together. Pei Ran originally wanted to greet Mr. Yun, but Mr. Yun had gotten carsick on the ride over, so he'd gone to his room as soon as he'd gotten off the bus.

When Pei Ran came back with the key card, Yan Zhun asked, "Do you want to go to the hot spring with them?"

Pei Ran shook his head, "I'd rather go back to the room." The president had booked everyone standard rooms, but the hotel was decent so even the standard room was plenty comfortable. Upon entering their room, Yan Zhun heard Pei Ran draw the curtain as he went to put down his luggage.

"Bed time?" Pei Ran said.

Yan Zhun took off his baseball cap and hung it aside, "Sure, are you sleepy?"

"I meant you." Pei Ran paused, "Didn't you go to bed at five last night?" The TZG leader had retired due to wrist problems, and a substitute had to take his place. For the sake of better teamwork, TZG had hurriedly arranged extra training sessions during this time. Yan Zhun often accompanied their training and stayed up late.

Anyone would be tired if he went to bed at five o'clock, woke up at noon to pack luggage, then travelled for nearly two hours on a bumpy bus.

Yan Zhun asked, "Did I wake you up?"

"No, Lin Xuhuan told me."

Yan Zhun nodded, took his phone from his pocket, and sent Lin Xuhuan a threatening sticker. He then muted it before throwing it on the table. Yan Zhun took off his coat, leaving on only a thin T-shirt, then lied down on the bed. Hotel beds were usually too soft, which wasn't good for the back, but it was nice once in a while.

He felt sleepy as soon as he closed his eyes. Half a minute later, he reopened his eyes and saw Pei Ran standing by the bed looking at the phone. Yan Zhun turned on his side and called out, "Teacher Pei."

They were finalizing the time for dinner in the class chat group. They had reserved the underground restaurant of the hotel in advance. Pei Ran texted "got it" along with the others in the group and asked, "Hmm?"

Yan Zhun said lazily, "Come and sleep with me for a while."

Pei Ran raised his head, a bit startled, and saw Yan Zhun looking at him as if he could fall asleep any second. A moment later, with their coats piled together, Pei Ran was spooned by Yan Zhun as they lay down in bed.

It wasn't exactly a hug, Yan Zhun only put his arm on Pei Ran's waist lightly. Yan Zhun asked, "What time is dinner?"

The dinner wasn't for the plus-ones. After all, they were all classmates; strangers tagging along would make it awkward.

"Six," Pei Ran said. "I'll come back early and bring you something to eat. What would you like?"

"No, I'll call room service. Have fun."

"Okay."

A few seconds later: "But don't be too late."

"Okay."

Yan Zhun's voice was very low, almost a whisper: "Remember that your boyfriend will be waiting for you."

"Okay." Pei Ran smiled silently. "I know."

The person behind him stopped speaking.

Yan Zhun leaned sideway and fell asleep with his lips only inches away from Pei Ran's neck.

When it was time for dinner, Pei Ran quietly got out of bed. Scared that he might wake Yan Zhun up, he only turned on a bathroom light and left after hastily getting ready in the dim light.

He arrived just on time, so most of his classmates had already gotten there. Pei Ran was looking around for an available seat when he saw Mr. Yun put down his cup and wave to him. "Pei Ran, come and sit next to me."

Mr. Yun was over 50 years old. He had some gray hair near his temples and was showing signs of balding, but he still looked energetic.

The seat on his left was empty, and on his right sat Luo Qingshan. Noticing that Pei Ran hadn't moved, Mr. Yun urged him again. Pei Ran hesitated but eventually sat down. Mr. Yun looked at him, then asked, "Why is your coat so big?"

Pei Ran stopped and looked down to discover that he was wearing Yan Zhun's coat. The room had been dark when he'd left, and he hadn't looked carefully enough.

"It's not mine," he said.

Luo Qingshan couldn't see Pei Ran at all because of the

person in between. After hearing this, he lowered his head and emptied his glass. Mr. Yun had asked him to sit next to him, but he didn't say anything specifically important. He just asked Pei Ran how he had been doing the past two years and how his college life was.

Pei Ran answered the questions one by one, then asked, "Sir, how has your health been?"

"It's OK. Nothing serious." Mr. Yun said lightly, "My wife frets too much and asked me to resign to rest. So I did that."

Someone nearby asked, "Sir, you still drink? Won't the missus scold you?"

"She's in the room," he said. "Just two cups, don't tell her."

Luo Qingshan said, "Not happening. You gave me standing penalty every day in high school. Today I'll have my revenge."

Mr. Yun turned and smacked him on the head, "Bad boy!" There was a burst of laughter and the atmosphere on the table became lively at once.

Since they were all grown-ups now, alcohol was inevitable. Pei Ran lowered his head to eat in silence and stayed out of the chaos. Only when people raised their glasses did he join the rest. At the end, most of the boys became tipsy. They sat on the other side to play some drinking games. Luo Qingshan was the loudest among them. The table became empty immediately.

Pei Ran put down his chopsticks and checked if he had received any new messages. Mr. Yun turned around after wrapping up his conversation with another student, asking, "Why didn't Yan Zhun come with you?"

"He's resting in the room." Then a bit surprised, Pei Ran asked, "You know him?"

Pei Ran soon realized that he shouldn't have been so surprised; Yan Zhun had gone to the same high school as him, so it wouldn't have been strange for Mr. Yun to have substituted for Yan Zhun's classes or acted as proctor for his exams.

However, Mr. Yun nodded and said, "I know this person. I once saw him when he came to our class to stuff something in your desk."

Pei Ran was stunned. "Stuff something? For me?" he asked.

Noticing his surprise, Mr. Yun smiled. "What, you forgot? Those textbooks."

Pei Ran froze upon hearing that.

Seeing his expression, Mr. Yun asked, "What's wrong?"

"Nothing..." Pei Ran recovered his voice, and his heart beat a little fast, "Sir... When did you see it?"

"I can't possibly remember." Mr. Yun touched his cup. "During lunch break one day."

The reason he remembered it was lunch break was that he had also gotten two new textbooks and wanted to put them on Pei Ran's desk while the classroom had been empty.

However, a student had beat him to it. He did not only give Pei Ran textbooks, but he'd also seemed to be holding a packet of candies in white packaging.

Luo Qingshan came over with a glass in hand and interrupted their conversation.

"Mr. Yun, let me have a toast to you. I made quite a bit of trouble for you in high school..."

Mr. Yun snorted and picked up the glass. "You should indeed. A lot of my gray hair is thanks to you."

Luo Qingshan smiled. "Pei Ran, let's have a toast?"

Pei Ran answered the toast, clinking his glass robotically with Mr. Yun's.

He hadn't paid any attention to who asked for a toast and

whose glass he clinked. The people beside him were chatting noisily. He sat down with his head lowered, and the fragments in his head were finally piecing together. More students came to offer a toast to Mr. Yun. No matter who offered it, the people at the table also had to drink. Pei Ran had drunk a couple of glasses when someone suddenly put a hand on his shoulder.

"Stop drinking, xiao-Ran," Luo Qingshan said. "You'll feel sick if you get too drunk."

Pei Ran moved away from his hand. Just as he was about to speak, his phone rang.

Yan Zhun:
I'm awake.

Pei Ran didn't cover it when he looked at his screen. Luo Qingshan saw the content at a glance. Full of alcohol and food, someone had already suggested that they wrap up.

Luo Qingshan pursed his lips and loudly proposed, "There's a KTV here. How about we order a room and play for a bit?"

Someone immediately agreed.

Pei Ran got up and put on his coat. "Mr. Yun, I have to excuse myself. Have a good time."

"I'm not going to join you young people's activities." Mr. Yun looked up at him. "Let's walk together?"

Pei Ran nodded. The coat was oversized enough that he had to fold up his sleeves. Because of alcohol, his cheeks were red, but his eyes were clear.

Luo Qingshan cut in, "You've both drunk a lot. Let me walk you back."

Before Pei Ran could speak, Mr. Yun refused first, "Don't bother; we're not drunk, so don't worry. You go have fun."

Pei Ran left the room with Mr. Yun and got on the elevator in silence.

As they their destination, Mr. Yun suddenly said, "Of the entire class, I'm actually most worried about you."

Surprised, Pei Ran turned to look at him. Mr. Yun was still looking ahead. The elevator door opened. He touched his own hair, then spoke slowly, "Well, I can retire now knowing you're okay."

Pei Ran suddenly remembered that back in high school Mr. Yun had also looked ahead like this before patting him on the shoulder. Then he'd said that the punishment had been finalized; those people wouldn't dare bully him again. He'd reminded Pei Ran to study hard and to not get distracted. He'd spoken in such an easy tone without any criticism, nor did he scold him or try to change him. His "different" sexual orientation had seemed trivial to Mr. Yun's.

Pei Ran tried to open his mouth as Mr. Yun walked out of the elevator. In the end, he didn't say anything. He just bowed solemnly and silently behind him.

When Pei Ran swiped his card to open the door, the bathroom door also opened.

The heat rushed out into the room, and Yan Zhun came out with a pair of loose black pants and wet hair. The two doors were close, so they almost bumped into each other.

There were droplets of water near Yan Zhun's collarbones. He had the smell of hotel shower gel, which was different but pleasant. Yan Zhun raised his eyebrow as Pei Ran stepped in. Before Pei Ran could react, he bent to lean over.

Pei Ran stood still and opened his mouth automatically. The expected kiss didn't come.

Instead, Yan Zhun sniffed, "Did you drink?"

Pei Ran paused, then pursed his lips. "Just a little."

"I don't think so. I can smell it." Yan Zhun stood up straight. "Your clothes..."

"Sorry," Pei Ran said. "The room was too dark when I left. I'll take it off now."

Yan Zhun had just finished a good nap and was in a pleasant mood. He stretched out his arms to stop Pei Ran from taking off his clothes. "Don't worry, keep it on for a while. I like it when you wear my clothes."

Pei Ran didn't take off the coat until he took a shower.

Yan Zhun was lying on the bed talking on the phone. It was from the coach. He looked at the clothes hanging on the back of his chair and answered it absentmindedly. After some serious discussions, the coach asked, "Why do I keep hearing water sound? Are you in the hot spring?"

"Pei Ran is taking a shower."

There was a awakward silence.

Then the coach said, "I won't keep you then," and hung up.

Yan Zhun didn't bother to explain. He threw his phone aside, took out his iPad, and sat down near the headboard, where he opened his folder of game saves and randomly picked a game from the perspective of the free man.

Pei Ran didn't come out of the bathroom until he began to watch a second match. He stuffed the dirty clothes into his bag and lay down beside Yan Zhun.

Maybe the president had assigned it by mistake, but they'd gotten a room with a single king size bed. They hadn't bothered asking for a change, however.

Yan Zhun was always serious when he watched gameplay, but this time he was very impatient. He kept fast forwarding through it until finally he turned to look at Pei Ran.

Pei Ran had washed his hair and dried it in the bathroom.

His hair was soft. Since he'd gotten into bed, he'd been looking up at Yan Zhun.

Yan Zhun felt a little funny, "What are you looking at?"

Pei Ran seemed a little distracted. After a few seconds, he said, "You."

Sensing that he was not in the right mood, Yan Zhun turned down the volume. "What is it?"

Pei Ran pursed his lips, then relaxed. After doing that several times, he asked, "Why didn't you come to get to know me in high school?"

Yan Zhun was caught off guard by that question, and the corner of his lips tensed.

Pei Ran said, "I always thought that the textbooks and uniform had been from someone else."

Yan Zhun looked away slightly. Why not exactly, it was because he was not certain at that time. Not certain whether he'd sent those things out of some pointless compassion and pity, or some other emotions. He'd had no experience and hadn't known what it was like to like someone.

"But I'm happy," Pei Ran said softly.

"What?"

Pei Ran looked away, then back again, looking shy but determined. "I'm happy to know that you're the one who sent me those things." The iPad was turned off now. It was squeezed to the edge of the bed, nearly about to fall to the carpet.

Yan Zhun pressed Pei Ran into the bed, kneeled beside Pei Ran's waist with his legs apart, held Pei Ran's face with his hands, and kissed him urgently. Their lips opened and they devoured each other, their tongues twisting with passion. The room filled with slick and suggestive noses.

Pei Ran had always thought that he would do better in the

next kiss, but he never did. He was still groaning with barely any air left, but this time Yan Zhun didn't let him go.

When the hem of his shirt was lifted, Pei Ran felt the heat overtaking him. Sweat beaded on his forehead. Yan Zhun finally finished the kiss. Pei Ran gasped heavily. Before he could slow down, he heard Yan Zhun ask, "Are you ticklish?"

Pei Ran opened his eyes halfway, not understanding where that came from, "A little bit." Before he finished speaking, Yan Zhun suddenly lifted his chin and kissed his Adam's apple.

Pei Ran's body stiffened, electricity running through his veins. Pei Ran had been spending the night at the TZG base every Saturday of late. They often kissed, but nothing beyond.

Yan Zhun had held back every time; cold showers were never pleasant. But now, upon lifting something between them, even just by a little, there was no stopping.

Then, the doorbell brought some sense back for Yan Zhun.

He straightened, looking over Pei Ran, and his throat tightened. Pei Ran's clothes had been pushed up to his neck. There were several pink marks on his body. The loose waist of his pants had also shifted down, revealing a small strip of white underwear.

His lips were red, his face flushed, and his eyes were moist. The doorbell rang again.

Yan Zhun took a deep breath and said in a hoarse voice, "I'll go get the door." Pei Ran suddenly hooked his legs to stop him the moment when Yan Zhun got up.

Before Pei Ran could speak, he was pushed down by Yan Zhun again. Yan Zhun lifted Pei Ran's head and gave him a kiss on the chin, "Do you know what it means to hook your boyfriend with your legs?"

Pei Ran's heart was pounding. He nodded slowly, "I do."

After not getting any response, the person outside began knocking on the door physically—

"Pei Ran! Are you in there?" It was Luo Qingshan.

Pei Ran was startled. He wanted to raise his head, but his neck was held by Yan Zhun, and they kissed again.

The knocking on the door continued.

"It's Luo Qingshan."

"I need to talk to you!"

"Pei Ran?"

After a long time, the noise finally stopped.

On top of the carpet, the boys' clothes were piled together casually. Pei Ran sat at the head of the bed with his legs bent. He lowered his head and held Yan Zhun's wrist. Even his ears were blushing, "Okay, that's it... Yan Zhun."

Yan Zhun kissed him and reached for something on the table. He handed the packing to Pei Ran and said in a low voice, "Teacher Pei, help me put it on."

Pei Ran's face suddenly became more flushed. He lowered his head. His hands were shaking as he tried to tear open the package. He finally managed to open it, but now he was struggling to put it on.

"Sorry." Pei Ran's voice was soft. "I've never done it before... Just a moment."

Yan Zhun paused, took his hand and asked, "Never? But before..."

"Never."

Yan Zhun didn't know what to say.

Pei Ran said, "I'm sort of germophobic."

Yan Zhun swallowed several times and asked bluntly, "So me, but not him?"

Pei Ran didn't say a word. After a moment, he looked up

and said, "It's on."

Yan Zhun silently lowered his head to kiss Pei Ran's knee and closed his eyes momentarily. His breathing was a complete mess now.

Back in high school, the city leaders once came to the school for inspection. The teachers had asked all the students to tuck their clothes into their pants when they did morning exercises. At that time, everyone else looked like nerdy bookworms. Only Pei Ran had stood out with his long legs and trim waist, looking fresh and proper.

Pei Ran's ankle was tightly held in someone else's grasp. He felt a tiny bite on his calf. He wanted to hide from it, but the more he tried, the harder Yan Zhun gripped his ankles.

At the end of it, Yan Zhun buried his face into Pei Ran's shoulder and said, "In high school, my homeroom teacher thought I was dating someone."

Pei Ran covered his eyes with the back of his hand. He didn't understand why Yan Zhun was telling him this, but he still answered dazedly, "Hmm?"

"I was staring at another class during the entire morning exercise." Yan Zhun said it very slowly, with a burning desire he didn't usually have in his voice.

He took Pei Ran's hand away and kissed his eyes, then the tip of his nose. They were too close. Pei Ran's every organ could feel Yan Zhun's body.

Pei Ran could barely see anything when he heard Yan Zhun said to him sweetly, "Beautiful legs, Teacher Pei."

Early next morning, Yan Zhun got up a little later than usual, but with his self-discipline, it was no later than 10.

When he woke up, the first thing he did was to look at the

person beside him. Pei Ran was still asleep. Yan Zhun touched his forehead and got up only after he was sure that everything was good. Yan Zhun called the front desk and ordered two sets of breakfast, then he cleaned up the garbage on the floor.

In truth, there was nothing to clear besides two condom packets. His aim at the garbage last night had gone amiss, and they'd ended up around the can. When Pei Ran woke up, he heard something from the balcony.

As soon as he moved, he felt a subtle ache all over his body. It was not strong, but it still made him stop getting up.

He turned his head towards the balcony. The curtain was only slightly open. Although the sunshine was not strong, Pei Ran still couldn't help squinting. He saw Yan Zhun open the door of the balcony with something in his hand. Pei Ran blinked a few times before he could see it clearly. In an instant, all his drowsiness was gone—Yan Zhun was holding his underwear.

And it was washed.

Last night, his legs had been so sore and numb that Yan Zhun had needed to help him to the shower. After cleaning up, he'd gone to sleep without a care in the world. When Yan Zhun came back from drying his underwear, he saw Pei Ran lying on the bed, staring at him.

"You're up?" Yan Zhun stepped forward and touched his forehead again. "I ordered breakfast. It just got here. Get up and have some."

Pei Ran looked up, "You just took..."

Yan Zhun's tone was casual: "I was worried you would feel dirty if it was left in the bathroom. I washed it."

This was the first time Pei Ran had someone else wash his underwear, as far as he could remember.

He closed his eyes and remembered last night. His cheeks were blushing, but his expression didn't show any sign of embarrassment. He just kept silent for a bit, then said, "Okay."

Breakfast was congee with lean pork, light and palatable. Yan Zhun said, "I've extended the room for one more day."

Pei Ran paused, "Hmm?"

"I was worried that you wouldn't get enough sleep." Yan Zhun looked down. "Does it still hurt?"

Pei Ran shook his head. Yan Zhun had been excellent with prep. He really didn't feel much pain.

But it was true that his legs were sore. After a quick discussion, they decided to sleep a little longer and not go back with the bus.

Nearing noon, messages kept popping up in the group chat. When Yan Zhun came out of the bathroom, he happened to see Pei Ran changing clothes. "Weren't you planning to sleep a little longer?"

"Yeah," Pei Ran put on his trousers, "but I still have to say goodbye to my teacher."

Yan Zhun glanced at the scarf he took out and said, "Do you have to wear that much?" The hotel had heating all the way from the room to the lobby.

Pei Ran hesitated, then explained, "It's too obvious. The marks on me..."

Although Pei Ran didn't grow up spoiled with care, he also never exactly experienced many hardships in life. In addition, his skin was paler than most boys, so his skin reddened very easily from Yan Zhun's touches.

He'd checked himself while in the shower. There were marks all over: on his waist, his neck, and his legs.

Pei Ran thought of the moment when Yan Zhun had kissed

his calf. He couldn't help but look down and speed up putting on his scarf.

Yan Zhun paused, "I'll go down with you."

Noon was the peak check-out time of the hotel, especially since it was the holidays, so the queue was not short.

Luo Qingshan was sitting on the sofa in the lobby yawning nonstop. The president sitting next to him couldn't help but ask, "What did you do last night?"

"Nothing. I didn't sleep well." Luo Qingshan took a sip of water and looked around. "Where's Pei Ran? Why hasn't him come down yet? He's always on time."

The president said, "I think they extended their stay for another day. They're probably still sleeping."

Luo Qingshan choked on the water and his face turned red, "They... are not checking out?" Just as he finished speaking, the elevator door beside them slowly opened. Pei Ran and Yan Zhun stepped out side by side. Pei Ran was covered from head to toe in layers, with only his head showing. One felt warm just looking at him.

Yan Zhun on the other hand only wore a sweatshirt, long black sleeves half rolled up to his elbows, and his collarbones peeking through the neckline. Luo Qingshan saw them go to the sofa beside him and said goodbye to Mr. Yun in a daze.

He'd noticed the marks on Yan Zhun's arm at once: like cat scratches. They were pink, nothing serious.

There were no cats in this hotel. He couldn't help looking up. Yan Zhun's collar was loose and there were two red marks on the right side of his Adam's apple.

They stood shoulder to shoulder. Although there was no excessive contact, Luo Qingshan could sense their intimacy at a glance.

He remembered that he had knocked on the door for a long time, but no one had answered him last night. He stopped breathing for two seconds, clenched and unclenched his fist, then stared at Pei Ran in disbelief.

He and Pei Ran had never gotten to home base. He was straight before. In high school, he'd been ignorant and hadn't known how men could have sex with each other. Later, in college, the small motels nearby were too dirty, and there were scandals about hidden spy cameras.

He and Pei Ran never went to those places.

Luo Qingshan had originally booked a hotel on the night of his birthday. Then, in a surprising turn of events, he'd accidentally drunk too much and had that fiasco with Su Nian. The room had been wasted since nobody had gone. In the end, Su Nian had taken him to a shabbier hotel to make do. He stared at them in disbelieve as they said goodbye to their teacher and classmates. When he walked by, Luo Qingshan couldn't help blurting out, "Pei Ran."

Pei Ran stopped and looked at him.

Luo Qingshan asked, "Last night... Why didn't you open the door?" He saw Pei Ran unconsciously lean a little towards Yan Zhun, and Pei Ran didn't speak for a few seconds.

"Private matter." Pei Ran then turned to the president and said, "We're headed up then. Take care and goodbye."

Pei Ran hadn't sleep well last night, so he fell asleep soon after getting back to his room.

Yan Zhun sat at the head of the bed, watching games with his headphone on, and turning to glance occasionally at Pei Ran.

Pei Ran slept on his side. Yan Zhun looked at him quietly

for a while and touched the lovebite near Pei Ran's shoulder with his fingertip. With the light of the iPad, he could clearly see that it had faded a lot. Yan Zhun rubbed it gently until the color became darker, stopping only when he felt satisfied.

When he was watching the third game, Yan Zhun's phone suddenly rang. He muted it immediately and then looked at the person next to him. Pei Ran had opened his eyes.

"Keep resting, don't worry." Yan Zhun said, planning to take the call outside.

Pei Ran grabbed his arm with barely any strength. His voice was slightly hoarse, "It's ok. I've had enough sleep. You can take it here."

Yan Zhun ruffled his hair and turned on the speaker. It was from the coach, who went straight to the point.

"Wei can't play anymore. He'll retire after this competition. It's so urgent that I've been asked to pick youth trainees... You need to make your decision soon." The coach said, "I've met these trainees. Not good enough. There is also a lack of leadership in the team, the current three members... I'm not sure."

Yan Zhun said, "I see. I'll give you my answer next week."

"Okay, I hope it's good news. Why haven't you come back yet? Isn't it just for one night?"

"I extended for another day."

The coach paused, then said, "Then you and Pei Ran, well, have fun."

Pei Ran listened to this call sleepily. A while after it ended, he looked up and said, "Are you going to go pro?"

Yan Zhun did not answer but asked, "Will you let me?"

Pei Ran was confused. "It's up to you."

"You are my boyfriend, I am under your control."

Realizing that this was what he'd said before in front of the convenience store, Pei Ran covered his eyes and felt shy. He sat up slowly, leaned lazily on Yan Zhun's arm, took out his phone and looked for something for a long time.

Yan Zhun's phone rang, and Pei Ran said, "I sent you a contact on WeChat."

Yan Zhun was at a lost, "Who is it?"

"A physical therapist." Pei Ran said, "He's good at what he does. The massages are nice." Pei Ran had learned piano as a child and now, he painted. After working for a long time, his would feel discomforin his wrists. The therapist had been introduced to him by his mom.

"Okay," Yan Zhun answered. Then, after a while, he asked, "Wasn't I good at massages?"

Last night, when Yan Zhun had held Pei Ran, he'd held his hands the whole time, clasping their fingers tightly together.

Pei Ran's hands had gone red.

Then Yan Zhun had noticed and given him a hand massage. Pei Ran had fallen asleep to the subtle pressure on his hands.

Pei Ran paused, then said, "It's different."

It was raining gently outside, and they didn't plan to enjoy the hot springs. They ended up lying in bed.

Pei Ran got up to wash his face. After the bathroom door was closed, Yan Zhun took out his phone again and forwarded the E-contract that the coach sent him last week to his father.

A couple of days later, Yan Zhun still hadn't received any response about the contract. He didn't say anything further either, until the next week, he received a phone call from his mother asking him how to add back WeChat contacts that had been previously blocked. It was the weekend when the call came in, and Yan Zhun was still sleeping in the base. His first reaction after he answered the phone was to look around. It was empty, and no one was there.

Yan Zhun hadn't unblocked anyone who had been blocked. He closed his eyes again, "I don't know. I'll look into it."

"Good," his mother said. "Your father blocked you. He tried to figure out how to unblock you for quite some time, still couldn't figure it out."

Then came the voice of his father: "I asked you to check online for me. Why are you calling him?"

Yan Zhun was speechless. So that was why he hadn't gotten any response. After a few seconds, he couldn't help but chuckle. His mother also laughed.

After that, she asked, "Have you considered it seriously?"

"Yes."

"What about school?"

"I can handle it."

Yan's father said something in the distance. Yan Zhun couldn't hear it clearly. A few seconds later, Yan's mother said gently, "It's not a small matter after all. You'd better come home. Let's discuss in person more carefully."

Yan Zhun got ready quickly. When he went downstairs, he saw Pei Ran sitting on his chair playing games. He seemed to be playing with Lin Xuhuan.

Yan Zhun had told the coach his intentions that he'd decided, and they'd discussed it enough. They were just missing a signed contract now. And though nothing really counted without a contract, a new computer had already been added to the training room. Yan Zhun had yet to officially join, but occasionally he played with the team as a group of four.

He pushed the training room door open. Lin Xuhuan had

just been knocked down on the ground, shouting that his opponent was cheating and asked Pei Ran to shoot at the enemy quickly. Pei Ran couldn't even see the enemy from his angle. He saw Yan Zhun come in and said, "Cover yourself, I'll let Yan Zhun play for me..." Pei Ran was about to step out to swap with Yan Zhun when someone pressed against his back.

Yan Zhun leaned down to hold his mouse just like how he'd taught him to press the gun that time, but this time he leaned closer. Pei Ran smelled mint on him.

Yan Zhun asked, "Location?"

Lin Xuhuan was also stunned for a moment, but soon he recovered. "Behind the tree at 75, I shot him down. He's probably healing." Yan Zhun held the gun calmly and cleanly knocked the enemy down. He was just about to release the mouse when he suddenly found something. The game character he was controlling had changed his ID, although it was still dressed in the default outfit.

"111Believer." Yan Zhun read out loud; it was in English.

Pei Ran answered, "Here."

Yan Zhun looked down and smiled. His voice still raspy from waking up, he asked, "What does it mean?"

Pei Ran was quiet for a few seconds. "It means I want to be your fan."

Yan Zhun said, "Then you are my first fan. I'll give you some personal benefits."

"Shit... Ah no, not you, bro." Lin Xuhuan couldn't bear it any longer, "But will you help me first, please."

Pei Ran had woken up late that day. When he'd gone downstairs to get himself some water, he'd been caught by Lin Xuhuan. Without saying a word, he'd been forced to play the game with him.

Yan Zhun casually pulled a chair to sit next to Pei Ran, watching him play until the cell phone rang briefly.

Mimi:
Hello, friend. Mimi gave birth recently. The kittens all have beautiful colors. The father is a little chubby orange cat. You already graduated, right? If you are interested, you can take one home.

Yan Zhun zoomed in on the picture and saw several kittens, still with their eyes closed. Mimi was a stray cat that he'd once kept for a few months. Rather, not kept—his father was allergic to cats, and, at that time, the base had been too small. He never took the cat home, but he would feed it after school every day. Later, the cat had gotten sick, and he'd taken it to the vet and helped it find an adoptive family.

Yan Zhun suddenly remembered that the first time he'd seen Pei Ran had been thanks to Mimi. On that day, he'd gone to feed her as usual. As soon as he'd turned around the corner, he'd seen Pei Ran there, too, feeding the cat sausages.

The sausages had been put on the ground. Pei Ran had been crouching, distanced slightly from the cat. He'd stretched out his hand, as if trying to touch it. He'd looked a bit funny.

Seeing that the cat was being fed, Yan Zhun had turned around to leave, but then he'd seen Pei Ran take out a bag of tissues from his backpack. Every time he'd petted the cat, he'd wipe his hands. Again and again, touch and then wipe...

Yan Zhun collected his thoughts, then typed slowly.

Approved:
No, my boyfriend is germophobic. We can't.

Time always flew when it came to finals season. On the first day of winter vacation, the first snow of the year happened to fall upon the city, and the world turned white overnight.

However, no one in the base was interested in watching the snow. Either they were training or scrolling through their Weibo on their phones. Today, TZG officially announced their new free man and team leader: TZG-GOD.

The team said he would play in the opening match the day after tomorrow. As the top team in the country, the sudden change of leader was undoubtedly major news, not to mention it going to a new player who was completely unheard of.

It caused a heated discussion online, and the comment section of that official post was swamped with question marks. It was so chaotic that Lin Xuhuan and others were all distracted.

Only Yan Zhun was still practicing in the training mode when the phone rang: "You already signed a contract with that club?! Have you ever respected me or your mother?" His father, who'd just received the tickets from him, was enraged. "How dare you send tickets to me!"

Yan Zhun said, "My mother agreed."

At first, Yan Zhun's father was speechless in anger. Then, he said, "I didn't agree!"

"It's good enough. You've gotten people to check over the contract several times by now."

"Of course you should be diligent with these things! Any mistake or omission will lead to serious consequences—"

"Will you come to the game or not?" Yan Zhun interrupted. "There are too many people, so it could be hard to find yours. If you do come, I'll send someone to pick you up."

The other side was silent for half a minute before: "We'll talk later!" And then the call ended.

Yan Zhun threw his mobile phone aside and got up for a cup of water. Lin Xuhuan grabbed him and said, "Bro, those people on Weibo are talking nonsense. Don't be angry."

When Yan Zhun had been in e-sports before, the PUBG sector had not yet been popular. He'd only played a few small games in cybercafes, none of which had any recordings. Naturally, few people recognized him.

Later, when "111GOD" appeared in the ranking of Asian service, it was also speculated that he was a scripter.

As a result, under the posts of TZG official account and Yan Zhun's new account, not only were the haters complaining, but TZG fans were also complaining, saying that it was better to let the second team or the youth trainees join.

"Why should I be angry?"

"You're not?" asked Lin Xuhuan. Even he couldn't hold his anger after reading some comments.

Yan Zhun took his clothes out of his hand and said, "Skills prove everything." Yan Zhun went to the kitchen to pour himself his cup of water. Instead of rushing back to training, he took out his phone and went to the balcony. Pei Ran had finished his exams last week, and now he was going to an art exhibition with his parents. The chat history had been left at last night's conversation. The latest were a ticket screen shot from Pei Ran, and a notice of a video call ending.

Approved:
Little fan

Pei Ran:
Here

Yan Zhun didn't know what to say. He wasn't good at texting. He just wanted to chat with Pei Ran in his free time.

A moment later, he typed: "It's snowing here." Before the message was sent out, his phone buzzed.

Pei Ran:
[image attachment]

Pei Ran:
It's snowing today.

Yan Zhun opened the picture, looked at it, then saved it.

Approved:
Same here.

Approved:
I miss you, teacher Pei.

The next day was game day.

Yan Zhun woke up early in the morning and saw a message on his phone. It'd been sent two hours ago.

Pei Ran:
... My flight has been cancelled

Yan Zhun quickly replied. He didn't get a return text even after he finished washing and changing his clothes. The line was busy when he called. As such, he was visibly in a bad mood when he got on the car on their way to the venue.

Once they got there, a lot of fans were waiting for them. For one thing, they wanted to cheer up the team. For another, they wanted to see the new leaer.

The car stopped, and the first three veteran players got out of the car and waved cheerfully at the fans. Before the fans could respond, they saw another boy coming out of the car.

He was wearing a black and red TZG uniform and a baseball cap. He was taller than the other players. Standing in the middle of the crowd, he looked like a celebrity who mistakenly entered the otaku party.

The new free man walked too quickly. It took only a few seconds for him to get off the bus and enter the venue. During this period, he had been looking down at his phone, and his expression was worse than the fans who were dissatisfied with the new arrangement of the team.

The present fans were left speechless.

After arriving backstage, Yan Zhun checked again to make sure that Pei Ran's flight had indeed been cancelled.

"All right, phones away," The coach said. "There are some changes in the tactics of the first round. Listen up."

There were pre-competition adjustments before almost evert game. The coach was excited, trying to cheer them up. He didn't stop until the staff came in to remind them that it was go-time. Yan Zhun zipped up his team uniform and handed his phone to the coach before going out. "If Pei Ran calls, could you answer it in my stead?"

"Sure," the coach said. "Your parents are here, third row."

"Okay." Yan Zhun passed through the aisle and was just about to walk on the field. Suddenly he noticed something and turned to look in the direction of the emergency exit.

Then he stopped.

Standing in front of him, Lin Xuhuan only heard him say, "I'll be back in two minutes." Pei Ran, wearing a white down jacket, was still breathing heavily. He'd been stopped by the security guard outside the emergency exit. He'd been about to make a phone call when someone grabbed his wrist.

Yan Zhun waved the security guard away and took Pei Ran inside. They barely had any time. Yan Zhun brought him into an empty utility room nearby. "Why didn't you reply?"

Knowing that he had made it, Pei Ran sighed in relief. "I was on the high-speed rail. There was no signal, and my phone died midway. I borrowed a charger from the taxi driver."

"There were still tickets for high-speed rail?" It was the winter holidays, and it was close to the Spring Festival, so it was hard to book tickets. "Yes," said Pei Ran, "They were standing tickets." Yan Zhun's throat bobbed. This room was the closest to the venue. They could easily hear the excitement from the audience and the commentators.

There was ten minutes left before the competition. The commentators began to introduce today's teams. Pei Ran heard them talk about Yan Zhun. "The new player of TZG, God? I've heard of him here and there. It's said that this one was a youth trainee in TZG a few years ago, but he quit early, so few people know about him."

"I've met him in the game, very good, super powerful."

"TZG players had not entered yet? Wait, no, player Huan loves to enter early and interact with the camera..."

Pei Ran listened quietly for a while, his heart beat a little faster. He found that he liked to hear people praise Yan Zhun.

"They're talking about you," Pei Ran said. "It's time for you to go now."

Yan Zhun said, "I'm not ready yet."

He raised his hand and ruffled Pei Ran's messy hair. He reminded him in a low voice, "Teacher Pei, add a buff for me."

The utility room was a little narrow, there was barely any room left when two boys stood there. Pei Ran blinked a few times, then agreed.

The swaying golden spotlight accidentally stopped at the window of the room. The commentator was still talking about 111GOD, and the other teams walked onstage one by one.

Pei Ran took a step forward, raised his head slightly, and kissed Yan Zhun's lips among the chaos.

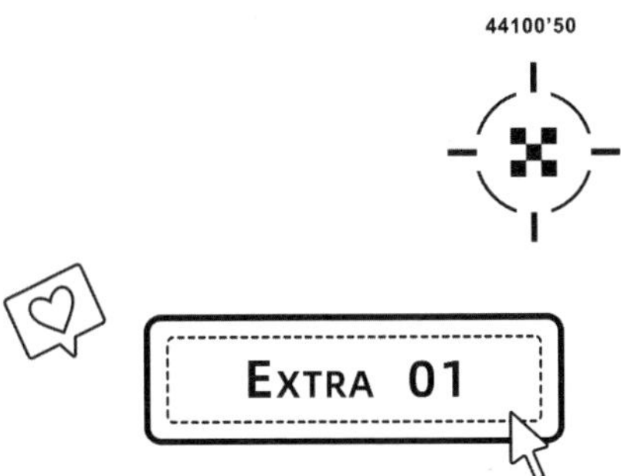

Extra 01

It was your typical hot summer day, with noisy cicadas, and fans buzzing overhead. Even the breeze felt like hot air.

The sharp school bell tore through the sullen atmosphere. When the teachers left, the classroom finally revitalized with a bit of energy. Yan Zhun closed his textbook and took his phone out from his desk to reply to Lin Xuhuan.

As soon as he began typing, the classmate sitting in front of him turned around and continued their discussion from the last break. "If you don't come this time, that's it. We won't have any class matches in senior year. You should think it over," said the front desk guy.

Yan Zhun looked down at the messages. The weather was so hot that even his tone was lazy, "I can't play."

"Come on," the front desk guys said. "Our class is not that good at playing basketball. Look, if we win the game the day after tomorrow, I'll buy you half a month's breakfast!"

Breakfast was not expensive. However, going to the school canteen in summer was so frustrating that only young lovers were willing to queue for each other. Yan Zhun threw the phone back into the drawer, raised his right hand to lean on the table, and explained, "Hand injury. I really can't play."

His wrist had been smashed two days ago. It wasn't serious, but it was still sore whenever he moved.

"All right," the front desk said helplessly. "We'll find someone else." Yan Zhun threw all of his textbooks into the drawer and lay down to sleep.

This weather was made for resting spirits. The two students in front of him were constantly chattering, and the conversation was heard by him clearly:

"What class are we playing against in the first round?"

"Class three."

"Damn, class three is very good at basketball. What's the name of that one in their class... Luo something?"

"Luo Qingshan, the one with the buzz cut."

"It's him. I heard that he once got into fight with the boys next class in first year. He won't play dirty, will he?"

"No, I've played with him. He's aggressive. I didn't dare to confront him anyway." Here, the boy briefly paused for two seconds, then he lowered his voice and said mysteriously, "But I know something."

"What?"

"I hear he's gay."

Silence.

"He's with a boy in their class. That guy represented our school and won the prize in some art competition. He was praised by the principal during the flag ceremony last time. His name is Pei Ran."

"How disgusting. Is it true?"

"Of course! I saw them holding hands for a long time on

the second floor of the school library last Wednesday... It's fine, I didn't feel sick when I saw it."

"Wow, you don't have that tendency, do you—"

Knock knock.

A dull knock interrupted the conversation. Both of them were surprised, and then they looked back as one. Yan Zhun raised his head a little, arms hiding his face such that only his eyes peeked through. Maybe it was because he was tired, but his eyelids were drooping, and his mood had just plummeted.

The two guys in front thought they'd been too loud and had woken him up. They were about to apologize when Yan Zhun asked, "When is the competition?"

"Huh?"

"Aren't we having a class match?"

"Yes..." the guy in front of him finally responded. "At four in the afternoon the day after tomorrow, at the school basketball court... Are you coming? Didn't you hurt your hand?"

"By that day, it'll be fine." After saying that, Yan Zhun looked at the other person. His voice sounded cold amidst the warm stuffy air. "I want to nap. Can you keep it down?"

After Yan Zhun bent down again, the two people sitting in front of him looked at each other for a moment, then both shut their mouths.

The competition organized by the school was much bigger than the small matches organized by the students themselves.

It was very hot that day, and the boys were warming up in their basketball jerseys. A huge crowd of students from the participating classes were cheering them on. The referee was the gym teacher. After a whistle, all the players entered the court. Everyone's attention immediately focused on the same place. Luo Qingshan, wearing a loose jersey, looked at the man standing in front of him, "Bro, are you Yan Zhun? Is this my first time playing with you?"

Yan Zhun hummed and looked down to warm up his wrist.

Luo Qingshan said, "I don't really control myself when playing. If I accidentally hurt you, don't get mad. If you can't stand it, let the substitute take your place."

Yan Zhun finally took a look at him and said, "You too." Luo Qingshan had heard and seen Yan Zhun before, but when they stood face to face, he realized to his surprise that Yan Zhun was a little taller than him. But it didn't matter. There may occasionally be one or two who looked decent among the game otaku kind, but they were usually bad at sports.

His belief disintegrated five minutes after the start of the game. When Yan Zhun broke through his score again, others on Luo Qingshan's team temporarily called a timeout. The rest areas of the two teams were very close. Yan Zhun wiped his sweat carelessly, and then he heard people across from him yell out playfully. "What's the matter? You failed to stop Yan Zhun several times. You lost your motivation to fight now that Pei Ran is not here?"

Panting heavily, Luo Qingshan took the water from the girl and took a big gulp of it. He went down the steps and said, "Yes, why hasn't teacher let him go yet? What a chatterbox."

After he pause, the players returned to where they should be. Just as Luo Qingshan got into position, his shoulder was patted lightly. "Pei Ran came. Do your best. Pass the ball to me if you can't make it." Yan Zhun raised his hand to wipe off the sweat from his chin and looked at the audience quietly. It was so hot that no matter how enthusiastic the audience was, they couldn't bear the stuffy heat.

Girls were all holding some sort of fan, with their black hair blowing messily; boys were not as elegant, many had either pants rolled up to their knees, or their bellies exposed. Pei Ran stood in the crowd holding his backpack in front of him. His clothes were neat and fresh. He was looking at Luo Qingshan quietly.

His expression was much calmer than the people around him. He looked distant but proper. Luo Qingshan was about to blow Pei Ran a kiss when the whistle blasted.

He quickly ran up and said with a smile, "Bro, my wife is here. Help me out here. I'll treat you to smoke later." The game started so fast that he wasn't sure if Yan Zhun heard it at first.

It wasn't until Yan Zhun earned ten points in a row that Luo Qingshan thought, *this guy must be a little deaf.*

"Yan Zhun, enough. We're nearly twenty points ahead of them." The guy who sat in front of him passed by. Hearing Yan Zhun's panting, he couldn't help but say, "Isn't your hand hurting? Why are you still trying so hard? Take a rest and let the substitute take your place. We're almost done anyways."

"I can do it," said Yan Zhun.

The final score was unexpected to everyone. When it came to the end, Luo Qingshan's class had basically given up. At the end of the game, the whistle was blown. Yan Zhun stopped running, lifted up the corner of his clothes and wiped the sweat on his eyelashes. The girls' discussion was not loud enough for Yan Zhun to hear. Pei Ran, however, could hear them very clearly standing in the crowd. "The boy from class eight is so hot. He's also amazing at basketball."

"You didn't know? Even in grade ten, many girls from upper grades went to see him outside his class, and there were girls in our class who wrote him love letters..."

"Ah! Who was it? What's his name?"

"I think it's... Yan—"

"Hey, class three, get out of the way!" A shout in the distance interrupted their conversation. Several girls heard the sound and looked up. They saw the basketball coming straight at them. One of the students from the next class was so excited after the win that, in the spur of the moment, he'd attempted a three-pointer from way too far.

However, the ball deviated. Not only did it not touch the backboard, it went straight for the audience. The basketball was coming in Pei Ran's direction, he stood in front the student audience and behind the girls who were waiting to give the players water. It was too late to hide elsewhere.

Pei Ran raised his hand wanting to cover his face when he heard a heavy "bang." The ball was blocked by a boy who'd arrived just in time. The basketball hit his wrist heavily, then rolled across the ground.

Yan Zhun frowned, bent down to pick up the ball, and threw it back to the court. The person in front of Pei Ran had dodged. The boy of class eight, who were the star of the girls' discussion, was now standing in front of him with his back towards Pei Ran. Pei Ran could even hear his deep and rapid panting. Pei Ran slowly put down his hand and wanted to say "Thank you," but then his sight was blocked by Luo Qingshan, who rushed towards him.

Luo Qingshan stood in their midst and gasped for breath. He took the water from Pei Ran's hand and drank it. After that, he turned back and said, "Stop trying if you don't know how to throw a 3-pointer! You almost hit someone!"

That student apologized in horror. Luo Qingshan said, "If you hit him, you're done!"

Pei Ran called out his name. "Don't be like this, it's just a mistake. It didn't hit me."

Luo Qingshan said a few more words, then he took Pei Ran's hand and went to the bench nearby to rest. Luo Qingshan exchanged a few words with his classmates. Looking back, he saw Pei Ran open his backpack to take out a bottle of unopened water.

Pei Ran barely walked out two steps and was grabbed by Luo Qingshan. "Where are you going, babe?"

Others looked at them awkwardly when they heard the word "babe."

Pei Ran looked down. "The boy from class eight helped block the ball. I wanted to give a bottle of water as thanks."

Luo Qingshan tugged harder and said, "He just won against your boyfriend. I'm not letting you do that."

Pei Ran said nothing.

"And good thing I was fast, or he would have hit you."

No, actually, the boy stopped very steadily, Pei Ran thought.

Seeing that he was silent, Luo Qingshan directly took the water from his hand, unscrewed it, took a drink, then said with a smile, "Now I've drunk from it, you can't give it away... Come on, let's go to the Japanese restaurant next door."

Before leaving the court, Pei Ran looked back.

That boy didn't join the class eight celebration. He still stood under the backboard, head quietly lowered as he wiped away his sweat. It didn't look like he was that excited about winning. The setting sun gently illuminated the ground, creating a slender shadow.

When they went to college, Luo Qingshan found out that Yan Zhun was his roommate and couldn't help thinking about that basketball match. "My leg wasn't feeling good that day, or you would have lost. If you don't believe it, you can have a game with me next time."

"Oh."

"By the way, you blocked the ball for my babe that time..." Luo Qingshan coughed twice, "I don't know if you remember, Pei Ran, who used to be my classmate, is my boyfriend."

Yan Zhun stopped. "I remember."

Luo Qingshan didn't notice the few seconds of silence. He said, "I'm just being upfront about it. If he comes to our dorm in the future, please don't mind. In fact, he came here a few days ago. You were playing games with headphones on that day. He was embarrassed to come in because you were here."

"Really. Next time he can come in, I don't mind."

With the roommate's approval, Luo Qingshan called Pei Ran to their dorm that afternoon. When Pei Ran came, Yan Zhun was smoking on the balcony.

He leaned against the wall and was watching a game, wearing only one earbud. Hearing footsteps, he looked up and met Pei Ran's gaze, who paused, then nodded politely.

Yan Zhun quickly recollected himself. He nodded expressionlessly, and then turned around to stub out the cigarette, throwing it into the garbage can next to him. He heard Pei Ran push open their dormitory door then close it gently.

Luo Qingshan called out "babe" from inside.

Yan Zhun stared at the extinguished cigarette butt in the garbage can for a while. He took out his cigarette box and got out another one, lit it in his mouth, then turned around and walked downstairs.

He didn't remember me. Yan Zhun thought.

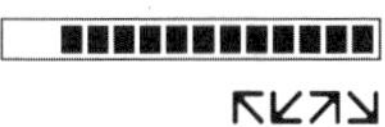

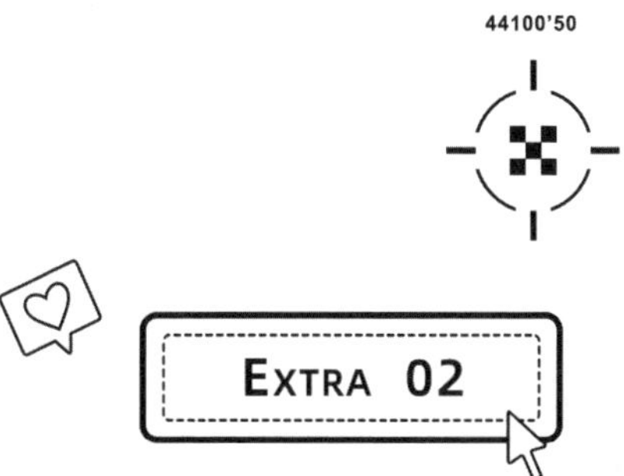

Extra 02

Recently, the teams that would represent China in the PUBG Global Invitational were finally announced. As the top team in China, TZG successfully received the invitation for next month's international tournament. Once the line-up of the team was decided, it immediately caused heated responses. In the field of e-sports, PUBG had always been less popular than MOBA games because the viewer experience wasn't as exciting. However, the discussion had remained heated during this period for an obvious reason:

TZG just won the championship of a major competition last month. In the last round, the new team leader TZG-GOD, who had been on the team for less than a season, had successfully gotten first place with a super record of 11 kills.

The killing spree recording from his point of view had spread across the Internet. Any player who saw it could only sign in admiration. Players all around the world had been discussing it passionately when the members of TZG had arrived last week in Germany, the venue of the international tournament. They'd been training for six consecutive days since then. TZG had just finished a training match. All of the members went back to the training room to rest.

The two big sofas in the training room were all occupied at this time. Although their rooms were just a few steps away, no one was willing to get up and move. Their schedule had been all over the place lately. Since their arrival, they had been filming video campaigns and taking photoshoots for several days, as per the organizing committee's request.

During the training, some people couldn't stop from yawning. The only clear-headed player in the room was sitting in his seat, idly playing with his mobile phone. Yan Zhun was browsing his boyfriend's Weibo.

Yan Zhun's account had been made by his coach. In just a few months, he had nearly a million fans, growing faster than some celebrities. However, he followed fewer than ten blogs.

Aside from the official team account, his teammates and sponsors, all there was left was one artist with about twenty thousand fans. Before Yan Zhun returned to the team, Pei Ran had already posted artwork of him. After Yan Zhun became famous post-debut, a lot of onlookers came to his Weibo. Now there were more than seven thousand comments under that post, making all types of speculations.

Pei Ran had asked "What should I do?", "How should I reply?" several times on the phone last night. His tone had been so confused and flustered that Yan Zhun couldn't help laughing. Today, he found a new post on Pei Ran's home page.

P&EI:
I liked God very much even before he became a professional player. I drew the TZG uniform because I was working on a private commission from a fan of one of the TZG members. I don't know any inside stories. I'm just a fan. Please do not

over-speculate, thank you. God probably followed me by mistake. Please don't ping him in the comments. I'm a man, not a girl... Thank you again, and I'm no longer taking any commissions.

"I see that some fans have set up a Weibo fan page for you. It has over 100,000 fans. Would you like to follow it?" Afraid to disturb others' rest, the coach whispered beside him. "It's good. Not everyone is treated like this."

"No." Yan Zhun tapped on the screen without raising his head, "I'm just a pro player. I don't need fans."

"You don't know how lucky you are." Wei laughed. He shook his phone. "Days ago, my fans were still fighting for me. They said that no one could replace me. They advised me to go back and play... Now they freaking told me to take good care of my injury and wished me a happy retirement."

The coach nodded, "The society is so cruel." Yan Zhun didn't listen to their banter. He read the first sentence of Pei Ran's post several times. Originally, he wanted to comment on it, but in the end, he reposted it.

TZG-GOD:
Thanks to Teacher P for supporting me. I also like your art very much.

That night they had a video call, and Pei Ran frowned and said with frustration, "You typed two extra spaces."

"Shaky hands," said the team leader who had killed 11 enemies in a single game. Yan Zhun wiped his face and hung up the towel. "When will you come?" Pei Ran's passport had just expired and was awaiting renewal.

"My ticket is next Tuesday." Pei Ran turned off the Weibo notifications with a guilty conscience, "You'd better delete it."

The coach had talked with them. The team was not against their relationship, but they didn't agree with them coming out publicly. After all, the consequences were unknown. The team felt that they shouldn't take the risk.

"Am I not allowed to help promote my favorite artist?"

Trying to hide his smile, Pei Ran said sternly, "Yan Zhun."

"I don't want to." Yan Zhun looked down at him and couldn't help taking a few screenshots. "You can delete it yourself next week when you get here."

On the day of Pei Ran's flight to Cologne, the PUBG Global Invitational officially began. When Pei Ran arrived at the hotel, the TZG members had already left. He left his luggage with the staff and rushed to the venue.

The coach arranged for him to sit in the front row, but he still couldn't see the players' faces clearly, so he had to rely on the big screen. As soon as he sat down, the players entered one after another. Pei Ran was sitting next to several Chinese girls. When Yan Zhun appeared on the screen, they were screaming so wildly that they nearly startled Pei Ran. Only when the spotlight shifted elsewhere did they quiet down. Pei Ran took out his phone and sent a message to the coach, informing him of his arrival.

"Ahhh! I got GOD's WeChat ID!"

Pei Ran's fingers paused as he looked at the girl beside him.

The lighting in the audience was quite dim. He couldn't see her face clearly. All he knew was that she gave off the very image of a feminine soft girl. "Really?! How did you get it?"

"Shh... I bought it from a TZG staff."

"Badass!!! Did you add him?"

"I'll wait until the game is over." The girl couldn't help smiling. "I made sure to ask. GOD doesn't have a girlfriend."

"I'm rooting for you, sister. Set the most beautiful picture of yourself as the icon."

Pei Ran quietly put his phone into his pocket. The girls chatted excitedly for a long time before stopping.

When the competition was about to start, the girls around Pei Ran finally took a look at him. "Ah, you must be Chinese too! Are you also an international student?" She smiled.

Pei Ran shook his head, "I came just for the game."

"Wow, a true fan. You travelled abroad just to watch the PUBG competition? Which team are you a fan of? TZG or WWP? Or which member's fan?"

Pei Ran was quiet for a while.

The girl misinterpreted the silence. "Do you like foreign teams? My friend, too—"

"No." The stage light was on, and Pei Ran looked forwards.

Seeing that Pei Ran didn't really want to chat, the girl pursed her lips and nodded. She was just about to turn her gaze back to the stage when Pei Ran turned to smile at her:

"I like TZG's GOD. I'm his fan."

In the opening match, TZG played a great game. Although they only got the second-place "chicken butt," the whole team killed 14 enemies, which immediately widened the gap between TZG and other teams on the killing list.

TZG members stepped down amidst loud cheering from the audience. Lin Xuhuan stretched. "Ah, I've already prepared what to say for the winner interview for entering the finals."

"Too soon," said the coach. "Don't you think you've been flamed online enough?"

"It's okay. They're used to me blabbering."

The coach rolled his eyes without saying a word. As soon as he looked back, he saw that Yan Zhun had put on his down jacket and zipped up tightly to hide his uniform.

The coach stopped him and said, "They haven't decided where to go for dinner yet."

"I'm not going. Enjoy yourselves." Yan Zhun lowered his hat, put on a mask and carried his own equipment bag.

The coach instantly understood. "I can get someone bring Pei Ran along to dinner."

"I'll take him back to the hotel." Yan Zhun said.

Everyone suddenly felt nosy. Although he knew that Yan Zhun was sensible, the coach still patted him and reminded, "We're still in the middle of a competition. Discipline is key."

Lin Xuhuan was close by and had good ears. He said, "Don't worry. The hotel has great sound proofing, I've tried."

Yan Zhun picked up a pillow to throw it in Lin Xuhuan's face. "Bye."

In March, the temperature in Cologne was close to freezing. Pei Ran stood in a corner at the venue hall, looking down at his phone.

All of a sudden, his backpack was pulled gently. Pei Ran turned around and saw the familiar black brim. Yan Zhun had disguised himself thoroughly. His low voice came through the mask, "Have you been waiting for a long time?"

"No, I just came out." As soon as Pei Ran finished, his phone rang. He originally planned to go back to the hotel by himself, so he'd called a car in advance, and now the car had arrived. Pei Ran said, "I didn't have time to cancel it."

"Just in time." Yan Zhun put on his mask. "Let's go back."

On their way back to the hotel, Yan Zhun's phone kept ringing. He ignored it, letting it ring.

He trained late last night and got up to play the game with barely any sleep. He'd been wound up tight from the morning. Only after he got into the car with Pei Ran did his shoulders finally relax. The back seat was very spacious, but they still sat shoulder to shoulder. Under the disguise of the thick sleeves, they held hands. Yan Zhun moved forward before Pei Ran even asked. He put his head against Pei Ran's shoulder. "I didn't sleep well last night." He said in a low voice.

Pei Ran shifted, wanting to make Yan Zhun more comfortable. "Have some sleep. When we arrive, I'll let you know."

At the hotel, Yan Zhun fell asleep instantly. Pei Ran went to the staff to pick up his luggage and took a shower.

There was no direct flight from Mancheng to Cologne, so, after landing, he'd been on a train for two hours. He couldn't stand not washing. Yan Zhun was still sleeping when he came out from the bathroom.

Pei Ran decided to call for room service after he woke up. As soon as he pressed the "don't disturb" button, he heard a stuffy voice from the bed, "Not ready yet?"

"Oh, I'm ready." Pei Ran paused. "I thought you were asleep. Do you want to have dinner?"

"No." Yan Zhun opened his eyes. "Come here." Yan Zhun treated him like a stuffed animal and hugged him tight. "I haven't showered yet, but the inside layer was covered by the team uniform at all times, so they're not dirty. Do you mind?"

"Not at all," said Pei Ran.

Yan Zhun then lowered his head and buried his face in Pei Ran's neck, smelling the bath gel on his body.

He hadn't seen Pei Ran for nearly two weeks. On the desk, Yan Zhun's phone was vibrating again. Pei Ran asked, "Do we have to tell the coach that we're at the hotel?"

"We're not kids."

Pei Ran had to tell the truth: "My neck is a little itchy."

Yan Zhun paused for two seconds and chuckled. The breath

hit on Pei Ran's neck, tickling it more. Yan Zhun slowly sat up and handed his phone to Pei Ran.

Pei Ran looked at him blankly.

"Didn't you want to delete the post?"

Pei Ran remembered the post and looked down. Yan Zhun had as many as 10 new WeChat messages from his coach. "You'd better reply to these first." Then, he glanced at the bottom of the screen and looked away. "There's a friend request."

Yan Zhun lay back down and replied to the texts in front of Pei Ran, then opened the new friend prompt.

Baa has sent a friend request.

Baa:
QAQ! ~

Baa has sent a friend request.

Baa:
God, accept please ~ ~

Yan Zhun never gave his personal number to others casually. He stared at the verification message for a few seconds before he came to realize that it was his fan.

Yan Zhun frowned. As soon as he was about to refuse, he found that the person next to him was staring at his phone. "I have never given my number to fans."

Pei Ran paused, and then said, "I know."

He gave a brief rundown of what happened at the venue today. With that, Pei Ran hesitated for a moment and said, "Actually... You can add fans if you want."

Lin Xuhuan and other members had all added a few fans, which were all super fans who would send gifts and gratuity crazily during live streams.

As long as you don't talk to them nonstop or add too many.

Yan Zhun interrupted his thoughts. "What did you tell her?"

Pei Ran was confused. "What?"

"She asked which player you liked. What was your answer?"

"I said I like GOD."

Yan Zhun had originally wanted to tease him, but he'd forgotten that Pei Ran was brutally honest all the time and would answer honestly to whatever he was asked.

Yan Zhun rejected the friend request and said, "No. One fan is enough. I can't deal with more."

Pei Ran blurted, "You've already accepted one?"

"Yep, an artist who is very good at painting. He confessed to me on Weibo."

Pei Ran was speechless.

"But he won't let me repost from him. Don't you think he'll stop being my fan?"

Pei Ran's ears were red. "No he won't."

"I'm not sure. He doesn't really seem to want to have anything to do with me." As soon as Yan Zhun finished speaking, his lips were kissed.

"Told you he won't," Pei Ran said.

That was the end of the role play. Yan Zhun lifted his hand to his forehead and kissed him back gently yet firmly.

For lovers who'd been separated for a couple of days, even a little contact could cause sparks.

Yan Zhun kissed him for a while, and then raised his head and said, "Don't kiss me these days. I can't help it."

Yan Zhun knew his priorities. He couldn't go too far during the tournament. He might need to meet with the coach later.

Pei Ran pursed his wet lips and said, "Oh." A few seconds later, he added, "But you can kiss me."

Yan Zhun was speechless.

Sometimes he suspected Pei Ran did it on purpose. After lying for half an hour, Yan Zhun called room service, and the waiter soon brought up the dinner.

Afraid that Pei Ran would feel dirty, Yan Zhun washed the dishes and chopsticks. When he came out, Pei Ran was on the phone, peeling shrimp with gloves, and the speaker was on.

"If you have time, you can go to the Cathedral. There are many street artists there," said a soothing female voice.

Realizing that Pei Ran was on the phone with his family, Yan Zhun quietly sat on one side to avoid disturbing him.

Mother and son spoke for a while before wrapping up.

"Are you staying with Yan Zhun?" Pei Ran's mother asked.

Yan Zhun was stunned, turning to look at Pei Ran with open surprise

Pei Ran hummed.

"He must be very busy at this time. You should book a new room." Pei's mom said.

"I will discuss with him."

After hanging up, Pei Ran turned around and saw Yan Zhun's surprised expression. He explained, "Some time ago, she found that I was always watching your games, so I told her. Do you mind?"

Of course Yan Zhun didn't mind. It was just, after knowing this, he became wide awake and even a little nervous.

As a result, he was still looking at the ceiling after Pei Ran fell asleep. After a moment, Yan Zhun quietly got up, casually put on a coat, and walked to the balcony with his phone. He clicked the contact he had just added back a while ago.

Approved:
Dad, what are you up to

No response. He sent his mother another message.

Mom:
We just woke up. Wait a minute. He's a slow typer.

BeStrictWithYourself:
What?

Approved:
Miss you. Wanna chat with you

Approved:
How have you been doing of late

Yan Zhun's father pushed his glasses up and squinted at the words on his phone. Flattery was a trap.

BeStrictWithYourself:
Much better, without you around

Approved:
Ok, I have a discovery. I'd like to tell you more about it

BeStrictWithYourself:
Wait a minute

Approved:
I found out that I like men

After sending this message, Yan Zhun muted the notifications from his father and booked a week-long stay at a hotel for after the competition. Then, he turned back to the room.

Yan Zhun had been standing outside too long; he was cold. So he lay outside covers, wanting to be warm before getting inside. A hand came out and touched the back of his hand.

Pei Ran had awakened to the cold and half opened his eyes. Yan Zhun didn't have time to say anything before Pei Ran moved closer, then caught hold of him and gave him half the covers. "Are you cold? Come over a bit. I'm warm."

"Okay."

Soon, Pei Ran's breathing slowed. Night shrouded the town. A few snowflakes fell slowly and melted after touching the human world. Cologne fell into a romantic snowy night. The city was in a dream. The lovers cuddled and fell asleep.

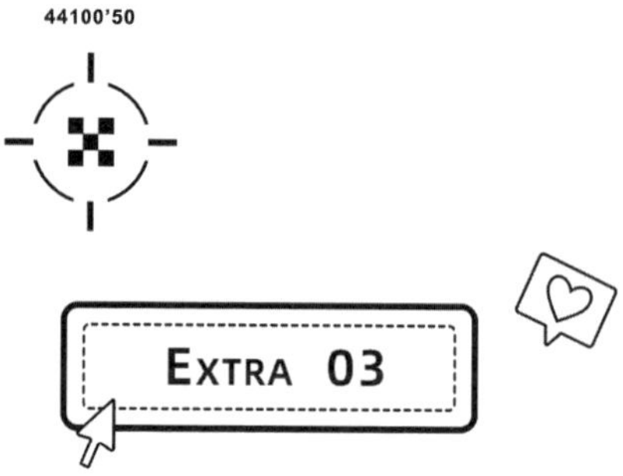

Mancheng Airport, 10 PM.

Although it was late at night, there were still many people around the pickup area. Some were holding up LED boards and some were carrying their cameras. Some travelers thought that they were waiting on a celebrity.

Until the girl holding the sign leaned slightly, revealing the words on the board: "Congratulations to TZG on the Star Cup." In the arrival hall, several members of the TZG team, hands in their pockets and wearing masks, were walking towards the exit, surrounded by team staff.

The coach was walking at the front. He hung up the call and looked back. "There are few restaurants still open so late. How about going to Haidilao hotpot before heading home?"

Lin Xuhuan rubbed his belly. "Hurry up, I'm starving."

"That's because you didn't have airplane meals," said the raider, walking beside him.

Lin Xuhuan yawned. "I was too sleepy. As soon as I opened my eyes, the flight had already arrived." They'd played in the tournament for four days in a row. Then they'd flown back immediately after the championship interview.

At first, they'd planned to come back tomorrow, but Yan Zhun changed the booking, and so did the others. "The assistant coach has already gone to Haidilao to get a seat. It's not far from the airport. I asked him to order in advance. We'll make it when we get there." The coach took his cell phone and asked, "What would you like to eat?"

These hungry boys almost repeated the entire menu.

"What about Yan Zhun?" The coach asked, looking back.

The team leader had been checking his phone since landing.

Lin Xuhuan sneaked up on him. "Bro, what are you looking at—" Yan Zhun turned his phone aside, and Lin Xuhuan only caught a glimpse of an interface similar to the gift-giving page on the live steaming platform. "Damn, bro, you're watching pretty girls stream and sending them gifts!" Lin Xuhuan sputtered, and then he wondered, "But that doesn't seem to be our streaming platform..."

Yan Zhun didn't want to pay attention to him. He raised his head and said, "Enjoy yourselves. I don't want to eat."

"Not hungry?" The coach paused and picked up the phone, "Then I'll ask someone to send you back to the base..."

"No, I won't go back to the base tonight."

The others understood instantly.

When the TZG team members came out from the airport, the fans suppressed their screams, but the cheer of "GOD!" was still hard to suppress.

There were so many fans around them that Yan Zhun couldn't take a taxi to leave alone, so he followed the team's car to Haidilao and waited for two minutes before he got up, wanting to leave out the back door.

"Yan Zhun, wait." The coach stood up. "I'll walk you out."

Yan Zhun raised his eyebrows and said nothing.

Approaching the back door, the coach said, "Captain, don't you think you meet with Pei Ran a little too frequently?"

Yan Zhun put one hand in his pocket and didn't look back, "So should I meet with you more frequently instead?"

The coach choked, "I'm worried that your relationship with him might be exposed. Actually, some fans have found out that you are in a relationship recently..."

Yan Zhun stopped and said, "Have I ever missed training?"

"Not at all," said the coach. "I'm just worried. If they knew you're dating a man..."

Yan Zhun said lightly, "I don't care."

The coach paused and swallowed what he wanted to say.

Yan Zhun put on his hat and covered his eyes with its brim. "Bye. Bon Appétit." After getting on a taxi, Yan Zhun put on his earphones again.

The phone went back to the live streaming page just before. Yan Zhun was using a live streaming software that had just been launched. Compared to the professional ones, it was a bit simple and had only a few functions. However, it was enough for an artist to start streaming.

There was only one word "Drawing" in the intro of the channel that Yan Zhun was watching. There were more than 3000 audience online, and the number was so pitiful that you could tell it was not fake. The host didn't turn on the video at himself and seldom spoke. He just focused on sketching lines and occasionally picked up a few comments to answer questions. The voice of the host was very soft and pleasant, "How many pictures is the host going to draw? I'll call it a day after finishing this one."

“Will the host offer a course? No, and I won’t do live streaming much in the future.”

“It’s GOD of the TZG team that I’m drawing.” The host paused for a moment, then elaborated. “He’s a professional player of the PUBG video game. He’s very good at it. He won the championship of the national invitational and was also the king of killing last year.”

Yan Zhun smiled and clicked on the comment section.

> Does the teacher like GOD very much?

The comment didn’t get a response from the host, but some fans soon replied:

> Yes, the first picture that got popular of teacher P is of GOD! And at that time, GOD wasn’t even famous. It must be true love.

> Teacher P’s desktop wallpaper is that picture of GOD

No answer from the host... Yan Zhun minimized the app and sent a message to his boyfriend on WeChat.

Yan Zhun:
I want to video call.

In his headphones, his boyfriend said, “Just a moment, I have a message to reply to.”

Teacher Pei:
Not now. I’m busy with something... How about later?

Teacher Pei:
Are you back at the hotel?

Yan Zhun:
Well, later then.

Yan Zhun went back to the stream, changed his ID, and then charged 2000 yuan into the account, which was divided into 100-yuan gifts and sent to Pei Ran’s channel one by one.

Pei Ran froze for several seconds before he said, “Wait, you don’t need to send me gifts. Don’t waste your money.”

The gifts were still appearing on the screen. Panicked, Pei

Ran shouted out the ID, "This... 'I like GOD,' please don't buy me gifts. Just watch my stream. I really don't need them."

Hearing what he wanted to hear, Yan Zhun smiled with satisfaction. Then, he changed his ID and bought gifts again...

Does teacher like GOD? sent a macaron

"Why again..." Pei Ran frowned, "Yes, you..."

When did teacher start liking GOD? sent a macaron

Pei Ran said vaguely, "A long time ago. Are you changing your ID again and again to send gifts? Don't do it. You can type. I'll answer you."

What does teacher like best about GOD? sent a macaron

"Every aspect. Stop it. Is there a button to turn off the gift-sending option?"

Has teacher watched GOD's games? sent a macaron

There was no response this time.

Yan Zhun raised his eyebrows and changed his ID into "What did teacher have for dinner?" He was just about to send more gifts when a page jumped out suddenly.

You have been asked to leave the channel by **P&EI**

Yan Zhun was speechless. He tried re-entered the stream.

You have been banned by **P&EI**, please try to enter the room again in **1 hour**

Yan Zhun was at a loss. Without the interference of gifts, Pei Ran's pace quickened. The audience said that they couldn't keep up with the progress, even just after a slight distraction.

A comment of "Can you draw another one" floated from the top. Pei Ran glanced at it. Although no one else could see it, he still shook his head, "I'm not free later. Let's call it a day after this." Pei Ran had rented a room not far from campus for convenience after going into third year. At the moment, there was only a slight noise from the computer fan in the room.

Pei Ran was very concentrated when drawing. He was wearing noise reduction earphones, and he was playing soft music as the background sound of his streaming at a very low volume. The rainstorm that just started outside the window was blocked from his world.

During this, he moved his head and glanced at a comment

> Was that a door opening? Are you in dorms?

Pei Ran didn't think too much about it, "No, I'm renting an apartment."

> You live alone? Please be careful.

"I live alone most of the time. Sometimes..." Pei Ran paused for a moment. "Don't worry. This neighborhood is very safe—"

Before he could finish his sentence, his view was suddenly obstructed. He instantly froze on the spot. His hand moved unconsciously, and a line which clearly didn't belong appeared on the drawing. Pei Ran was blindfolded.

The person's palm was big and cold, pressing on his eyes with a bit of strength. He couldn't help leaning back.

When the earphones were pulled out, he could feel the person behind him bending down and approaching, and said in a soft voice, "Freeze. Where is the money?"

Pei Ran couldn't register what was happening. His heart-beat was racing. He caught a whiff of the man. Rain, nicotine, and the faint touch of Cologne.

"You..."

Sensing that he wanted to turn back, the man held on to his neck with the other hand, "Don't move if you don't want get hurt."

Pei Ran said nothing.

"Behave, as long as you are obedient—"

"Did you smoke?"

Silence.

Pei Ran pushed the hand away and looked up at the person behind him.

The person who had half an hour ago sent him a message saying that he was back at the hotel and wanted to have a video call, was now standing behind him.

His collar was disheveled, and rain had soaked through his hair and shirt. He looked like he'd had quite a journey. "It's from Lin Xuhuan." The hand on Pei Ran's neck loosened. Yan Zhun looked down at him and said, "I didn't smoke."

Pei Ran wanted to ask him how and when he came back. Then, he realized something and looked at the computer:

> Gosh! What's going on?!

> Burglary?! So scary...

> I have reported to the administrator!

> What use is an administrator?

> I'm in class, so someone else please call the police!

> I'm calling now, who knows where the host lives?!

> ... Huh? I feel like it's a joke?

Pei Ran hurriedly explained, "It's not a burglary. I'm fine. Don't call the police. It's my friend pranking me.

"It's really OK. No one is threatening me with a knife and asking me to lie. It's my friend." Pei Ran looked at the screen, habitually read out the comments in a low voice, "'How can a friend come to you in the middle of the night...' Because he lives here when he doesn't work."

Yan Zhun said, "Cohabitant."

"Yes, we will occasionally coh—" Pei Ran stopped half way.

Yan Zhun chuckled. He ruffled Pei Ran's hair lightly then said, "I'll go shower."

When the bathroom door closed, Pei Ran blinked several

times and smoothed out his hair.

He drank a mouthful of water, then ignored the overwhelming comments on the right side of the screen: "Two men cohabiting?" and "Hahaha, they don't know what 'cohabit' means." He then lowered his head and continued drawing.

When Yan Zhun came out of the shower, Pei Ran had turned off his computer and was standing on the balcony with his back to him. He bowed his head to respond to the messages on his phone.

The air was still moist and cool after the heavy rain with speckles of light in the distance. Pei Ran sighed a relief after sending the messages. His shoulder relaxed. Yan Zhun leaned over and put his chin on his shoulder.

Yan Zhun, "Why did you start stream suddenly?"

"My former teacher participated in the research and development of a painting-lesson software. He recognized my style from my Weibo and asked me to help boost its popularity. I couldn't refuse... I don't think I helped much." Pei Ran turned and looked at him. "Only this time. I won't do this anymore."

They were close to each other. When Yan Zhun hummed, Pei Ran could even feel the tremor of his voice box.

Pei Ran pursed his lips. "I thought you were coming back tomorrow."

"Homesick, so I changed the ticket," Yan Zhun said. "Are you tired after streaming for three hours?"

"A little bit. It's tiring to read the comments and chat with them. I get distracted... How did you know I had been streaming for three hours?"

Pei Ran paused, suddenly remembering that fool who had been sending macarons to him. His eyes widened, "Did you watch it? Where did you see it?"

Yan Zhun laughed, "There was a reminder on your Weibo. I saw it as soon as I got off the plane." Pei Ran didn't know that he'd shared this information on Weibo. He'd probably forgotten to unclick some options when he logged in.

Pei Ran said, "There's no need to buy me gifts."

"Haven't you always done that for me?"

Pei Ran blurted out, "Never."

"Come on, teacher Pei." Yan Zhun said jokingly, "I recognized the account you used in my live streaming room."

Pei Ran didn't respond.

Pei Ran had indeed registered a secret account. When Yan Zhun was attacked by antis, Pei Ran would send him gifts to block out the flames.

Yan Zhun saw Pei Ran's ears turn red. He reached out, wanting to pinch them.

"Have you ever thought about stopping live streaming?" Pei Ran said suddenly.

Yan Zhun thought that Pei Ran didn't want him to be cursed at and said, "I'm not affected by the anti-fans."

"No," Pei Ran said. "It's so tiring. I feel exhausted after sitting for three hours. Training is already tiring for you, if you sit and play for another few hours, your back will hurt."

"Live streaming is more profitable. The team has signed a contract with the platform. And I'm not doing it frequently. Lin Xuhuan and them stream twice as long every month."

"Are you short on money?" Pei Ran looked at him. "I also have savings. You don't have to work so hard."

Yan Zhun gazed at him. "Will teacher Pei sponsor me?"

Pei Ran said solemnly, "I can do that."

Right after his words, Yan Zhun leaned forward, and they kissed. Pei Ran had always been calm and self-disciplined in his daily life. His mood and tone were always very distant, giving others a feeling that he was difficult to approach.

Yan Zhun enjoyed disturbing Pei Ran.

Right now, Pei Ran was lying on the bed. The buttons of his pajamas all parted. His fair skin was bare in the air, and his pants had been pulled down. Only a bedside lamp was on in the room. Pei Ran's ears were flushed, his lips were wet with saliva, and his nipples were rising up and down along with his heavy breathing.

His nipples were in Yan Zhun's mouth again. Pei Ran's heart was about to jump out, "Not there, Yan Zhun..."

The tip of Yan Zhun's tongue swirled around affectionately, and he looked up at Pei Ran. He pushed Pei Ran's bangs aside, lowered his head to kiss Pei Ran's eyelids, which were tinted scarlet, put his warm palm on Pei Ran's inner thigh, and said in a raspy voice, "Open your legs, teacher Pei."

Although they had done it many times, whenever he heard Yan Zhun say these words, Pei Ran would still blush with embarrassment. He hummed assent. Then, as soon as he raised his ankles, he was forced to open his legs even farther by Yan Zhun, who was holding his thighs.

When his length was in Yan Zhun's mouth, Pei Ran almost forgot how to breathe.

He arched himself to grasp Yan Zhun's hand and said in a panic, "No, Yan Zhun... You don't need to do this..."

There was no response. Pei Ran put his fingers in Yan Zhun's hair, but did not dare to press further. "Yan Zhun..."

Pei Ran couldn't stand Yan Zhun giving him oral sex at all. The simultaneous pleasure and shame hit him all at once. When he reached orgasm, his shoulders were arched, his toes were tightly curled, and his ankles were trembling.

Pei Ran gasped and grabbed the sheet. When Yan Zhun released him, he was still immersed in the afterglow of the orgasm. Yan Zhun leaned up again, squeezed his chin and gave him a sweet kiss.

"Teacher Pei, you seem to like it very much." Yan Zhun said as if he was bewitching him, "You shudder every time my tongue touches you."

There was a heavy rain outside again, hitting the window mercilessly, but Pei Ran could only hear Yan Zhun.

Pei Ran looked at him into his eyes for a few seconds and suddenly hummed.

Yan Zhun paused. He liked to tease Pei Ran in bed. Although Pei Ran let him mess around and his body reacts very passionately, he seldom answered his dirty talk.

When Yan Zhun suspected that he had heard it wrong, Pei Ran suddenly hugged him.

Just after the orgasm, Pei Ran didn't have much strength. He put his face on Yan Zhun's neck. His usually cool voice was wrapped with strong lust.

Pei Ran said, "come in, Yan Zhun."

At four o'clock in the morning, the phone on the bedside table pinged several times.

It was picked up, turned off and thrown away again.

The sheets were all wrinkled, and half of the bedding fell to the floor. The condom wrappers were all over the floor, and the boy's panting became smaller and smaller gradually.

Pei Ran really couldn't make a sound anymore.

He was kneeling down on the bed. The man's hands pushed his buttocks down, and there were traces of kissing from his neck to the waist. Pei Ran just had a rest for less than half a minute before hearing the sound of plastic tearing.

Feeling Yan Zhun intruding again, Pei Ran helplessly grasped the sheet, and even his voice seemed to have been ravaged, "Yan Zhun... It's sore, too much, I can't..."

"You can, Teacher Pei." Yan Zhun's collarbones were soaked with sweat. His thumb brushed across where their body connected and he praised hoarsely, "You're still very tight."

By the end of it, it was bright outside.

Pei Ran felt for his sore underbelly. Lying on the bed, He couldn't even open his eyes.

"Teacher Pei, open your legs."

Pei Ran was shocked and shook his head, "I really can't do it. Yan Zhun, I'm going to be broken."

His tone was so serious that Yan Zhun couldn't help but smile as he lowered his head to kiss the tip of Pei Ran's ear. "You won't. Open your legs. I'll clean it up for you."

Pei Ran was still struggling internally whether to believe him or not when he felt the hot towel covering his body, and his muscles immediately relaxed. He seemed to be drawn into the vortex of exhaustion, couldn't even gather any energy to open his eyelids.

In a half-asleep state, he was held up and covered with something silky soft.

The corner of his mouth was kissed, and the man's low voice seeped into his dream.

"Good night, Teacher Pei."

When Yan Zhun woke up, Pei Ran was still sleeping. The person who usually kept an eight-hour sleep habit was now breathing steadily with his eyes closed and no signs of waking up.

Yan Zhun closed his eyes again with satisfaction. After

half a minute, he remembered that there seemed to be a live interview to do this afternoon. He fumbled out his phone. The moment it was turned on, countless messages poured in. Yan Zhun frowned, muted his phone and glanced at the screen lazily.

Almost all of them were WeChat texts from the coach:

Yan Zhun! Something's wrong! Why the hell don't you turn on your cell phone

Call me back as soon as you see it! It's urgent!

Someone fucking outed you! Reply now!

Pei Ran didn't open his eyes until dusk.

He looked at the warm light coming in through the crack of the window. For a moment, he couldn't tell whether it was sunrise or sunset. Pei Ran stood up and looked around. There was no one in the room. His first reaction was to look for his phone.

He had received numerous messages, including a reminder of turning digital gifts into cash from the live streaming platform, thanks sent by his teacher, and Yan Zhun's message.

Yan Zhun:
Teacher Pei, I have an interview this afternoon and am going back to base. I asked the housekeeper to help make soup. Tell me when you wake up and I'll send it to you.

Yan Zhun:
Teacher Pei, I may not be able to meet you in the evening. I'll have the soup delivered to you. [Pig kneeling down]

Yan Zhun:
Still sleeping? You must be hungry.

Pei Ran smiled and lay back again to type.

Pei Ran:
I'm up. Don't bother auntie. I'll just have dinner by myself.

Yan Zhun:
No way

Yan Zhun:
You have to eat something good to nourish your body.

Nourish...

Pei Ran's ears suddenly turned red again.

Pei Ran:
No, it's really ok. Are you finished?

Yan Zhun:
Not yet. I've had it delivered. Remember to eat the soup.

Pei Ran:
OK, don't forget to have dinner.

Yan Zhun:
Sure.

Yan Zhun:
Teacher Pei.

Pei Ran:
Yes.

Yan Zhun:
Send me a voice message.

Pei Ran was startled.

Pei Ran:
...What do you want me to say?

Yan Zhun:
Whatever. I want to hear your voice.

Pei Ran blinked, dumbfounded. After a few seconds, he pressed the voice button.

"Then you... should finish early. I'll wait for you at home."

After chatting with Yan Zhun, Pei Ran quit the chat and replied to other messages one by one. It was not until Lin Kang's new message came in that Pei Ran found that Lin Kang had sent him more than ten WeChat messages that day. At Lin Kang's text, Pei Ran paused half way through a yawn.

Lin Kang:
My gosh! Pei Ran, did you see Weibo!!

Lin Kang:
You and Yan Zhun have been exposed!!!

Lin Kang:
Oh no, to be exact, Yan Zhun has been exposed! It didn't mention you...

Lin Kang had known about their relationship for a long time, so he came to find Pei Ran the moment when he saw it.

Pei Ran's brain hummed for a while, but he calmed down quickly. He took a deep breath and opened the Weibo link sent from Lin Kang.

An insider revealed in many PUBG forums that GOD, the captain of TZG, is homosexual

That person didn't say many words but uploaded a few photos. The photo seemed to be taken in the school drawing studio. In the picture, he and Yan Zhun were kissing, and there were two more of them leaving the studio.

But these photos put mosaic on him, leaving only Yan Zhun's face.

Truly valid evidence.

Pei Ran looked at the name of the person who posted it. It was a series of random letters, followed by the number 123.

It was a very common random ID, but Pei Ran thought it looked very familiar.

He was about to click into the account's home page when an unrecognized number called. Pei Ran picked up. "Hello?"

"Pei Ran... It's me."

Pei Ran was quiet for a second. He wanted to hang up.

"Don't!" Luo Qingshan quickly stopped him. "Pei Ran, I... saw Weibo. Are you ok?"

Pei Ran said nothing.

"I've already told you that it's not safe to date Yan Zhun. You can never know when the whole world will find out."

Luo Qingshan said, "Although it didn't affect you this time, who can be sure about next time? Pei Ran, don't you care that people know you are gay?"

Pei Ran suddenly thought of something. He frowned and held his cell phone silently.

Luo Qingshan thought he was moved by him, and continued, "You must be very afraid now, right? It's OK. That person didn't expose you at first, and certainly will not later. But Yan Zhun's situation will be watched by many fans moving forward. How about this, you stay away from him for a period of time to avoid being photographed again—"

Pei Ran suddenly interrupted him, "diwgaahh123."

Luo Qingshan paused. "Huh?"

"This account is yours, isn't it? Luo Qingshan."

Luo Qingshan was stunned, and his cold sweat came out immediately. He said with a fake smile, "What are you talking about? How could it—"

"In the past, the forum sent a notification to your phone. I've seen it." Pei Ran coldly interrupted him "If I log in with your mobile phone number, it should be this account."

Luo Qingshan was astounded. He had never used forums before, nor posted anything with that account, so he was sure that no one knew his ID. Who could believe that Pei Ran still recall a system notification that was sent so long ago?

Luo Qingshan opened his mouth. It took while to squeeze past the knot in his throat, "You're misremembering, I—"

"Luo Qingshan." Pei Ran's voice was full of disgust. It was the coldest Luo Qingshan had never heard him be. "You really make me sick."

At the TZG team interview:

After several hours of crisis management, the TZG team

had completely calmed down. The coach stood with his hands on waist, looking at Yan Zhun, who was receiving an interview not far away.

Everyone thought that TZG's interview this afternoon would be cancelled. Unexpectedly, not only did it go on as usual, even the person in the center of the news appeared in front of the camera.

The coach looked at Yan Zhun, who was handling the questions with ease, and suddenly came to the conclusion that even if the sky collapsed, it really didn't matter after all.

His phone rang. The coach saw the caller's name and went to the balcony with his phone immediately.

He answered, "Pei Ran?"

"Yes, thanks for picking up. Is Yan Zhun okay?"

"He's fine. He's having an interview right now. Don't worry, it won't affect you at all. Yan Zhun has asked me to remove your photos. I contacted the admin of those platforms, and they should be deleted immediately. Your name will never appear on the Internet—"

Pei Ran interrupted him, "What about Yan Zhun?"

The coach thought of the host's question just now, which asked Yan Zhun what he would like to say about the news this afternoon. Was he in love?

Yan Zhun's expression was neutral, and his tone was flat. "No comment. Yes."

He'd practically admitted it.

Then the host started, "The other person—"

"That's enough." Yan Zhun smiled. "Let's focus on me."

The coach recollected his thought and said, "Yan Zhun... He's fine, seriously. To tell you the truth, I have prepared for the consequence of officially forcing him to withdraw from the team, but it didn't come to that. The higher ups told me to ask him to be careful. As long as no more explicit photos are exposed in the future... then it's fine. The higher ups aren't against homosexuality. It's not as bad as we thought. You can rest assured, Pei Ran." The coach smiled. "The biggest impact of this... the boy will probably lose a lot of female fans."

Pei Ran was relieved. "That's good. Sorry to disturb you. I'll thank you later."

Hanging up the phone, the coach was relieved as well. He put away the phone and went back. Halfway there, he realized something was wrong.

What did Pei Ran just say? Why did he feel strange about it? It was already seven o'clock in the evening after the interview. The TZG members walked out of the building together.

"Food!" Lin Xuhuan cried out.

The raider asked, "Can you stop thinking about eating every day?"

"I was so worried that I haven't had any meals all day. Am I not supposed to have something to eat when the matter is solved? Bro, are you coming?"

"No," said Yan Zhun.

The coach said, "You'd better not meet with Pei Ran for the time being..."

"I know." Yan Zhun lowered his eye and said, "I'll go back to the base."

Yan Zhun walked at the back of the group and looked at his phone to confirm: Pei Ran still hadn't replied to him.

Lin Xuhuan said, "I want to go to the Japanese buffet on Boya Street, or let's have seafood? Crabs are in season right now... BabePei?"

Yan Zhun stopped and looked up at once. Pei Ran, dressed

in white, was standing at the gate of the building. He was standing with his back straight, looking proper and solemn.

Upon hearing Lin Xuhuan's voice, Pei Ran looked over and straightened. He called out, "Yan Zhun."

Yan Zhun had seen the camera facing Pei Ran outside the building.

He stepped forward quickly, took off his team jacket and put it on Pei Ran. Then he took off his hat and put it on Pei Ran's head. The brim of his hat nearly covered half of Pei Ran's face.

Yan Zhun turned to the coach and said, "I'll take him to the basement—" Yan Zhun's hand was held before he could finish speaking.

Pei Ran's hands were smaller than Yan Zhun's. He wrapped his fingers around Yan Zhun's, and then he laced their fingers together.

"No." said Pei Ran.

Yan Zhun took a deep breath and said, "Teacher Pei, be good. Many people are taking pictures outside."

"I'm fine." Pei Ran raised his chin, and his eyes were showing from beneath the brim of the hat. "I'm not afraid to be known by others, Yan Zhun."

Yan Zhun looked at Pei Ran quietly. This person who had always looked clean when going out hadn't even covered the lovebites on his arms and neck tonight. His eyes were still swollen from last night. He looked like he'd just woken up, and his whole body was in a mess that didn't match Pei Ran's usual self.

But Pei Ran was more vivid, more lovely, and more attractive than ever.

It was often said that feelings would change. As time went

by, the passion of love would turn into boredom.

This was not true for him. Yan Zhun thought that he would only love Pei Ran more and more every day.

Pei Ran asked, "Shall we go home?"

Yan Zhun's eyes were drowned in complex emotions.

He held his hand carefully and said in a serious voice, "Yes, let's go home."

Limerence

If you have any questions, please send e-mail to
info@vialactea.ca